THE

SAINT AND HIS SAVIOUR:

THE

PROGRESS OF THE SOUL IN THE KNOW-LEDGE OF JESUS.

BY

C. H. SPURGEON.

"Christ in all."—Col. iii. 11.

ISBN 1 871676 01 0

Christian Focus Publications Ltd

Houston   Tain
Texas   Ross-shire

FOREWORD

"The special work of our ministry is to lay open Christ, to hold up the tapestry and unfold the mysteries of Christ. Let us labour therefore to be always speaking somewhat about Christ, or tending that way. When we speak of the law, let it drive us to Christ; when of moral duties, let them teach us to walk worthy of Christ. Christ, or something tending to Christ, should be our theme, and mark to aim at."

SIBBS.

This quotation from Sibbs is one which was epitomised in the life and preaching of Spurgeon.

'The Saint and His Saviour' is a supreme example of Spurgeon's heart warming concern that we would learn of and experience the ways of Christ with His people. From the believers first meeting until "the ransomed of the Lord shall return" are described.

The Publishers are pleased to commend this book in the prayer that your experience will concur with the sub-title of this book,

'The progress of the soul in the knowledge of Jesus'.

W H M MacKenzie
Inverness
April 1989.

THE SAINT AND HIS SAVIOUR.

CONTENTS.

———◆———

THE SAINT AND HIS SAVIOUR.

I.

The Despised Friend.

"We esteemed him not."—ISA. liii. 3.

IT would not be easy for some of us to recall
the hour when we first heard the name of Jesus.
In very infancy that sweet sound was as familiar
to our ear as the hush of lullaby. Our earliest
recollections are associated with the house of
God, the family altar, the Holy Bible, the
sacred song, and the fervent prayer. Like
young Samuels, we were lighted to our rest by
the lamps of the sanctuary, and were awakened
by the sound of the morning hymn. Many a
time has the man of God, whom a parent's
hospitality has entertained, implored a blessing
on our head, desiring in all sincerity that we

B

might early call the Redeemer blessed; and to his petition a mother's earnest "Amen" has solemnly responded. Ours were happy portions and goodly heritages; but nevertheless, being "born in sin, and shapen in iniquity," these heavenly privileges did not of themselves avail to give us love to Jesus and pardon by his blood.

We are often compelled to weep over sins aggravated by light as clear as noonday,—ordinances undervalued from their very frequency,—warnings despised, although accompanied with tears from a parent's eye,—and loathings felt in the heart, if not expressed by the lips, to those very blessings which were the rich benisons of heaven. In our own persons we are witnesses to the fact of innate depravity, the birth-plague of man; and we can testify to the doctrine that grace, and grace alone, can change the heart. The words of Isaiah are ours with an emphasis, notwithstanding all the hallowed influences which surrounded us: and in uttering the confession, "We esteemed him not," the haunts of our childhood, the companions of our youth, and the sins of our manhood, unanimously confirm our truthfulness.

Starting, then, with our own experience, we

are led to infer that those who were denied our advantages will certainly be compelled to adopt the same humble language. If the child of pious parents, who by divine power was in youth brought to know the Lord, feels constrained to acknowledge that once he did not esteem the Saviour, shall the man whose education was irreligion, whose childhood was riot, whose youth was license, and whose maturity was crime, be able to adopt language less humiliating? No; we believe that all men of this class, who are now redeemed from the hand of the enemy, will readily acknowledge that they were the blind neglecters of the beauties of our glorious Emmanuel. Aye, more, we venture to challenge the "Church of the first-born" to produce a single saint who did not once pass by the cross with indifference, if not contempt.

Whether we review the "noble army o martyrs," "the goodly fellowship of the prophets," "the glorious company of the apostles, or "the holy Church throughout all the world, we shall not discover a single lover of the adorable Redeemer who will not join the general confession, "We esteemed him not."

Pause, attentive reader, and ask thyself whether thou dost esteem him *now*; for possibly it may happen that thou hast not as yet seen in him any " beauty that thou shouldest desire him," nor canst thou subscribe to the exclamation of the spouse, "Yea, he is altogether lovely." Should this be thine unhappy condition, a meditation thereon may, under the Holy Spirit's influence, be of much use to thee; and I beseech thee, while we unfold the secrets of what was once our prison-house, be thou intensely anxious that by any means thou also mayest escape a bondage which deprives thee of joy here, and will shut thee out from bliss hereafter.

We propose to endeavour first of all to bring the fact of our light estimation of Jesus vividly before our eye; then, secondly, we will discuss the causes of this folly; and, thirdly, seek to excite emotions proper to such a mournful contemplation.

I. Let us go to the potter's house, and view the unshapen clay which we once were; let us remember "the rock whence we were hewn," and the "hole of the pit from which we were digged," that we may with deeper feeling repeat the text, "We esteemed him not." Let us here seriously peruse the diary of memory, for there the witnesses of our guilt have faithfully recorded their names.

We pause, and consider first *our overt acts of sin*, for these lie like immense boulders on the sides of the hill of life, sure testifiers to the rock within.

Few men would dare to read their own autobiography, if all their deeds were recorded in it; few can look back upon their entire career without a blush. "We have all sinned, and come short of his glory." None of us can lay claim to perfection. True, at times a forgetful self-complacency bids us exult in the virtue of our lives; but when faithful memory awakes, how instantly she dispels the illusion! She waves her magic wand, and in the king's palaces frogs arise in multitudes; the pure rivers at her glance become blood; the whole land is creeping with loathsomeness. Where we imagined purity, lo, imperfection ariseth. The snow-wreath of satisfaction melts before the sun of truth; the nectared bowl of gratulation is embittered by sad remembrances; while, under the glass of honesty, the deformities and irregularities of a life apparently correct are rendered, alas! too visible.

Let the Christian, whose hair is whitened by

the sunlight of heaven, tell his life-long story.
He may have been one of the most upright and
moral, but there will be one dark spot in his
history, upon which he will shed the tear of
penitence, because then he knew not the fear of
the Lord.   Let yon heroic warrior of Jesus
recount his deeds; but he too points to deep
scars, the offspring of wounds received in the
service of the Evil One.   Some amongst our
chosen men, in their days of unregeneracy,
were notorious for guilt, and could well write
with Bunyan*—" As for my own natural life, for
the time that I was without God in the world,
it was, indeed, according to the course of this
world and the spirit that now worketh in the
children of disobedience (Eph. ii. 2, 3).   It was
my delight to be taken captive by the devil at
his will (2 Tim. ii. 26), being filled with all unrighteousness; the which did also so strongly
work, both in my heart and life, that I had but
few equals, both for cursing, swearing, lying,
and blaspheming the holy name of God."   Suffice it, however, that by each of us open sins
have been committed, which manifest that "we
esteemed him not."

   Could we have rebelled against our Father

* Grace Abounding.

with so high a hand, if his Son had been the
object of our love? Should we have so perpetually trampled on the commands of a venerated
Jesus? Could we have done such despite to
his authority, if our hearts had been knit to his
adorable person? Could we have sinned so
terribly, if Calvary had been dear to us? Nay;
surely our clouds of transgressions testify our
former want of love to him. Had we esteemed
the God-man, should we so entirely have neglected his claims? could we have wholly forgotten
his loving words of command? Do men insult
the persons they admire? Will they commit
high treason against a king they love? Will
they slight the person they esteem, or wantonly
make sport of him they venerate? And yet we
have done all this, and more; whereby the least
word of flattery concerning any natural love to
Christ is rendered to our now honest hearts as
hateful as the serpent's hiss. These iniquities
might not so sternly prove us to have despised
our Lord had they been accompanied by some
little service to him. Even now, when we do
love his name, we are oft unfaithful, but *now*
our affection helps us "to creep in service where
we cannot go;" but *before* our acts were none
of them seasoned with the salt of sincere affec-

tion, but were all full of the gall of bitterness.
O beloved, let us not seek to avoid the weight
of this evidence, but let us own that our gracious
Lord has much to lay to our charge, since we
chose to obey Satan rather than the Captain of
salvation, and preferred sin to holiness.

Let the self-conceited Pharisee boast that he
was born free—we see on our wrists the red
marks of the iron; let him glory that he was
never blind—our eyes can yet remember the
darkness of Egypt, in which we discerned not
the morning star. Others may desire the
honour of a merited salvation—we know that
our highest ambition can only hope for pardon
and acceptance by grace alone; and well we remember the hour when the only channel of that
grace was despised or neglected by us.

The Book of Truth shall next witness against
us. The time is not yet erased from memory
when this sacred fount of living water was un-
opened by us, our evil hearts placed a stone over
the mouth of the well, which even conscience
could not remove. Bible dust once defiled our
fingers; the blessed volume was the least sought
after of all the books in the library.

Though now we can truly say that His word
is "a matchless temple where we delight to be,

to contemplate the beauty, the symmetry, and the magnificence of the structure, to increase our awe, and excite our devotion to the Deity there preached and adored;"* yet at one sad period of our lives we refused to tread the jewelled floor of the temple, or when from custom's sake we entered it, we paced it with hurried tread, unmindful of its sanctity, heedless of its beauty, ignorant of its glories, and unsubdued by its majesty.

Now we can appreciate Herbert's rapturous affection expressed in his poêm :—

> " Oh book ! infinite sweetness ! let my heart
> Suck every letter, and a honey gain,
> Precious for any grief in any part ;
> To clear the breast, to mollify all pain."

But *then* every ephemeral poem or trifling novel could move our hearts a thousand times more easily than this "book of stars," "this god of books." Ah ! well doth this neglected Bible prove us to have esteemed Jesus but lightly. Verily, had we been full of affection to him, we should have sought him in his word. Here he doth unrobe himself, showing his inmost heart. Here each page is stained with drops of his blood, or emblazoned with rays of his glory. At

* Boyle.

every turn we see him, as divine and human, as dying and yet alive, as buried but now risen, as the victim and the priest, as the prince and saviour, and in all those various offices, relationships and conditions, each of which render him dear to his people and precious to his saints. Oh let us kneel before the Lord, and own that "we esteemed him not," or else we should have walked with him in the fields of Scripture, and held communion with him in the spice-beds of inspiration.

The Throne of Grace, so long unvisited by us, equally proclaims our former guilt. Seldom were our cries heard in heaven; our petitions were formal and lifeless, dying on the lip which carelessly pronounced them. Oh sad state of crime, when the holy offices of adoration were unfulfilled, the censer of praise smoked not with a savour acceptable unto the Lord, nor were the vials of prayer fragrant with precious odours!

Unwhitened by devotion, the days of the calendar were black with sin; unimpeded by our supplication, the angel of judgment speeded his way to our destruction. At the thought of those days of sinful silence, our minds are humbled in the dust; and never can we visit the mercy-seat without adoring the grace which affords despisers a ready welcome.

But why went not " our heart in pilgrimage?" Why sung we not that "tune which all things hear and fear?" Why fed we not at "the Church's banquet," on this "exalted manna?" What answer can we give more full and complete than this—" We esteemed him not?" Our little regard of Jesus kept us from his throne: for true affection would have availed itself of the ready access which prayer affords to the secret chamber of Jesus, and would thereby have taken her fill of loves. Can we now forsake the throne? No; our happiest moments are spent upon our knees, for there Jesus manifests himself to us. We prize the society of this best of friends, for his divine countenance "giveth such an inward decking to the house where he lodgeth, that proudest palaces have cause to envy the gilding." We delight to frequent the shades of secrecy, for there our Saviour allows us to unbosom our joys and sorrows, and roll them alike on him.

O Lamb of God! our prayerlessness bids us confess that once we considered thee to have neither form nor comeliness.

Furthermore, our *avoidance of the people of*

God confirms the humiliating truth. We who now stand in the "sacramental host of God's elect," glorying in the brotherhood of the righteous, were once "strangers and foreigners." The language of Canaan was to our ear either an unmeaning babble at which we scoffed, a harsh jargon which we sought not to imitate, or an "unknown tongue" above our powers of interpretation. The heirs of life were either despised as "earthen pitchers," the work of the hands of the potter, or we removed from their society, conscious that we were not fit compeers for "the precious sons of Zion, comparable to fine gold." Many have been the weary looks which we cast upon the time-piece when, in pious company, the theme has been too spiritual for our grovelling understanding; full often have we preferred the friendship of the laughing worldling to that of the more serious believer.

Need we ask the source of this dislike? The bitter stream is not like the river of Egypt, silent as to its source: it proclaims its own origin plainly enough; and the ear of self-partiality cannot be deaf to the truthful sound— "Ye loved not the servants, because ye esteemed not their master; ye dwelt not amid the brethren, for ye had no friendship towards the firstborn of the family."

One of the plainest evidences of alienation from God is a want of attachment to his people. In a greater or less degree this once existed in each of us. True, there were some Christians whose presence always afforded us pleasure; but we must be aware that our delight in their company was occasioned more by the affability of their manners, or the winning style of their address, than by the fact of their intrinsic excellence. We valued the gem for its setting, but a common pebble in the same ring would have equally engrossed our attention. The saints, *as saints*, were not our chosen friends, nor could we say, "I am a companion of *all those* that fear thee." All hail, thou leader of the host! we boldly own that from the moment when we first loved thy person, all thy followers have been dear to us, there's not a lamb amongst thy flock we would disdain to feed; thy servants may be mocked by contempt, persecuted by cruelty, branded with infamy, oppressed by power, humbled by poverty, and forgotten by fame; but to us they are the "excellent of the earth," and we are not ashamed to call them brethren.

Such sentiments are the finest products of esteem for the Redeemer, and their former absence is conclusive evidence that we then "esteemed him not." We have no further need of aid in this self-condemnation.

Broken Sabbaths start like warrior clansmen from the wild heath of neglected time; they point to *the deserted sanctuary,* for which they would execute a dread revenge did not the shield of Jesus cover us; for, lo! their bows are stringed with *neglected ordinances,* and their arrows are *despised messages of mercy.*

But wherefore these accusers? *Conscience* the ranger of the soul, hath seen enough. He will affirm that he hath beheld the ear closed to the wooing voice of the friend of sinners; that full often the eyes have been averted from the cross when Jesus himself was visibly set forth. Let him give in his own evidence. Hear him. He saith:—I have witnessed the barring of the heart to the entrance of Jesus; I have seen the whole man in arms to repair the breaches which a powerful minister had caused; I have been present when the struggle against the Saviour has been as fierce as the ravening wolf. In vain the sprinkled blood to rivet the attention—heedless of Calvary or Gethsemane, this mad soul refused to see the beauties of the Prince of Life, but rather spurned him from the heart which was his lawful throne. The sum and substance of my declaration is, "We esteemed him not."

Away then, O pride! we know that "without the sovereign influence of God's extraordinary and immediate grace, men do very rarely put off all thy trappings, till they who are about them put on their winding-sheet;"* but if aught can lay thee in the grave, the retrospect of our treatment of our loving Lord might avail to do it. Pause then, O Christian, and thus soliloquize: " I once scorned him who loved me with an everlasting love, I once esteemed him as a root out of a dry ground. I served him not, I cared not for his blood, his cross, or his crown; and yet I am now become one of his own children. Verily, to grace I will for ever sing :—

'Great God of wonders! all thy ways
    Are matchless, godlike, and divine,
But the fair glories of thy face
    More godlike and unrivalled shine:
Who is a pardoning God like thee?
Or who hath grace so rich and free?'"

* Clarendon.

II. We now enter upon an examination of
the latent causes of this sin.   When the disease
is removed, it may be useful to learn its origin,
that we may serve others and benefit ourselves.

Our coldness towards the Saviour resulted
primarily from *the natural evil of our hearts.*
We can plainly discern why the dissolute and
reprobate entertain but little affection for purity
and excellence: the self-same reason may be
given for our disregard of the incarnation of
virtue in the person of our Lord Jesus.   Sin
is a madness, disqualifying the mind for sober
judgment; a blindness, rendering the soul incapable of appreciating moral beauty; it is in fact
such a perversion of all the faculties, that under
its terrible influence men will "call evil good,
and good evil; they will put darkness for light,
and light for darkness; bitter for sweet, and
sweet for bitter."*   To us in our fallen condition fiends often appear more fair than angels,
we mistake the gates of hell for the portals of
bliss, and prefer the garnished lies of Satan
to the eternal verities of the Most High.   Revenge, lust, ambition, pride, and self-will, are too
often exalted as the gods of man's idolatry;
while holiness, peace, contentment, and humility,

* Isaiah v. 20.

are viewed as unworthy of a serious thought. O sin, what hast thou done! or rather, what hast thou undone! Thou hast not been content to rob humanity of its crown, to drive it from its happy kingdom, to mar its royal garments, and despoil its treasure; but thou hast done more than this! It sufficed not to degrade and dishonour; thou hast even wounded thy victim; thou hast blinded his eyes, stopped his ears, intoxicated his judgment, and gagged his conscience; yea, the poison of thy venomed shaft hath poured death into the *fountain*. Thy malice hath pierced the *heart* of manhood, and thereby hast thou filled his veins with corruption and his bones with depravity. Yea, O monster, thou hast become a murderer, for thou hast made us *dead* in trespasses and sins!

This last word opens up the entire mystery; for if we are spiritually dead, it is of course impossible for us to know and reverence the Prince of glory. Can the dead be moved to ecstasies, or corpses excited to rapture? Exercise your skill on yonder lifeless body. It has not yet become a carnival for worms. The frame is still complete, though lifeless. Bring hither lute and harp; let melodies most sweet, and harmonies unequalled, attempt to move the

c

man to pleasure: he smileth not at the swelling strain, he weepeth not at the plaintive cadence; yea, could the orchestra of the redeemed pour forth their music, he would be deaf to the celestial charm.

Will you assault the city by another gate? Place then before those eyes the choicest flowers that e'er were grown since Eden's plants were blasted. Doth he regard the loveliness of the rose or the whiteness of the lily? Nay, the man knoweth no more of their sweetness than doth the water of Nilus of the lotus which it beareth on its bosom. Come, ye gales of Araby, and winds laden with the spicy odours of Ceylon; let the incense of fragrant gums, of frankincense and myrrh, smoke before him; yet, motionless as a statue, the nostril is not distended, nor doth pleasure sit upon the lip. Aye, and ye may bring to your aid more powerful means. Ye may combine the crash of the avalanche, the roar of the cataract, the fury of the ocean, the howling of the winds, the rumbling of the earthquake, and the roll of the thunder: but these sounds, united into one godlike shout, could not arouse the slumberer from his fatal couch. *He is dead*, doth in one word solve the mystery. So also we, though quickened by the Holy

Ghost, were once dead in sin, and hence "we esteemed him not." Here is the root of all our misdeeds, the source of all our iniquity.

When we are asked to point out the parent of light, we turn our finger to the sun above; and if the question be proposed, Whence cometh evil? we point within us to an evil heart of unbelief which departeth from the living God.

The secondary causes of the folly which we once committed lie very near the surface, and may repay a moment's observation. *Self-esteem* had much to do with our ill-treatment of "the sinner's Friend." Conceit of our own deserts made us indifferent to the claims of one who had procured for us a perfect rightcousness. "The whole need not a physician;" and we felt insulted by the language of a gospel which spoke to us as undeserving beings. The Cross can have little power where pride conceals the necessity of a pardon; a sacrifice is little valued when we are unconscious of our need thereof. In our own opinion we were once most noble creatures; the Pharisee's oration would have sincerely enough emanated from us. A few little trifles there might be which were not quite correct, but in the main we thought ourselves "rich and increased in goods;" and even when under the powerful voice of law we were made to discern our poverty, we yet hoped by future obedience to reverse the sentence, and were utterly unwilling to accept a salvation which required a renunciation of all merit and simple trust on the crucified Redeemer. Never until all the work of our hands had been unravelled, and our fingers themselves had become powerless, would we cease from our own labour, and leaving the spider's-web of man's doings, array ourselves in the garment of free justification. No man will ever think much of Christ till he thinks little of himself. The lower our own views of ourselves become, the higher will our thoughts of Jesus be raised; and only when self-annihilation is complete will the Son of God be our "all in all."

Vain glory and self-esteem are fruitful parents of evil. Chrysostom calls self-love one of the devil's three great nets; and Bernard styles it "an arrow which pierceth the soul through, and slays it; a sly, insensible enemy, not perceived." Under the sad influence of this power we commonly love him best who does us the most harm; for the flatterer who feeds our vanity with pleasing cries of "Peace, peace," is far more regarded than that sincere friend, the blessed Jesus, who earnestly warns us of our ill estate. But when

self-confidence is removed—when the soul is
stripped by conviction—when the light of the
spirit reveals the loathsome state of the heart
—when the power of the creature fails, how
precious is Jesus! As the drowning mariner
clutches the floating spar—as the dying man
looks to some great physician—as the criminal
values his pardon, so do we then esteem the deliverer of our souls as the Prince of the kings
of the earth. Self-loathing begets an ardent
passion for the gracious "lover of our souls,"
but self-complacency hides his glories from us.

Love of the world has also its share in using
this dear friend so ill. When he knocked at
the door we refused him admittance, because
another had already entered. We had each
chosen another husband to whom we basely
gave away our hearts. "Give me wealth,"
said one. Jesus replied, "Here am I; I am
better than the riches of Egypt, and my reproach is more to be desired than hidden treasures." The answer was, "Thou art not the
wealth that I seek for; I pant not for an airy
wealth like thine, O Jesus! I do not care for a
wealth above in the future—I desire a wealth
here in the present; I want a treasure that I
can grasp *now*; I want gold that will buy me a

house, a farm, and estate; I long for the sparkling jewel that will adorn my fingers; I ask thee
not for that which is hereafter; I will seek for
that when years have passed away."

Another of us cried, "I ask for health, for I
am sick." The best Physician appears, and
gently promises, "I will heal thy soul, take
away thy leprosy, and make thee whole." "Nay,
nay," we answered, "I ask not for that, O Jesus!
I ask to have a *body* that is strong, that I may
run like Asahel or wrestle like an Hercules;
I long to be freed from pain of body, but I do
not ask for health of soul, that is not what
I require." A third implored for happiness.
"Listen to me," said Jesus, "my ways are ways
of pleasantness, and all my paths are peace."
"Not the joy for which I sigh," we hastily replied; "I ask the cup filled to the brim, that I
may drink it merrily; I love the jovial evening,
and the joyous day; I want the dance, the revelry,
and other fair delights of this world; give your
hereafter to those who are enthusiasts—let
them live on hope; I prefer this world and the
present."

Thus did we each in a different fashion set
our affection on things below, and despise the
things above. Surely he was no ill painter who

thus sketched us to the life with his graphic
pencil: "The interpreter took them apart again,
and had them into a room where was a man that
could look no-ways but downwards, with a muckrake in his hand; there stood also one over his
head with a celestial crown in his hand, and
proffered him that crown for his muckrake; but
the man did neither look up nor regard, but
raked to himself the straws and dust of the floor."

While we love the world, "the love of the
Father is not in us;"* nor the love of Jesus the
son.   Two masters we cannot serve.   The world
and Jesus never will agree.   We must be able
to sing the first portion of Madame Guion's
stanza before we can truly join in its concluding
words:

> "Adieu! ye vain delights of earth,
>   Insipid sports, and childish mirth,
>   I taste no sweets in you;
>   Unknown delights are in the Cross,
>   All joy beside to me is dross;
>   And Jesus thought so too."

It would be a great omission did we not observe
that our *ignorance of Christ* was a main cause
of our want of love towards him.   We now see
that to know Christ is to love him.   It is im-

* 1 John ii. 15.

possible to have a vision of his face, to behold his person, or understand his offices, without feeling our souls warmed towards him. Such is the beauty of our blessed Lord, that all men, save the spiritually blind, pay willing homage to him. It needs no eloquence to set forth Christ to those who see him by faith, for in truth he is his own orator; his glory speaks, his condescension speaks, his life speaks, and, above all, his death speaks; and what these utter without sound, the heart receiveth willingly.

Jesus is " curtained from the sight of the gross world" by the wilful unbelief of mankind, or else the sight of him would have begotten veneration for him. Men know not the gold which lies in the mine of Christ Jesus, or surely they would dig in it night and day. They have not yet discovered the pearl of great price, or they would have sold their all to buy the field wherein it lies. The person of Christ strikes eloquence dumb when it would describe him; it palsies the artist's arm when with fair colours he would portray him; it would o'ermatch the sculptor to carve his image even were it possible to chisel it in a massive block of diamond. There is nought in nature comparable to him. Before his radiance the brilliance of the sun is dimmed; yea, nothing can compete with him, and heaven itself blushes at its own plainness of countenance when his "altogether lovely" person is beheld. Ah, ye who pass him by without regard, it is well said by Rutherford, "Oh if ye knew him, and saw his beauty, your love, your heart, your desires, would close with him and cleave to him. Love, by nature, when it seeth, cannot but cast out its spirit and strength upon amiable objects, and good things, and things love-worthy; and what fairer thing is there than Christ?" The Jewish world crucified him because they knew not their king; and we rejected him because we had not seen his adaptation to our wants, and believed not the love he bore to our souls. We can all thus soliloquize with Augustine:— "There was a great dark cloud of vanity before mine eyes, so that I could not see the sun of justice and the light of truth; I, being the son of darkness, was involved in darkness; I loved my darkness, because I knew not thy light; I was blind, and loved my blindness, and did walk from darkness to darkness; but Lord, thou art my God, who hast led me from darkness and the shadow of death; hast called me into this glorious light, and behold I see." Those days of soul-eclipse are gone, but never can we too much bewail them. Sad were those hours when the morning-star shone not, when the Cross had no charms, and the glorious Redeemer no esteem; could tears obliterate them from the annals of the past, our eyes should empty their cisterns ere our cheeks should be dry—could prayers recall them, we would besiege the throne with incessant supplications. They are gone, alas! beyond the arm of even omnipotence to restore them; but we rejoice to see their iniquity blotted out and their sin entirely covered.

The river of sinful neglect of Jesus has doubtless other tributary sources which we cannot now tarry to notice. Contemplation need not here wander in a maze, she hath a path laid straight before her; unchain her feet and bid her conduct you over the field of memory, that with her you may count the other rills which fed this noxious stream.

III. We come now to the practical part of our meditation, and consider the emotions which ought to be excited by it.

First, then, we think *deep penitential sorrow* will well become us. As tears are the fit moisture for the grave, as ashes are a fit crown for the head of mourning, so are penitential feelings the proper mementoes of conduct now forsaken and abhorred. We cannot understand the christianity of those men who can narrate their past history with a kind of self-congratulation. We have met with some who will recount their former crimes with as much gusto as the old soldier tells his feats in arms. Such men will even blacken themselves to render their case more worthy of regard, and glory in their past sins as if they were ornaments to their new life. To such we say, Not thus thought Paul; when speaking to the Romans, he said, "whereof ye are now ashamed." There are times when it is proper, beneficial, and praise-worthy for a converted man to tell the sad tale of his former life; free grace is thus glorified, and divine power extolled, and such a story of experience may serve to bring about faith in others who think themselves too vile; but then let it be done in a right spirit, with expressions of unfeigned regret and repentance. We object not to the narration of the deeds of our unregenerate condition, but to the mode in which it is too often done. Let sin have its monument, but let it be a heap of stones cast by the hands

of execration—not a mausoleum erected by the
hands of affection. Give it the burial of Absalom
—let it not sleep in the sepulchre of the kings.

Can we, beloved, enter the dark vault of our
former ignorance without a feeling of oppressive
gloom? Can we traverse the ruins of our mis-
spent years without sighs of regret? Can we
behold the havoc of our guilt, and smile at the
destruction? Nay. It is ours to bewail what we
cannot efface, and abhor what we cannot retract.

O fellow-heir of the kingdom, let us go
together to the throne of Jesus, that our tears
may bathe his feet; that, like Mary, we may
make our grief a worshipper of his person.
Let us seek some alabaster-box of very precious
ointment wherewith to anoint him, or at any
rate let our eyes supply a tribute of true
gratitude. We approach his sacred person, and
on his feet we see the impress of his love deep-
cut by the piercing nails. Come now, my
heart! bewail that wound, for thou didst make
it; the soldier was but thy servant who did
thy bidding, but the cruel act was thine.
Note well his hands which firmly grasp thee;
they too have their scars; and weep at the
remembrance that these were made for thee.
For thee he bore the ignominy of the cross, the

pain of crucifixion. Turn not thine eyes away until the hole of the side has been well pondered. See there that frightful gash, deep mine which reacheth to his heart. And this, my soul, was done for thee! dost thou not love the sufferer? Yea, thou dost, with a love as deep and bottomless as the ocean; but forget not that once thou didst despise him. Many a time hast thou slighted this gracious friend; thy husband was once hated by thee; thy beloved has often received contumely and scorn from thee. Not long ago thou didst mock, despise, and insult him. Hard words hast thou spoken of him, and ill deeds hast thou done to him. His wooings thou didst disregard, the tender offerings of love thou didst trample under foot, and the deep anguish which he endured for thee was in thine ears an idle tale. What! are the fountains dry? When will thy sorrow find better cause for coining itself in tears? Canst thou afford a silly story of a love-sick maid a tear or two, and shall not this—thyself and Jesus—move thy soul? He loved, and thou didst hate; he died, yet thou didst scoff his agonies; he saved thee, and yet thou didst refuse to be his child. O base ingratitude! Clouds might be fit mourners to weep thee away in showers; but yet we are.

oft hard as the granite rock, and cold as the mountain which storeth up its snow, which it might well afford to lavish forth in rivers. We should long to feel the sweet pleasure of repentance, for indeed it is no common delight. Howe has excellently described the joy of penitential grief in his " Delight in God : "—

" There is pleasure mingled with such tears, and with those mournings which are not without hope, and which flow naturally and without force from a living principle within, as waters from their still freshly-springing fountain. When the soul finds itself unbound and set at liberty, when it can freely pour out itself to God, dissolve kindly and melt before him, it doth it with regret only at what it hath done and been, not at what it is now doing, except that it can do it no more; affecting even to be infinite herein, while it yet sees it must be confined within some bounds. It loves to lie in the dust and abase itself; and is pleased with the humiliation, contrition, and brokenness of heart which repentance towards God includes in it. So that as God is delighted with this sacrifice, so *it* is with the offering of it up to him. Many men apprehend a certain sweetness in revenge; such a one finds it only in this just revenge upon himself. How unexpressible a pleasure accompanies its devoting itself to God, when bemoaning itself, and returning with weeping and supplication, it says, 'Now, lo! I come to thee, thou art the Lord my God, I have brought thee back thine own, what I had sacrilegiously alienated and stolen away, the heart which was gone astray, that hath been so long a vagabond and fugitive from thy blessed presence, service, and communion. Take now the soul which thou hast made; possess thy own right; enter upon it; stamp it with the entire impression of thine own seal, and mark it for thine. Other lords shall no more have dominion. What have I to do any more with the idols wherewith I was wont to provoke thee to jealousy? I will now make mention of thy name, and of thine only. I bind myself to thee in everlasting bonds, in a covenant never to be forgotten.'"

Let not a libation of tears be the only offering at the shrine of Jesus; *let us also rejoice with joy unspeakable*. If we have need to lament our sin, how much more to rejoice at our pardon! If our previous state moves us to tears, shall not our new condition cause our hearts to leap for joy? Yes, we must, we will praise the Lord for his sovereign, distinguishing grace. We owe him an eternal song for this change in our position; he has made us to differ, and this from mere unmerited mercy, since we, like others, "esteemed him not." He certainly did not elect us to the high dignity of union with himself because of any love we had toward him, for we confess the very reverse. It is said of the writer's sainted predecessor, Dr. Rippon, that when asked why God chose his people, he replied, "Because he chose them;" and when the question was repeated, he answered yet again, "Because he *did* choose them, and if you ask me a hundred times I can give you no other reason." Verily it is "even so Father, because so it seemed good in thy sight." Let our gratitude for divine grace leap forth in praise; let our whole man be vocal to *his* honour who has elected us in sovereignty, redeemed us by blood, and called us by grace.

Should we not also be moved to *the deepest prostration of spirit* at the remembrance of our guilt? Ought not the subject of our present contemplation to be a stab in the very heart of pride? Come hither, Christian, and though now arrayed in the garments of salvation, behold here thy former nakedness. Boast not of thy riches, remember how sorry a beggar once thou wast. Glory not in thy virtues, they are exotics in thy heart; remember the deadly plants—the native growth of that evil soil. Stoop thyself to the earth, and though thou canst not veil thyself with wings as angels do, let repentance and self-abhorrence serve thee instead thereof. Think not that humility is weakness; it shall supply the marrow of strength to thy bones. Stoop, and conquer; bow thyself, and become invincible. The proud man has no power over his fellows; the beasts of the forest tremble not at the loftiness of the giraffe, but the crouching lion is the monarch of the plain. He who esteems himself but little, stands on a vantage-ground with his fellow-men. Like an Eastern house, the heart has a lowly entrance, and every guest must bow his head ere he can cross the threshold. He who has felt his own ruin will not imagine any to be hopeless; nor will he think them too fallen to be worthy his regard. Though he may be a priest or Levite in the temple of his God, he will not feel degraded if he stain his hands in binding up the wounds of the victims of evil. Like the friend of publicans and sinners, he will seek out the sick who need a physician. Christianity has founded a colony for the outcasts of society. The founder of Rome welcomed to his new-built city the dregs of all the nations of the earth; so let every Christian believe that Zion's inhabitants are to be gathered from haunts of sin and chambers of vice. How prone are we to forestal the damnation of men! How often do we write in our book of doom the names of many whom we afterwards discover to have been "ordained unto eternal life!" The astronomer will believe that the most erratic comet will yet accomplish its journey, and revisit our sphere; but we give up those for lost, who have not wandered one-half the distance from the centre of light and life. We find an excuse for inaction in the fancied hopelessness of sinners; while fastidious delicacy, by the fear of pollution, seeks to mask at once our indolence and pride. If we had right views of *ourselves*, we should judge none too base to be reclaimed, and should count it no dishonour to bear upon the shoulders of our sympathy, the most wandering of the flock. We have amongst us too much of the spirit of "Stand by, for I am holier than thou." Those whom Jesus would have grasped by the hand, we will scarcely touch with a pair of tongs; such is the pride of many professors, that they need but the name to be recognised at once as the true successors of the ancient Pharisees. If we were more like

Christ, we should be more ready to hope for the hopeless, to value the worthless, and to love the depraved. The following anecdote, which the writer received from the lips of an esteemed minister of the Church of England, may perhaps, as a fact, plead more forcibly than words. A clergyman of a parish in Ireland, in the course of his visitations, had called upon every one of his flock with but one exception. This was a woman of most abandoned character, and he feared that by entering her house he might give occasion of offence to gainsayers, and bring dishonour upon his profession. One Sabbath, he observed her among the frequenters of his church, and for weeks after he noticed her attention to the word of life. He thought, too, that amid the sound of the responses he could detect one sweet and earnest voice, solemnly confessing sin, and imploring mercy. The bowels of his pity yearned over this fallen daughter of Eve; he longed to ask her if her heart were indeed broken on account of sin; and he intensely desired to speak with her concerning the abounding grace which, he hoped, had plucked her from the burning. Still, the same delicacy of feeling forbade him to enter the house; time after time he passed her door with longing look, anxious

for her salvation, but jealous of his own honour.
This lasted for a length of time, but at last it
ended. One day, she called him to her, and with
overflowing tears which well betrayed her bursting heart, she said, *" O sir! if your Master had
been in this village half as long as you have, he
would have called to see me long ago; for surely
I am the chief of sinners, and therefore have
most need of his mercy."* We may conceive the
melting of the pastor's heart, when he saw his
conduct thus gently condemned by a comparison
with his loving Master. From that time forth
he resolved to neglect none, but to gather even
the "outcasts of Israel." Should we, by our
meditation, be constrained to do likewise, we
shall have derived no little benefit, and possibly
some soul may have reason to bless God that our
thoughts were directed into such a channel.
May the gracious Spirit, who has promised to
" lead us into all truth " by his holy influences,
sanctify to our profit this visit to the house of our
nativity, exciting in us all those emotions which
are congenial to the subject, and leading us to
actions in harmony with the grateful retrospect.

TO THE UNCONVERTED READER.

My Friend,—Although this book was written chiefly for the Lord's family, yet it may please the gracious Spirit to bless it to thine own soul. With this desire let me seriously entreat thee well to consider the condition thou art in. Thou art one who esteems not Jesus. This is a state, sad in itself by reason of thy loss of present delight in him; but how much more terrible if thou dost remember the eternal consequences of refusing Christ. He is thine only real hope, and yet thou rejected him. Thy salvation can only come through him, and yet thou dost wilfully remove thyself from him. A few more years will bring thee to the threshold of another world. It will go ill with thee if thou dost still " neglect this great salvation." Death will soon loosen thy girdle and break thy strength. What wilt thou do in the last hour of extremity without a Saviour? Judgment will follow on the heels of

dissolution; and when the insulted Saviour sits
upon the judgment-seat, how wilt thou face him?
Wilt thou be able to bear the fury of his incensed
majesty? As oil, the softest of substances, doth
burn the most fiercely, so doth love when it is
angered. I bid thee bethink thyself, how thou
wilt endure his ire. The eyes which once flowed
with tears shall flash lightnings on thee. The
hands which were nailed to the cross of redemption shall seize the thunderbolts of vengeance,
and the voice which once in melting tones said,
"Come, ye weary," shall pronounce in thundering words the sentence, "Depart, ye cursed!"

Art thou so besotted as to venture on so
hazardous a course as continued rebellion? Dost
thou wish to lie down in torment, and make thy
bed in hell?

O my brother-immortal! tarry here and
ponder thy woeful estate; and may the Spirit
now manifest to thee thy lost and helpless condition, that, so stripped of self, thou mayest seek
my Master's righteousness. He says:—"*I love
them that love me, and they that seek me early
shall find me.*"

II.

𝕱𝖆𝖎𝖙𝖍𝖋𝖚𝖑 𝖂𝖔𝖚𝖓𝖉𝖘.

"Faithful are the wounds of a friend."—Prov. xxvii. 6.

The death in sin, which we so much lamented in the last chapter, is now happily a thing of the past with us. Divine grace has quickened us; heavenly influence has preserved us; and faithful promises have secured our spiritual immortality. It is now our delightful duty to adore the love which, even when we were dead in sins, was still planning deeds of kindness towards us; and which in its own appointed time enlisted Omnipotence in our behalf, whereby we received life from the dead.

In order to raise our hearts heavenward, and tune our lips to the psalmody of praise, let us, by the Spirit's gracious assistance, review the way whereby the Lord led us to himself.

Like ourselves, many of our readers will admit

that the first they ever knew of Jesus was in the character of a faithful friend wounding us for sin.   Though at that time we knew not that love was mixed with every blow, yet now we perceive it to have been the kind plan of a gracious Saviour to bring us to himself.   The Roman emperor conferred freedom on a slave by smiting him on the ear: and Jesus sets us at liberty by a blow upon our heart.

I. We shall dwell first upon the fact that *all saved persons have been wounded*.   Neither in the Church militant nor the host triumphant is there one who received a new heart, and was reclaimed from sin, without a wound from Jesus. The pain may have been but slight, and the healing may have been speedy; but in each case there has been a real bruise, which required a heavenly physician to heal.

1. With some, this wounding commenced in *early* life; for as soon as infancy gave place to childhood, the rod was exercised upon certain of us.   We can remember early convictions of sin, and apprehensions of the wrath of God on its account.   An awakened conscience in our most tender years drove us to the throne of mercy. Though we knew not the hand which chastened

our spirit, yet did we "bear the yoke in our youth." How many were "the tender buds of hope" which we then put forth, alas! too soon to be withered by youthful lusts; how often were we "scared with visions" and terrified with dreams, while the reproof of a parent, the death of a playfellow, or a solemn sermon made our hearts melt within us! Truly, our goodness was but " as the morning cloud and the early dew ;" but who can tell how much each of these separate woundings contributed toward that killing by the law, which proved to be the effectual work of God? In each of these arousings we discover a gracious purpose ; we trace every one of these awakenings to His hand who watched over our path, determined to deliver us from our sins. The small end of that wedge which has since been driven home, was inserted during these youthful hours of inward strife; the ground of our heart was then enduring a ploughing preparatory to the seed.

Let none despise the strivings of the Spirit in the hearts of the young; let not boyish anxieties and juvenile repentances be lightly regarded. He incurs a fearful amount of guilt who in the least promotes the aim of the Evil One by trampling upon a tender conscience in a child. No one knows the age of the youngest

child in hell; and therefore none can guess at
what age children become capable of conversion.
We at least can bear our testimony to the fact
that grace operates on some minds at a period
almost too early for recollection. Nor let it be
imagined that the feelings of the young are slight
and superficial—they are frequently of the deepest
character. The early woundings of the Saviour
are made upon hearts not yet rendered callous by
worldliness and sensuality. The Christian whose
lot it was to be smitten in his childhood, will
well remember the deep searchings of heart and
the keen convictions of soul which he endured.

O beloved, how much have we to bless our
Jesus for, and how much for which to reprove
ourselves! Did we not stifle our conscience,
and silence the voice of reproof? Were we not
deaf to the warning voice of our glorious Jesus?
When he smote us sorely, we returned not to
kiss his rod, but were as refractory as the bullock
unaccustomed to the yoke. Our most solemn
vows were only made to be broken; our earnest
prayers ceased when the outward pressure was
removed; and our partial reformations passed
away like dreams of the night. Blessed be *His*
name, he at last gave us the effectual blow of
grace; but we must for ever stand in amazement

at the patience which endured our obstinacy, and persevered in its design of love.

2. Many of the Lord's beloved ones have felt the wounds to be exceedingly *painful.* There are degrees in the bitterness of sorrow for sin; all have not the same horrible apprehensions of destruction; but some there be who have drank the very wormwood and gall of repentance. Usually, such persons have been great sinners previously, or become great saints in after life. They love much because they feel that much has been forgiven; their fearful bondage increases their gratitude for glorious liberty; and the wretchedness of their natural poverty enhances their estimation of the riches of Jesus. The painful process is thus a gainful one; but when it is endured it is indeed an exceeding fiery furnace— an oven that burneth with vehement heat. He who hath had his feet fast in the stocks of conviction will never forget it till his dying day. Well do some of us call to mind the season when our true Friend smote our heart, with what we then thought the hand of a cruel one. Our mirth was turned into mourning, our songs to lamentations, our laughter into sighing, and our joys to misery. Black thoughts haunted our benighted soul—dreary images of woe sat upon

the throne of our imagination—sounds akin to
the wailings of hell were frequent in our ears,
unitedly making our entire man so full of
agony that it could be compared to nothing but
the portal of hell.   During this period, our
prayers were truly earnest when we could pray;
but at times a sense of tremendous guilt bound
our lips, and choked our utterance.   Now and
then a faint gleam of hope lit up the scene for a
moment, only to increase the gloom upon its
departure.   The nearer we approached to our
Lord, the more sternly (we thought) he repelled
us; the more earnest our attempts at amendment, the more heavy the lash fell upon our
shoulders.   The law grasped us with iron hand,
and smote us with the scourge of vengeance;
conscience washed the quivering flesh with
brine; and despondency furnished us with a bed
of thorns, upon which our poor mangled frame
found a hard couch.   By night we dreamed of
torment, by day we almost felt its prelude.   In
vain did we ask Moses to propitiate an angry
God; in vain did we attempt by vows to move
his pity : " the Breaker " * broke our hearts with
his heavy hammer, and seemed intent to make
our agonies intolerable.   We dared not touch

* Mic. ii. 13.

the hem of his garment, lest "Depart from me!" should be the only word he would afford us. A fearful looking-for of judgment and of fiery indignation wrought in us all manner of fears, suspicions, tremblings, despondings, and despairings.

Old Burton was no ill limner when he thus painted the soul under the pressure of a burden of guilt:—"Fear takes away their content, and dries the blood, wasteth the marrow, alters their countenance, 'even in their greatest delights—singing, dancing, feasting—they are still (saith Lemnius) tortured in their souls.' It consumes them to nought. 'I am like a pelican in the wilderness (saith David of himself, temporarily afflicted): an owl, because of thine indignation.'* 'My heart trembleth within me, and the terrors of death have come upon me; fear and trembling are come upon me, &c., at death's door.' 'Their soul abhorreth all manner of meat.'† Their sleep is (if it be any) unquiet, subject to fearful dreams and terrors. Peter, in his bonds, slept secure, for he knew God protected him. Tully makes it an argument of Roscius Amerinus' innocency (that he killed not his father) because he so securely slept. Those martyrs in the pri-

* Ps. cii. 6, 10; lv. 4.   † Ps. cvii. 18.

mitive Church were most cheerful and merry in
the midst of their persecutions; but it is far
otherwise with these men: tossed in a sea, and
that continually, without rest or intermission,
they can think of nought that is pleasant; "their
conscience will not let them be in quiet;" in perpetual fear and anxiety, if they be not yet ap-
prehended, they are in doubt still they shall be
ready to betray themselves. As Cain did, he
thinks every man will kill him; 'and roar for
the grief of heart,'* as David did, as Job did.†
'Wherefore is light given to him that is in
misery, and life to them that have a heavy
heart? Which long for death; and if it come
not, search it more than treasures, and rejoice
when they can find the grave.' They are generally weary of their lives: a trembling heart
they have, a sorrowful mind, and little or no
rest. *Terror ubique tremor, timor undique et
undique terror:* 'tears, terrors, and affrights, in
all places, at all times and seasons.' *Cibum et
potum pertinacitèr aversantur multi, nodum in
scirpo quæritantes, et culpam imaginantes ubi
nulla est,* as Wierus writes,‡ 'they refuse many of
them meat and drink, cannot rest, aggravating

* Ps. xxxviii. 8.   † Job xx. 3, 21, 22, &c.
‡ De Lamiis, lib. iii. c. 7.

still, and supposing grievous offences where there are none.' God's heavy wrath is kindled in their souls, and, notwithstanding their continual prayers and supplications to Christ Jesus, they have no release or ease at all, but a most intolerable torment, and insufferable anguish of conscience; and that makes them, through impatience, to murmur against God many times, to think hardly of him, and even, in some cases, seek to offer violence to themselves. In the morning they wish for evening, and for morning in the evening; for the sight of their eyes which they see, and fear of heart."*

Hart knew the deep woundings of this faithful Friend; witness the following lines :—

> " The Lord, from whom I long backslid,
>   First check'd me with some gentle stings ;
> Turn'd on me, look'd, and softly chid,
>   And bade me hope for greater things.

> " Soon to his bar he made me come
>   Arraign'd, convicted, cast, I stood,
> Expecting from his mouth the doom
>   Of those who trample on his blood.

> " Pangs of remorse my conscience tore,
>   Hell open'd hideous to my view ;
> And what I only heard before,
>   I found, by sad experience, true.

* Deut. xxviii. 65, 66.

" Oh! what a dismal state was this,
    What horrors shook my feeble frame!
But, brethren, surely you can guess,
    For you, perhaps, have felt the same."

Doubtless, some of our readers will cry out
against such a description as being too harsh;
our only answer is, we have felt these things in
a measure, and we testify what we do know.
We do not, for one moment, teach that all or
that many are thus led in a path strewn with
horrors, and shrouded in gloom; but we hope
to be acknowledged, by those who have experienced the same, to have uttered no strange
thing, but the simple tale, unexaggerated and
unadorned. We need no better evidences to
convince all Christian men of our truthfulness
than those with which our own pastorate has
furnished us. Many have we seen in this condition; and we hope that not a few have been,
by our instrumentality, led into the liberty
wherewith Christ makes men free.

Such terrible things are not necessary to true
repentance, but they do at times accompany it.
Let the man who is now floundering in the
slough of Despond take heart, for the slough
lieth right in the middle of the way, and the
best pilgrims have fallen into it. Your case,

O soul under spiritual distress, is by no means singular; and if it were so, it would not be necessarily desperate, for Omnipotence knoweth nothing of impossibilities, and grace stayeth not for our demerits. A dark cloud is no sign that the sun has lost his light; and dark black convictions are no arguments that God has laid aside his mercy. Destruction and wrath may thunder, but mercy can speak louder than both. One word from our Lord can still the waves and winds. Get thee beneath the tree of life, and not a drop of the shower of wrath will fall on thee. Fear not to go, for the cherubims which you see are not guards to prevent your approach, but ministers who will welcome your coming. Oh! sit not down in sullen despair, harden not thine heart, for it is a friend that wounds thee. He has softened thee in the furnace; he is now welding thee with his hammer. Let him slay thee, but do thou still trust in him. If he had meant to destroy thee, he would not have showed thee such things as these: love is in his heart when chiding is on his lips; yea, his very words of reproof are so many "tokens for good." A father will not lift his hand against another man's child, but he exercises discipline upon his own; even so the Lord your God

chastens his own, but reserveth retribution for
the children of wrath in another state of being.
Bethink thee, also, that it is no small mercy to
feel thy sin; this proves that there is no mortification in thy frame, but life is there. To feel
is an evidence of life; and spiritual sorrow is a
clear proof of life in the soul. Moreover, there
are thousands who would give worlds to be in
the same condition as thou art; they are grieving because they do not have those very feelings
which are in thy case thy burden and plague.
Multitudes envy thee thy groans, thy tears, and
meltings; yea, some advanced saints look at
thee with admiration, and wish that their hearts
were as tender as thine. Oh! take courage; the
rough usage of to-day is an earnest of loving
dealings by-and-bye. It is in this manner
the sheep is brought into the fold by the bark-
ing of the dog; and in this fashion the ship
is compelled by the storm to make for the
nearest haven. Fly to Jesus, and believe his
grace.

  3. A portion of the redeemed have had this
season of wounding *protracted* for a long time.
It was not one heavy fall of the rod, but stroke
after stroke, repeated for months, and even years,
in continual succession. John Bunyan was for

many years an anxious and desponding seeker
of mercy; and thousands more have trodden
the valley of darkness for as long a time.
Winters are not usually long in our favoured
clime, but some years have seen the earth
covered with snow and fettered in ice for many
a dreary month; so also many souls are soon
cheered by the light of God's countenance, but
a few find, to their own sorrow, that at times
the promise tarries. When the sun sets we
usually see him in the morning; but Paul,
when in a tempest at sea, saw neither sun,
moon, nor stars, for three days: many a tried
soul hath been longer than this in finding light.
All ships do not make speedy voyages: the
peculiar build of the vessel, the winds, the
waves, and the mistakes of the captain, all
affect the time of the journey. Some seeds
send forth their germs in a few days; others
abide long in darkness, hidden under the clods.
The Lord can, when it is his good pleasure,
send conviction and comfort as rapidly in succession as the flash of lightning and the clap of
thunder; but at times he delays it for purposes
which, though we know not now, we shall know
hereafter. Men shall not have an Easter until
they have had Lent; but God's Lents are not

all of the same duration.   Let none, then, foolishly imagine that they have entered a long
lane which will have no turning; let them consider how long they were in sin, and they will
have little cause to complain that they are so
long in humiliation. When they remember their
own ignorance, they will not think they are detained too long in the school of penitence.   No
man has any right to murmur because he is
waiting a little for the King of mercy; for if he
considereth what he waits for, he will see it to
be well worthy of a thousand years' delay. God
may say, " *To-day* if ye will hear *my* voice;" but
thou, O sinner, hast no right to demand that he
should hear *thine* at all, much less to-day. Great
men often have petitioners in their halls, who
will wait for hours, and come again and again
to obtain promotion: surely, the God of heaven
should be waited for by them that seek him.
Thrice happy is he that getteth an early inter-
view, and doubly blest is he who getteth one
at all. Yet it does at times seem hard to
stand at a door which opens not to repeated
knocking — "hope deferred maketh the heart
sick:" and it may be, some reader of this
volume is driven to doubt the eventual result
of his strivings and prayers; he may be crying,

" My life is spent with grief, and my years with sighing."

" How oft have these bare knees been bent to gain
   The slender alms of one poor smile in vain ?
   How often tir'd with the fastidious light
   Have my faint lips implor'd the shades of night ?
   How often have my nightly torments pray'd
   For ling'ring twilight, glutted with the shade ?
   Day worse than night, night worse than day appears ;
   In fears I spend my nights, my days in tears :
   I moan unpitied, groan without relief,
   There is no end or measure of my grief.
   The branded slave, that tugs the weary oar,
   Obtains the Sabbath of a welcome shore ;
   His ransom'd stripes are heal'd ; his native soil
   Sweetens the mem'ry of his foreign toil :
   But ah ! my sorrows are not half so blest ;
   My labours find no point, my pains no rest :
   I barter sighs for tears, and tears for groans,
   Still vainly rolling Sisyphæan stones."

Cease thy complaint, O mourner, the angel is on his way, and faith shall quicken his flight ; while thou art yet speaking He hears, yea, before thou callest again, He may answer thee.

4. Divine sovereignty displays itself in the manner whereby souls are brought to Jesus ; for while many, as we have said, are smitten with deep wounds, there are perhaps a larger number whose smartings are *less severe,* and their suffering *far less acute.* Let us never make apologies for the superficial religion too common

in the present day; above all, let us never lead
others to mistake fancies for realities, and evan-
escent feelings for enduring workings of grace. We
fear too many are deluded with a false religion,
which will be utterly consumed when the fire
shall try all things; and we solemnly warn our
readers to rest short of nothing less than a real
experience of grace within, true repentance,
deep self-abhorrence, and complete subjection
to salvation by grace. Yet we do believe and
know that some of the Lord's family are, by his
marvellous kindness, exempted from the exceeding rigour of the terrors of Sinai, and the excessive griefs engendered by the working of the
Law. God openeth many hearts with gentle
picklocks, while with others he useth the crow-
bar of terrible judgments. The wind of the
Spirit, which bloweth *where* it listeth, also
bloweth *how* it pleaseth: it is oftentimes a
gentle gale, not always a hurricane. When the
lofty palm of Zeilan putteth forth its flower,
the sheath bursts with a report which shakes
the forest, but thousands of other flowers of equal
value open in the morning, and the very dewdrops hear no sound; so many souls blossom in
mercy, and the world hears neither whirlwind
nor tempest Showers frequently fall upon this

earth too gently to be heard, though truly at other seasons the rattling drops proclaim them; grace also "droppeth, like the gentle dew from heaven," on souls whom Jesus would favour, and they know nothing of heavy hail and drenching torrents.

Let none doubt their calling because it came not with sound of the trumpet; let them not sit down to measure their own feelings by those of other men, and because they are not precisely the same, at once conclude that they are no children of the kingdom. No two leaves upon a tree are precisely alike—variety is the rule of nature; the line of beauty runs not in one undeviating course; and in grace the same rule holds good. Do not, therefore, desire another man's repentance, or thy brother's apprehensions of wrath. Be not wishful to try the depth of the cavern of misery, but rather rejoice that thou hast a partial immunity from its glooms. Be concerned to flee for refuge to Jesus; but ask not that the avenger of blood may almost overtake thee. Be content to enter the ark like a sheep led by its shepherd; desire not to come like an unruly bullock, which must be driven to the door with stripes. Adore the power which is not bound down to a unity of

method, but which can open the eye by the clay
and spittle, or by the simple touch of the finger.
Jesus cried, with a loud voice, "Lazarus, come
forth!" but the restoration was as easily
effected when he gently said, "Maid, arise!"
Zaccheus was called from the tree with a voice
that the crowd could hear; but it was a still
voice which in the garden said, "Mary!"
Can any man say but that equal benefits flowed
from these varied voices? It is arrogance for
any man to map out the path of the Eternal, or
dictate to Jesus the methods of his mercy. Let
us be content with gentle wounds, and let us
not seek heavy blows as a proof of his faithfulness.

Much more might have been discoursed concerning *the means* used by Providence to break
the hard heart. Bereavement, disappointment,
sickness, poverty, have had their share of uses;
the Word preached, Scriptures read or reproofs
received, have all been owned to conversion. It
would be interesting to register the diverse ways
of Jehovah's doings with sinners; and it would
be found a valuable occupation for a gathering
of Christians in an evening party, if the question is passed round to each, and one acts as
recorder for the rest; thus interesting informa-

tion may be obtained, and unprofitable talking avoided.

II. We now seek to justify our assertion that *these wounds are inflicted by " the friend," Christ Jesus*. Our readers will observe that Jesus' name has not often occurred in the course of this chapter, but this has had its reasons; in order that our words might be somewhat in accordance with the state of the soul during the operation of conviction, for then it discerns not Jesus, and knows nothing of his love. A faint idea of his saving power may arise, but it is only the hush between the succeeding gusts of wind. There is an atonement, but the tried conscience rejoices not therein, since the blood has never been applied; HE is able to save unto the uttermost, but since the man has not come unto God by him, he as yet participates not in the salvation. Nevertheless, an unseen Jesus is a true Jesus; and when we see him not, he is none the less present, working all our works in us. We would insist strongly on this point, because a very large number of mourning sinners ascribe their sorrow to any source but the right one.

1. We know those at present in the prison-

house of conviction who believe themselves to be tormented by the devil, and are haunted by the dreadful thought that he is about to devour them, since hell seems to have begun in their souls. May the sacred Comforter render our words profitable to a heart so exercised. It is not an evil one who convinces the soul of sin, although the troubled spirit is prone to impute its arousings to the machinations of the devil. It is never the policy of the Prince of darkness to disturb his subjects; he labours to make them self-satisfied and content with their position; spiritual uneasiness he looks upon with most crafty suspicion, since he sees therein the cause of desertion from his evil army. We do not assert that none of the terrors which accompany conviction are the works of the devil, for we believe they are; but we maintain that the inward disturbance which originates the commotion is a work of love—a deed of divine compassion, and comes from no other fountain than eternal affection. The dust which surrounds the chariot may rise from beneath, but the chariot itself is paved with the love of heaven. The doubts, the despairings, and the hellish apprehensions may be the work of Diabolus, but the real attack is headed by Emmanuel, and it is from very fear that the true assault may be successful that Satan attempts another. Jesus sends an army to drive us to himself, and then the Prince of the powers of the air dispatches a host to cut off our retreat to Calvary. So harassed is the mind when thus besieged, that like the warriors in old Troy, it mistakes friends for foes, not knowing how to discern them in the darkness and confusion. Let us labour a moment to point out the helmet of Jesus in the battle, that his blows may be distinguished from those of a cruel one.

The experience which we have pictured leads us to abhor sin. Can Satan be the author of this? Is he become a lover of purity, or can an unclean spirit be the father of such a godly feeling? An adept in sin himself, will he seek to reveal its vileness? If indeed it delights him to see a soul unhappy here, would he not far rather allow a present bliss, in the malicious prospect of a certain future woe for his victim? We believe Satan to be exceedingly wise, but he would be penny wise and pound foolish if he should inflict a temporary torment on the sinner here, and so by his over haste lose his great object of ruining the man for ever. Devils may drive swine down a steep place into the sea; but

they never influenced swine to bemoan their
condition, and beg to be made sheep. Satan
might carry Jesus to a pinnacle of the Temple
to tempt him; but he never carried a publican
to the house of prayer to smite on his breast
and cry, "God be merciful to me a sinner!"
Nothing which leads to Jesus can be of the Evil
One, by this we may judge whether our inward
trouble be of God or no.   That which draws us
to Jesus hath something of Jesus in it; the
waggons which fetch us to our Joseph may have
rumbling wheels, but they are sent by *Him*.
When our enemy cannot hinder the voice of
God from being heard in the heart, he mingleth
therewith such horrid yellings and howlings
that the coming sinner is in doubt whether the
voice come from heaven or hell; howbeit, the
question may be answered in this manner—if it
be a harsh, reproving voice which is heard, then
Satan is angry, and is but counterfeiting, to
prevent the word of God from having effect;
but if it be a sweet voice seeking to draw the
soul from an earnest and thorough repentance,
then it cometh wholly from hell. O sinner,
let a friend warn thee of the syren-song of a
smiling devil—it will be thine eternal shipwreck
if thou dost not seal thine ears, and neglect his

enchanting music; but, on the other hand, be not afraid of the devil when he howleth like a Cerberus, for thus doth he seek to affright thee from the gate of heaven; stay not for him, but be firmly persuaded that the inward goad which urges thee forward is in the hand of Jesus, who desires to hasten thee to the house of refuge which he has builded. Do not think that thy sharp pains are given thee by the old murderer, for they are the effects of the knife of "the beloved Physician." Many a man under a surgical operation cries out as if he were about to be killed; but if patience had its perfect work, he would look to the end more than to the means. It is hard indeed to rejoice under the heavy hand of a chastising Jesus; but it will be somewhat easier to thee if thou bearest in mind that Jesus, and not the devil, is now smiting thee for thy sins.

2. Very common also are the cases where the genuineness of conviction is doubted, because it is conceived to be merely an awakened conscience, and not the real lasting work of Jesus by his Holy Spirit. Well may this cause anxiety, if we reflect that the mere awakenings of conscience so often prove to be of no avail. How many reformations have been commenced by the

command of conscience, and have soon crumbled beneath temptation like an edifice of sand at the approach of the sea! How many prayers have been forced forth like untimely figs by the warmth of a little natural feeling! but such prayers have been displaced by the old language of indifference or iniquity. It is but just, therefore, that the anxious inquirer should very honestly examine his feelings whether they be of God.

Conscience is that portion of the soul upon which the Spirit works in convincing of sin; but conscience cannot of itself produce such a real death to sin as must be the experience of every Christian. It may, when stirred up by a powerful sermon or a solemn providence, alarm the whole town of Man-soul; but the bursting of the gates and the breaking of the bars of iron must come from another hand.

Natural conscience may be distinguished from supernatural grace by its being far more easily appeased. A small sop will suffice to stop the mouth of a conscience which, with all its boasted impartiality, is yet as truly depraved as any other portion of the man. We marvel at the Christian minister when he speaks of conscience as " God's vicegerent," styling it the judge who cannot be bribed, whereas the slightest observation would suffice to convince any man of the corruption of the conscience. How many commit acts with allowance which are gross sins, but concerning which their unenlightened conscience utters no threat; and even when this partial censor does pronounce sentence of condemnation, how easily will the slightest promise of reformation avert his wrath, and induce him to palliate the sin!

Conscience, when thoroughly aroused, will speak with a thundering voice; but even his voice cannot wake the dead—spiritual resurrection is the work of Deity alone. We have seen men swept with a very tornado of terrible thoughts and serious emotions; but the hot wind has passed away in an hour, and has left no blessing behind it. There is no healing beneath the wings of a merely natural repentance, and its worthlessness may be proved by its transitory existence.

Conscience will be content with reformation; true grace will never rest till it receives a knowledge of regeneration. Let us each be anxious to be possessors of nothing short of a real inwrought sorrow for sin, a deep sense of natural depravity, a true faith in the Lord Jesus, and actual possession of his Spirit; whatever is short of this, lacks the vital elements of religion. If such is our feeling *now*—if we now pant for Jesus in all his glorious offices to be ours for ever, we need not fear but that *He* has wounded us in love, and is bringing us to his feet. If we now feel that nothing but the blood and righteousness of Christ Jesus can supply the wants we deplore, we may rejoice that grace has entered our heart, and will win the victory. A soul under the influence of the Holy Ghost will be insatiable in its longings for a Saviour; you might as well attempt to fill a ship with honour, or a house with water, as a truly emptied soul with aught save the Lord Jesus. Is thy soul hungering with such a hunger that husks will not content thee? Art thou thirsting until "thy tongue cleaveth to thy mouth" for the living water of life? Dost thou abhor all counterfeits, and look only for the good gold of the kingdom? Art thou determined to have Christ or die? Will nothing less than Jesus allay thy fears? Then be of good cheer; arise, *He* calleth thee; cry unto him, and he will assuredly hear.

Again, *we think an excellent test may be*

found in the length of time which these feelings have endured. The awakenings of an unrenewed conscience soon pass away, and are not usually permanent in their character. Arising in a night, they perish also in a night. They are acute pains, but not chronic; they are not a part of the man, but simply incidents in his history. Many a man drops the compliment of a tear when justice is at work with him; but wiping that tear away, sunshine follows the shower, and all is over. Hast thou, my reader, been a seeker of the Lord for a very little while? I beseech thee take it not for granted that thou art under the influence of the Spirit, but plead with God that thine own instability may not afresh be manifest in again forgetting what manner of man thou art. O ye whose momentary warmth is but as the crackling of blazing thorns, this is not the fire from heaven; for that glorious flame is as eternal as its origin, being sustained by Omnipotence. O ye Pliables, who turn back at the first difficulty, crowns and kingdoms in the realms of the blessed are not intended for such as you! Unstable as water, ye shall not excel! Your lying vows have been so often heard in heaven, that justice frowns upon you. How have ye

lied unto God, when ye have promised in the
hour of sickness to turn to him with full purpose
of heart? How will your violated promises be
swift witnesses to condemn you, when God
shall fetch from the archives of the past the
memorials of your treachery!

What can be more worthy of your solemn
consideration than the words of Solomon—
"He that being often reproved hardeneth his
neck, shall suddenly be destroyed, *and that
without remedy.*" * It will go hard with some
of you, my readers, who have abounded with
hypocritical repentances when the Lord shall
bring you into judgment. Ye have no excuse
of ignorance; ye cannot cloak your guilt with
darkness; "ye knew your duty, but ye did it
not." You vowed in deceit; you prayed in
mockery; you promised with falsehood. Surely,
your own lips will say "Amen!" to the anathema
which shall call you "cursed;" and the chambers of your memory will, from their sin-
stained walls, reverberate the sentence, "Cursed!
cursed! cursed!"

But has the penitent reader been under the
hand of God for some time? Have his impressions been abiding? Do they bring forth the

* Prov. xxix: 1.

fruits of real longing after Jesus? Then let him be of good cheer. The river which drieth not is the river of God; the lighthouse which endureth the winds and waves is founded on a rock; and the plant which is not plucked up our heavenly Father hath planted. The stony-ground hearer lost his verdure when the sun had arisen with burning heat; but if out of an honest and good heart you have received the word which abideth for ever, you are one of those upon the good ground. When the light remains in one position for a long time, it is not likely to be an *ignis fatuus;* but that which leapeth continually from place to place, even the peasant knows to be the will-o'-the-wisp, and nothing more. True stars fall not; shoot-ing stars are no stars at all, but sundry gases which have long enough held together, and blaze at bursting. Rivers which, like Kishon, only flow with temporary torrents, may be useful to sweep away an invading army, but they cannot fertilise the surrounding country: so temporary conviction may bring destruction upon a host of sins, but it is not the river which makes glad the city of God. The works of God are abiding works; he buildeth no houses of sand which fall at the rise of the flood, or the rushing of the wind. Hast thou, O convinced soul, been long under the hand of sorrow? then take heart, this is all the more likely to be the hand of the Lord. If thou feelest, at all seasonable hours, a strong desire to seek his face, and pour out thine heart before him, then doubtless thou art one of those who shall be called—"sought out," and thou shalt dwell in "a city not forsaken." The morning cloud goeth because it is but a cloud; but the rain and the snow return not to heaven void, but water the earth, and make it bring forth and bud: if thy soul buddeth with desires, and bringeth forth prayers and tears, then have we hope for thee that God hath sent his word from above to dwell in thine heart.

Best of all, *when we are put out of all heart with our doings and with our own capabilities;* then indeed the Lord is there. So long as we cling in the least degree to self, we have ground to distrust the reality of the work within. The Spirit is a humbling spirit, and God sends him that he may humble us. Every wound given by the Saviour is accompanied by the voice, "This is against thy self-righteousness." Without this process of cutting and wounding, we should imagine ourselves to be something, whereas we are nothing; we should think our fig-leaves to be as excellent as court robes, and our own filthy rags as white as the spotless robe of Jesus. Hast thou, my friend, been learning the lesson, that "whatsoever is of nature's spinning must be all unravelled before the righteousness of Christ is put on?" * Dost thou now perceive that "nature can afford no balsam fit for soul cure?" Art thou despairing of all healing from the waters of Abana and Pharpar? And wilt thou now gladly wash in Jordan and be clean? If it be so with thee, then thou art no stranger to the influences of Jesus' grace upon thine heart; but if not, all thy repentances, thy tears, thy sighs, thy groans, must go for nothing, being but dross and dung in the sight of the rein-trying Jehovah. Self is the fly which spoils the whole pot of ointment; but Jesus is the salt which makes the most poisonous river to become pure. To be weaned from our own works is the hardest weaning in the world. To die not only to all ideas of past merit, but to all hopes of future attainments, is a death which is as hard as that of the old giant whom Greatheart slew. And yet this death is absolutely requisite before salvation.

* Thomas Wilcocks.

for unless we die to all but Christ, we can never
live with Christ.

The carnal professor talks very much of faith,
of sanctification, of perfection; but therein he
offers sacrifice to himself as the great author
of his own salvation: like the Pharaoh of
old, he writes upon the rocks, "I conquered
these regions by these my shoulders." But not
so he who has really been taught by the God of
heaven; he bows his head, and ascribes his deliverance wholly to the grace of the covenant
God of Israel. By this, then, can thy state be
tested—Is *self* annihilated, or is it not? Art
thou looking upward, or art thou hoping that
thine own arm shall bring salvation? Thus
mayest thou best understand how thy soul
standeth with regard to a work of grace. That
which strippeth the creature of all comeliness,
which marreth the beauty of pride, and staineth
the glory of self-sufficiency, is from Jesus; but
that which exalteth man, even though it make
thee moral, amiable, and outwardly religious, is
of the devil. Fear not the blow which smites
thee to the ground—the lower thou liest the
better; but shun that which puffeth up and
lifteth thee to the skies. Remember the Lord
hath said, " And all the trees of the field shall

know that I the Lord have brought down the
high tree, have exalted the low tree, have dried
up the green tree, and have made the dry tree
to flourish." * Be thou ever one of the low
trees, for then Jesus will regard thee. He
putteth down the mighty from their seats, but
he exalteth the humble and meek. None are
nearer mercy's door than those who are farthest
from their own; none are more likely to get a
good word from Jesus than they who have not
one word to say for themselves. He that is
clean escaped from the hands of self, hath not a
step between himself and acceptance. It is a
good sign of a high tide of grace, when the
sands of our own righteousness are covered.
Take heart that Christ loveth thee, when thou
hast no heart for the work of self-saving. But
never, never hope that a devout carriage, re-
spectable demeanour, and upright conversation,
will justify thee before God—

> "For love of grace
> Lay not that flattering unction to your soul;
> It will but skin and film the ulcerous place,
> Whiles rank corruption, mining all within,
> Infects unseen."

Once more: *when our sorrowful feelings*

* Ezek. xvii. 24.

*drive us to a thorough renunciation of sin, then
we may hope.* How many there are who talk
most rapidly of a deep experience, of corruption,
and of indwelling sin, who never heartily renounce their evil ways! But how vain is all
their idle talk, while their lives show that they
love sin, and delight in transgression! He that
is sorry for past sin, will be doubly careful to
avoid all present acts of it. He is a hypocrite
before God who talketh of a work within when
there is no work without. Grace will enter a
sinful heart, even though it be exceeding vile;
yet it will never make friendship with sin, but
will at once commence to drive it out. He has
altogether mistaken the nature of divine grace,
who conceives it possible that he can be a par-
taker of it and yet be the slave of lust, or allow
sin to reign in his mortal body. The promise
runs—"Let the wicked *forsake* his way, and the
unrighteous man his thoughts, and let him return unto the Lord, and he will have mercy
upon him; and to our God, for he will abundantly pardon;" but we read not of a single word
of comfort to him who goeth on in his iniquity.
Though the high and lofty One will stoop over
a wounded sinner, he will never do so while the
weapons of rebellion are still in his hands.

"There is no peace, saith my God, unto the wicked." Justice will never raise the siege simply because of our cries, or promises, or vows: the heart shall still be invested with terrors as long as the traitors are harboured within its gates. The Spirit saith, by the mouth of Paul, "For godly sorrow worketh repentance to salvation not to be repented of. For behold this self-same thing, that ye sorrowed after a godly sort, what carefulness it wrought in you, yea, what clearing of yourselves, yea, what indignation, yea, what fear, yea, what vehement desire, yea, what zeal, yea, what revenge! In all things ye have approved your-selves in this matter."* That is no true re-pentance to eternal life which hath not such blessed companions as these. Isaiah saith, "By this, therefore, shall the iniquity of Jacob be purged; and this is all the fruit to take away his sin; when he maketh all the stones of the altar as chalkstones that are beaten in sunder, the groves and images shall not stand up."† No sooner does penitence enter the heart than down goeth every idol, and every idolatrous altar. He whom the Lord calleth will, like

* 2 Cor. vii. 10, 11.   † Isa. xxvii. 9.

Gideon,* cast down the altar of Baal, cut down
the grove, and burn the bullock; like Phineas,†
his javelin will pierce through lusts; and, as the
sons of Levi‡ at the bidding of Moses, he will
go through the camp, and slay the nearest and
dearest of his bosom sins—his hand shall not
spare, neither shall his eye pity: right hands
will be cut off, and right eyes plucked out; sin
will be drowned in floods of godly sorrow, and
the soul will desire to be free from that which
it hateth, even to detestation. As Thomas Scott
remarks, in his *Treatise on Repentance,* "This
is the grand distinction betwixt true repentance
and all false appearances. Though men be
abundant in shedding tears, and make the most
humiliating confessions, or most ample restitution; though they openly retract their false
principles, and are zealous in promoting true
religion; though they relate the most plausible
story of experiences, and profess to be favoured
with the most glorious manifestations; though
they have strong confidence, high affections,
orthodox sentiments, exact judgment, and ex-
tensive knowledge: yet, except they 'do works
meet for repentance, all the rest is nothing

* Judg. vi. 28.   † Num. xxv. 7.
‡ Ex. xxxiii. 26, 27.

they are still in their sins. For the tree is known by its fruit; and 'every tree that bringeth not forth good fruit is hewn down, and cast into the fire.' Yea, though Cain's terror, Judas's confession and restitution, Pharaoh's fair promises, Ahab's humiliation, Herod's reverencing the prophet, hearing him gladly, and doing many things—the stony-ground hearer's joy—together with the tongue of men and angels, the gifts of miracles and prophecies, and the knowledge of all mysteries, were combined in one man, they would not prove him a true penitent, so long as the love of one lust remained unmortified in his heart, or the practice of it was *allowed* in his life." Ask thyself, then, this all-important question, How is my soul affected by sin? Do I hate it? do I avoid it? do I shun its very shadow? do I sincerely renounce it, even though by infirmity I fall into it? Rest assured if thou canst not give a satisfactory answer to these questions thou art yet very far from the kingdom; but if, with an honest heart, thou canst declare that sin and thyself are at an utter enmity, then "the seed of the woman" is begotten in thine heart, and dwelleth there the hope of glory.

Believer, the hour is fresh in our memory

when the divorce was signed between ourselves
and our lusts. We can rejoice that we have
now dissolved our league with hell. But, oh
how much we owe to sovereign grace! for we
had never left the garlic and fleshpots of Egypt
if the Passover had not been slain for us. Our
inward man rejoiceth greatly at the recollection
of the hour which proclaimed eternal war between "the new creature in Christ Jesus" and
the sin which reigned unto death. It was a
night to be remembered: we crossed the Rubi-
con—peace was broken—old friendships ceased
—the sword was unsheathed, and the scabbard
thrown away. We were delivered from the
power of darkness, and brought into "the kingdom of God's dear Son;" and henceforth we no
'onger serve sin, but the life which we live in
the flesh is a life of dependance on the Son of
God, who loved us and gave himself for us. Let
us testify that we never knew what it was to
have peace with God until we had ceased to
parley with sin. Not one drop of true comfort
did we receive until we had foresworn for ever
the former lusts of our ignorance: till then
our mouths were filled with wormwood and gall,
until we had cast out our iniquities as loathsome and abominable; but now, having re-

nounced the works of darkness, "we have peace with God, through our Lord Jesus Christ, by whom also we have received the atonement."

If thou, O reader, canst satisfactorily answer the solemn inquiries here proposed to thee, thy case is assuredly in the hands of Jesus the Lord; if thou hast continually bewailed thy sin, hast renounced thine own works, and escaped from thy lusts, then thou art none other than one called of God to grace and glory. Be thou assured that natural conscience can never rise to such a height as this—it may skim the surface, but it cannot mount aloft. Mere nature never poured contempt on human righteousness, and never severed man from his sins. It needs a mighty one to carry away the gates of the Gaza of our self-sufficiency, or to lay our Philistine sins heaps upon heaps. God alone can send the sun of our own excellency back the needed degrees of humility, and he alone can bid our sins stand still for ever. It is Jesus who hath smitten, if he hath with one blow uncrowned thee, and with another disarmed thee. He is wont to perform wonders; but such as these are his own peculiar miracles. None but He can kill with one stone two such birds as our high-soaring righteousness and low-winged

lust. If Goliath's head is taken from his
shoulders, and his sword snatched from his
hand, no doubt the conqueror is the Son of
David. We give all glory and honour to the
adorable name of Jesus, the Breaker, the Healer,
our faithful Friend.

3. It frequently occurs that the circumstances
of the person at the time of conversion afford
grave cause to doubt the divine character of the
woundings which are felt. It is well known
that severe sickness and prospect of death will
produce a repentance so like to genuine, godly
sorrow, that the wisest Christians have been
misled by it. Many have we seen and heard of
who have expressed the deepest contrition for
past guilt, and have vehemently cried for mercy,
with promises of amendment apparently as sincere as their confessions were truthful—who have
conversed sweetly of pardon, of joy in the Spirit,
and have even related ecstasies and marvellous
manifestations; and yet, with all this, have
proved to be hypocrites, by returning at the
first opportunity to their old courses of sin and
folly. It hath happened unto them according
to the proverb, "The dog hath returned to his
vomit, and the sow that was washed to her
wallowing in the mire."

Pious Mr. Booth writes, "I pay more attention to people's lives than to their deaths. In all the visits I have paid to the sick during the course of a long ministry, I never met with *one*, who was not previously serious, that ever recovered from what he supposed the brink of death, who afterwards performed his vows and became religious, notwithstanding the very great appearance there was in their favour when they thought they could not recover." We find also, ready to our hand, in a valuable work,* the following facts, which are but specimens of a mass which might be given :—"A certain American physician, whose piety led him to attend, not only to people's bodies, but to their souls, stated that he had known a hundred or more instances in his practice, of persons who, in prospect of death, had been apparently converted, but had subsequently been restored to health. Out of them all he did not know of more than three who devoted themselves to the service of Christ after their recovery, or gave any evidence of genuine conversion. If, therefore, they had died, as they expected, have we not reason to believe that their hopes of heaven would have proved terrible delusions?

* Arvine's Cyclopædia of Anecdotes.

"A pious English physician once stated that
he had known some three hundred sick persons
who, soon expecting to die, had been led, as they
supposed, to repentance of their sins, and saving
faith in Christ, but had eventually been restored
to health again. Only ten of all this number, so
far as he knew, gave any evidence of being really
regenerated. Soon after their recovery they
plunged, as a general thing, into the follies and
vices of the world. Who would trust, then, in
such conversions?"

Such examples serve as a holy warning to us
all, lest we too should only feel an excitement
produced by terror, and should find the flame of
piety utterly quenched when the cause of alarm
is withdrawn. Some of us can trace our first
serious thoughts to the bed of sickness, when, in
the loneliness of our chamber, "We thought
upon our ways, and turned our feet unto his
testimonies."* But this very circumstance
was at the time a source of doubt, for we said
within ourselves, "Will this continue when my
sickness is removed, or shall I not find my
apathy return, when again I enter on the business
of the world?" Our great anxiety was not lest
we should die, but lest living we should find

* Prov. cix. 59.

our holy feelings clear gone, and our piety evaporated. Possibly our reader is now sick, and this is his trouble: let us help you through it. Of course, the best proof you can have of your own sincerity is that which you will receive when health returns, if you continue steadfast in the faith of Jesus, and follow on to know him. Perseverance, when the pressure is removed, will discover the reality of your repentance. The natural wounds inflicted by Providence are healed soon after the removal of the rod, and folly is not thereby brought out of the heart; but when Jesus smites for sin, the wounds will smart even when the instrumental rod of correction is removed, while "the blueness of the wound cleanseth away evil." * We, who had many mock repentances ere we really turned to the living God, can now see the main spring of our error. Every thief loves honesty when he finds the jail uneasy; almost every murderer will regret that he slew a man when he is about to be executed for his crime: here is the first point of distinction which we beg our reader to observe.

That repentance which is genuine ariseth not so much from dread of punishment as from fear

* Prov. xx. 30.

G

of sin. It is not fear of damning, but fear of sinning, which make the truly humbled cry out for grace. True, the fear of hell, engendered by the threatenings of the law, doth work in the soul much horror and dismay; but it is not *hell* appearing exceeding *dreadful*, but *sin* becoming exceeding *sinful* and abominable, which is the effectual work of grace. Any man in his reason would tremble at everlasting burnings, more especially when by his nearness to the grave the heat of hell doth, as it were, scorch him; but it is not every dying man that hates *sin*—yea, none do so unless the Lord hath had dealings with their souls. Say then, Dost thou hate hell or hate sin most? for, verily, if there were no hell, the real penitent would love sin not one wit the more, and hate evil not one particle the less. Wouldest thou love to have thy sin and heaven too? If thou wouldest, thou hast not a single spark of divine life in thy soul, for one spark would consume thy love to sin. Sin to a sin-sick soul is so desperate an evil that it would scarce be straining the truth to say that a real penitent had rather suffer the pains of hell without his sins than enter the bliss of heaven with them, if such things were possible. Sin, *sin*, sin, is the accursed thing which the living soul hateth.

Again: *saving repentance will most easily manifest itself when the subjects of our thoughts are most heavenly.* By this we mean, if our sorrow only gushes forth when we are musing upon the doom of the wicked, and the wrath of God, we have then reason to suspect its evangelical character; but if contemplations of Jesus, of his cross, of heaven, of eternal love, of covenant grace, of pardoning blood and full redemption bring tears to our eyes, we may then rejoice that we sorrow after a godly sort. The sinner awakened by the Holy Spirit will find the source of his stream of sorrow not on the thorn-clad sides of Sinai, but on the grassy mound of Calvary. His cry will be, "O sin, I hate thee, for thou didst murder my Lord;" and his mournful dirge over his crucified Redeemer will be in plaintive words—

"'Twas you, my sins, my cruel sins,
　His chief tormentors were;
Each of my crimes became a nail,
　And unbelief the spear;
'Twas you that pull'd the vengeance down
　Upon his guiltless head;
Break, break, my heart, oh burst mine eyes,
　And let my sorrows bleed."

Ye who love the Lord, give your assent to this our declaration, that love did melt you more

than wrath, that the wooing voice did more
affect you than the condemning sentence, and
that hope did impel you more than fear. It
was when viewing our Lord as crucified, dead,
and buried that we most wept. *He* with *his*
looks made us weep bitterly, while the stern
face of Moses caused us to tremble, but never
laid us prostrate confessing our transgression.
We sorrow because our offence is against *Him*,
against his love, his blood, his grace, his heart
of affection. Jesus is the name which subdues
the stubborn heart, if it be truly brought into
subjection to the Gospel. He is the rod which
bringeth waters out of the rock, he is the
hammer which breaketh the rock in pieces.

Furthermore, *saving repentance will render
the conscience exceedingly tender, so that it will
be pained to the quick at the very recollection of
the smallest sin*. Natural repentance crieth out
at a few master-sins, which have been most
glaring and heinous—the more especially if
some visitor point them out as crimes of the
blackest dye; but when it hath executed one or
two of these on the gallows of confession, it is
content to let whole hosts of less notorious of-
fenders escape without so much as a reprimand.
Not so the man whose penitence is of divine

origin—he hates the whole race of the Evil One; like Elijah he will cry, "Let none escape;" he will cut up to the best of his power every root of bitterness which may still remain, nor will he willingly harbour a single traitor in his breast. The secret sins, the every-day offences, the slight errors (as the world has it), the harmless follies, the little transgressions, the peccadilloes, all these will be dragged forth to death when the Lord searcheth the heart with the candle of his Spirit.

Jesus never enters the soul of man to drive out one or two sins, nor even to overcome a band of vices to the exception of others; his work is perfect, not partial; his cleansings are complete baptisms; his purifyings tend to remove all our dross, and consume all our tin. He sweeps the heart from its dust as well as its Dagons; he suffers not even the most insignificant spider of lust to spin its cobweb, with allowance, on the walls of his temple. All heinous sins and private sins, youthful sins and manhood's sins, sins of omission and of commission, of word and of deed, of thought and of imagination, sins against God or against man, all will combine like a column of serpents in the desert to affright the new-born child of heaven; and he will desire to see the head of every one of them broken beneath

the heel of the destroyer of evil, Jesus, the seed
of the woman. Believe not thyself to be truly
awakened unless thou abhorrest sin in all its
stages, from the embryo to the ripe fruit, and in
all its shades, from the commonly allowed lust
down to the open and detested crime. When
Hannibal took oath of perpetual hatred to the
Romans, he included in that oath plebeians as
well as patricians; so if thou art indeed at
enmity with evil, thou wilt abhor all iniquity,
even though it be of the very lowest degree.
Beware that thou write not down affright at
one sin as being repentance for all.

There are, doubtless, other forms and phases
of doubt, but our space does not allow us to
mention more, nor does the character of the
volume require that we should expatiate on
more of these than are the most usual causes of
grief to the Lord's people. We beseech the
ever-gracious Spirit to reveal the person of
Jesus to every smitten sinner; to anoint his
eyes with eye-salve, that he may see the heart
of love which moves the hand of rebuke, and
to guide every mourning seeker to the cross,
whence pardon and comfort ever flow. It is
none other than Jesus who thus frowns us to
our senses, and chastises us to right reason;

may the Holy Ghost lead every troubled one to believe this encouraging doctrine, then shall our heart's desire be granted.

We cannot, however, bring our remarks to a close until again we have urged the duty of self-examination, which is at once the most important and most neglected of all religious exercises.

When we think how solemn is the alternative "*saved*" or "*damned*," we cannot but importune our readers, as they love their souls, to "examine themselves whether they be in the faith." Oh! remember it will be all too late to decide this question soon, since it will cease to be a question. The time will have passed for hopeful changes and gracious discoveries; the only changes will be to torments more excruciating, and discoveries then will but reveal horrors more and more terribly astounding. We wonder not that men should anxiously inquire concerning their position; we might marvel more that the most of them are so indifferent, so utterly careless to the things of the kingdom of heaven. It is not our body, our estate, our liberty, concerning which there is this question at law, it is a suit of far weightier nature—our eternal existence in heaven or hell. Let us narrowly inspect our innermost feelings; let

us search what manner of men we be; let us
rigidly scrutinise our heart, and learn whether
it be right with God or no.   Let not the good
opinion of our fellow-men mislead us, but let us
search for ourselves, lest we be found like the
mariner who bought his bags of one who filled
them not with biscuit but with stones, and he,
relying on the merchant's word, found himself
in the broad ocean without a morsel of food.
Yet if good men tell us we are wrong, let us not
despise their opinion, for it is more easy to
deceive ourselves than the elect.   He was not
far from truth who said, " We strive as hard to
hide our hearts from ourselves as from others,
and always with more success; for, in deciding
upon our own case, we are both judge, and
jury, and executioner; and where sophistry
cannot overcome the first, or flattery the second,
self-love is always ready to defeat the sentence
by bribing the third—a bribe that in this case
is never refused, because she always comes up
to the price." *   Since we are liable to be self-
deceived, let us be the more vigilant, giving
most earnest heed to every warning and reproof,
lest the very warning which we slight should be
that which might have shown us our danger.

* Colton.

Many tradesmen are ruined by neglecting their books; but he who frequently casts up his accounts will know his own position, and avoid such things as would be hazardous or destructive. No ship was ever wrecked by the captain's over-anxiety in taking his longitude and latitude; but the wailing sea bears sad witness to the fate of careless mariners, who forgot their chart, and wantonly steered onward to rocks which prudent foresight would easily have avoided. Let us not sleep as do others, but rouse ourselves to persevering watchfulness, by the solemn consideration that if we be at last mistaken in our soul's condition, the error can never be amended. Here, if one battle be lost, a hopeful commander expects to retrieve his fortunes by future victory; but let us once fail to overcome in the struggle of life, our defeat is everlasting. The bankrupt merchant cheers his spirit with the prospect of commencing trade again—business may yet prosper, competence may yet bless him, and even wealth may deign to fill his house with her hidden treasures; but he who finds himself a bankrupt in another world, without God, without Christ, without hope, must abide for ever penniless, craving, with a beggar's lip, the hopeless boon of one poor drop

of water to cool his burning tongue. When
life is over with the unrighteous, all is over—
where the tree falleth there it must for ever lie;
death is the Medusa's head, petrifying our condition—he that is unholy, shall be unholy still;
he that is unjust, must be unjust still. If there
were the most remote possibility of rectifying
our present errors in a future state of existence,
we might have some excuse for superficial or
infrequent investigation; this, however, is utterly
out of the question, for grace is bounded by the
grave. If we be in Christ, all that heaven
knows of unimaginable bliss, of inconceivable
glory, of unutterable ecstasy, shall be ours most
richly to enjoy; but if death shall find us out
of Christ, horrors surpassing thought, terrors
beyond the dreamings of despair, and tortures
above the guess of misery, must be our doleful,
desperate doom. How full of trembling is the
thought, that multitudes of fair professors are
now in hell: although they, like ourselves, once
wore a goodly name, and hoped, as others said
of them, that they were ripening for glory;
whereas they were fattening for the slaughter,
and were drugged for execution with the cup of
delusion, dreaming all the while that they were
drinking the wines on the lees, well refined.

Surely, among the damned, there are none more horribly tormented in the flame than those who looked to walk the golden streets, but found themselves cast into outer darkness, where there is weeping, and wailing, and gnashing of teeth. The higher the pinnacle from which we slip, the more fearful will be our fall; crownless kings, beggared princes, and starving nobles, are the more pitiable because of their former condition of affluence and grandeur: so also will fallen professors have a sad pre-eminence of damnation, from the very fact that they were once esteemed rich and increased in goods. When we consider the vast amount of unsound profession which prevails in this age, and which, like a smooth but shallow sea, doth scarcely conceal the rocks of hypocrisy—when we review the many lamentable falls which have lately occurred among the most eminent in the Church, we would lift up our voice like a trumpet, and with all our might entreat all men to be sure of their grounds of trust, lest it should come to pass that sandy foundations should be discovered when total destruction has rendered it too late for anything but despair.

O age of profession, put thyself in the crucible! O nation of formalists, take heed lest ye

receive the form and reject the Spirit! O
reader, let us each commence a thorough trial of
our own spirits!

> " Oh! what am I?   My soul awake,
> And an impartial survey take:
> Does no dark sign, no ground of fear
> In practice or in heart appear?

> " What image does my spirit bear?
> Is Jesus form'd and living there?
> Say, do his lineaments divine
> In thought, and word, and action, shine?

> " Searcher of hearts! oh search me still,
> The secrets of my soul reveal;
> My fears remove, let me appear
> To God and my own conscience clear.

> " May I at that bless'd world arrive,
> Where Christ through all my soul shall live,
> And give full proof that He is there,
> Without one gloomy doubt or fear."

III. We close our chapter by the third remark—*the wounds of our Jesus were faithful.*
Here proof will be entirely an unnecessary
excess, but we think meditation will be a profitable engagement.   Ah! brethren, when we
were groaning under the chastening hand of
Jesus, we thought him cruel; do we think so ill
of him now?   We conceived that he was wroth
with us, and would be implacable; how have
our surmises proved to be utterly unfounded!

The abundant benefit which we now reap from the deep ploughing of our heart is enough of itself to reconcile us to the severity of the process. Precious is that wine which is pressed in the winefat of conviction; pure is that gold which is dug from the mines of repentance; and bright are those pearls which are found in the caverns of deep distress. We might never have known such deep humility if *He* had not humbled us. We had never been so separated from fleshly trusting had He not by his rod revealed the corruption and disease of our heart. We had never learned to comfort the feeble-minded, and confirm the weak, had He not made us ready to halt, and caused our sinew to shrink. If we have any power to console the weary, it is the result of our remembrance of what we once suffered—for here lies our power to sympathise. If we can now look down with scorn upon the boastings of vain, self-conceited man, it is because our own vaunted strength has utterly failed us, and made us contemptible in our own eyes. If we can now plead with ardent desire for the souls of our fellow-men, and especially if we feel a more than common passion for the salvation of sinners, we must attribute it in no small degree to the fact that we have been

smitten for sin, and therefore knowing the
terrors of the Lord are constrained to persuade
men. The laborious pastor, the fervent minister,
the ardent evangelist, the faithful teacher, the
powerful intercessor, can all trace the birth of
their zeal to the sufferings they endured for sin,
and the knowledge they thereby attained of its
evil nature. We have ever drawn the sharpest
arrows from the quiver of our own experience.
We find no sword-blades so true in metal as
those which have been forged in the furnace of
soul-trouble. Aaron's rod, that budded, bore
not one half so much fruit as the rod of the covenant, which is laid upon the back of every chosen
child of God; this alone may render us eternally
grateful to the Saviour for his rebukes of love.

We may pause for a moment over another
thought, if we call to mind our deep depravity.
We find within us a strong and deep-seated
attachment to the world and its sinful pleasures;
our heart is still prone to wander, and our
affections yet cleave to things below. Can we
wonder then that it required a sharp knife to
sever us at first from our lusts, which were
then as dear to us as the members of our body?
so foul a disease could only be healed by frequent
draughts of bitter medicine. Let us detest the

sin which rendered such rough dealing necessary, but let us adore the Saviour who spared not
the child for his crying. If our sin had been
like the hyssop on the wall, our own hand
might have gently snapped the roots; but having
become lofty as a cedar of Lebanon, and firmly
settled in its place, only the omnipotent voice of
Jehovah could avail to break it: we will not
therefore complain of the loudness of the thunder, but rejoice at the overturning of our sin.
Will the man who is asleep in a burning house
murmur at his deliverer for shaking him too
roughly in his bed? Would the traveller, tottering on the brink of a precipice, upbraid the
friend who startled him from his reverie, and
saved him from destruction. Would not the
harshest words and the roughest usage be
acknowledged most heartily as blows of love and
warnings of affection. Best of all, when we view
these matters in the light of eternity, how little
are these slight and momentary afflictions compared with the doom thereby escaped, or the bliss
afterwards attained! Standing where our ears
can be filled with the wailings of the lost, where
our eyes are grieved by sights of the hideous
torments of the damned--contemplating for an
instant the fathomless depth of eternal misery,

with all its deprivation, desperation, and aggra-
vation—considering that we at this hour might
have been in our own persons enduring the
doom we deprecate,—surely it is easy work to
overlook the pain of our conviction, and bless
with all sincerity "the hand which rescued us."
O hammer which broke our fetters, how can we
think ill of thee! O angel which smote us on
the side, and let us out of the prison-house, can
we do aught but love thee! O Jesus, our
glorious deliverer, we would love thee, live to
thee, and die for thee! seeing thou hast loved
us, and hast proved that love in thy life and in
thy death. Never can we think thee unmer-
ciful, for thou wast mercifully severe. We are
sure not one stroke fell too heavily, nor was one
pang too painful. Faithful thou wast in all thy
dealings, and our songs shall exalt thee in all
thy ways, even when thou causest groans to
proceed from our wounded spirits. And when
our spirits shall fly toward thy throne of light,
though in their unceasing hallelujahs thy
tender mercies and lovingkindnesses shall claim
the highest notes, yet, midst the rapturous
hosannahs, shall be heard the psalm "of remembrance" sounding forth our praise for the rod of
the covenant and the hand of affliction. While

here on earth we hymn thy praise in humbler strains, and thus adore thy love—

"Long unafflicted, undismay'd,
In pleasure's path secure I strayed,
Thou mad'st me feel thy chastening rod,
And straight I turned unto my God.

"What though it pierced my fainting heart,
I bless the hand that caused the smart
It taught my tears awhile to flow,
But saved me from eternal woe.

"Oh! hadst thou left me unchastised,
Thy precepts I had still despised,
And still the snare, in secret laid,
Had my unwary feet betrayed.

I love thee, therefore, O my God,
And breathe towards thy dear abode,
Where, in thy presence fully blest,
Thy chosen saints for ever rest."

TO THE UNCONVERTED READER.

FRIEND,—In this chapter thou hast parted company with the Christian. Thou couldst join with him while he esteemed not Jesus, but now that Christ has begun to wound the conscience of his child, thou biddest him adieu, and proudly boasteth that thou art not one of so miserable a character. Notwithstanding this, I am loath to part with thee until I have again expostulated with thee.

Thou thinkest it a blessing to be free from the sad feelings we have been describing, but let me tell thee it is thy curse—thy greatest, deadliest curse that thou art a stranger to such inward mourning for thy guilt. In the day when the Judge of heaven and earth shall divide tares from wheat, thou wilt see how terrible it is to be an unregenerate sinner. When the flames of hell get hold upon thee, thou wilt wish in vain for that very experience which now thou dost set at nought. It will not be all May-day with thee; thine hour of death is as

sure as another man's, and then a better than I
shall convince thee of thine error. Laugh not
at weeping souls, account them not to be in a
pitiable plight; for sad as their condition appears, it is not half so sad as thine, and there
is not one of all those moaning penitents who
would change places with thee for an hour.
Their grief is greater joy than thy bliss; thy
laughter is not so sweet as their groans; and
thy pleasant estate is despicable compared with
their sorest distress. Besides, remember those
who are now in such darkness will soon see
the light, but thou shalt soon walk in increasing
and unceasing darkness. Their sorrows shall
be ended; thine are not yet commenced, and
when commenced shall never know a conclu-
sion. Theirs is *hopeful* distress; thine will be
hopeless agony. Their chastisement comes from
a loving Jesus; thine will proceed from an angry
God. Theirs has for its certain end ETERNAL
SALVATION; thine EVERLASTING DAMNATION. Oh!
bethink thee for a moment, wouldst thou rather
choose to have painless mortification and so
perish, than to feel soreness in thy wounds and
then receive a cure? Wouldst thou rather lie
and rot in a dungeon than bruise thyself by
climbing the wall to escape? Surely thou

wouldst endure anything rather than be damned
and I bid thee take this for truth, that thou
shalt either repent or burn; thou shalt either
shed tears of penitence here, or else shriek in
vain for a drop of water in that pit which
burneth with fire unquenchable. What sayest
thou to this? Canst thou dwell with devouring
flames? Canst thou abide the eternal burnings?
Ah! be not mad, I entreat thee. Why shouldst
thou destroy thyself? What good will come of
it when thy blood shall be laid at thine own
door? Hast thou not sinned? Why then
think it foolish to repent? Has not God
threatened his fierce wrath to him that goeth
on in his iniquity? Why then despise those
whom grace has turned, and who therefore are
constrained to bid thee turn from the error of
thy sinful ways? May the Lord stay thy madness in time, and give thee repentance, otherwise, "Tophet is ordained of old: the pile
thereof is fire and much wood; the breath of
the Lord, like a stream of brimstone, doth
kindle it." *

* Isa. xxx. 33.

III.

Jesus Desired.

"Oh that I knew where I might find him!"—Job xxiii. 3.

AWHILE the woundings of Jesus are given in the dark, and we do not recognise the hand which smiteth us; but it is not always to be so. Incessant disappointments put us out of all heart with the former refuges of our souls, and renewed discoveries make us sadly aware of the superlative evil dwelling in our flesh; stripped thus of all covering without, and trembling at our own shameful impotence, we hail with gladness the news of a Saviour for sinners. As on the frail raft, the almost skeleton mariners, having long ago devoured their last morsel, raise themselves with all their remaining strength to catch a glimpse of a passing sail, if haply it may bring relief, so doth the dying sinner receive with eagerness the message of coming grace. He **might have** scorned the terms of mercy once, but, like a city long besieged, he is now too glad to receive peace at any price. The grace which in his high estate he counted as a worthless thing, is now the great object of his combined desires. He pants to see the Man who is "mighty to save," and would count it honour to kiss his feet or unloose the latchet of his shoes. No cavilling at sovereignty, no murmuring at self-humiliation, no scorning the unpurchasable gifts of discriminating love; the man is too poor to be proud, too sick to struggle with his physician, too much afraid of death to refuse the king's pardon because it puts him under obligation. Happy is it for us if we understand this position of utter helplessness into which we must all be brought if we would know Christ!

It is one of the strange things in the dealings of Jesus, that even when we arrive at this state of entire spiritual destitution, we do not always become *at once* the objects of his justifying grace. Long seasons frequently intervene between our knowledge of our ruin, our hearing of a deliverer, and the application of that deliverer's hand. The Lord's own called ones frequently turn their eyes to the hills, and find no help coming therefrom; yea, they wish to look unto

him, but they are so blinded that they cannot
discern him as *their* hope and consolation. This
is not, as some would rashly conclude, because
he is not the Saviour for such as they are. Far
otherwise. Unbelief crieth out, "Ah! my vileness disqualifies me for Christ, and my exceeding
sinfulness shuts out his love!" How foully doth
unbelief lie when it thus slandereth the tender
heart of Jesus! how inhumanly cruel it is when
it thus takes the cup of salvation from the only
lips which have a right to drink thereof! We
have noticed in the preaching of the present day
too much of a saint's gospel, and too little of a
sinner's gospel. Honesty, morality, and goodness, are commended not so much as the *marks*
of godliness, as the *life* of it; and men are told
that as they sow, so they shall reap, without the
absolutely necessary caveat that salvation is not
of man, neither by man, and that grace cometh
not to him that worketh, but to him that
believeth on Him that justifieth the ungodly.
Not thus spake our ancient preachers when in
all its fulness they declared—

> "Not the righteous, not the righteous—
> Sinners, Jesus came to save."

The words of a much calumniated preacher
are not less bold than true :—

"There is nothing in men, though never so vile, that can debar a person from a part in Christ. Some will not have Christ, except they can pay for him; others dare not meddle with Christ, because they are such vile and wretched creatures, that they think it impossible that Christ should belong to such wretched persons as they are. You know not (saith one) what an abominable sinner I am; you look upon others, and their sins are but ordinary, but mine are of a deep dye, and I shall die in them: the rebellion of my heart is another kind of rebellion than is in others. Beloved, let me tell you freely from the Lord, let men deem you as they will, and esteem yourself as bad as you can, I tell you from the Lord, and I will make it good, there is not that sinfulness that can be imagined in a creature that can be able to separate or debar any of you from a part in Christ; even though you are thus sinful, Christ may be your Christ. Nay, I go further; suppose one person in this congregation should not only be the vilest sinner in the world, but should have all the sins of others, besides what he himself hath committed; if all these were laid upon the back of him, he should be a greater sinner than now he is; yet, if he should bear all the sins of

others, as I said, there is no bar to this person,
but Christ may be his portion. ' He bore the
sins of many' (saith the text), but he bare
them not as his own, he bare them for many.
Suppose the many, that are sinners, should have
all their sins translated to one in particular, still
there is no more sin than Christ died for, though
they be all collected together. If other men's
sins were translated upon you, and they had
none, then they needed no Christ; all the need
they had of Christ were translated to you, and
then the whole of Christ's obedience should be
yours. Do but observe the strain of the Gospel,
you shall find that no sin in the world can be a
bar to hinder a person from having a part in
Christ; look upon the condition of persons (as
they are revealed in the Gospel) to whom Christ
is reached out; and the consideration of their
persons will plainly show to you that there is no
kind of sinfulness can bar a person from having
a part in Christ. Consider Christ's own expression, 'I came to seek and to save that
which was lost; I came not to call the righteous,
out sinners, to repentance; the whole need not
a physician, but they that are sick;' here still
the persons are considered in the worst condition (as some might think) rather than in the

best.   Our Saviour is pleased to express himself
in a direct contrary way to the opinion of men.
' I came not to call the righteous, but sinners ;'
the poor publican that had nothing to plead for
himself went away more justified than the proud
pharisee, who pleaded with God, ' I thank thee
that I am not such an one.'

"Men think righteousness brings them near
to Christ ; beloved, our righteousness is that
which puts a man away from Christ ; stumble
not at the expression, it is the clear truth of
the Gospel ; not simply a doing of service and
duty doth put away from Christ ; but upon the
doing of duty and service to expect acceptance
with Christ or participation in Christ—this kind
of righteousness is the only separation between
Christ and a people ; and whereas no sinfulness
in the world can debar a people, their righteousness may debar them."*

Possibly some may object to such terms as
these as being too strong and unguarded, but a
full consideration of them will show that they
are such as would naturally flow from the lips
of a Luther when inculcating faith alone as the
means of our salvation, and are fully borne out
by the strong expressions of Paul when writing

* Crisp.

to the Romans and Galatians. The fact is, that very strong terms are necessary to make men see the whole of this truth, for it is one which of all things the mind can least receive.

If it were possible to make men clearly understand that justification is not in the least degree by their own works, how easy would it be to comfort them! but herein lies the greatest of all difficulties. Man cannot be taught that his goodness is no increase to God's wealth, and his sin no diminution of divine riches; he will for ever be imagining that some little presents must be offered, and that mercy never can be the gratuitous bounty of Heaven. Even the miserable creature who has learned his own bankruptcy and beggary, while assured that he cannot bring anything, yet trembles to come naked and as he is. He knows he cannot do anything, but he can scarcely credit the promise which seems too good to be true—" I will heal their backsliding, I will love them *freely :* for mine anger is turned away from him."* Yea, when he cannot deny the evidence of his own eyes, because the kind word stares him in the face he will turn away from its glories under

* Hos. xiv. 4.

the sad supposition that they are intended for all men save himself. The air, the stream, the fruit, the joys and luxuries of life, he takes freely, nor ever asks whether these were not intended for a special people; but at the upper springs he stands fearing to dip his pitcher, lest the flowing flood should refuse to enter it because the vessel was too earthy to be fit to contain such pure and precious water: conscious that in Christ is all his help, it yet appears too great a presumption even to touch the hem of the Saviour's garment. Nor is it easy to persuade the mourning penitent that sin is no barrier to grace, but that " where sin abounded, grace did much more abound;" and only the spirit of God can make the man who knows himself as nothing at all, receive Jesus as his all in all. When the Lord has set his heart on a man, it is not a great difficulty that will move him from his purpose of salvation, and therefore "he devises means that His banished be not expelled from him."* By the divine instruction of the Holy Ghost, the sinner is taught that Jesus is the sinner's friend, adapted to his case, and "able to save unto the uttermost." Even then, too often, the work is not complete; for the soul now

* 2 Sam. xiv. 14.

labours to find him whom it needs, and it often happens that the search is prolonged through months of weariness and days of languishing. If the Church, in the canticles, confesses, "By night on my bed I sought him whom my soul loveth: I sought him, but I found him not. I will rise now, and go about the city in the streets, and in the broad ways I will seek him whom my soul loveth; I sought him, but I found him not," surely, even if our reader's history does not confirm the fact that grace is sometimes hidden, he will at least assent to the probability of it, and pray for the many who are crying, "Oh that I knew where I might find him!"

May Jesus smile on our humble endeavour to trace the steps of our own soul, so that any who are in this miserable condition may escape by the same means! O ye prisoners of hope, who are seeking a Redeemer who apparently eludes your grasp, let your earnest prayer accompany your reading, while you fervently cry—

> " Saviour, cast a pitying eye,
>   Bid my sins and sorrows end:
>   Whither should a sinner fly?
>   Art not thou the sinner's friend?
>   Rest in thee I gasp to find,
>   Wretched I, and poor, and blind.

" Didst thou ever see a soul
    More in need of help than mine?
Then refuse to make me whole;
Then withhold the balm divine:
But if I do want thee most,
Come, and seek, and save the lost.

" Haste, oh haste to my relief;
From the iron furnace take;
Rid me of my sin and grief,
For thy love and mercy's sake;
Set my heart at liberty,
Show forth all thy power in me.

" Me, the vilest of the race,
Most unholy, most unclean;
Me, the farthest from thy face,
Full of misery and sin;
Me with arms of love receive;
Me, of sinners chief—*forgive !*" *

We propose—

I. To mark the *hopeful signs* connected with this state of heart;

II. To give *certain excellent reasons* why the soul is permitted to tarry in it; and

III. To hold forth sundry *plain directions* for behaviour in it, and escape from it.

I. It is our pleasant duty to note the *hopeful signs* which gladden us when reviewing this state.

1. We are cheered by observing that *the*

* C. Wesley.

longing of the spirit is now entirely after Jesus—
"Oh that I knew where I might find *Him!*"
Once, like the many whom David mentions, the
inquiry was, "Who will show us *any* good?"
A question indiscriminately addressed to any
and all within hearing, demanding with eagerness any good in all the world. But now the
desires have found a channel, they are no longer
like the wide-spread sheet of water covering
with shallow depth a tract of marsh teeming
with malaria and pestilence, but having found a
channel, they rush forward in one deep and rapid
stream, seeking the broad ocean, where sister
streams have long since mingled their floods.

Of most men the complaint is true, that they
will "bore and thread the spheres" with the
"quick, piercing eye" of the astronomer, or
"cut through the working wave" to win the
pearl, or wear themselves away in smoky toil,
while as "subtle chymics" they divest and strip
the creature naked, till they find the callow
principles within their nests; in fine, will do
anything and everything of inferior importance,
but here are so negligent that it is truly asked,

> " What hath not man sought out and found
>   But his dear God?"*

* Herbert.

When the heart can express itself in the words of our text, it is far otherwise, for to it every other subject is trivial, and every other object vain. Then, too, there was the continual prayer after pardon, conversion, washing, instruction, justification, adoption, and all other spiritual blessings; but now the soul discerns all mercies bound up in one bundle in Jesus, and it inquires no more for cassia, aloes, and camphire, but asks for Him who hath the savour of all good ointments. It is no small mark of grace when we can esteem Jesus to be all we want. He who believeth there is gold in the mine, and desires to obtain it, will not be long before he hath it; and he who knoweth Jesus to be full of hid treasures of mercy, and seeketh him diligently, shall not be too long detained from a possession of him. We have never known a sinner anxious for Jesus—for Jesus only—who did not in due time discover Jesus as his friend, "waiting to be gracious."

Our own experience recalls us to the period when we panted for the Lord, even for Him, our only want. Vain to us were the mere ordinances—vain as bottles scorched by the simoom, and drained of their waters. Vain were ceremonies—vain as empty wells to the thirsty

Arab. Vain were the delights of the flesh—bitter as the waters of Marah, which even the parched lips of Israel refused to drink. Vain were the directions of the legal preacher—useless as the howling of the wind to the benighted wanderer. Vain, worse than vain, were our refuges of lies, which fell about our ears like Dagon's temple on the heads of the worshippers. One only hope we had, one sole refuge for our misery. Save where that ark floated, north, south, east, and west, were one broad expanse of troubled waters; save where that star burned, the sky was one vast field of unmitigated darkness. Jesus, Jesus, Jesus! he alone, he without another, had become the solitary hiding-place against the storm. As the wounded, lying on the battle-field, with wounds which, like fires, consume his moisture, utters only one monotonous cry of thrilling importunity, "Water, water, water!" so did we perpetually send our prayer to heaven, "Jesus, thou Son of David, have mercy on me! O Jesus, come to me!"

> "Gracious Lord! incline thine ear,
> My requests vouchsafe to hear;
> Hear my never-ceasing cry—
> Give me Christ, or else I die.

" Wealth and honour I disdain,
  Earthly comforts, Lord, are vain ;
  These can never satisfy,
  Give me Christ, or else I die.

" Lord, deny me what thou wilt,
  Only ease me of my guilt ;
  Suppliant at thy feet I lie,
  Give me Christ, or else I die.

" All unholy and unclean,
  I am nothing else but sin ;
  On thy mercy I rely,
  Give me Christ, or else I die.

" Thou dost freely save the lost,
  In thy grace alone I trust ;
  With my earnest suit comply,
  Give me Christ, or else I die.

' Thou dost promise to forgive
  All who in thy Son believe ;
  Lord, I know thou canst not lie,
  Give me Christ, or else I die.

' Father, does thy justice frown ?
  Let me shelter in thy Son !
  Jesus, to thy arms I fly,
  Come and save me, or I die."

As he that tantaliseth thirst with painted
rivers—as he that embittereth hunger's pangs
by the offering of pictured fruits, so were they
who spoke of ought else save Christ and him
crucified. Our heart ached with a void the
whole earth could not fill; it heaved with a

desire as irresistible as the mountain torrent, and as little able to be restrained as the volcano when swelling with its fiery lava. Every power, every passion, every wish, moved onward in one direction. Like to an army pressing upwards through a breach, did our united powers rush forward to enter the city of salvation by one door—that door Jesus the Lord. Our soul could spare no portion of itself for others; it pressed the whole of its strength into the service to win Christ, and to be found in him. And oh! how glorious did Jesus then seem! what would we not have given to have had the scantiest morsel of his grace? "A kingdom for a horse!" cried the routed monarch. "A kingdom for a look—a world for a smile—our whole selves for one kind word!" was then our far wiser prayer. Oh what crushing we would have endured, if in the crowd we could have approached his person! what trampling would we have borne, if our finger might have touched the lowest hem of his garments! Bear us witness, ye hours of ardent desire, what horrors we would have braved, what dangers we would have encountered, what tortures we would have suffered, for one brief glimpse of *Him* whom our souls desired to know! We could have

trodden the burning marl of hell at his bidding,
if his face had but been in prospect; and as for
Peter's march upon the deep, we would have
waded to our very necks without a fear, if it
were but with half a hope of a welcome from
the Lord on the other side. He had no robbers
then to share his throne, no golden calf to provoke him to jealousy. *He* was the monarch
reigning without a rival. No part of our heart
was then shut up from him; he was welcomed
in every chamber of our being. There was not
a tablet of the heart which was not engraven
with his name, nor a string of our harp which
did not vibrate with his praise, nor an atom of
our frame which would not have leaped for very
joy at the distant sound of his footsteps. Such
a condition of longing alone for Jesus is so
healthy, that many advanced believers would
be well-nigh content to retrace their steps, if
they might once more be fully occupied with
that desire to the exclusion of every other.

If my reader be fully resolved to satisfy his
hunger only with the manna which cometh
down from heaven—if he be determined to
slake his thirst at no stream save that which
gusheth from the Rock—if he will accept no
cordial of comfort save that which is com-

pounded of the herbs of Gethsemane—it is, it must be, well with him. If none but Jesus is thy delight, take heart. Augustine cast away Tully's works because there was no Christ in them; if thou, like him, dost renounce all but Christ, Christ will never renounce thee.

2. Another pleasing feature of this case is, *the intense sincerity and ardent earnestness of the soul.* Here is an " Oh !"—a deep, impassioned, burning ejaculation of desire. It is no fanciful wish, which a little difficulty will presently overcome—it is no effervescence of excitement, which time will remove; but it is a real want, fixed in the core of the heart so firmly, that nothing but a supply of the need can silence the importunate petition. It is not the passing sigh, which the half-awakened heave as a compliment to an eloquent discourse or a stirring tract,—it is not the transient wish of the awe-struck spectator who has seen a sudden death or a notable judgment,—it is not even the longing of a soul in love for a time with the moral excellences of Christ; but it is the prayer of one who needs must pray, who cannot, who dare not, rest satisfied until he find Jesus—who can no more restrain his groaning than the light clouds can refuse to fly before the violence of

the wind. We have, we hope, many a time
enjoyed nearness to the throne of grace in
prayer; but perhaps never did such a prayer
escape our lips as that which we offered in the
bitterness of our spirit when seeking the Saviour. We have often poured out our hearts
with greater freedom, with more delight, with
stronger faith, with more eloquent language;
but never, never have we cried with more vehemence of unquenchable desire, or more burning
heat of insatiable longing. There was then no
sleepiness or sluggishness in our devotion; we
did not then need the whip of command to
drive us to labours of prayer; but our soul could
not be content unless with sighs and lamentations—with strong crying and tears it gave vent
to our bursting hearts. Then we had no need
to be dragged to our closets like oxen to the
slaughter, but we flew to them like doves to
their windows; and when there we needed no
pumping up of desires, but they gushed forth
like a fountain of waters, although at times we
felt we could scarcely find them a channel.

Mr. Philpot justly observes, " When the Lord
is graciously pleased to enable the soul to pour
out its desires, and to offer up its fervent breath-
ings at his feet, and to give them out as He

gives them in, then to call upon the Lord is no point of duty, which is to be attended to as a duty; it is no point of legal constraint, which must be done because the Word of God speaks of it; but it is a feeling, an experience, an inward work, which springs from the Lord's hand, and which flows in the Lord's own divine channel. Thus when the Lord is pleased to pour out this ' Spirit of grace and of supplication,' we must pray; but we do not pray *because* we must; we pray because we have no better occupation, we have no more earnest desire, we have no more powerful feeling, and we have no more invincible and irresistible constraint. The living child of God groans and sighs, because it is the expression of his wants·—because it is a language which pours forth the feelings of his heart—because groans and sighs are pressed out of him by the heavy weight upon him. A man lying in the street with a heavy weight upon him will call for help; he does not say, 'It is *my duty* to cry to the passers-by for help;' he cries for help because he wants to be delivered. A man with a broken leg does not say, ' It is *my duty* to send for a surgeon;' he *wants* him to set the limb. And a man in a raging disease does not say, 'It is

my duty to send for a physician;' he *wants* him
to heal his disease. So when God the Holy
Spirit works in a child of God, he prays, not
out of a sense of duty, but from a burdened
heart; he prays, because he cannot but pray;
he groans, because he cannot but groan; he
sighs, because he must sigh, having an inward
weight, an inward burden, an inward experience,
in which, and out of which, he is compelled to
call upon the Lord." *

The supplication of the penitent is no mecha-
nical form of devotion, followed for the sake of
merit; it is the natural consequence of the
wounding of Jesus; and its offerer knows no
more of merit in presenting it than in breathing,
or any other act which necessity prevents him
from suspending. This " Oh!" is one which will
not rise once and then sink for ever; it is not
the explosion of a starry rocket, succeeded by
darkness; but it will be an incessant ejaculation
of the inner man. As at some of our doors
every hour brings a post, so at the door of
mercy every hour will hear a prayer from such
an one; in fact, the soul will be full of prayer
even when it is not in the exercise itself—even
as a censer may be filled with incense when no

* Sermon on Prayer and its Answer

fire is burning in it. Prayer will become a state of the soul, perpetual and habitual, needing nothing but opportunity to develop itself in the outward act of petitioning at the feet of mercy. It is well when Mr. Desires-awake is sent to court, for he will surely prevail. Violence taketh the kingdom by force; hard knocks open mercy's door; swift running overtakes the promise; hard wrestling wins the blessing.

When the child crieth well, his lungs are sound; and when the seeker can with impetuous earnestness implore pardon, he is most surely not far from health. When the soil of our garden begins to rise, we know that the bulb will soon send forth its shoot; so when the heart breaketh for the longing which it hath unto God's testimonies, we perceive that Jesus will soon appear to gladden the spirit.

3. We are rejoiced to observe *the sense of ignorance which the seeker here expresses—* "*Oh that I knew* where I might find him!" Men are by nature very wise in matters of religion, and in their own opinion they might easily set up for Doctors of Divinity without the slightest spiritual enlightenment. It is a remarkable fact that men who find every science in the world to be too much for them, even

when they have but waded ankle-deep into the
elements thereof, can yet affect to be masters
of theology, and competent, yea, infallible
judges in matters of religion.   Nothing is more
easy than to pretend to a profound acquaintance with the religion of the cross, and even
to maintain a reputation as a well-taught and
highly-instructed disciple of the Lamb; and,
at the same time, nothing is more rare than
really to be taught of God, and illuminated by
the Spirit; and yet without this the religion of
Jesus never can be really understood.   Natural
men will array themselves in robes of learning,
ascend the chair of profession, and thence teach
to others doctrines with which they fancy
themselves to be thoroughly conversant; and if
a word were hinted of their deficiency in knowledge, and their inherent inability to discern
spiritual things, how wrathful would they become, how fiercely would they denounce the
bigotry of such an assertion, and how furiously
would they condemn the cant and fanaticism
which they conceive to be the origin of so
humiliating a doctrine!

To be as little children, and bend their necks
to the yoke of Jesus, the Master, is quite out of
the question with the men of this generation,

who love to philosophise the Word, and give
what they call "intellectual" views of the
Gospel. How little do they suspect that, professing themselves to be wise, they have become
fools! How little do they imagine that their
grand theories and learned essays are but
methods of the madness of folly, and, like paint-
ings on the windows of their understanding,
assist to shut out the light of the Holy Spirit.
Self-conceit in men who are destitute of heavenly
light, unconsciously to them doth exercise itself
on that subject upon which their ignorance is
of necessity the greatest. They will acknowledge that when they have studied astronomy,
its sublimities are beyond them; they will not
arrogate to themselves a lordship of the entire
regions of any one kingdom of knowledge: but
here, in theology, they feel themselves abundantly qualified, if they have some readiness in
the original languages, and have visited the
schools of the universities; whereas a man
might with as much justice style himself professor of botany, because he knows the scientific
names of the classes and orders, although he
has never seen one of the flowers thus named
and arranged—for what can education teach of
theology but names and theories? Experience

alone can bring the things themselves before
our eyes, and in the light of Jesus can we alone
discern them. We are pleased, therefore, to
discover in the utterance of the awakened soul
a confession of ignorance. The man inquires
"Where he can find the Lord?" He is self-
confident no longer, but is willing to ask his
way to heaven; he is prepared to go to the
very dame-school of piety, and learn the alpha-
bet of godliness. He may be distinguished for
his learning, but now a little child may lead
him; his titles, his gown, his diploma, his
dignity, all these are laid aside, and down he sits
at the feet of Jesus to begin again, or rather to
commence learning what he never knew before.

Conviction of ignorance is the doorstep of
the temple of wisdom. "It is said in the Creed
that Christ descended into hell : *descendit ut
ascendat*—He took his rising from the lowest
place to ascend into the highest; and herein
Christ readeth a good lecture unto us—he
teacheth us that humility is the way to glory." *
Seneca remarked, "I suppose that many might
have attained to wisdom, had they not thought
that they had already attained it." †   We

* Ephr. Udall's Sermons.
† Seneca de Irâ, lib. iii. c. 36.

must first be emptied of every particle of fleshly
wisdom, ere we can say that "Christ is made
unto us wisdom." We must know our folly,
and confess it, before we can be accepted as the
disciples of Jesus. It is marvellous how soon
he doth unfrock us of our grand apparel, and
how easily our wisdom disappears like a bubble
vanishing in air. We were never greater fools
than when our wisdom was the greatest in our
own esteem; but as soon as real wisdom came,
straightway our opinion of ourselves fell from
the clouds to the bottom of the mountains.
We were no divines or doctors when we were
under the convincing hand of the Spirit; we
were far more like babes for ignorance, and we
felt ourselves to be very beasts for folly.* Like
men lost in a dark wood, we could not find our
paths; the roads which were once apparent
enough, were then hedged up with thorns; and
the very entrance to the narrow way had to be
pointed out by Evangelist,† and marked by a
light. Nevertheless, blessed is he who desireth
to learn the fear of the Lord, for he shall find
it the beginning of wisdom.

Nor, in the present case, hath a sense of
ignorance driven the man to pry into secrets

* Ps. lxxiii. 22.   † Bunyan's Pilgrim.

too deep for human wisdom. He doth not exclaim, "Oh that I knew where sin took its origin, or how predestination meeteth the agency of man!" No; he seeks only this, "Oh that I knew where I might find *Him!*" Many are puzzling themselves about abstract questions while their eternal interests are in imminent peril; such men are like the man who counted the stars, but taking no heed to his feet, fell into a pit and perished. "We may sooner think to span the sun, or grasp a star, or see a gnat swallow a leviathan, than fully understand the debates of eternity. . . . . Too great an inquisitiveness beyond our line is as much a provoking arrogance as a blockish negligence of what is revealed, is a slighting ingratitude."* The quickened spirit disdains to pluck the wild flowers of carnal knowledge; he is not ambitious to reach the tempting beauties blooming on the edge of the cliffs which skirt the sea of the unrevealed; but he anxiously looks around for the rose of Sharon, the lily of the valley. He who thus studieth only to know Christ, shall soon, by the assistance of the Holy Spirit, learn enough to spell out his own salvation.

* Charnock's Divine Attributes.

4. An evidence of grace is presented to us by *the absence of all choice as to where the Saviour is discovered.* "Oh that I knew where I might find him!" Here is no stipulation; Jesus is wanted, and let him be wherever he may, the soul is prepared to go after him. We, when in this state of experience, knew little of sect or denomination. Before our conviction we could fight for names, like mercenaries for other men's countries. The mottoes of our party were higher in our esteem than the golden rules of Christianity; and we should have been by no means grieved at the conflagration of every other section of professors, if our own might have been elevated on the ruins. Every rubric and form, every custom and antiquity, we would have stained with our blood, if necessary, in order to preserve them; and mightily did we shout concerning our own Church, "Great is Diana of the Ephesians." Not a nail in the church-door but we reverenced it—not a vestment which we did not admire; or, if we loved not pomp, simplicities were magnified into our very household gods. We hated popery, but were essentially papistical; for we could have joined His Unholiness in all his anathemas, if he would but have hurled them against those who differed

from *us*. · We too did, in our own fashion, curse
by bell, book, and candle, all who were not of
our faith and order; and could scarcely think it
possible that many attained salvation beyond
the pale of our Church, or that Jesus deigned to
give them so much as a transient visit.

How changed we were when, by Divine grace,
the sectarianism of our ungodliness did hide its
head for shame! We then thought that we
would go among Methodists, Baptists, Episco-
palians, Independents, Presbyterians, or anywhere, so that we could but find a Redeemer for
our guilty souls. It is more than probable that
we found it necessary to shift our quarters, and
attend the very house which we lately detested,
to bow with the people whom once we held in
abhorrence. All the fancies of our former lives
dissolved before the heat of our desire. The
huntsman loveth the mountain which shadeth
his valley more than all its giant brothers; but
nevertheless, when in hot pursuit of the cha-
mois, he leapeth from cɪag to crag, and asks not
what is the name of the rock upon which the
object of his chase hath bounded; so the sinner,
ardently following after the Saviour, will pursue
him whithersoever he goeth.

Nor at such seasons did we regard the respect-

ability of the denomination or the grandeur of
the structure in which God was adored. The
chapel in the dark alley, the despised and deserted church, the disreputable schoolroom,
were now no longer noticed with a sneer; but
whether under the vaulted sky of heaven, the
cobwebbed thatch of a barn, the dingy ceiling
of a village station, or the magnificent roof of
the temple of the great assembly, we only
sought one thing, and that one thing found, all
places were on a level. No praising a church
for its architectural beauty—no despising a
meeting-house for its aboriginal ugliness; both
buildings were valued not by their figure but by
their contents; and where Jesus was more easily
to be found, there did we make our haunt. It
is true our servants, our ploughmen, and our
paupers, sat with us to hear the same word; but
we did not observe the difference, though once
perhaps we might have looked aghast if any but
my lady in satin, or my lord in superfine broad-
cloth, had ventured into a pew within the range
of our breath. To us the company mattered not,
so long as the Master of the Feast would but
reveal himself. The place might be uncon-
secrated, the minister unordained, the clerk
uneducated, the sect despicable, and the service

K

unpretending, but if Jesus did but show his
face there it was all we wished for.   There is no
authentic account of the dimensions, the fashion,
or furniture, of the room in which Jesus suddenly
appeared and pronounced his " peace be unto
you." Nor do we think that any one of the
assembly even so much as thought thereof while
their Lord was present. It is well when we are
content to go whithersoever the Lamb doth
lead. Doubtless, the catacombs of Rome, the
glens of Scotland, and the conventicles of England, have been more frequented by the King of
kings than cathedrals or chapels-royal : therefore do the godly count it little where they
worship, looking only for His presence which
maketh a hovel glorious, and deprecating His
absence, which makes even a temple desolate.
We would in our anxious mood have followed
Jesus in the cave, the mountain, the ravine, or
the catacomb, so that we might but have been
within the circle of his influence.

Nor would we have blushed to have sought
Jesus among his kinsfolk and acquaintance—the
sick, the poor, the uneducated, but yet sincere
children of light. How did we then delight to
sit in that upper room where stars looked
between the tiles, and hear the heavenly con-

versation which, from a miserable pallet surrounded by ragged hangings, an enfeebled saint
of the Lord did hold with us! Like divers, we
valued the pearl, even though the shell might
be a broken one, nor did we care where we went
to win it. When those creaking stairs trembled
beneath our weight, when that bottomless chair
afforded us uneasy rest, and when the heat and
effluvia of that sick-room drove our companion
away, did we not feel more than doubly repaid
while that friend of Jesus told us of all *his* love,
his faithfulness and grace? It is frequently the
case that the most despised servants of the
Lord are made the chosen instruments of comforting distressed souls, and building them up
in the faith. The writer confesses his eternal
obligations to an old cook, who was despised as
an Antinomian, but who in her kitchen taught
him many of the deep things of God, and
removed many a doubt from his youthful mind.
Even eminent men have been indebted to humble
individuals for their deliverance: take, for instance, Paul, and his comforter, Ananias; and
in our own day, Bunyan, instructed by the
holy women at Bedford. True seekers will
hunt everywhere for Jesus, and will not be
too proud to learn from beggars or little chil-

dren. We take gold from dark mines or muddy streams; it were foolish to refuse instruction in salvation from the most unlettered or uncouth. Let us be really in earnest after Christ, then circumstance and place will be lightly esteemed.

We remark also that there is no condition for distance in this question, it is only "where;" and though it be a thousand miles away, the man has his feet in readiness for the journey. Desire o'erleapeth space; leagues to it are inches, and oceans narrow into straits. Where, at one time, a mile would tire the body, a long journey after the Word is counted as nothing: yea, to stand in the house of God for hours during service is reckoned a pleasure and not a hardship. The Hindoo devotee, to find a hopeless salvation, will roll himself along for hundreds of miles: it seems but natural that we, when searching for eternal life, should count all things but loss for the excellency of the knowledge of Christ Jesus our Lord. Mary Magdalene only needed to know where they had laid her Lord, and her resolve was, "I will take him away;" for surely, she thought, her bodily strength could never fail under such a burden, and she measured the power of her body by the might of her love.

So do destitute sinners, who need a Saviour, altogether laugh at hazards or hardships which may intervene. Come mountain or valley, rapid or rock, whirlpool or tempest, desire hath girded the traveller with an omnipotence of heart, and a world of dangers is trodden beneath the feet, with the shout of Deborah—" O my soul, thou hast trodden down strength."

"I doubt not," said Rutherford to Lady Kenmure, "that if hell were betwixt you and Christ, as a river which ye behoved to cross ere ye could come at him, but ye would willingly put in your foot, and make through to be at him, upon hope that he would come in himself into the deepest of the river, and lend you his hand." Doubtless it is so with thee, reader, if thou art as we have described.

We think also we may be allowed to add, that the earnest inquirer does not object to any position of humiliation which may be required of him ere he can " see Jesus." It is only demanded " where?" and though the reply may be, " There, in yonder cell of penitence, on your bended knees, stripped of all your glories, shall you alone behold him," no delay will reveal the lurking pride; but an instantaneous and joyful obedience will manifest that the one absorbing passion has entirely swallowed up all ideas of dignity, honour, and pride.

Like Benhadad, when in danger, hearing that the king of Israel is a merciful king, we will consent to put sackcloth on our loins, and ropes upon our necks, and go in unto him, hoping for some words of favour. We make a surrender at discretion, without reserve of the arms of our sins or the baggage of our pleasures. He that is down so low as to be wholly submissive, will find that even justice will not smite him. Mercy always flieth near the ground. The flower of grace groweth in the dells of humility. The stars of love shine in the night of our self-despair. If truth lie not in a well, certainly mercy doth. The hand of justice spares the sinner who has thrown away both the sword of rebellion and the plumes of his pride. If we will do and be anything or everything, so that we may but win Christ, we shall soon find him to be everything to us. There is no more hopeful sign of coming grace than an emptiness of our own selfish terms and conditions, for he resisteth the proud, but giveth grace unto the lowly.

Thus have we tried to sum up all the promises which this state affords, but cheering though they be, we fear few will accept the comfort they afford; for " as he that poureth vinegar upon nitre, so is he that singeth songs to a sad heart;" and it is generally in vain to condole a patient under an operation by any reflections on the benefit thereof, seeing that while the pain lasteth he will still cry out and groan. Nevertheless, we who have escaped cannot refrain from singing without the walls of the dungeon, in the hope that some within may hear and take heart. Let us say to every mourner in Zion, Be of good cheer, for " He who walked in the garden, and made a noise that made Adam hear his voice, will also at some time walk in your soul, and make you hear a more sweet word, yet ye will not always hear the noise and din of his feet when He walketh."* Ephraim is bemoaning and mourning† "when he thinketh God is far off, and heareth not; and yet God is like the bridegroom, standing only behind a thin wall,‡ and laying to his ear, for he saith himself, I have surely heard Ephraim bemoaning himself." " I will surely have mercy upon him, saith the Lord."

Be thou of good cheer, O seeker; go on, for hope prophesies success, and the signs of thy

* Rutherford. † Jer. xxxi. 18.
‡ Cant. ii. 9.

case prognosticate a happy deliverance. None
who are like thee have failed at last; persevere,
and be saved.

II. We are now arrived at our second division,
wherein we proposed to consider *the reasons
of this tarrying*. May our Divine Illuminator
enlighten us while we write!

We believe that many are delayed because
they seek not rightly, or because they seek not
eagerly, with these we have just now nothing to
do; we are dealing with the genuine convert, the
sincere searcher, who yet cannot find his Lord.
To the exercised mind no question is more
hard to answer than this, "Why doth he not
hear?" but when delivered from our distress,
nothing is more full of joy than the rich discovery that "he hath done all things well."

If our reader be now in sorrow, let him
believe what he cannot see, and receive the
testimony of others who now bear witness that
"God's way is in the sea, and his path in the
deep waters."

1. We now perceive that *it afforded pleasure
to Jesus* to view the labours of our faith in pursuit after him. Jesus doth often hide his face
from his children, that he may hear the sweet

music of their cry. When the woman of Canaan came before our Lord, he answered her
not a word; and when her importunity did
somewhat prevail, a harsh sentence was all she
obtained. Yet the blessed Jesus was not angry
with her, but was pleased to behold her faith
struggling amid the waves of his seeming
neglect, and finding anchorage even on that
hard word which appeared like a rock ready to
wreck her hopes. He was so charmed with her
holy daring and heavenly resolution, that he
detained her for a time to feast his eyes upon
the lovely spectacle. The woman had faith in
Christ, and Jesus would let all men see what
faith can do in honour of its Lord.

Great kings have among their attendants
certain well-trained *artistes* who play before
them, while they, sitting with their court, behold their feats with pleasure. Now, *Faith* is
the king's champion, whom he delights to put
upon labours of the most herculean kind.
Faith hath, when bidden by its Master, stopped
the sun and chained the moon; it hath dried
the sea and divided rivers; it hath dashed bul-
warks to the ground; quenched the violence of
fire; stopped the mouths of lions; turned to
flight the armies of the aliens, and robbed death

of its prey. *Importunity* is the king's running
footman; he hath been known to run whole
months together without losing his breath, and
over mountains he leaps with the speed of
Asahel; therefore doth the Lord at times try
his endurance, for he loveth to see what his own
children can perform. *Prayer*, also, is one of
the royal musicians; and although many do
prefer his brother, who is called Praise, yet this
one hath ever had an equal share of the king's
favour. His lute playeth so sweetly that the
heavens have smiled with sunshine for the space
of three years and six months* at the sound
thereof; and when again the melodious notes
were heard, the same skies did weep for joy,
and rain descended on the earth. Prayer hath
made God's axe of vengeance stay in mid air,
when hastening to fell the cumberer to the
ground; and his sword hath been lulled to sleep
in its scabbard by the soft sonnets of prayer,
when it sung of pardons bought with blood.
Therefore, because Jesus delighteth in these
courtiers whom he hath chosen, he doth ever
find them work to do, whereby they may minister unto his good pleasure. Surely thou who
walkest in darkness, and seest no light, thou

* James v. 17, 18.

mayst be well content to grope thy way for a
while, if it be true that this midnight journey
is but one of the feats of faith which God is
pleased that thou shouldst perform. Go on
then in confidence.

2. We may sometimes regard this delay as *an
exhibition of Divine sovereignty.* God is not
bound to persons nor to time; as he giveth to
whom he pleaseth, so doth he bestow his favours
in his own time and manner. Very frequently
the prayer and the answer attend each other, as
the echo doth the speaker's voice. Usually it
is, "Before they call I will answer, and while
they are yet speaking I will hear." But Divine
prerogative must be manifested and maintained,
and therefore he doth sometimes give temporary
denials or protracted delays. Through some of
our squares the right of way is private, and in
order to maintain the right, although the road
is usually open, yet there are gates which at
times are closed for a season, lest any should
imagine that they could demand a passage; so,
although mercy be free and speedy, yet it is not
always immediate, that men may know that the
giver has a right to refuse. Jesus is no paid
physician, who is bound to give us his calls;
therefore he will sometimes step in late in the

day, that we may remember he is not our debtor. Oh! our hearts loathe the pride which bows not to Divine sovereignty, but arrogantly declares God to be under obligations to his creatures. Those who are full of this satanic spirit will not assert this in plain language, but while they cavil at election, talking with impious breath about " partiality," " injustice," "respect of persons" and such like things, they too plainly show that their old nature is yet unhumbled by Divine grace.   We are sure of this, that no convinced sinner, when under a sense of his ill-desert, will ever dispute the justice of God in damning him, or quarrel with the distinguishing grace which Heaven giveth to one and not to another. If such a person has not yet been able to subscribe to the doctrine of sovereign, discriminating, electing grace, we wonder not that he hath found no peace; for verily Jesus will have him know that his bounties are in his own hand, and that none can lay any claim to them.   Herbert, in his *Country Parson*, says, " He gives no set pension unto any, for then, in time, it will lose the name of charity with the poor, and they will reckon upon it, as on a debt;" truly it would be even so with the lovingkindnesses of the Lord, if they were always bestowed where man at first

desires them.   There is nothing over which the
Lord is more jealous than his crown—his sovereignty—his right to do as he will with his own.
How grateful should we be that he uses such
lenient and gentle means to preserve his dignity; and that while he might, if he pleased,
block up the gates of salvation for ever, he doth
only for a moment cause them to be closed, that
we may sing the more loudly when we obtain
an entrance through them.

3. *A ministry devoid of gospel grace* is a frequent cause of long delay in finding the Saviour.
Some of us in the days of our sorrow for sin
were compelled by circumstances to sit under a
legal preacher who did but increase our pain,
and aggravate our woe.   Destitute of all savour
and unction, but most of all wanting in a clear
view of Jesus the Mediator, the sermons we
heard were wells without water, and clouds
without rain.   Elegant in diction, admirable in
style, and faultless in composition, they fell on
our ears even as the beautiful crystals of snow
fall upon the surface of a brook, and only tend
to swell its floods.   Good morality, consistent
practice, upright dealing, amiable behaviour,
gentle carriage, and modest deportment, were
the everyday themes of the pulpit; but, alas!

they were of as little service to us as instructions
to dance would be to a man who has lost both
his legs. We have often been reminded by such
preachers, of the doctor who told a poor penniless widow that her sick son could easily be
cured if she would give him the best wine, and
remove him at once to Baden-Baden—the poor
creature's fingers staring all the while through
the tips of her worn-out gloves, as if they
wished to see the man who gave advice so pro-
foundly impracticable.

Far be it from us to condemn the preaching
of morality by such men, for it is doubtless all
they can preach, and their intentions being
good, it is probable they may sometimes be of
service in restraining the community from acts
of disorder; but we do deny the right of many
to call themselves Christian ministers, while
they constantly and systematically neglect to
declare the truths which lie at the very foundation of the Gospel. A respected bishop of the
Episcopalian denomination,* in addressing the
clergy of the last century, said, "We have long
been attempting to reform the nation by moral
preaching. With what effect? None. On the
contrary, we have dexterously preached the

* Bishop Lavington.

people into downright infidelity. We must change our voice; we must preach Christ and him crucified; nothing but the Gospel is the power of God unto salvation." We fear that in some measure this is the case even now— would that we dared to hope otherwise! Let such of us as are engaged in the work of the ministry take heed to ourselves, and to our doctrine, that we cause no needless pain, and retard no man's progress to a Saviour; and let our reader look to his own soul's salvation, and select his pastor, not for his eloquence, learning, amiability, or popularity, but for his clear and constant testimony to the Gospel of Christ. The witness of the pulpit must be incessantly evangelical, nor is a single exception to be allowed. A venerable divine justly writes, " Faithful preachers *never* preach mere philosophy, nor mere metaphysics, nor mere morality."* How many poor souls may now be in bondage by your lifeless preaching, O ye who love anything better than the simple Gospel! What are ye but polished bolts on the dungeon-door of the distressed, or well-dressed halberdiers, affrighting men from the palace of mercy? Ah! it will be well for some if they shall be

* Emmons.

able to wash their hands of the blood of souls, for verily in the cells of eternal condemnation there are heard no yells of horror more appalling than the shrieks of damned ministers. Oh, to have misled men—to have ruined their souls for ever !

Happy suicide,* who by his own hand escapes the sound of the curses of those he victimized! happy in comparison with the man who will for ever hear the accusing voices of the many who have sunk to perdition through the rottenness of the doctrine which he offered them for their support. Here, on our knees we fall, and pray for grace that we may ever hold up Jesus to the sinner; not doctrine without Jesus, which is as the pole without the brazen serpent, but Jesus —a whole Jesus—to poor lost sinners. We are sure that many convinced souls have tarried long in the most distressing condition, simply because, by reason of the poverty of their spiritual food, their weakness was so great that the cry of Hezekiah was theirs — "This day is a day of trouble; for the children are come to the birth, and there is not strength to bring forth."† May our glorified Jesus soon come into his Church, and raise up shepherds after his

* Mr. Sadleir.   † Isa. xxxvii. 3.

own heart, who, endowed with the Holy Spirit, full of sympathy, and burning with love, shall visit those who are out of the way, and guide the wanderer to the fold. Such men are still to be found. O reader, search them out, sit at their feet, receive their word, and be not disobedient to the commands which they utter from heaven.

4. *Misapprehension of the nature of salvation,* in some cases, delays the happy hour of Christ's appearance. A natural tendency to legal ideas dims the mind to the perception of the doctrine of Jesus, which is grace and truth. A secret desire to do something in part to aid Jesus, prevents us from viewing *him* as "all our salvation, and all our desire." Humbled though we have been by the cutting down of all our righteousness, yet the old root will sprout—"at the scent of water it will bud;" and so long as it does so, there can be no solid peace, no real cleaving to Christ. We must learn to spell the words *law* and *grace,* without mingling the letters.

While sick men take two kinds of medicine there is little hope of a cure, especially if the two draughts are compounded of opposing ingredients; the bird which lives on two trees builds its nest on neither; and the soul halting

L

between grace and works can never find rest
for the sole of its foot. Perhaps, my reader, a
secret and well-nigh imperceptible self-trust is
the very thing which shuts out Christ from thy
soul. Search and look.

Not a few seekers are expecting some extraordinary sign and wonder ere they can believe.
They imagine that conversion will come upon
them in some marvellous manner, like Mary's
visitation by the angel. Naaman-like, they are
dreaming that the prophet will strike his hand
over the place, and they shall recover. "Go
wash in Jordan seven times" has not enough
mystery in it for their poor minds: "Except
they see signs and wonders they will not believe."
Let none, however, hope for miracles; wonders do occur: some are brought to Jesus by
vision and revelation, but far more are drawn
by the usual means of grace, in a manner which
is far removed from the marvellous. The Lord
is not in the whirlwind, the Lord is not in the
fire; but usually he speaketh in the still small
voice. Surely it should be enough for us, if we
find pardon in the appointed method, without
desiring to have rare and curious experiences,
with which, in after years, we may gratify our
own self-love, and elevate ourselves as singular

favourites of heaven. Regeneration is indeed a supernatural work, but it is usually a silent one. It is a pulling down of strongholds, but the earth shakes not with the fall; it is the building of a temple, but there is no sound of hammer at its erection; like the sunrise, it is not heralded by the blast of trumpet, nor do wonders hide beneath its wings. We know who is the mother of mystery; do we desire to be her children? Strange phantoms and marvellous creatures find their dwelling-place in *darkness;* light is not in relationship with mystery; let none be hoping to find it so. *Believe and live* is the plan of the Gospel; if men would but lay aside their old ideas, they would soon find Jesus as their very present help; but because they look for unpromised manifestations, they seek in vain, until disappointment has taught them wisdom.

5. Although the seeking penitent hath renounced all known sin, yet *it may be that some sin of ignorance yet remains unconfessed, and unrepented of,* which will frequently be a cause of great and grievous delay.

God, who searcheth Jerusalem with candles, will have us examine ourselves most thoroughly. He has issued a search-warrant to conviction,

which giveth that officer a right to enter every
room of our house, and command every Rachel
to rise from her seat lest the images should be
beneath her. Sin is so skilful in deception, that
it is hard to discover all its lurking places;
neither is it easy to detect its character when
brought before our eyes, since it will often
borrow the garb of virtue, and appear as an
angel of light; nor should we ourselves use
sufficient diligence in its destruction, if the
delay of the needed mercy did not urge us to a
more vigorous pursuit of the traitors who have
brought us into grief. Our gracious Lord, for
our own sake, desires the execution of our secret
sins, and by his frowns he puts us upon the
watch lest we should indulge or harbour them.

Never, perhaps, shall we again possess so deep
a horror of sin as in that moment when we
well-nigh despaired of deliverance from it, and
therefore never shall we be so fully prepared to
exterminate it. Eternal wisdom will not allow
a season so propitious to pass without improve-
ment; and having melted our heart in the furnace till the scum floateth on the surface, it doth
not allow it to cool until the dross hath been
removed. Look to thyself, O seeker, for peradventure the cause of thy pain lieth in thine

own heart. How small a splinter prevents the healing of a festered wound; extract it, and the cure is easy. Be wise; what thou doest do quickly, but do it perfectly; thus shalt thou make sure work for eternity, and speed the hour of thine acceptance. Be sure sin will find *thee* out, unless thou dost find *it* out. A warrior stimulated the valour of his soldiers by simply pointing to the enemy and exclaiming, " *Lads, there they are, if you do not kill them, they will kill you.*" Thus would we remind thee, that sin will destroy *thee* if thou dost not destroy *it*. Be concerned, then, to drive it from thine heart.

6. *Usefulness in after life* is often increased by the bitter experience with which the soul is exercised while seeking after Jesus; but as this has already received our attention, we will close our meditations on the reasons for protracted delay, by the simple remark, that it is of far more importance to a penitent to use every means for obtaining the Saviour's blessing, than to inquire into the motives which have hitherto made him deaf to his petitions. Earnestly do we entreat the mourner to strive to enter in at the straight gate, and to continue his cry—" Oh that I knew where I might find him !"

III. It is now our pleasant duty to direct the troubled spirit to *the means of obtaining speedy and lasting peace*. May the God who opened the eyes of the desolate Hagar in the wilderness, and guided her so that she saw a well of water whereat she filled her empty bottle, use us as his finger to point the thirsting, dying sinner to the place where *He* stands, who once said, "If any man thirst, let him come unto me and drink." Our rules shall be expressed in simple words—that the wayfaring man, though a fool, may not err therein.

1. *Go where he goes*. Dost thou desire to present a petition to the king—wilt thou not go to his palace to do it? Art thou blind—where shouldst thou sit but at the way-side, begging? Hast thou a sore disease—where is there a place more fitting for thee than the porch of Bethesda, where my Lord doth walk? Art thou palsied—wilt thou not desire to be in his presence, though on thy bed thou be let down to the spot where he standeth? Did not Obadiah and Ahab journey through the whole land of Israel to find Elijah? and wilt not thou visit every place where there is hope of meeting Jesus? Dost thou know where his haunts are? Hast thou not heard that he dwelleth on the hill of

Zion, and hath fixed his throne of mercy within the gates of Jerusalem? Has it not been told thee that he ofttimes cometh up to the feast, and mingleth with the worshippers in his temple? Have not the saints assured thee that he walketh in the midst of his Church, even as John, in vision, saw him among the golden candlesticks? Go, then, to the city wh ch he hath chosen for his dwelling-place, and wait within the doors which he hath deigned to enter. If thou knowest of a gospel minister, sit in the solemn assembly over which he is president. If thou hast heard of a church which has been favoured with visits from its Lord, go and make one in the midst of them, that when he cometh he may bid thee put thine hand into his side, and be not faithless but believing. Lose no opportunity of attending the word: Thomas doubted, because he was not there when Jesus came.

Let sermons and prayers be thy delight, because they are roads wherein the Saviour walketh. Let the righteous be thy constant company, for such ever bring Him where they come. It is the least thing thou canst do to stand where grace usually dispenseth its favour. Even the beggar writes his petition on the flag-stone of a frequented thoroughfare, because he

hopeth that among the many passers, some few
at least will give him charity; learn from him
to offer thy prayers where mercies are known to
move in the greatest number, that amid them
all there may be one for thee. Keep thy sail
up when there is no wind, that when it blows
thou mayst not have need to prepare for it; use
means when thou seest no grace attending them,
for thus wilt thou be in the way when grace
comes. Better go fifty times and gain nothing
than lose one good opportunity. If the angel
stir not the pool, yet lie there still, for it may be
the moment when thou leavest it will be the
season of his descending. "Being in the way,
the Lord met with me," said one of old; be
thou in the way, that the Lord may meet with
thee. Old Simeon found the infant Messiah in
the Temple; had he deserted its hallowed courts
he might never have said, "Mine eyes have seen
thy salvation." Be sure to keep in mercy's way.

2. *Cry after Him.* Thou hast been lying in
his path for many a day, but he has not turned
his eye upon thee. What then? Art thou
content to let him pass thee by? Art thou
willing to lose so precious an opportunity?
No! thou desirest life, and thou wilt not be
ashamed to beg aloud for it: thou wilt not fear

to take him for an example of whom it is written,
"When he heard that it was Jesus of Nazareth,
he began to cry out and say, Jesus, thou Son of
David, have mercy on me! And many charged
him that he should hold his peace; but he cried
the more a great deal, Thou Son of David, have
mercy on me!" It is an old proverb, "We lose
nothing by asking," and it is an older promise,
"Ask and ye shall receive." Be not afraid of
crying too loudly. It is recorded, to the honour
of Mordecai, that he cried with a loud cry; and
we know that the kingdom of heaven suffereth
violence. Think it not possible to pray too
frequently, but at morning, at noon, and at
eventide, lift up thy soul unto God. Let not
despondency stop the voice of thy supplication,
for He who heareth the young ravens when they
cry, will in due time listen to the trembling
words of thy desire. Give Him no rest until he
hear thee; like the importunate widow, be thou
always at the heels of the great One; give not
up because the past has proved apparently fruit-
less, remember Jericho stood firm for six days,
but yet when they gave an exceeding great
shout, it fell flat to the ground. "Arise, cry
out in the night: in the beginning of the watches
pour out thine heart like water before the face

of the Lord. Let tears run down like a river day and night: give thyself no rest; let not the apple of thine eye cease." * Let groans, and sighs, and vows keep up perpetual assault at heaven's doors.

> "Groans fresh'd with vows, and vows made salt with tears;
> Unscale his eyes, and scale his conquered ears:
> Shoot up the bosom-shafts of thy desire,
> Feather'd with faith, and double-fork'd with fire;
> And they will hit: fear not, where heaven bids come,
> Heav'n's never deaf, but when man's heart is dumb."

Augustine sweetly writes, "Thou mayest seek after honours, and not obtain them; thou mayest labour for riches, and yet remain poor; thou mayest dote on pleasures, and have many sorrows. But our God of his supreme goodness says, Who ever sought *me*, and found me not? whoever desired me, and obtained me not? whoever loved me, and missed of me? I am with him that seeks for me: he hath me already that wisheth for me; and he that loveth me is sure of my love." Try whether it be not so, O reader, for so have we found it.

3. *Think of his promises.* He has uttered many sweet and gracious words, which are like the call of the hen, inviting thee to nestle beneath

* Lam ii 18, 19.

his wings, or like white flags of truce bidding
thee come without fear. There is not a single
promise which, if followed up, will not lead thee
to the Lord. *He* is the centre of the circle, and
the promises, like radii, all meet in *him*, and
thence become Yea and Amen. As the streams
run to the ocean, so do all the sweet words of
Jesus tend to himself: launch thy bark upon
any one of them, and it shall bear thee onward
to the broad sea of his love. Lost on a dreary
moor, the wanderer discovers his cottage by the
light in the window casting a gleam over the
darkness of the waste; so also must we find out
" our dwelling-place " by the lamps of promise
which our Saviour hath placed in the windows
of his word. The handkerchiefs brought from
the person of Paul healed the sick; surely the
promises, which are the garments of Christ, will
avail for all diseases. We all know that the key
of promise will unfasten every lock in Doubting
Castle; will we be content to lie any longer in
that dungeon when that key is ready to our
hand? A large number of the ransomed of the
Lord have received their liberty by means of a
cheering word applied with power. Be thou
constant in reading the word and meditation
thereon. Amid the fair flowers of promise

groweth the rose of Sharon—pluck the promises, and thou mayst find *Him* with them. *He*
feedeth among the lilies—do thou feed there
also. The sure words of Scripture are the footsteps of Jesus imprinted on the soil of mercy—
follow the track and find *Him*. The promises
are cards of admission not only to the throne,
the mercy-seat, and the audience-chamber, but
to the very heart of Jesus. Look aloft to the
sky of Revelation, and thou wilt yet find a
constellation of promises which shall guide thine
eye to the star of Bethlehem. Above all, cry
aloud when thou readest a promise, " Remember
thy word unto thy servant, on which thou hast
caused me to hope."

4. *Meditate on his person and his work.* If
we were better acquainted with Jesus, we should
find it more easy to believe him. Many souls
mourn because they cannot make themselves believe; and the constant exhortations of ministers
persuading them to faith, cause them to sink
deeper in the mire, since all their attempts
prove ineffectual. It were well for both if they
would remember that the mind is not to be
compelled to belief by exhortation or force of
will; a small acquaintance with the elements of
mental science would suffice to show them that

faith is a result of previous states of the mind,
and flows from those antecedent conditions, but
is not a position to which we can attain without
passing through those other states which the
Divine laws, both of nature and of grace, have
made the stepping-stones thereto. Even in
natural things, we cannot believe a thing simply
because we are persuaded to do so; we require
evidence; we ask, "What are we to believe?"
we need instruction on the matter before we
can lay hold upon it. In spiritual things especially we need to know what we are to believe,
and why. We cannot by one stride mount to
faith, and it is at least useless, not to say cruel,
to urge us to do so, unless we are told the grounds
on which our faith must rest. Some men endeavour to preach *sinners to Christ*; we prefer to
preach *Christ to sinners*. We believe that a faithful exhibition of Jesus crucified will, under the
Divine blessing, beget faith in hearts where fiery
oratory and vehement declamation have failed.
Let this be borne in mind by those who are be-
wailing themselves, in the words of John Newton:

> "Oh, could but I believe,
>   Then all would easy be;
> I would, but cannot—Lord, relieve!
>   My help must come from thee."

Thou wilt not long have need to pray in this
fashion if thou canst obey the rule we would put
before thee, which is, meditate on Jesus; reflect
upon the mystery of his incarnation and redemption; and frequently picture the agonies of
Gethsemane and Calvary. The cross not only
demands faith, but causes it. The same Christ
who requires faith for salvation doth infuse
faith into all those who meekly and reverently
meditate upon his sacrifice and mediation. We
learn to believe in an honest man by an acquaintance with him, even so (although faith be
the gift of God, yet he giveth it in the use of the
means) it cometh to pass that by frequent consideration of Jesus, we know him, and therefore
trust in him. Go thou to the gloomy brook of
Kedron, make Gethsemane thy garden of retirement, tread the blood-stained Gabbatha, climb
the hill of Calvary, sit at the foot of the accursed
tree, watch the victim in his agonies, listen to
his groans, mark his flowing blood, see his head
bowed on his breast in death, look into his open
side; then walk to the tomb of Joseph of Arima-
thea, behold him rise, witness his ascension, and
view him exalted far above principalities and
powers, as the mediator for sinful men: thus
shalt thou see and believe, for verily hard is

that unbelief which can endure such sights; and if the Holy Spirit lead thee to a true vision of them, thou shalt believe inevitably, finding it impossible longer to be incredulous. A true view of Calvary will smite unbelief with death, and put faith into its place. Spend hours in holy retirement, tracing his pilgrimage of woe, and thou shalt soon sing,

> " Oh how sweet to view the flowing
> Of his soul-redeeming blood;
> With Divine assurance knowing
> That he made my peace with God!'

5. *Venture on Him.* This is the last but best advice we give thee, and if thou hast attended to that which precedes it, thou wilt be enabled to follow it. We have said " venture," but we imply no venture of risk, but one of courage. To be saved it is required of thee to renounce all hope of salvation by any save Jesus—that thou hast submitted to. Next thou art called upon to cast thyself entirely on him, prostrating thyself before his cross, content to rely wholly on *Him.* Do this and thou art saved, refuse and thou art damned. Subscribe thy name to this simple rhyme—

> " I'm a poor sinner, and nothing at all,
> But Jesus Christ is my all in all;"

and, doing this, thou art secure of heaven.

Dost thou delay because of unworthiness? Oh do not so, for he invites thee just as thou art. Thou art not too sinful, for he is "able to save unto the uttermost." Think not little of his power or his grace, for he is infinite in each; only fall flat upon his gracious declaration, and thou shalt be embraced by his mercy. To believe is to take Jesus at his word, and when all things deny thee the hope of salvation, still to call *Him* yours. Now we beseech thee launch into the deep, now cut thy moorings and give up thyself to the gale, now leave the rudder in *his* hands, and surrender thy keeping to *his* guardianship. In this way alone shalt thou obtain peace and eternal life.

May the Directing Spirit lead us each to Him in whom there is light, and whose light is the life of men.

TO THE UNCONVERTED READER.

FRIEND,—Love to thy soul constrains us to set apart this small enclosure for thine especial benefit. Oh that thou hadst as much love for thine own soul as the writer has! Though he may have never seen thee, yet remember when he wrote these lines he put up an especial prayer for thee, and he had thee on his heart while he penned these few but earnest words.

O Friend, thou art no seeker of Jesus, but the reverse! To thine own confusion thou art going *from* him instead of *to* him! Oh, stay a moment and consider thy *ways*—thy *position*—thine *end!*

As for thy *ways*, they are not only wrong before God, but they are uneasy to thyself. Thy conscience, if it be not seared with a hot iron, is every day thundering at thee on account of thy paths of folly. Oh that thou wouldst turn from thine error, while the promise is yet within hearing, " Let the wicked forsake his way, and the unrighteous man his thoughts;

and let him return unto the Lord, and he will
have mercy upon him, and unto our God, for he
will abundantly pardon." Be not betrayed into
a continuance in these ways in the vain hope
that thy life will be prolonged to an indefinite
period, wherein thou hopest to accomplish repentance; for life is as frail as the bubble on the
breaker, and as swift as the Indian arrow. To-
morrow may never come, oh use "to-day"—

> " *Now*, is the constant syllable ticking from the clock
>   of time ;
> *Now*, is the watchword of the wise; *Now*, is on the
>   banner of the prudent.
> Cherish thy to-day, and prize it well, or ever it be
>   engulphed in the past ;
> Husband it, for who can promise if it shall have a
>   to-morrow ?" *

" To-morrow is a fatal lie—the wrecker's
beacon—wily snare of the destroyer;" be wise,
and see to thy ways while time waits for thee.

Consider next thy *position*. A condemned
criminal waiting for execution; a tree, at the
root of which the axe is gleaming ; a target, to
which the shaft of death is speeding; an insect
beneath the finger of vengeance waiting to be
crushed ; a wretch hurried along by the strong
torrent of time to an inevitable precipice of doom.

* Tupper's *Proverbial Philosophy.*

Thy present position is enough to pale the cheek of carelessness, and move the iron knees of profanity. A man asleep in a burning house, or with his neck upon the block of the headsman, or lying before the mouth of a cannon, is not in a more dangerous case than thou art. Oh bethink thee, ere desolation, destruction, and damnation, seal up thy destiny, and stamp thee with despair!

Be sure, also, that thou consider thy *latter end*, for it is thine whether thou consider it or no. Thou art ripening for hell; oh, how wilt thou endure its torments! Ah! if thou wouldst afford a moment to visit, in imagination, the cells of the condemned, it might benefit thee for ever. What! fear to examine the house in which thou art to dwell? What! rush to a place and fear to see a picture of it? Oh let thy thoughts precede thee, and if they bring back a dismal story, it may induce thee to change thy mind and tread another path! Thou wilt lose nothing by meditation, but rather gain much thereby. Oh let the miseries of lost souls warn thee lest thou also come into this place of torment! May the day soon arrive when thou canst cry after the Lord, and then even thou shalt be delivered!

IV.

Jesus Pardoning.

"The blood of Jesus Christ his Son cleanseth us from all sin."—1 JOHN i. 7.

———

" I will praise thee every day,
  Now thine anger's turn'd away.
  Comfortable thoughts arise
  From the bleeding sacrifice.
  Jesus is become at length,
  My salvation and my strength;
  And his praises shall prolong,
  While I live, my pleasant song."

LET our lips crowd sonnets within the compass of a word; let our voice distil hours of melody into a single syllable; let our tongue utter in one letter the essence of the harmony of ages: for we write of an hour which as far excelleth all the days of our life as gold exceedeth dross. As the night of Israel's passover was a night to be remembered, a theme or bards, and an incessant fountain of grateful song, even so is the time of which we now speak, the never-to-be-forgotten hour of our emancipation from guilt, and of our justification in Jesus.

Other days have mingled with their fellows till, like coins worn in circulation, their image and superscription are entirely obliterated; but this day remaineth new, fresh, bright, as distinct in all its parts as if it were but yesterday struck from the mint of time. Memory shall drop from her palsied hand full many a memento which now she cherishes, but she shall never, even when she tottereth to the grave, unbind from her heart the token of the thrice-happy hour of the redemption of our spirit. The emancipated galley-slave may forget the day which heard his broken fetters rattle on the ground; the pardoned traitor may fail to remember the moment when the axe of the headsman was averted by a pardon; and the long-despairing mariner may not recollect the moment when a friendly hand snatched him from the hungry deep: but O hour of forgiven sin! moment of perfect pardon! our soul shall never forget thee while within her life and being find an immortality.

Each day of our life hath had its attendant

angel; but on this day, like Jacob at Mahanaim, hosts of angels met us. The sun hath
risen every morning, but on that eventful morn
he had the light of seven days. As the days
of heaven upon earth—as the years of immortality—as the ages of glory—as the bliss of
heaven, so were the hours of that thrice-happy
day. Rapture divine, and ecstasy inexpressible,
filled our soul. Fear, distress, and grief, with
all their train of woes, fled hastily away; and in
their place joys came without number. Like
as terrors fly before the rising sunlight, so
vanished all our dark forebodings, and

> " As morn her rosy steps in the eastern clime,
>   Advancing, sowed the earth with orient pearl,"

so did grace strew our heart with priceless gems
of joy. "For, lo, the winter was past; the
rain was over and gone; the flowers appeared
on the earth; the time of the singing of birds
was come; and the voice of the turtle was
heard in our land; the fig-tree put forth her
green figs, and the vines with the tender grape
gave a good smell, when our Beloved spake,
and said, 'Arise, my love, my fair one, and come
away.'" Our buried powers, upspringing from
the dark earth, where corruption had buried

them, oudded, blossomed, and brought forth
clusters of fruit. Our soul was all awake to
gladness; conscience sang approval; judgment
joyfully attested the validity of the acquittal;
hope painted bright visions for the future; while
imagination knew no bounds to the eagle-flight
of her loosened wing. The city of Mansoul
had a grand illumination, and even its obscurest
lanes and alleys were hung with lamps of brilliance. The bells of our soul rang merry peals,
music and dancing filled every chamber, and
every room was perfumed with flowers. Our
heart was flooded with delight; like a bottle
full of new wine, it needed vent. It contained
as much of heaven as the finite can hold of in-
finity. It was wedding-day with our soul, and
we wore robes fairer than ever graced a bridal.
By night angels sang—" Glory to God in the
highest, on earth peace, goodwill towards
men;" and in the morning, remembering their
midnight melodies, we sang them o'er again.
We walked in Paradise; we slept in bowers of
amaranth; we drank draughts of nectar from
goblets of gold, and fed on luscious fruits
brought to us in baskets of silver.

"The liquid drops of tears that we once shed
Came back again, transform'd to richest pearl;"

the breath we spent in sighs returned upon
us laden with fragrance; the past, the present,
the future, like three fair sisters, danced around
us, light of foot and gladsome of heart. We
had discovered the true alchymist's stone, which,
turning all to gold, had transmuted all within
us into the purest metal. We were rich, im-
mensely rich; for Christ was ours, and we were
heirs with Him.

Our body, too, once the clog and fetter of our
spirit, became the active partner of our bliss.
Our eyes were windows lighted up with happiness; our feet were young roes bounding with
pleasure; our lips were fountains gushing with
song, and our ears were the seats of minstrels.
It was hard to contain our rapture within the
narrow bounds of prudence. Like the insects
leaping in the sunshine, or the fish sporting in
the stream, we could have danced to and fro in
the convulsions of our delight. Were we sick,
our pleasure drowned our pain; were we
feeble, our bliss renewed our strength. Each
broken bone praised Him; each strained sinew
blessed Him; our whole flesh extolled Him.
Every sense was the inlet of joy, and the outlet
of praise. As the needle stayeth at the pole,
so did our quivering frame rest on Him. We

knew no thought beyond, no hope above, the perfect satisfaction of that hour; for Christ and his salvation had filled us to the very brim.

All nature appeared to sympathise with us We went forth with joy, and were led forth with peace; the mountains and the hills broke forth before us into singing, and all the trees of the field clapped their hands. The fields, the floods, the sky, the air, the sun, the stars, the cattle, the birds, the fish—yea, the very stones seemed sharers of our joy. They were the choir, and we the leaders of a band, who at the lifting of our hand poured forth whole floods of harmony.

Perhaps our birthday found the earth wrapped in the robes of *winter*, but its snowy whiteness was all in keeping with the holiday of our spirit. Each snow-flake renewed the assurance of our pardon, for we were now washed whiter than snow. The burial of the earth in its winding-sheet of white betokened to us the covering of our sins by the righteousness of Jesus. The trees, festooned with ice-drops, glittered in the sun as if they had coined stars to shine upon us; and even the chill blast, as it whirled around us, appeared but an image of that power which

had carried our sins away, as far as the east is
from the west.   Sure, never was winter less
wintry than then, for in a nobler sense than the
poet* we can affirm—

> " With frequent foot,
> Pleas'd have I, in my cheerful morn of life,
> Trod the pure snows, myself as pure."

Grace enabled us to find a song where others
did but murmur.

It may be we were brought to love the glorious Redeemer in the *spring-time* of the year;
and if so, our quickened spirit found all around
it the counterpart of the world within. We,
too, like the little flowers, were rising from
our tombs; like the sweet birds, expecting
brighter days, we sung the songs of promise;
like the rippling brooks, unbound from our
captivity, we leaped in hasty joy; and, like the
woodlands, we were " prodigal of harmony."
The mountains, lifting their green heads to
the sky, we charged to tell our Maker how we
desired to approach his footstool; and the valleys, bleating with the flocks, were bidden to
commend us to the notice of the great Shepherd
of the sheep. The falling rains we thanked as

* Thomson.

emblems of him who cometh down "like rain upon the mown grass;" and the smiling sun we owned as a type of his great Lord, who bringeth healing beneath his wings.

> " We walk'd
> The sunny glade, and felt an inward bliss
> Beyond the power of kings to purchase."

Aye, and beyond the power of kings to guess if they, too, had not felt the same. As the portals of earth were opening for the coming of the summer, so were we preparing for glorious days of happiness and fruitfulness. Everything in creation was in keeping with our condition, as if nature were but a dress made by a skilful hand, fitting our new-born soul in every part. We were supremely blest. Our heart was like a bell dancing at bridal joys, and the world was full of bells chiming with it. We were glad, and nature cried, " Child, lend me thine hand, and we will dance together, for I too am at case since my great Lord hath loosed me from my wintry fetters; come on, favoured one, and wander where thou wilt, for

> " 'The soft'ning air is balm;
> Echo the mountains round; the forest smiles;
> And every sense, and every heart is joy.'

Come on, then, and sport with me on this our
mutual feast."

If in *summer* we brought forth fruits meet
for repentance, and were planted in the garden
of the Lord, the soil on which we trod was
prolific of emblems of our own condition, and
of creatures sympathising with our joy; and
the sky which canopied our dwelling-place was
woven like a tapestry with praises of our Lord.
When the rainbow bridged the sky, we hailed
it as the sign of the eternal covenant made with
us by Him who keepeth truth to all generations;
if the steaming river sent its exhalation to the
clouds, we put our song upon its altar that it
might ascend with it; if the dewdrops sparkled
on the breast of morn, " the dew of our youth"
rejoiced at their kindred beauty; or if the soft
winds breathed odours, we bade them receive
another burden, while we perfumed them with
the name of Jesus. Whether we walked
the sea-side, and thought the waves washed
blessings to our feet, or found beneath the
high rock a grateful shelter from the heat,
or drank the stream whose waters were
sweeter to our taste than e'er before, we were
by every object drawn upward evermore to
contemplate the Lord our Redeemer, who in

every scene of nature was set forth in minia-
ture. All summers had been winters compared
with this; for now we had flowers in our heart,
a sun in our soul, fruits in our spirit, songs in
our thoughts, and joy and heat in our affections. Till then we never knew the glory of
this mighty world, because we did not know it
to be our Father's and our own; but then we
looked from the hill-top on the wide-spread
scene with the eyes of a young heir just come
to his estate, or a fresh-crowned monarch whose
fair dominions stretch beneath his feet far as
the eye can see. Then we felt, in *fact*, what we
had only heard in poetry, the noble birthright
of a regenerated man—

> " His are the mountains, and the valleys his;
> And the resplendent rivers. His to enjoy,
> With a propriety that none can feel;
> But who, with filial confidence inspir'd,
> Can lift to heaven an unpresumptuous eye,
> And smiling say, ' My Father made them all.'
> Are they not his by a peculiar right,
> And by an emphasis of interest his,
> Whose eye they fill with tears of holy joy,
> Whose heart with praise, and whose exalted mind
> With worthy thoughts of that unwearied love,
> That plann'd, and built, and still upholds, a world
> So cloth'd with beauty for rebellious man ? "

O happy spirit ! tuned aright to unison with a

fair earth, man's first inheritance, lost till by
grace again we call it ours, and know it to be
beautiful. Words fail to describe the Divine
rapture of the spirit; and however well a poet
may paint nature as *he* sees it, yet though he
succeed to his own satisfaction, the new-born
child of God, whose feelings are richer even
than the wealth of poesy, will feel that he hath
but poorly pencilled what his now enlightened
eye beholds with raptures of delight. This
world is a great music-box, and he who hath
the key can set it playing, while others with
open mouth are wondering whence the song
proceedeth. Nature is a colossal organ, and
the frail fingers of man may move its keys to
thunders of music; but the organist is usually
unseen, and the world knows not how such
majestic sounds are begotten. Summer is
earth in court-dress; and if the heart be so, it
will know to what court summer belongeth,
and will call him friend.

Need we reiterate our joys by laying *autumn*
also under contribution? Truly, if then we
found our Lord, the ripened fruit did taste
more lusciously than ever. The yellow suit in
which the year was clad shone in our eyes
like burnished gold. Even as old Autumn—

> "Joy'd in his plenteous store,
> Laden with fruits that made him laugh, full glad
> That he had banish'd hunger,"

so did we rejoice that our hunger and thirst were satisfied with ripe fruit from the tree of life. The harvest-home echoed to our heart's glad shouts, and the vintage songs kept tune with our loud rejoicings.

All seasons of the year are alike beautiful to those who know how to track the Creator's footsteps along the road of providence, or who have found a token of his grace, and therefore bless the hour in which it came. There is neither stick nor stone, nor insect, nor reptile, which will not teach us praise when the soul is in such a state as that whereof we now are musing :—

> "There's music in the sighing of a reed;
> There's music in the gushing of a rill;
> There's music in all things, if men had ears;
> Their earth is but an echo of the spheres." *

The one pardoning word of the Lord of all absolution hath put music into all things, even as the trump of the archangel shall breathe life into the dead. Those drops of atoning blood have put fair colours upon all creation, even as

* Byron.

the sunrise paints the earth, which else had
been one huge blot of darkness.

How doubly dear do all our mercies become
at the moment when Christ shines on us! the
bread of our table is well-nigh as holy as the
bread of Eucharist; the wine we drink tastes as
sacred as that of His consecrated cup; each meal
is a sacrament, each sleep hath its Jacob's vision;
our clothes are vestments, and our house a
temple. We may be sons of poverty, but when
Jesus comes, for that day at least, he strews our
floor with sand of gold, and plants upon the
roof hard-by the ancient house-leek, flowers of
sweet contentment, of which heaven need not be
ashamed. We are made so happy in our low
estate at that transporting word of grace which
gives us liberty, that we do not envy princes
their crowns, nor would their wealth tempt us
from the happy spot where our Lord deigns to
~ive us his company.

Oh that blest day! again our memory rushes
back to it, and rapture glows even at its mention.
Many days have passed since then; but as the
one draught of sweet water refreshes the camel
over many a mile of desert, so doth that
happy hour still cheer us as we remember it.
Beginning of the days of heaven! Firstborn

of morning! Prophet of blessings! Funeral of
fears! Birthday of hope! Day of our spirit's
betrothal! Day of God and day of mercy!—oh
that we had power to sing the joy which kindles
our passions to a flame while we review thee! or
rather, oh that we had grace to hymn His
praise who made thee such a day! Doth the
stranger inquire, What hath so distinguished
that day above its fellows? the answer is already
knocking at the door of our lips to obtain an
egress. We were released from the thraldom
of sin, we were delivered from the scourges of
conscience, we were ransomed from the bondage
of law, we were emancipated from the slavery
of corruption; death vanished before the quickening of the Holy Ghost, poverty was made
rich with infinite treasures of grace, and hunger
felt itself satisfied with good things. Naked
before, we on that day put on the robes of
princes; black, we washed ourselves clean in a
bath of blood; sick, we received instant healing; despairing, we rejoiced with joy unspeakable. Ask her who has had the issue of her
blood stanched by a touch; ask yon healed
demoniac, or his companion who throws away
the crutch of his long halting, why on that day
of recovery they were glad; and they will

N

exhibit their own persons as reasons for their joy: so, O wondering gazer, look on us and solve the mystery of our enthusiastic song. We ourselves are our own answer to your inquiries.

Let us summon memory again to lead the choir, while all that is within us doth bless His holy name. " He spake and it was done;" " He said, Let there be light, and there was light." He passed by, in the greatness of his love and in the plenitude of his power, and bade us live. O eyes of beauty, how were ye outdone by his sweet looks! He was fairer than the sons of men, and lovelier than a dream when he manifested himself unto us. Lying by the pool of mercy, we pined away with disappointment, for none would put us into the healing water; but his love stayed not for an instant, he said, "Take up thy bed and walk." Ah, where shall thunders be found which will lend us voices? where floods which can lend us uplifted hands? for we need these to utter half His praise. Angels, your sonnets and your golden canticles are poor, poor things for our sweet Lord Jesus. He deserveth notes which your voices cannot afford, and music which dwells not within the strings of your most melodious harps. He must be his own poet, for none but he can sing himself. *He* knows, and only he, that depth of love within his bleeding heart, some drops of which we drank on that auspicious morning of redemption. He can tell, and only he, the transporting sound of that sweet assurance which laid our fears to rest in his own sepulchre. He alone can testify what he hath wrought; for, as for us, we were asleep on the mount of joy; "when God turned back the captivity of Zion, we were like men that dreamed; our mouth was filled with laughter, and our tongue with singing."* *He*, our Light, did light a candle around us; our "conversation was in heaven;" our soul made us like the chariots of Amminadib;

> "Our rapture seem'd a pleasing dream,
>   The grace appear'd so great."

We cried out in wonder, love, and praise, "Whence is this to me?† and what am I, and what is my Father's house, that the Lord hath visited me, and brought me hitherto."‡ Our dark and loathsome prison still made our garments to smell of its mouldiness, and this quickened our gratitude for our deliverance.

* Ps. cxxvi. 1, 2.
† Luke i. 43.   ‡ 2 Sam. vii. 18.

Like Jonah, fresh from the whale's belly, we were willing enough for service of any kind; all too glad to have come up alive from "the bottoms of the mountains," where we feared that "the earth with her bars was about us for ever." Never did lark spring from his cage-door to the sky with half such speed as that which we made when we obtained our liberty from the iron bondage; no young roe e'er bounded so nimbly over the hills as did our hearts when they were "like hinds let loose." "We could almost re-tread the steps of our pilgrimage to sing once more that song of triumph over a host of sins buried in the sea of forgetfulness, or drink again of the wells of Elim, or sit beneath those seventy palm-trees.

Dear spot of ground where Jesus met us! dear hour which brought us to his feet! and precious, precious lips of Jesus, which spoke us free! That hour shall lead the song, and every hour shall join the chorus of—"UNTO HIM THAT LOVED US, AND WASHED US FROM OUR SINS IN HIS OWN BLOOD, AND HATH MADE US KINGS AND PRIESTS UNTO GOD AND HIS FATHER, TO HIM BE GLORY AND DOMINION FOR EVER. AMEN."

Had it been in our power to have handled the

poet's style and measure, we might more fully
have expressed our emotions; but if our pen be
not that of a ready writer, at least our heart is
inditing a good matter. We close by an interesting account of conversion, illustrating its intense darkness, and its succeeding unspeakable
light. It is an extract from that valuable and
interesting biography, entitled, *Struggles for
Life.* After hearing a powerful sermon, he
goes home much impressed:—" I spoke to no
one, and did not dare to lift my eyes from my
feet, as I expected the earth to open and swallow
me. The commotion of my soul was altogether
such as language cannot describe. I crept to
my room, locked the door, and fell upon my
knees; but no words came. I could not pray.
The perspiration was oozing from every pore.
How long I lay on my knees I know not:
happily, this fearful agony of mind did not last
long, or I should have died. Some hours
elapsed—hours like ages; in which I *felt* myself
before the throne of righteous judgment, and
while the process was going on I was dumb.
Had the salvation of my soul depended upon a
word, I could not have uttered it. But he who
had smitten, graciously healed. As if they had
been slowly unfolded before me, there appeared

these never-to-be-forgotten words:—' THE
BLOOD OF JESUS CHRIST CLEANSETH US FROM
ALL SIN.'

"I had read and heard these wonderful words
often, but now they appeared new to me. I
gazed, believed, loved, and embraced them.
The crisis was past. A flood of tears rushed
from my eyes; my tongue was set at liberty.
I prayed, and perhaps it was the first time in
my life that I really did pray.

"For three days after this I was filled with
indescribable joy. I thought I saw heaven,
with its blessed inhabitants, and its glorious
king. I thought he was looking on me with
unutterable compassion, and that I recognised
Him as Jesus, my Saviour, who had laid me
under eternal obligation. The world, and all
its concerns, appeared utterly worthless. The
conduct of ungodly men filled me with grief
and pity. I saw everything in an entirely new
light: a strong desire to fly to heathen lands,
that I might preach the good news to idolaters,
filled my heart. I longed to speak about the
grand discovery I had made, and felt assured
that I had but to open my lips to convince
every one of the infinite grace of Christ,
and the infinite value of salvation. And I

thought my troubles over, and that, henceforth, the same scenes of joy and hallowed
peace were to pass before my eyes, and fill my
heart."

Such feelings are not the lot of all to the
same degree; but an exceedingly large proportion of the Lord's redeemed will recognise this
experience as "the path of the just;" and some
who read will rejoice to see here a fair copy of
their inner life at this very moment.

May the God of all grace bring each of us to
this fair land of Beulah, this palace of delights,
this chamber of bliss. Amen.

TO THE UNCONVERTED READER.

FRIEND,—Thou art amazed at this, for it sounds like a wild legend or fairy tale. Thou knowest nothing of such joy; this is a spring from which thou hast never drawn living water. How much dost thou lose by thine impenitence, and how poor are the things which recompense thy loss! What are thy delights but bubbles? what thy pleasure but sweet poisons? and what thy most substantial bliss but a deceptive, illusive vision of the night? Oh that thou wert able to judge between genuine and counterfeit, real and fictitious! Sure one grain of right reason would teach thee the superiority of spiritual joys to mere carnal excitements. Thou art not so far bereft of judgment as to put any one of thine high carnival days in competition with the time of pardoned sin. Thou wilt not venture to compare thy sweetest wine with that wine of heaven which flows into the lips of the sinner who is forgiven; nor wilt thou bring thy music into rivalry with that which welcomes the returning prodigal. Answer these two questions, we beseech thee, What doth it profit thee to sin against God? and, What shall it profit thee, at last, if thou shouldst gain the whole world and lose thine own soul? Will a few carnal merriments repay thee for unnumbered woes? Will transient sunlight make amends for everlasting darkness? Will wealth, or honour, or ambition, or lust, furnish thee with an easy pillow when thou shalt make thy bed in hell? In hell thou shalt be if thou hast not Christ. Oh! remember God is just; and, because he will be just, PREPARE TO MEET THY GOD!

V.

Joy at Conversion.

"The Lord hath done great things for us; whereof we are glad."—Ps. cxxvi. 3.

"O love, thou bottomless abyss!
My sins are swallowed up in thee;
Covered is my unrighteousness,
Nor spot of guilt remains on me;
While Jesus' blood, through earth and skies,
Mercy, free, boundless mercy cries.
With faith I plunge me in this sea;
Here is my hope, my joy, my rest;
Hither when hell assails I flee;
I look into my Saviour's breast;
Away, sad doubt, and anxious fear!
Mercy is all that's written there.
Fixed on this ground will I remain,
Though my heart fail, and flesh decay;
This anchor shall my soul sustain,
When earth's foundations melt away;
Mercy's full power I then shall prove,
Loved with an everlasting love."

HE who dares to prescribe one uniform standard of experience for the children of God, is either grievously ignorant or hopelessly full of self-esteem. Facts teach us that in the highway to heaven there are many paths, not all equally near to the middle of the road, but nevertheless trodden by the feet of real pilgrims. Uniformity is not God's rule; in grace as well as providence he delights to display the most charming variety. In the matter of conversion this holds good of its attendant rejoicing, for all do not alike sing aloud the same rapturous song. All are glad, but all are not alike so. One is quiet, another excitable; one is constitutionally cheerful, another is inclined to melancholy: these will necessarily feel different degrees of spiritual ecstasy, and will have their own peculiar modes of expressing their sense of peace with God.

It is true, God usually displays unto the newly regenerate much of the riches of his grace; but there are many who must be content to wait for this till a future period. Though he dearly loves every penitent soul, yet he does not always manifest that love. God is a free agent to work where he will and when he will, and to reveal his love even to his own elect in his own chosen seasons. One of the best of the Puritans hath wisely written, "God oftentimes works grace in a silent and secret way, and takes sometimes five, sometimes ten, sometimes twenty years—yea, sometimes more—before he will make a clear and satisfying report of his own work upon the soul. It is one thing for God to work a work of grace upon the soul, and another thing for God to show the soul that work. Though our graces are our best jewels, yet they are sometimes at first conversion so weak and imperfect that we are not able to see their lustre."   All rules have exceptions; so we find there are some who do not rejoice with this joy of harvest, which many of us have the privilege of remembering.

Let none conceive, therefore, that our book pretends to be an infallible map from which none will differ; on the contrary, it thinks itself happy if it shall suit the experience of even a few, and shall break the chains of any who are enslaved by the system of spiritual standards set up by certain men against whom it enters its earnest protest. Like the tyrant Procrustes, some classes of religionists measure all men by themselves, and insist that an inch of divergence from their own views must entail upon us present and eternal severance from those whom they delight to speak of as the peculiar people, who through much tribulation must enter the kingdom of heaven. Thus much by way of caution; we now proceed.

The style of our last chapter scarcely allowed us to ask the question, Whence this happiness? or if it suggested itself, we were too much in haste to express our gladness to reply to the inquiry. We will now, however, sit down coolly and calmly to review the causes of that exceeding great joy; and, if possible, to discover God's design in affording us such a season of refreshing. Those who are now mourning the loss of the peaceful hours, sweet still to their memory, may perhaps be cheered by the Ebenezers then erected, and by them may be guided again to the Delectable Mountains. Great Light of the soul, illuminate us each while meditating on thy former mercies!

I. We shall discuss *the causes* of the happiness which usually attends a sense of pardon. The study of experience is one far more calculated to excite our admiration of the wisdom, love, and power of God than the most profound researches which contemplate only the wonders of nature and art. It is to be regretted that master-minds have not arisen who could reduce a science so eminently practical and useful into some kind of order, and render it as rich in its literature as the science of medicine or the study of mind. An exceedingly valuable volume might be written as a book of spiritual family medicine for the people of God, describing each of the diseases to which the saint is subject, with its cause, symptoms, and cure; and enumerating the stages of the growth of the healthy believer. Such a compilation would be exceedingly interesting, and its value could scarcely be estimated. In the absence of such a guide, let us continue our musings by the help of such little experience as we may have acquired.

1. Among the many things which contribute to the ravishing sweetness of our first spiritual joy, we must mention *the case wherein it found us.* We were condemned by God and by our conscience, and harassed by fears of the immediate execution of the wrath of God upon us. We were exercised, both day and night, by sorrows for the past and forebodings of the future; impending destruction prevented sleep, and the sense of guilt made life a burden. "When," says one, "the usual labours of the day required that I should sleep, and my body, toiled and wasted with the disquiet of my mind,

made me heavy, and urged it more, yet I was afraid to close my eyes lest I should awaken in hell; and durst not let myself sleep till I was by a weary body beguiled into it, lest I should drop into the pit before I was aware. Was it any wonder then that the news of pardon and forgiveness was sweet to one in such a case— whereby I was made to lie down in safety, and take quiet rest, while there was none to make me afraid? 'For so He giveth his beloved sleep.'" * It is but natural that rest should be exceeding sweet after such a period of disquietude. We expect that the sailor will exhibit his joy in no ordinary manner when, at last, after a weary and tempestuous voyage, he puts his foot upon his native shore. We did not wonder when we heard of festivities in the islands of the West among the slaves who were declared free for ever. We do not marvel at the shouts of soldiers who have escaped the hundred hands of death in the day of battle. Shall we then make it a matter of surprise when we behold justified men exulting in their liberty in Jesus, and their escape from fearful perdition? We think it but in the ordinary course of things that when, like the Psalmist, we have received

* Halyburton.

answers to our prayers, we should also sing like him, "Come and hear, all ye that fear God, and I will declare what he hath done for my soul. I cried unto him with my mouth, and he was extolled with my tongue. I will go into thy house with burnt-offerings: I will pay thee my vows, which my lips have uttered, and my mouth hath spoken when I was in trouble. Thou hast turned for me my mourning into dancing: thou hast put off my sackcloth, and girded me with gladness, to the end that my glory may sing praise to thee, and not be silent. O Lord my God, I will give thanks unto thee for ever." Men put dark colours into the picture to make the lights more apparent; and God useth our black griefs to heighten the brightness of his mercies. The weeping of penitence is the sowing of jewels of joy. The poet * sang in another sense that which we may well quote here—

" And precious their tears as that rain from the sky,†
   Which turns into pearls as it falls in the sea."

Spiritual sorrow is the architect of the temple of praise; or at least, like Hiram, it floateth on

---

* Moore.

† "The Nisan, or drops of spring-rain, which the Easterns believe to produce pearls if they fall into shells."—*Richardson.*

its seas the cedars for the pillars of the beautiful house. To appreciate mercies we must feel miseries; to value deliverance we must have trembled at the approach of destruction. Our broken chains make fine instruments of music, and our feet just freed from fetters move right swiftly, dancing to the song: we *must* be glad when our bondage is yet so fresh in our memory. Israel sang loud enough when, in the sea of Egypt, her oppressors were drowned, because she knew too well from what a thraldom she was rescued. Shushan was glad, and rest was in the city, when the Jews had clean escaped from the wiles of Haman. No Purim was ever kept more joyously than that first one when the gallows were still standing, and the sons of the evil counsellor yet unburied. We may mourn through much of the long pilgrimage to heaven, but the first day is dedicated to feasting, because yesterday was spent in slavery. Were we always mindful of the place from whence we came out, perhaps we should be always rejoicing.

2. *There is given unto us at this period a peculiar outpouring of grace* not always enjoyed in after days. The heart is broken—it needs soft lineaments wherewith it may be bound; it hath been wounded by the robbers, and left half

o

dead upon the road—it is meet that the good physician should pour in oil and wines; it is faint—it needs a cordial; it is weak—it is therefore carried in the bosom of love. He who tempers the wind to the shorn lamb breathes gently on the new-born child of grace. He gives it milk—the ready-prepared nutriment of heaven; he lays it in the soft cradle of conscious security, and sings to it sweet notes of tender love. The young plant receives double attention from the careful gardener; so do the young plants of grace receive a double portion of sunlight by day, and of the dew by night.

The light wherein for the first time we discover Christ is usually clear and sparkling, bringing with it a warming force and reviving influence to which we have been strangers before. Never is it more truly sweet to see the light, or a more pleasant thing to the eyes to behold the sun, than when he shines with mild and benignant rays upon our first love. Grace then is grace indeed; for then it effectually operates on us, moving us to hearty affection and burning zeal, while it absorbs the passions in one object, wrapping us up in itself. So rich are the manifestations of Jesus to our souls at that hour, that in after life we look back to that time as "the days of our espousals;" so ardent are we then in love to our Lord, that in succeeding years we are often compelled to ask for the same grace, desiring only that it may be with us as in months past.

Though our head shall be anointed with fresh oil every day of our life, yet on the first coronation morning the fullest horn is emptied upon us. A man may have such a clear and glorious revelation of Christ to his soul, and such a sense of his union with Jesus on that beginning of days, that he may not have the like all his life after. "The fatted calf is not every day slain; the robe of kings is not every day put on; every day must not be a festival day or a marriage day; the wife is not every day in the bosom; the child is not every day in the arms; the friend is not every day at the table; nor the soul every day under the manifestations of Divine love."* Jacob only once saw the angels ascending and descending; Samuel did not hear from God every night. We do not read that the Lord appeared to Solomon save that once in vision. Paul was not for ever in the third heaven, nor was John in the Spirit every Lord's-

* Brooks.

day. Grace is at all times a deep, unfathomable sea, but it is not always at flood-tide.

When we are going to our Jesus he will send waggons to fetch us to his own country—he will come out to meet us in great pomp, and will introduce us to the king; but when we are safely settled in Goshen he will love us equally, but it may be he will not make so great a point of honouring us with high days and festivals. Christ will array his chosen ones in goodly attire, and bind flowers about their brows, on the day of their union to him; but, perhaps, to-morrow he may, for their benefit and his glory, "plunge them into the ditch, so that their own clothes shall abhor them." It may be we have a greater sense and sight of grace at first than we do afterwards, and this is the reason of our greater joy.

3. *The exceeding value of the things revealed* naturally produces a sense of unutterable delight when perceived by faith. It is no joy at a fictitious boon—but the benefit is real, and in itself of a nature calculated to excite wonder and praise. The mercies received are discovered to be inestimably precious, and hence there springs at once emotions of joyous gratitude. He would scarce be of a sane mind who would not

smile upon the receipt of a treasure which would free him from heavy liabilities, and secure him an abundant provision for life. When the naked are clothed, when the hungry are fed, and when beggars are elevated from dunghills to thrones, if they exhibit no signs of gladness, they give grave cause to suspect an absence of reason. And can a sinner receive a royal pardon, a princely robe, a promise of a crown, and yet remain unmoved? Can he banish hunger at the King's own table, and feel the embraces of his reconciled Monarch, and restrain his joy? Can he behold himself adopted into the family of God, made joint heir with Christ, and an inheritor of the kingdom of heaven, and still behave himself coldly? No! he must—he will rejoice,—

> " For should he refuse to sing
> Sure the very stones would speak.

It is no small thing to receive a succession of mercies—all priceless, all unmerited, all eternal, and all our own. Justification in itself is a " joy worth worlds ;" but when its attendants are seen at its heels, we can only say with the Queen of Sheba, "There is no heart left in me." It is not enough that we are washed and clothed, but there is our Father's banqueting house open to us—we are feasted—we hear music—a fair crown is set upon our head, and we are made kings and priests unto our God; and, as if all this were little, he gives to us himself, and makes himself our Lord, our God.

Can a mortal become possessor of Christ, of his person, his attributes, his all—and can ne then restrain the bliss which must find his heart a vessel all too narrow to contain it? Surely sweetness is only sweetness when we discern *Him* as our everlasting Friend—ours entirely, ours securely, ours eternally.

> "Known and unknown, human, divine!
>   Sweet human hand, and lips, and eye,
>   Dear heavenly friend that canst not die,
> MINE, MINE—for ever, ever MINE!" *

Truly, the believer might be excused if at the first recognition of the Redeemer as his *own*, own Friend, he should become sick of love, or faint with overflowing happiness. Rhoda opened not the gate for gladness when she heard Peter's voice; who shall wonder if the believing penitent should behave like one who is in a dream, and should lay himself under the imputation of madness! Conceive the rapturous delights of

* In Memoriam.

the sailors of Columbus when they hailed the land, or their beaming countenances when they found it to be a goodly country, abounding with all wealth; picture the heroic Greeks when from the mountain-tops they saw the flood which washed their native shore, and shouted—"The sea! the sea!" and you may then look on another scene without wonder—a company of pardoned sinners, singing with all their heart and soul and strength the praise of One who hath done great things for them, whereof they are glad.

4. *At this season the spirit lives nearer to its God*, and thus it dwells nearer heaven. The things of the world have less power to charm us when we have but lately proved their vanity; the flesh hath scarcely ceased to smart with the pain caused by the burnings of sin, and we are the more afraid of the fire; we have just escaped the paw of the lion and the jaw of the bear, and, having the fear of these before our eyes, we walk very near to the Shepherd. Bear witness, ye saints of God, to the holy dew of your youth, for which, alas! you now mourn. Can ye not remember how ye walked with God, how calm was your frame, how heavenly your spirit! Ye never saw the face of man when ye left your

chambers till ye had seen the face of God;
nor did ye shut your eyes in slumber on your
beds till ye had first commended your spirit to
your Father in heaven. How artless was your
simplicity! how fervid your prayerfulness! how
watchful your daily behaviour! What a marvellous tenderness of conscience characterised
you!—you trembled to put one foot before the
other, lest you should offend your God; you
avoided the very appearance of evil; you were
moved by the faintest whispers of duty; and all
the while what a quiet state of repose your soul
did swim in, and how pleasantly did you com-
mune with heaven! Grace had planted an
Eden around you, where you walked with
Jehovah amid the trees of the garden. You
were like Daniel by the river Ulai—THE MAN's
hand was on your shoulder, and his voice called
you, "Man, greatly beloved." You drank
out of your Master's cup, and fed out of his
hand, like the poor man's ewe-lamb in Nathan's
parable. Your eyes were up unto Him, as the
eyes of handmaidens to their mistresses; nor
could you afford the vain, harlot world so much
as an instant's gaze. In the religious shows of
old times they were wont to represent Meditation as a fair maiden, with her eyes fixed upon

a book which she was intently studying; around
her they placed young boys, dressed as fairies,
demons, or harlequins, who, with their dancing,
tricks, jokes, or frightful howlings, sought to
divert her from her reading; but she, nothing
moved, still continued wholly occupied therewith: now such were we at the young spring-
time of our piety, when we were first consecrated
to the Lamb. We were wholly engrossed with
Jesus, and nothing could draw us from him.
His name was the sum of all music; his person
the perfection of all beauty; his character the
epitome of all virtue; himself the total sum of
the riches, the glory, the love of an entire universe. "One sweet draught, one drop of the
wine of consolation from the hand of Jesus, had
made our stomachs loathe the brown bread and
the sour drink of this miserable life."* We
were wholly lost in admiring him, and could
only ask, "Who knoweth how far it is to the
bottom of our Christ's fulness? who ever
weighed Christ in scales?" or, "Who hath seen
the heights, and depths, and lengths, and
breadths of his surpassing love?"

Here is one grand secret of our greater flight
of joy at that time—we had then more wing

* Rutherford.

than now, for we had more communion with God. We were living on high, while men lay grovelling below; we were above the storms and tempests then, for we had entered into the secret place of the tabernacles of the Most High. We bathed our brow in the sunlight of an unclouded sky, standing on an eminence, up whose lofty sides the clouds knew not how to climb. Did we live nearer to our Lord now, we should beyond a doubt enjoy far more of the cream of life, and know less of its wormwood. We cannot expect to have the same *enjoyment* unless we be occupied in the same *employment*. He who goes away from the fire should not ask many times why he does not feel the same heat. The young convert is in a holy frame—he is most sure to be in a happy one. Distance from God is the source of the major part of our doubts, fears, and anxieties; live nearer to him, and we shall be all the further from the world, the flesh, and the devil, and so we shall be less molested by them. We cannot make the sun shine, but we can remove from that which may cast a shadow on us. Remove then thy sins, O weak believer, and thou mayst hope to see Him yet again!

5. Immediately after conversion *we are emi-*

nently careful to use all the means of grace, and
therefore we derive more comfort from them
than in after years, when we are more negligent
of them. The young convert is to be seen at
every prayer meeting, early or late; every religious service, even though it be at a considerable distance, finds him as an attendant; the
Bible is seldom closed, and the season for private
devotion is never neglected. In after days any
excuse will enable us to be absent from Divine
service with an easy conscience; but then it
would have been a high crime and misdemeanour
to have been absent at any available opportunity.
Hence the soul, feeding much on heavenly food,
waxeth fat, and knoweth nothing of the sorrows
of the hungry one who neglects the royal table.
The young footman on the heavenly race exerts
all his strength to win the race, and his progress
is thus far greater at first than afterwards, when
his breath a little fails him, or the natural
slothfulness of the flesh induces him to slacken
his pace. Would to God we could maintain
the speed of our youth! we should then retain
its comforts. We have met with some few of
the eminently holy who have enjoyed a continual feast ever since the day of their espousals;
but these were men who were constantly fervent

in spirit, serving their Lord with a diligent heart.
Why should it not be so with many more of
us? John Bunyan hath well written, "You that
are old professors, take you heed that the young
striplings of Jesus, that began to strip but the
other day, do not outrun you, so as to have that
Scripture fulfilled on you, 'The last shall be
first, and the first last,' which will be a shame
to you and a credit to them."* Oh! that we
were as obedient now as we were then to the
voice of the Word from heaven, then would
that voice be more sweet to our ears, and the
face of heaven would not be so full of frowns.
"The soul of the diligent shall be made fat," is
true in spiritual matters equally with temporal.
"Give diligence to make your calling and election sure; for if ye do these things, ye shall
never fall, for so an entrance shall be administered to you abundantly into the everlasting
kingdom of our Lord and Saviour Jesus Christ."
He that would be rich must still continue his
heed to his flocks and his herds. It is not one
venture which maketh the soul rich; it is continued perseverance in the business of salvation.
None but lively, active Christians can expect to
feel those ravishing joys, sweet comforts, and

* Heavenly Footman.

blessed delights which follow at the heels of a healthy soul. Stagnant water never sparkles in the sun—it is the flowing brook which shines like a vein of silver : set thy grace at work, and thy joys shall marvellously increase. If our bucket be empty, we had better ask ourselves whether it might not be full again were it sent down into the well. Truly, a neglect of means robs us of much consolation.

6. *Novelty* no doubt had some hand in the singular feelings of that joyous season. As an eminent saint says, "They were new things, wherewithal I was utterly unacquainted before, and this made them the more affecting." We have all felt the great exciting power of novelty in everyday-life, and the same influence exerts itself upon the inner life of the soul. At first, pardon, adoption, acceptance, and the kindred blessings, are new things, and, besides their own value, have the brightness of newly-minded mercies to recommend them to our notice. Prayer, praise, meditation, and hearing, are fresh exercises ; and, like a horse just brought to his labour, we are in haste to be engaged in them. "In the morning of life, before its wearisome journey, the youthful soul doth expand in the simple luxury of being —it hath not contracted

its wishes nor set a limit to its hopes." The
morning sun is shining on the yet glistening
hedgerows, and the dewdrops are all pearls; the
smoke of earth hath not yet darkened the skies,
and they are one pure firmament of azure.
There is more than a little of the Athenian in
every man; there is not one of us who is not
charmèd by something which has but lately
come to the light of observation. True, we
shall find the glories of the cross as marvellous
in after years as they are now, but now they are
so startling to us that we cannot but feel
astonishment and wonder. As he who after
a life of blindness at the first sight of the stars
would naturally lift up his hands in amazement,
so doth the man from whose spiritual eye the
film hath been removed, exult in his first vision
of the heavenly gifts of God. Never is the rose
more lovely than in its bud; so grace is never
more graceful than in its beginnings. The young
lambs frisk in the fields—they will assume a
steadier gait when they become "the sheep of
his pasture;" but till then let them show their
joy, for it is the necessary consequence of their
new-created being.

7. We are inclined to believe that the most
common cause is the fact that, *at first conversion,*

the soul relies more simply upon Christ, and looks more attentively at him than it does in after days, when evidences, good works, and graces, become more an object of regard than the person of Jesus. When the glorious Redeemer finds us lost and ruined in the fall—when he makes us deeply conscious of that ruin—then we take him, and him alone, for our treasure; but in future years he gives to us sundry rings, jewels, and ornaments, as love-tokens—and we most foolishly set our eyes more upon these than upon the Giver, and consequently lose much of the cheering effect of a constant view of the Saviour. At the first time of love we are too weak to venture on our own feet, but cling with both our arms around the neck of Jesus; there we find an easy carriage, which we lose when our overweening pride constrains him to set us on the ground to run alone. He who hath a speck in the eye of his faith, obscuring his vision of the Saviour, will find much pain resulting therefrom. That which removes us from the simplicity of our faith in Christ, although it be in itself most excellent, yet to us becomes a curse. Many of us might be willing to renounce all our experience, our graces, and our evidences, if we might but return to the

former childlike faith of our spiritual infancy.
To lie quietly afloat on the stream of free grace
is the very glory of existence, the perfection of
earthly happiness.

No seat is so pleasant as that which is
beneath the shadow of Jesus. We may fetch
our spices from afar, but they shall yield no
such fragrance as that which is shed from the
robes of the all-glorious Emmanuel, of whom it
is written, "All thy garments smell of myrrh,
and aloes, and cassia." Whatsoever spiritual
joy we have which springs not from Christ as
the Fountain, we shall find it sooner or later
bitter to our taste. The young convert is happy
because he drinks only from Jesus, and is yet
too full of infirmity to attempt the hewing of a
cistern for himself.

If we be unfaithful to Christ, we must not
expect many of his smiles. It matters little
what is the object of our delight, be it never so
lovely, if it become a rival of Jesus, he is grieved
thereby, and makes us mourn his absence.
"When we make creatures, or creature-com-
forts, or anything whatever but what we receive
by the Spirit of Christ to be our joy and our
delight, we are false to Christ."* He gave

* Owen.

himself wholly for us, and he thinks it ill that
will not give him sole possession of our heart.
Jesus, like his Father, is a jealous God—he will
not brook a rival. He will have us rejoice only
in *His* love, hearken only to *His* voice, and keep
our eyes constantly on him, and him only.
Beyond a doubt, were we in constant fellowship
with our loving Redeemer, we might always
retain a measure, if not the entire fulness, of
our early joy; and did we labour to improve in
our acquaintance ·with him, and our devotion
to him, our joy might possibly increase to an
indefinite degree, until our tabernacle on earth
would be like a house built upon the wall of
heaven, or at least in the suburbs of the city of
God. It is no wonder that so many lose their
first joy when we remember how many lose
their first love. "It may be," saith a holy
Puritan to the doubting soul, "it may be, if
thou hadst minded and endeavoured more after
community with God and conformity to God,
thou mightest at this time have looked upward,
and seen God in Christ smiling upon thee, and
have looked inward into thy soul, and seen the
Spirit of grace witnessing to thy spirit that thou
wert a son, an heir, an heir of God, and a joint-
heir with Christ. But thou hast minded more

thine own comfort than Christ's honour; thou
hast minded the blossoms and the fruit more
than Christ, the Root; thou hast minded the
springs of comfort more than Christ, the Fountain of life; thou hast minded the beams of the
sun more than the Sun of righteousness: and,
therefore, it is but a righteous thing with God
to leave thee to walk in a valley of darkness, to
hide his face from thee, and to seem to be as an
enemy to thee." Let us labour then to keep
our eye single, so shall our whole body be full
of light—light cheering and delightful beyond
what we can even dream. It is quite impossible
to define the limit of the happiness mortals may
experience in the condescending company of a
gracious Saviour; let us each seek to soar into
the loftiest air, that we may prove what is the
joy unspeakable and full of glory. Certain it is
that faith is the golden pipe which conducts the
living waters of the mount of God to the pilgrim
sons of Jehovah. Let us keep the course unob-
structed, and we may hope to drink deep
draughts of true delight.

It cannot be supposed that we have enume-
rated more than a small proportion of the
causes of this spiritual phenomenon; the rest
lie **beyond the writer's** limited experience, or do

not at this moment suggest themselves. These, perhaps, are the most frequent, and consequently the most apparent.

Should we have a reader who has lost his first love, it may be he will, by these suggestions, be able to detect the secret robber who has stolen his substance. If so, we beseech him, as he loves his own soul, to be in earnest to remedy the evil by driving out the insidious enemy. O spirit of God, restore unto us each "the years which the locust has eaten!"

II. We shall now endeavour to discover *the designs* of our heavenly Father in thus favouring us on that happy day of conversion. These are many, and most of them unknown: we must, therefore, be content to behold some of them; and may the contemplation excite wonder, gratitude, and love.

1. Doubtless *our Lord would have us ever remember that day*, and regard it with an especial interest; therefore did he crown it with lovingkindness and tender mercies. It was a birthday—he distinguished it with festivities; it was a marriage-day—he celebrated it with music; it was a resurrection—he did attend it with joyful sound of trumpet. He illuminated that

page of our biography that we might refer to it
with ease.   It was a high day, and he made it
high in our esteem by the marvellous grace
which he displayed towards us.   At the sign-
ing of Magna Charta, if on no other occasion,
the king and his courtiers would array themselves in all their dazzling robes and glittering
jewels; surely it is not unbecoming even in the
majesty of heaven to reveal something of its
glories when making peace with rebels.   The
black cap is but the fitting accompaniment of
the sentence of death; why should it be thought
unseemly that garments of praise should be displayed on the day of acquittal?   In heaven
there is held a solemn festival when heirs of
glory are begotten, and the heart of Jesus rejoices over the recovery of his lost sheep: we
need not wonder that the cause of such sublime
delights is himself made a sharer in them.
Men strike medals to commemorate great
national successes; should it be considered a
strange thing that Jesus giveth tokens to his
people in the day of their salvation?   We are
but too little mindful of the benefits of the
Lord; he doth therefore mark this day of the
calendar in golden letters, that we may be compelled to remembrance.

It can never happen to us again: we are
regenerated for all—saved in a moment from sin
and its consequences; it is meet that we should
make merry and be glad, for the dead are alive,
and the lost are found. The peace has just now
been welcomed with illuminations and with
national festivities; shall the eternal peace be
tween heaven and the soul be unattended witl
rejoicings? The greater the occasion, the more
proper is its remembrance—and what can be a
happier event to us than our salvation? therefore let it be had in perpetual remembrance,
and let "all kinds of music" unite to sound
its praise. Some among us honour the anni-
versary of the building of the house of the
Lord; but far more do we delight in the returning day which saw us placed as living stones in
the temple of Jesus. Bless the Lord, O our
souls, who hath forgiven all our iniquities and
healed all our diseases!

2. *Our wise and loving Lord graciously designed to give us something which might in all
after trials be a sweet staying to the soul when
a present sense of his love should be absent.*
How often have we been enabled to recover confidence in the day of our infirmity, by remembering "the years of the right hand of the

Most High!"* David, when his soul refused
to be comforted, found it good "to consider
the days of old," and to rehearse his former
"song in the night."   He declares that his
"spirit made diligent search,"—meaning that
he turned over the register and records of God's
former mercies, in order that some record, still
extant, might help him in his need.   When the
heir of heaven is in doubt as to his inheritance among them that are sanctified, it affords
no small degree of assurance to be able to turn
to the birthday register, and read "of Zion it
is said this man was born there;" this decides
the case at once in our favour.   In times of
contention, when we "see not our signs," we
shall find it eminently comfortable to look back
to the consecrated hour which witnessed our
acceptance in the beloved, for so shall we again
be able to assure ourselves of our election by a
remembrance of our calling.

We at times should have had no heart for
song if we had not found our harp already
tuned, having not yet become unstrung since
the hour of high festivity in the halls of
bounty.   Some despise Ebenezers, and talk
slightingly of the hope which issues from them;

* Ps. lxxvii. 10.

such persons can scarcely have had more than a superficial experience, or they would have learned far better.

The future would lie for ever in obscurity if we did not borrow a lamp from the hand of the past to cheer the gloom, and show where a sure foot-hold is to be found. This, then, is God's design in lighting up the hill Mizar of our first conversion, that it may cast a light, like Malvern's watch-fire, for many a mile beyond.

A pleasant anecdote is told of Mr. Kidd, once minister of Queensferry, near Edinburgh. He was one day very much depressed and discouraged, for want of that comfort which is produced by simple faith in Jesus. He therefore sent a note to Mr. L——, the minister of Culross, requesting a visit from him, that a brother's help might lift him out of his Slough of Despond. When the servant arrived at Culross, Mr. L—— told him that he was too busy to wait upon his master, but he was charged to deliver these words to him—"*Remember Torwood!*" The man, like Jonathan's lad, knew nothing of the matter, but Mr. Kidd understood it well, for at Torwood he had received manifestations of Jesus. Upon being reminded thereof, his dark-

ness vanished, and he joyfully cried out, " Yes,
Lord! I will remember *Thee*, from the hill
Mizar, and from the Hermonites !"   It may be
that in periods of gloom and distraction, that
place, that spot of ground where Jesus met with
us for the first time, will prove a very Bethel to
our spirits.   Here is wisdom in this day of joy,
let him that knoweth it be thankful.

3. *We had suffered so much in the time of
conviction that we needed much tenderness*, and
therefore He gave it to us.   There was no small
fear lest we should be swallowed up of sorrow,
and die under the pangs and throes of the new
birth, therefore did he tend us with the carefulness of a mother, and watch over us with
abundant compassions.   Like a sailor snatched
from the deep, we were ready to perish, and
should have expired in our deliverer's arms had
he not used the most compassionate arts to
restore us to life.   We were sore broken and
wounded, therefore did he place us in an in-
ärmary on the hills of Delight, where he made
all our bed in our sickness, poured out his best
wine with his own hand, fed us with royal
dainties, and all the while did watch us, lest
any should disturb our rest.   When we become
somewhat stronger, he leaves us to share with

our fellow-soldiers in the camp, whose rations are not quite so full of marrow and fatness.

The wise shepherds said to the pilgrim band, "Come in, Mr Feeblemind; come in, Mr. Ready-to-halt; come in, Mr. Despondency and Mrs. Much-afraid, his daughter." These were called by name because of their weakness, while the stronger sort were left to their own liberty. So also at their feast they made the viands suitable to the condition of the tender ones, " of things easy of digestion, and that were pleasant to the palate, and nourishing." Many of the promises are made specially for the feeble among the Lord's flock, to be heavenly *ambulances* for the wounded. When grace is young, and as yet but a spark, the kind hand of the Lord preserves it from the rough wind, and his own warm breath fans it to a flame. He doth not deliver the soul of his turtle-dove into the hand of its enemies, but for a while houseth it in the rock, or carrieth it in his hand. The tender plant of grace is covered all the day long, watered every moment, protected from the frost, and fostered in the warm air of communion and endearing fellowship. It should be accepted as a conclusive proof of the wisdom and prudence of our gracious God, that he sendeth the soft and refreshing showers upon the new-mown grass, and in that blessed manner effaces all the ill effects of the severe discipline of conviction. "If," says Austin, "one drop of the joy of the Holy Ghost should fall into hell, it would swallow up all the torments of hell;" assuredly it soon removes all the sadness produced by pains of repentance.

4. *The journey before us was exceeding long,* therefore did he refresh us before he sent us on our way. Elijah was made to eat once and again before his forty days of travelling—so must the spirit be refreshed before it sets out on its long pilgrimage. Jesus, in this hour of heaven, drops such tokens of love into the hands of his children that in after days they may recruit their strength by looking upon the heavenly earnest. The smiles, embraces, and assurances of that hour put spirit and mettle into the Christian warrior, enabling him to bid defiance to the stoutest enemies, and brave the greatest dangers. Before fighting, *feasting.* The angels met Jacob at Mahanaim before he heard of Esau's threatening approach. Paul was caught up into the third heaven before he was buffeted by the messenger of Satan. There should be cheering words at the buckling on of

the harness, for they will all be wanted by-and-by. God filleth the believer's bottle full when he starteth, for he hath a wide desert to traverse, a thirsty heart to carry, and few wells on the road. Although grace, like manna, must descend day by day—yet comforts, like the quails, come only at seasons, and we must gather enough at those times to last us many days. It is certain that the delights of the past afford the readiest means for exciting pleasure in the present, we carry from the fires of yesterday burning coals for the kindling of to-day. The ship hath more provisions on board when it starts upon its voyage than it is likely to have in a few weeks, and it then showeth all its flags and streamers which must soon be furled, and the canvas will be spread, which, though more useful, is not so glorious for show. The remembrance of the happy shore, and the gaiety of the departure, will support the spirit of the mariners when storms assail them, and the comforts then placed on board will be found none too many for the greatness of their toil upon the wide and stormy sea. Gurnal says that past experiences are like cold dishes reserved at a feast, from which the child of God can make a hearty

meal when there is nothing else on the table;
and when we consider how long a time has sometimes elapsed between one banquet and another,
it is doubtless intended that we should set aside
an abundant provision from the well-spread table
which furnishes the feast of the penitent's reception.   Take thy first joys, O little faith, and
drink full draughts of cordial from them.

5. *By the joy of his right hand, He put to
flight our hard thoughts of him.*   Deceived by
the outward appearance, we thought his chas-
tenings unkind; we attributed his wounds to
cruelty and enmity; nor could our mistake be
corrected until He displayed the richness of his
love in the most compassionate way—by restor-
ing our soul and renewing our strength.   Oh!
what a death-blow was his love to all our
unkind thoughts of him; how were we ashamed
to look at the dear friend whom we had so
basely slandered!   We saw it all then, clear as
noonday, and wept at the recollection of our
premature judgment and rash surmises.   The
Lord soon changed our thoughts concerning
his dealings.   We said, "It is enough; these
things are not against me: surely goodness and
mercy shall follow me all the days of my life."

We might to this hour have been mindful

of our agonies, if the succeeding joy had not obliterated all; so that, like the woman after her deliverance, "we remember no more the travail" for joy at the result. If we had only felt the sore woundings of his arm, and had never had a look at his sweet loving face, we might have written hard things against God as well as against ourselves; but now that he visiteth us in mercy, we gladly confess, "Thou hast dealt well with thy servant, O Lord, according unto thy word." When reaping the fruit of that rough sowing, we repent most truly of the impatience and unbelief which dared to lie against the Lord, and accuse him of unkindness. We retracted every word, and would have washed those feet with tears which we had bespattered with our vile suspicions, and kissed away every stain which our unbelief had put upon his pure, unmingled love.

6. *This cheering manifestation of mercy made us full of love to the good ways of holiness,* which we then found to be exceedingly pleasant. Henceforth we believe and know the King's highway to be a path of peace; and when at any time we lose the happiness once enjoyed, we look back to the time of love, and remembering how sweet was the service of Jesus, we

march forward with renewed vigour. We had heard the vile calumny that religion was a thing of misery and sadness, and that its followers were the companions of owls and lovers of lamentation; but the jubilant nature of our reception into the house of the saints laid bare the slander, and discovered the reverse of our gloomy apprehensions. We thought that glens, ravines, wildernesses, clouds, tempests, lions, dragons, and all kind of horrid things, were the sum-total of Christian experience; but instead thereof we were "led forth with peace;" where we feared a wilderness we found a Sharon, and the oil of joy was given us instead of the expected mourning.

We labour now to exhibit cheerfulness, since we firmly believe that this recommends the way to the wavering, and is the true method of honouring the God of all consolation. "This world is a howling wilderness to those alone who go howling through it;" but—

> "The men of grace have found
>   Glory begun below;
> Celestial fruits, on earthly ground,
>   From faith and hope may grow."

He who affirms that godliness is gloominess knoweth not what he saith. The Lord desireth to teach us, at the very beginning of our Christian career, that he would have us be happy, happy only in himself. He makes us glad when we are but beginners, and little in Israel, that we may see that we can be made blessed by simple faith, without any other assistance. "Christians might avoid much trouble," says Dr. Payson, "if they would only believe what they profess—that God is able to make them happy without anything else. They imagine, if such a dear friend were to die, or such and such blessings to be removed, they should be miserable; whereas, God can make them a thousand times happier without them. To mention my own case—God has been depriving me of one blessing after another; but as every one has been removed, he has come in and filled up its place; and now, when I am a cripple, and not able to move, I am happier than ever I was in my life before, or ever expected to be; and if I had believed this twenty years ago, I might have been spared much anxiety." This is the very thing our very gracious Jesus would teach us, if we were not so slow to learn; for, in the very first dawning of life, when graces and virtues are not yet developed, he makes himself so precious that we may know that he alone is the fountain of delights, and the very soul of rejoicing. He puts into us a constant love to his ways, by that delightful advent which he gives us at the very first step we take therein. It is of no use for the infidel to tell us our course will not end in bliss—it began with it, and we are compelled to believe that, if the same Jesus be Alpha and Omega too, the end must be eternal happiness.

7. We may also regard these great delights as *earnests of the future bliss of the righteous.* A pledge assures the wavering and confirms the weak; wisdom, therefore, bestows the earnest upon the young believer that he may be rendered confident of ultimate felicity. During our progress to the celestial city, our Lord is pleased to refresh our souls with sundry "drops of heaven," as the foretaste of that glorious rest which remains for his people, and this early joy is the first of a series of antepasts of heaven which we hope to receive while sojourning below. It is, so to speak, the enlisting money wherewith the young recruit is pledged to the king's service, and assured of his bounty.

The Apostle Paul tells us that the holy spirit of promise is the *earnest* of our inheritance. "The

original word, αρραβων, seems properly to denote
the first part of the price that is paid in any con-
tract as an earnest and security of the remainder,
and which therefore is not taken back, but kept
till the residue is paid to complete the whole
sum."* Such are the raptures of the newly-par-
doned soul—tokens which he will keep for ever, as
the first instalments of an eternal weight of glory,
and which he may safely retain as a portion of
his own inheritance. These spiritual joys are
like the cluster of grapes which the spies brought
from Eschol—they are sweet in themselves, but
they become more delightful still when they are
regarded as proofs that the land of Canaan is
fertile, and flowing with milk and honey. Thus
the rest of the Sabbath is described by Stennet
as "the antepast of heaven," and of its true
enjoyment he says—

> "This heavenly calm within the breast
> Is the dear pledge of glorious rest,
> Which for the Church of God remains—
> The end of cares, the end of pains."

The last of the seers, whom we feel constrained to quote in almost every page, makes
"Hopeful" victorious over the scoffing "Atheist"
by the simple expression, "What! no Mount

* Chandler.

Q

Zion? Did we not see from the Delectable Mountains the gate of the city?" These Sabbath mercies, delectable views, and days of espousals, are
a witness within the believer which all the sneers
of man, the malice of devils, and the doubts of
corrupt nature cannot disprove. Such things
are designed to be the true "internal evidence"
of the power of the Gospel.

The ends and purposes of God which we have
mentioned are far from despicable, and when we
remember the marvellously pleasant process by
which such great effects are produced, we would
desire to ascribe honour to that eternal wisdom
which can use rich wines as well as bitter
medicines in the cure of souls.

And now, reader, what dost thou say to these
things? Hast thou tasted the "thousand
sacred sweets" which are afforded by the hill of
Zion? Hast thou felt the "heaven begun
below" of which we have treated? If thou hast
not, then allow a word of advice which may well
be furnished from the subject:—*Never believe
the falsehood which pronounces true religion to
be a miserable thing,* for a more ungrounded
slander can never be imagined. The godly have
their trials as well as the rest of the human
family, but these are rather the effects of sin

than of grace. They find this world at times a
howling wilderness—but then the manna from
above, and the rock which follows them, combine
to prevent their howling as they pass through it,
and constrain the wilderness and the solitary
place to be glad for them. Some of them are of
a sorrowful countenance—but their gloom is the
result of temperament rather than of religion,
and if they had more grace, the wrinkles upon
their brows might become fewer.

The Gospel is in itself "glad tidings of *great
joy*;" can you suppose that misery is the result
of that which is essentially joyful? The very
proclamation of it is a theme for exulting song;*
how much more the reception of it? If the
hope of reconciliation be a just ground of
rejoicing, how much more the actual agreement
of the soul with its God? "We rejoice in God
through Jesus Christ, by whom we have received
the atonement."† To us there are express
precepts given to "rejoice in the Lord alway."‡
And that the exhortation might have its full
weight, and not be accounted hasty, it is solemnly
repeated, "and again I say, Rejoice." Hence,
therefore, we may safely conclude that the
genuine right temper and frame of a healthy

* Isa. lii. 7—10.   † Rom. v. 11.   ‡ Phil. iv. 4.

Christian mind will be an habitual joyfulness, prevailing over all the temporary occasions of sorrow which in this life must unavoidably beset us.

No trial can be thought of so heavy as to outweigh our great cause of joy; nor can the kingdom of God ever be in its constitution, even when attacked by the most furious assaults, anything other than "righteousness, and peace, and joy in the Holy Ghost."* "Nor," says Howe, in a letter to the bereaved Lady Russell, "is this a theory only, or the idea and notion of an excellent temper of spirit, which we may contemplate indeed, but can never attain to. For we find it also to have been the attainment and usual temper of Christians heretofore, that, 'being justified by faith, and having peace with God, they have rejoiced,' in hope of the glory of God, unto that degree as even to 'glory in their tribulations also;'† and in the confidence that they should 'be kept by the power of God through faith unto salvation,' they have therefore 'greatly rejoiced,' though with some mixture of heaviness (whereof there was need) from their manifold trials. But that their joy did surmount and prevail over their heaviness is manifest, for

* 1 Thes. v. 16   † Rom. v. 1, 3.

this is spoken of with much diminution, whereas they are said to 'rejoice *greatly*,' and 'with joy unspeakable and full of glory.' " *

If, when the believer is but a feeble thing, " carried away by every wind," he is, despite his weakness, able to rise to raptures of joy, who shall dare to suppose him unhappy when he has become strong in faith and mighty in grace? If the porch of godliness be paved with gold, what must be the interior of the palace? If the very hedgerows of her garden are laden with fruit, what shall we not find on the goodly trees in the centre? The blade yieldeth much, shall the ear be empty? Nay, " the ways of the Lord are right," and those who walk therein are blessed. Think not otherwise of them, but as you wish to share their " last end," think well also of the way which leadeth thither.

May the Lord direct his children, by his Holy Spirit, in reviewing this subject by prayer, to give all the glory of their mercies to the adorable person of Jesus.   Amen.

* 1 Pet. i 5, 6, 8.

TO THE UNCONVERTED READER.

FRIEND,—We have been answering questions concerning a joy with which thou canst not intermeddle—for thou art, to thine own loss and shame, a stranger from the commonwealth of Israel. But thou too hast a question or two which it were well to ask thyself. Whence that misery of which thou art at times the victim? Why dost thou tremble under an arousing sermon? Why doth the funeral knell grate on thine ear? What makes thy knees knock together at the sound of thunder? Why dost thou quiver at nightfall, though a leaf, all solitary, was the only thing which stirred within many a yard of thee? Why dost thou feel such alarm when pestilence is abroad? Why so anxious after a hundred remedies? Why so fearful if thou art but sick an hour? Why so unwilling to visit the grave of thy companion? Answer this, O soul, without reserve! Is it not that thou art afraid to die? It is! —thou knowest it is!

But, O my friend, fear death as much as thou
wilt, thou canst not escape it. On his pale
horse he is pursuing thee at no lame pace, but
at a rate which thou mayst guess of by the
wind or the flashing lightning. Noiseless is the
wing of time, dumb is the lip of death; but time
is none the less rapid for its silence, and death
not one whit the more uncertain because he
trumpets not his coming. Remember, while
thou art fearing, the messenger is hastening
to arrest thee. Every moment now gliding
away is another moment lost, and lost to one
who little can afford it. Oh! ere the wax hath
cooled which is sealing thy death-warrant, list
to a warning from God, for if the book of thy
doom be once sealed, it shall never be opened
for erasure or inscription. Hear Moses and the
prophets, and then hear the great Jesus speak:
—"The soul that sinneth it shall die." "He
will by no means spare the guilty." "Cursed
is every one that continueth not in all things
that are written in the book of the law to do
them." "Behold the day cometh that shall
burn as an oven, and all the proud, yea, and
ALL THAT DO WICKEDLY, shall be stubble; and
the day that cometh shall burn them up, saith
the Lord of Hosts, that it shall leave them

neither root nor branch." Regard then the
voice of Jesus, full of mercy :—"*The Son of
Man is come to seek and to save that which was
lost.*"

> " Sinner, is thy heart at rest?
> Is thy bosom void of fear?
> Art thou not by guilt oppress'd?
> Speaks not conscience in thine ear?
>
> ' Can this world afford thee bliss?
> Can it chase away thy gloom?
> Flattering, false, and vain it is;
> Tremble at the worldling's doom
>
> " Long the Gospel thou hast spurn'd,
> Long delay'd to love thy God,
> Stifled conscience, nor hast turn'd,
> Wooed though by a Saviour's blood.
>
> " Think, O sinner! on thy end;
> See the judgment-day appear;
> Thither must thy spirit wend,
> There thy righteous sentence hear.
>
> " Wretched, ruin'd, helpless soul,
> To a Saviour's blood apply;
> He alone can make thee whole—
> Fly to Jesus, sinner, fly." *

* Waterbury.

VI.

Complete in Christ.

"Ye are complete in Him."—COL. ii. 10.

THE pardoned sinner for awhile is content
with the one boon of forgiveness, and is too
overjoyed with a sense of freedom from bondage
to know a wish beyond. In a little time,
however, he bethinks himself of his position, his
wants, and his prospects : what is then his
rapture at the discovery that the roll of his
pardon is also an indenture of all wealth, a
charter of all privileges, a title-deed of all needed
blessings! Having received Christ, he hath
obtained all things in him. He looketh to that
cross upon which the dreadful handwriting of
ordinances hath been nailed; to his unutterable
surprise he beholds it blossom with mercy, and
like a tree of life bring forth the twelve manner
of fruits—yea, all that he requires for life, for
death, for time, or for eternity. Lo! at the
foot of the once accursed tree grow plants for

his healing, and flowers for his delight; from the bleeding feet of the Redeemer flows directing love to lead him all the desert through—from the pierced side there gushes cleansing water to purge him from the power of sin—the nails become a means of securing him to righteousness, while above the crown hangs visible as the gracious reward of perseverance. All things are in the cross—by this we conquer, by this we live, by this we are purified, by this we continue firm to the end. While sitting beneath the shadow of our Lord, we think ourselves most rich, for angels seem to sing, "Ye are complete in him."

"COMPLETE IN HIM!"—precious sentence! sweeter than honey to our soul, we would adore the Holy Spirit for dictating such glorious words to his servant Paul. Oh! may we by grace be made to see that they really are ours—for ours they are if we answer to the character described in the opening verses of the Epistle to the Colossians. If we have faith in Christ Jesus, love towards all the saints, and a hope laid up in heaven, we may grasp this golden sentence as all our own. Reader, hast thou been able to follow in that which has already been described as the "way which leads from banishment?" Then thou mayst take this choice sentence to thyself as a portion of thine inheritance; for weak, poor, helpless, unworthy though thou be in thyself, in *Him*, thy Lord, thy Redeemer, thou art complete in the fullest, broadest, and most varied sense of that mighty word, and thou wilt be glad to muse upon the wonders of this glorious position. May the great Teacher guide us into this mystery of the perfection of the elect in Jesus, and may our meditation be cheering and profitable to our spirits! As the words are few, let us dwell on them, and endeavour to gain the sweets which lie so compactly within this little cell.

Pause over those two little words, "*in Him*"— in Christ! Here is the doctrine of union and oneness with Jesus—a doctrine of undoubted truth and unmingled comfort. The Church is so allied with her Lord that she is positively one with him. She is the bride, and He the bridegroom; she is the branch, and He the stem; she the body, and He the glorious Head. So also is every individual believer united to Christ. As Levi lay in the loins of Abraham when Melchisedek met him, so was every believer chosen in Christ, and blessed with all spiritual blessings in heavenly places in him. We have been spared, protected, converted, justified, and accepted solely and entirely by virtue of our eternal union with Christ.

Never can the convinced soul obtain peace until, like Ruth, she finds rest in the house of her kinsman, who becomes her husband—Jesus the Lord. An eminent pastor, lately deceased,* said in one of his sermons, "Now, I am as sure as I am of my own existence that wherever God the Holy Ghost awakens the poor sinner by his mighty grace, and imparts spiritual life in his heart, nothing will ever satisfy that poor sinner but a believing assurance of eternal union with Christ. Unless the soul obtains a sweet and satisfactory consciousness of it in the exercise of a living faith, it will never 'enter into rest' this side eternity."

It is from oneness with Christ before all worlds that we receive all our mercies. Faith is the precious grace which discerns this eternal union, and cements it by another—a vital union; so that we become one, not merely in the eye of God, but in our own happy experience—one in aim, one in heart, one in holiness, one in communion, and, ultimately, one in glory.

This manifest union is not more real and actual than the eternal union of which it is the

* Rev. Joseph Irons, Camberwell.

revelation; it does not commence the union, nor does its obscurity or clearness in the least affect the certainty or safety of the immutable oneness subsisting between Jesus and the believer. It is eminently desirable that every saint should attain a full assurance of his union to Christ, and it is exceedingly important that he should labour to maintain a constant sense thereof; for although the mercy be the same, yet his comfort from it will vary according to his apprehension of it. A landscape is as fair by night as by day, but who can perceive its beauties in the dark?—even so we must see, or rather believe, this union to rejoice in it.

No condition out of Paradise can be more blessed than that which is produced by a lively sense of oneness with Jesus. To know and feel that our interests are mutual, our bonds indissoluble, and our lives united, is indeed to dip our morsel in the golden dish of heaven. There is no sweeter canticle for mortal lips than the sweet song, "My beloved is mine, and I am His:"—

" E'en like two bank-dividing brooks,
   That wash the pebbles with their wanton streams,
   And, having rang'd and search'd a thousand nooks,
   Meet both at length in silver-breasted Thames,
   Where in a greater current they conjoin;—
   So I my best beloved's am, so he is mine."

Verily the stream of life floweth along easily enough when it is commingled with him who is our life. Walking with our arm upon the shoulder of the beloved is not simply safe, but delightful; and living with his life is a noble style of immortality, which may be enjoyed on earth. But to be out of Christ is misery, weakness, and death—in short, it is the bud, of which the full-blown flower is damnation. Apart from Jesus we have nothing save fearful forebodings and terrible remembrances. Beloved, there is no Gospel promise which is ours unless we know what it is to be *in Him*. Out of him all is poverty, woe, sorrow, and destruction: it is only in him, the ark of his elect, that we can hope to enjoy covenant mercies, or rejoice in the sure blessings of salvation. Can we now entertain a hope that we are really hidden in the rock? Do we feel that we are a portion of Christ's body, and that a real union exists between us? Then may we proceed to unfold and appropriate the privileges here mentioned.

Ye are *complete* in Him. The word "complete" does not convey the whole of the meaning couched in the original word πεπληρωμένοι. It is upon the whole the best word which can be found in our language, but its meaning

may be further unveiled by the addition of other
auxiliary readings.

I. YE ARE COMPLETE IN HIM.—Let us consider the meaning of the phrase as it thus stands
in our own authorised version. We are *complete*. In all matters which concern our spiritual
welfare, and our soul's salvation, we are complete
in Christ.

1. *Complete without the aid of Jewish ceremonies.*—These had their uses. They were
pictures wherewith the law, as a schoolmaster,
taught the infant Jewish church; but now that
faith is come, we are no longer under a schoolmaster, for in the clear light of Christian knowledge we need not the aid of symbols:—

> "Finished are the types and shadows
>   Of the ceremonial law."

The one sacrifice has so atoned for us that we
need no other. In Christ we are complete
without any addition of circumcision, sacrifice,
passover, or temple service. These are now but
beggarly elements. They would be incum-
brances—for what can we need from them when
we are complete in Christ? What have we to
do with moon or stars, now that Christ hath
shone forth like the sun in his strength? Let

the dim lamps be quenched—they would but mock the dawn, and the sunlight would deride their unneeded glimmerings. We despise not the ceremonial law—it was " the shadow of good things to come," and as such we venerate it; but now that the substance hath appeared, we are not content with guesses of grace, but we grasp him who is grace and truth. How much more highly are we favoured than the ancient believers, for they by daily offerings confessed themselves to be incomplete! They could never stay their hand and say, " It is enough," for daily sin demanded daily lambs for the altar. The Jews were never made complete by their law, for their rites " could never make the comers thereunto perfect;" but this is our peculiar and superior privilege, that we are perfected by the one offering on Calvary.

2. *We are complete without the help of philo-sophy.*—In Paul's time, there were some who thought that philosophy might be used as a supplement to faith. They argued, contended, and . mystified every doctrine of revelation. Happy would it have been for them and the Church had they heeded the words of Paul, and kept entirely to the simplicity of the Gospel, glorying only in the cross of Christ! The

Christian has such a sublime system of doctrine that he never need to fear the vain speculations of an infidel science, nor need he ever call in the sophisms of the worldly wise to prop his faith—in Christ he is complete. We have never heard of a dying believer asking the aid of a worldly philosophy to give him words of comfort in the hour of dissolution. No! he has enough in his own religion—enough in the person of his Redeemer—enough in the comforts of the Holy Ghost. Never let us turn aside from the faith because of the sneer of the learned: this a Christian will not, cannot do—for we see *that* eternal evidence in our religion which we may call its best proof, namely, the fact that in it we are complete.

No man can add anything to the religion of Jesus. All that is consistent with truth is already incorporated in it, and with that which is not true it can form no alliance. There is nothing new in theology save that which is false. Those who seek to improve the Gospel of Jesus do but deface it. It is so perfect in itself that all additions to it are but excrescences of error; and it renders us so complete that aught we join with it is supererogation, or worse than that. David would not go to the fight in Saul's armour, for he had not proved it; so can we say, "the sling and stone are to us abundant weapons; as for the mail of philosophy, we leave that for proud Goliahs to wear." One of the most evil signs of our day is its tendency to rationalism, spiritualism, and multitudes of other means of beclouding the simple faith of our Lord Jesus: but the Lord's chosen family will not be beguiled from their steadfastness, which is the only hope of an heretical generation; for they know whom they have believed, and will not renounce their confidence in him for the sophistries of "the wise and prudent."

3. *Complete without the inventions of superstition.*—God is the author of all revealed and spiritual religion; but man would write an appendix. There must be works of supererogation, deeds of penance, acts of mortification, or else the poor papist can never be perfected. Yea, when he has most vigorously applied the whip, when he has fasted even to physical exhaustion, when he has forfeited all that is natural to man—yet he is never sure that he has done enough, he can never say that he is complete; but the Christian, without any of these, feels that he has gained a consummation by those last words of his Saviour—"It is finished!" The blood of his

agonising Lord is his only and all-sufficient
trust. He despises alike the absolutions and
the indulgences of priest or pontiff; he tramples
on the refuge of lies which the deceiver has
builded—his glory and his boast ever centring
in the fact that he is *complete in Christ.* Let
but this sentence be preached throughout the
earth, and believed by the inhabitants thereof,
and all the despots on its surface could not
buttress the tottering church of Rome, even for
a single hour. Men would soon cry out, "Away
with the usurper! away with her pretensions.
there is all in Christ; and what can she add
thereto, saving her mummeries, pollutions, and
corrupt abominations."

4. *We are complete without human merit, our
own works being regarded as filthy rags.*—How
many there are who, while waxing warm against
popery, are fostering its principles in their own
minds! The very marrow of popery is reliance
on our own works; and in God's sight the
formalist and legalist are as contemptible, if
found in an orthodox church, as if they were
open followers of Antichrist. Brethren, let us
see to it that we are resting alone in the righteousness of Jesus, that he is all in all to us.
Let us never forget that if we are perfect in him,

we are perfect only in him. While we would
diligently cultivate works of holiness, let us be
careful lest we seek to add to the perfect work
of Jesus. The robe of righteousness that nature
spins and weaves is too frail a fabric to endure
the breath of the Almighty, we must, therefore,
cast it all away—creature doings must not be
united with, or regarded as auxiliary to, Divine
satisfaction.

We would be holy, even as God is, but we
are still confident that this will not be supple-
menting the great righteousness which is ours by
imputation. No; though compassed with sin and
surrounded by our depravity, we know that we are
so complete in Jesus that we could not be more
so, even were we free from all these things, and
glorified as the spirits of just men made perfect.

Blessed completely through the God-man,
let our unbelief be ashamed, and let our admiration be fastened upon this interesting and
delightful state of privilege. Arise, believer!
and behold thyself "perfect in Christ Jesus.'
Let not thy sins shake thy faith in the all-
sufficiency of Jesus. Thou art, with all thy
depravity, still in him, and therefore complete.
Thou hast need of nothing beyond what there
is in him. In him thou art at this moment

just, in him entirely clean, in him an object of
divine approval and eternal love. *Now*, as thou
art, and where thou art, thou art still complete.
Feeble, forgetful, frail, fearful, and fickle in thyself, yet *in Him* thou art all that can be desired.
Thine unrighteousness is covered, thy righteousness is accepted, thy strength is perfected, thy
safety secured, and thy heaven certain. Rejoice,
then, that thou art "Complete in him." Look
on thine own nothingness and be humble, but
look at Jesus, thy great representative, and be
glad. Be not so intent upon thine own corruptions as to forget his immaculate purity, which
he has given to thee. Be not so mindful of
thine original poverty as to forget the infinite
riches which he has conferred upon thee. It
will save thee many pangs if thou wilt learn to
think of thyself as being *in Him*, and as being
by his glorious grace accepted in him, and
perfect in Christ Jesus.

II. YE ARE FULLY SUPPLIED IN HIM.—
Having him, we have all that we can possibly
require. The man of God is thoroughly furnished in the possession of his great Saviour.
He never need to look for anything beyond, for
in him all is treasured. Do we need *forgiveness*

for the past?   Pardons, rich and free, are with
Jesus.   Grace to cover all our sin is there;
grace to rise above our follies and our faults.
Is it *wisdom* which we lack?   He is made of
God unto us wisdom.   His finger shall point
out our path in the desert; his rod and staff
shall keep us in the way when we walk through
the valley of the shadow of death.   In our
combats with the foe do we feel want of
strength?   Is he not Jehovah, mighty to save?
Will he not increase power unto the faint, and
succour the fallen?   Need we go to Assyria, or
stay on Egypt, for help?   Nay, these are broken
reeds.   Surely, in the Lord Jehovah have we
righteousness and strength.   The battle is before
us, but we tremble not at the foe; we feel
armed at all points, clad in impenetrable mail,
for we are fully supplied in him.   Do we deplore
our ignorance?   He will give us *knowledge;* He
can open our ear to listen to mysteries unknown.
Even babes shall learn the wonders of his grace,
and children shall be taught of the Lord.   No
other teacher is required; He is alone efficient
and all-sufficient.   Are we at times distressed?
We need not inquire for *comfort,* for in him,
the consolation of Israel, there are fats full of
the oil of joy, and rivers of the wine of thanks-

giving. The *pleasures* of the world are void to us, for we have infinitely more joy than they can give in *Him* who has made us complete.

Ah! my reader, whatever exigencies may arise, we shall never need to say, "We have searched, but cannot find what we require; for it is, and ever shall be, found in the storehouse of mercy, even in Jesus Christ." " It hath pleased the Father that in him should *all* fulness dwell;" and truly none of the saints have ever complained of any failure in Him. Tens of thousands of them have drawn from this sacred well, yet is it as full as ever, and all who come to it are supplied with the full measure of their necessities. Jesus is not one single sprig of myrrh, but " *a bundle* of myrrh is my beloved unto me;" * not one mercy, but a string of mercies, for "my beloved is unto me as *a cluster* of camphire." "In Christ is a cluster of all spiritual blessings, all the blessings of the everlasting covenant are in his hands and at his disposal; and saints are blessed with all spiritual blessings in heavenly places in him. He is the believer's wisdom, righteousness, sanctification, and redemption. There is not a mercy we want but is in him, or a blessing we enjoy but what

* Sol. Song, i. 13, 14.

we have received from him.   He is the believer's
' *all in all.*' " * The word translated "complete"
is used by Demosthenes in describing a ship as
fully manned—and truly the Christian's ship,
from prow to stern, is well manned by her
captain, who himself steers the vessel, stills the
storm, feeds the crew, fills the sails, and brings
all safe to their desired haven. In every position
of danger or duty Christ himself is all-sufficient
for protection or support.   Under every conceivable or inconceivable trial, we shall find in
him sufficient grace : should every earthly
stream be dried, there is enough in him, in the
absence of them all.   His glorious person
is the dwelling-place of all-sufficiency. "In
Him dwelleth all the fulness of the Godhead
bodily;" as the fulness of Deity is sufficient to
create and sustain a universe of ponderous orbs,
and whole worlds of living creatures, can it be
supposed that it will be found unable to supply
the necessities of saints ?   Such a fear would be
as foolish as if a man should tremble lest the
atmosphere should prove too little for his breath,
or the rivers too shallow for his thirst. To
imagine the riches of the incarnate God to fail
would be to conceive a bankrupt God, or a

* Dr. Gill.

wasted infinite. Therefore, let us set up our banners in his name, and exceedingly rejoice.

III. A third reading is—YE ARE SATISFIED IN HIM.—Satisfaction is a jewel rare and precious. Happy is the merchant-man who finds it. We may seek it in *riches*, but it lieth not there. We may heap up gold and silver, pile on pile, until we are rich beyond the dream of avarice, then thrust our hands into our bags of gold, and search there for satisfaction, but we have it not. Our heart, like the horseleech, crieth, "Give, give." We may erect the palace and conquer mighty nations, but among the trophies which decorate the hall, there is not that precious thing which worlds cannot buy. But give us Christ, let us be allied to him, and our heart is satisfied. We are content in poverty—we are rich; in distress we have all, and abound. We are full, for we are satisfied in him.

Again, let us explore the fields of *knowledge*; let us separate ourselves, and intermeddle with all wisdom; let us dive into the secrets of nature; let the heavens yield to the telescope, and the earth to our research; let us turn the ponderous tome and pore over the pages of the

mighty folio; let us take our seat among the
wise, and become professors of science: but,
alas! we soon shall loathe it all, for "much
study is a weariness of the flesh." But let us
turn again to the fountain-head, and drink of
the waters of revelation: we are then satisfied.
Whatever the pursuit may be, whether we
invoke the trump of fame to do us homage,
and bid our fellows offer the incense of honour,
or pursue the pleasures of sin, and dance a giddy
round of merriment, or follow the less erratic
movements of commerce, and acquire influence
among men, we shall still be disappointed, we
shall have still an aching void, an emptiness
within; but when we gather up our straying
desires, and bring them to a focus at the foot of
Calvary, we feel a solid satisfaction, of which
the world cannot deprive us.

Among the sons of men there are not a few of
restless spirit, whose uneasy souls are panting
for an unknown good, the want of which they
feel, but the nature of which they do not comprehend. These will hurry from country to
country, to do little else but attempt a hopeless
escape from themselves; they will flit from
pleasure to pleasure, with the only gain of fresh
grief from repeated disappointments. It were

hard indeed to compound a medicine for minds thus diseased. Verily, the aromatics and balms of Araby, or the islands of the sea, might be exhausted ere the elixir of satisfaction could be distilled, and every mystic name in the vocabulary of the wise might be tried in vain to produce the all-precious charm of quiet. But in the Gospel we find the inestimable medicine already compounded, potent enough to allay the most burning fever, and still the most violent palpitations of the heart. This we speak from experience, for we too were once, like the unclean spirit, "seeking rest and finding none;" we once groaned for an unseen something, which in all our joys we could not find, and now, by God's great love, we have found the water which has quenched our thirst—it is that which Jesus gives, "the living water" of his grace. We revel in the sweets of the name of Jesus, and long for nought beside. Like Naphtali, we are satisfied with favour, and full of the blessing of the Lord. Like Jacob, we exclaim, "It is enough." The soul is anchored, the desire is "satiated with fatness," the whole man is rich to all the intents of bliss, and looketh for nothing more. Allen, in his *Heaven Opened*, represents the believer as soliloquising in the

following joyous manner :—" O happy soul, how
rich art thou! What a booty have I gotten!
It is all mine own. I have the promises of
this life, and of that which is to come. Oh!
what can I wish more? How full a charter is
here! Now, my doubting soul may boldly and
believingly say with Thomas, ' My Lord and my
God.' What need we any further witness? We
have heard his words. He hath sworn by his
holiness that his decree may not be changed,
and hath signed it with his own signet. And
now return to thy rest, O my soul! for the Lord
hath dealt bountifully with thee. Say, if thy
lines be not fallen to thee in a pleasant place,
and if this be not a goodly heritage? O
blasphemous discontent! how absurd and
unreasonable an evil art thou, whom all the
fulness of the Godhead cannot satisfy, because
thou art denied in a petty comfort, or crossed in
thy vain expectations from the world! O my
unthankful soul, shall not a Trinity content
thee? Shall not all-sufficiency suffice thee?
Silence, ye murmuring thoughts, for ever. I
have enough, I abound, and am full. Infinite-
ness and eternity is mine, and what more can
I ask?"

Oh may we constantly dwell on the blissful

summit of spiritual content, boasting continually in the completeness of our salvation IN HIM, and may we ever seek to live up to our great and inestimable privilege! Let us live according to our rank and quality, according to the riches conveyed to us by the eternal covenant. As great princes are so arrayed that you can read their estates in their garments, and discern their riches by their tables, so let our daily carriage express to others the value which we set upon the blessings of grace. A murmur is a rag which is ill-suited to be the dress of a soul possessed of Jesus; a complaining spirit is too mean a thing for an heir of all things to indulge. Let worldlings see that our Jesus is indeed a sufficient portion. As for those of us who are continually filled with rejoicing, let us be careful that our company and converse are in keeping with our high position. Let our satisfaction with Christ beget in us a spirit too noble to stoop to the base deeds of ungodly men. Let us live among the generation of the just; let us dwell in the courts of the great King, behold his face, wait at his throne, bear his name, show forth his virtues, set forth his praises, advance his honour, uphold his interest, and reflect his image. It is not becoming that princes of the blood should herd with beggars, or dress as they do; let all believers, then, come out from the world, and mount the hills of high and holy living; so shall it be proved that they are content with Christ, when they utterly forsake the broken cisterns.

IV. The text bears within it another meaning —YE ARE FILLED IN HIM:—so Wickliffe translated it, "𝔄nd ȝe ben fillið in 𝔥ym." A possession of Jesus in the soul is a filling thing. Our great Creator never intended that the heart should be empty, and hence he has stamped upon it the ancient rule that nature abhors a vacuum. The soul can never be quiet until in every part it is fully occupied. It is as insatiable as the grave, until it finds every corner of its being filled with treasure. Now, it can be said of Christian salvation, that it, and it alone, can fill the mind. Man is a compound being, and while one portion of his being may be full, another may be empty. There is nothing which can fill the whole man save the possession of Christ.

The man of hard calculation, the lover of facts, may feast his head and starve his heart;—the sentimentalist may fill up his full measure of emotion, and destroy his understanding;—the

poet may render his imagination gigantic, and
dwarf his judgment;—the student may render
his brain the very refinement of logic, and his
conscience may be dying:—but give us Christ
for our study, Christ for our science, Christ for
our pursuit, and our whole man is filled.   In
his religion we find enough to exercise the
faculties of the most astute reasoner, while yet
our heart, by the contemplation, shall be
warmed—yea, made to burn within us.   In
him we find room for imagination's utmost
stretch, while yet his kind hand preserves us
from wild and romantic visions.   He can satisfy
our soul in its every part.   Our whole man feels
that his truth is our soul's proper food, that its
powers were made to appropriate *Him*, while *He*
is so constituted that he is adapted to its every
want.   Herein lies the fault of all human
systems of religion, they do but subjugate and
enlist a portion of the man; they light up with
doubtful brilliance one single chamber of his
soul, and leave the rest in darkness; they cover
him in one part, and allow the biting frost to
benumb and freeze the other, until the man feels
that something is neglected, for he bears a
gnawing within him which his false religion
cannot satisfy.   But let the glorious Gospel of

the blessed Jesus come into the man, let the Holy Spirit apply the word with power, and the whole man is filled—every nerve, like the string of a harp, is wound up, and gives forth melody—every power blesses God—every portion is lighted up with splendour, and the man exclaims—

> "There rest, my long divided soul,
> Fixed on this mighty centre, rest."

"Shaddai," the Lord all-sufficient, is a portion large enough to afford us fulness of joy and peace. In Him, as well as in his house, "there is bread enough and to spare." In the absence of all other good things, he is an overflowing river of mercy, and when other blessings are present, they owe all their value to Him. He makes our cup so full that it runneth over, and so he is just what man's insatiable heart requires. It is a fact which all men must acknowledge, that we are never full till we run over—the soul never has enough till it has more than enough; while we can contain, and measure, and number our possessions, we are not quite so rich as we desire. *Pauperis est numerare pecus*—we count ourselves poor so long as we can count our wealth. We are never satisfied till we have more than will satisfy us. But in Jesus

there is that superabundance, that lavish richness, that outdoing of desire, that we are
obliged to exclaim, *" It is enough—I'm filled to
the brim."*

How desirable is that state of mind which
makes every part of the soul a spring of joys!
The most of men have but one well of mirth
within them; according to their temperament,
they derive their happiness from different powers
of the mind—one from bold imagination, another
from solitary meditation, and a third from memory; but the believer has many wells and
many palm-trees, for all that is within him is
blessed by God. As the waters cover the sea,
so has Divine grace flooded every portion of his
being. He has no "aching void," no "salt land,
and not inhabited," no "clouds without rain;"
but where once were disappointment and discontent, there are now "pleasures for evermore,"
for the soul is "filled in Him."

Seek then, beloved Christian reader, to know
more and more of Jesus. Think not that thou art
master of the science of Christ crucified. Thou
knowest enough of him to be supremely blest;
but thou art even now but at the beginning.
Notwithstanding all thou hast learned of him,
remember thou hast but read the child's first

s

primer; thou art as yet on one of the lower
forms; thou hast not yet a degree in the sacred
college. Thou hast but dipped the sole of thy
foot in that stream wherein the glorified are
now swimming. Thou art but a gleaner—thou
hast not at present handled the sheaves with
which the ransomed return to Zion. King Jesus
hath not showed thee *all* the treasures of his
house, nor canst thou more than guess the value
of the least of his jewels. Thou hast at this
moment a very faint idea of the glory to which
thy Redeemer has raised thee, or the completeness with which he has enriched thee. Thy joys
are but sips of the cup, but crumbs from under
the table. Up then to thine inheritance, the
land is before thee, walk through and survey
the lot of thine inheritance; but this know, that
until thou hast washed in Jordan, thou shalt be
but as a beginner, not only in the whole science
of Divine love, but even in this one short but
comprehensive lesson, "COMPLETE IN HIM."

TO THE UNCONVERTED READER.

FRIEND,—We will venture one assertion, in the full belief that thou canst not deny it—*thou art not entirely satisfied*. Thou art one of the weary-footed seekers of a joy which thou wilt never find out of Christ. Oh! let this chapter teach thee to forego thy vain pursuit, and look in another direction. Be assured that, as hitherto thy chase has been a disappointment, so shall it continue to the end unless thou dost run in another manner. Others have digged the mines of worldly pleasure, and have gained nothing but anguish and despair; wilt thou search again where others have found nothing? Let the experience of ages teach thee the fallacy of human hopes, and let thine own failures warn thee of new attempts.

But hark! sinner, all thou needest is in Christ. He will fill thee, satisfy thee, enrich thee, and gladden thee. Oh! let thy friend beseech thee, "Taste and see that the Lord is good."

VII.

Love to Jesus.

"Lord, thou knowest all things; thou knowest that I
love thee."—JOHN xxi. 17.

CHRIST rightly known is most surely Christ
beloved. No sooner do we discern his excellencies, behold his glories, and partake of his
bounties, than our heart is at once moved with
love towards him. Let him but speak pardon
to our guilty souls, we shall not long delay to
speak words of love to his most adorable person.
It is utterly impossible for a man to know
himself to be complete in Christ, and to be
destitute of love towards Christ Jesus. A believer may be in Christ, and yet, from a holy
jealousy, he may doubt his own affection to his
Lord; but love is most assuredly in his bosom,
for that breast which has never heaved with
love to Jesus, is yet a stranger to the blood of
sprinkling. He that loveth not, hath not seen

Christ, neither known him. As the seed expands in the moisture and the heat, and sends forth its green blade—so when the soul becomes affected with the mercy of the Saviour, it puts forth its shoots of love to him and desire after him.

This love is no mere heat of excitement, nor does it end in a flow of rapturous words; but it causes the soul to bring forth the fruits of righteousness, to its own joy and the Lord's glory. It is a principle, active and strong, which exercises itself unto godliness, and produces abundantly things which are lovely and of good repute. Some of these we intend to mention, earnestly desiring that all of us may exhibit them in our lives. Dr. Owen very concisely sums up the effects of true love in the two words, *adherence* and *assimilation:* the one knitting the heart to Jesus, and the other conforming us to his image. This is an excellent summary; but as our design is to be more explicit, we shall in detail review the more usual and pleasing of the displays of the power of grace, afforded by the soul which is under the influence of love to Christ.

1. One of the earliest and most important signs of love to Jesus is *the deed of solemn dedi-*

cation of ourselves, with all we have and are, most unreservedly to the Lord's service.

Dr. Doddridge has recommended a solemn covenant between the soul and God, to be signed and sealed with due deliberation and most fervent prayer. Many of the most eminent of the saints have adopted this excellent method of devoting themselves in very deed unto the Lord, and have reaped no little benefit from the re-perusal of that solemn document when they have afresh renewed the act of dedication. The writer of the present volume conceives that burial with Christ in Baptism is a far more scriptural and expressive sign of dedication; but he is not inclined to deny his brethren the liberty of confirming that act by the other, if it seem good unto them. The remarks of John Newton upon this subject are so cautious and sententious,* that we cannot forbear quoting them at length:—"Many judicious persons have differed in their sentiments with respect to the propriety or utility of such written engagements. They are usually entered into, if at all, in an early stage of profession, when, though the heart is warm, there has been little actual experience of its deceitfulness. In the

* See "Life of Grimshaw," p. 13.

day when the Lord turns our mourning into joy, and speaks peace, by the blood of his cross, to the conscience burdened by guilt and fear, resolutions are formed which, though honest and sincere, prove, like Peter's promise to our Lord, too weak to withstand the force of subsequent unforeseen temptation. Such vows, made in too much dependance upon our own strength, not only occasion a farther discovery of our weakness, but frequently give the enemy advantage to terrify and distress the mind. Therefore, some persons, of more mature experience, discountenance the practice as legal and improper. But, as a scaffold, though no part of an edifice, and designed to be taken down when the building is finished, is yet useful for a time in carrying on the work—so many young converts have been helped by expedients which, when their judgments are more ripened, and their faith more confirmed, are no longer necessary. Every true believer, of course, ought to devote himself to the service of the Redeemer; yea, he must and will, for he is constrained by love. He will do it not once only, but daily. And many who have done it in writing can look back upon the transaction with thankfulness to the end of life, recollecting it as a season of

peculiar solemnity and impression, accompanied
with emotions of heart neither to be forgotten
nor recalled. And the Lord, who does not
despise the day of small things, nor break the
bruised reed, nor quench the smoking flax,
accepts and ratifies the desire; and mercifully
pardons the mistakes which they discover, as
they attain to more knowledge of him and of
themselves. And they are encouraged, if not
warranted, to make their surrender in this
manner, by the words of the prophet Isaiah :—
'One shall say, I am the Lord's, and another
shall call himself by the name of Jacob, and
another shall *subscribe with his hand* to the
Lord, and surname himself by the name of
Israel.' "*

Whatever view we may take of *the form* of
consecration, we must all agree that the deed
itself is absolutely necessary as a firstfruit of the
Spirit, and that where it is absent there is none
of the love of which we are treating. We are
also all of us in union upon the point that
the surrender must be sincere, entire, uncon-
ditional, and deliberate; and that it must be
accompanied by deep humility, from a sense of
our unworthiness, simple faith in the blood of

* Isa. xliv. 5.

Jesus as the only medium of acceptance, and constant reliance upon the Holy Spirit for the fulfilment of our vows. We must give ourselves to Jesus, to be his, to honour and to obey, if necessary, even unto death. We must be ready with Mary to break the alabaster box, with Abraham to offer up our Isaac, with the apostles to renounce our worldly wealth at the bidding of Christ, with Moses to despise the riches of Egypt, with Daniel to enter the lion's den, and with the three holy children to tread the furnace. We cannot retain a portion of the price, like Ananias, nor love this present world with Demas, if we be the genuine followers of the Lamb. We consecrate *our all* when we receive *Christ* as all.

The professing Church has many in its midst who, if they have ever given themselves to Christ, appear to be very oblivious of their solemn obligation. They can scarce afford a fragment of their wealth for the Master's cause; their time is wasted, or employed in any service but that of Jesus; their talents are absorbed in worldly pursuits; and the veriest refuse of their influence is thought to be an abundant satisfaction of all the claims of heaven. Can such men be honest in their professions of attach-

ment to the Lamb? Was their dedication a
sincere one? Do they not afford us grave suspicion of hypocrisy? Could they live in such a
fashion if their hearts were right with God?
Can they have any just idea of the Saviour's
deservings? Are their hearts really renewed?
We leave them to answer for themselves; but
we must entreat them also to ponder the following questions, as they shall have one day to
render an account to their Judge. Doth not
God abhor the lying lip? And is it not lying
against God to profess that which we do not
carry out? Doth not the Saviour loathe those
who are neither cold nor hot? And are not
those most truly in that case who serve God
with half a heart? What must be the doom
of those who have insulted Heaven with empty
vows? Will not a false profession entail a fearful punishment upon the soul for ever? And is
he not false who serves not the Lord with all
his might? Is it a little thing to be branded
as a robber of God? Is it a trifle to break our
vows with the Almighty? Shall a man mock
his Maker, and go unpunished? And how
shall he abide the day of the wrath of God?

May God make us ever careful that, by his
Holy Spirit's aid, we may be able to live unto

him as those that are alive from the dead; and
since in many things we fall short of his perfect
will, let us humble ourselves, and devoutly seek
the moulding of his hand to renew us day by
day. We ought ever to desire a perfect life as
the result of full consecration, even though we
shall often groan that "it is not yet attained."
Our prayer should be—

> "Take my soul and body's powers;
> Take my memory, mind, and will;
> All my goods, and all my hours;
> All 1 know, and all I feel;
> All I think, or speak, or do;
> Take my heart—but make it new."*

2. *Love to Christ will make us "coy and
tender to offend."*—We shall be most careful
lest the Saviour should be grieved by our ill
manners. When some much-loved friend is
visiting our house, we are ever fearful lest he
should be ill at ease; we therefore watch every
movement in the family, that nothing may disturb the quiet we desire him to enjoy. How
frequently do we apologise for the homeliness
of our fare, our own apparent inattention, the
forgetfulness of our servants, or the rudeness of
our children. If we suppose him to be uncom-

* C. Wesley.

fortable, how readily will we disarrange our
household to give him pleasure, and how disturbed are we at the least symptom that he is not
satisfied with our hospitality. We are grieved
if our words appear cold towards him, or our
acts unkind. We would sooner that he should
grieve us than that we should displease him.
Surely we should not treat our heavenly Friend
worse than our earthly acquaintance; but we
should sedulously endeavour to please Him in
all things who pleased not himself. Such is the
influence of real devotion to our precious Redeemer, that the more the mind is pervaded
with affection to him, the more watchful shall
we be to give no offence in anything, and the
more sorrow shall we suffer because our nature is
yet so imperfect that in many things we come
short of his glory. A believer, in a healthy
state of mind, will be extremely sensitive; he
will avoid the appearance of evil, and guard
against the beginnings of sin. He will often
be afraid to put one foot before another, lest he
should tread upon forbidden ground; he will
tremble to speak, lest his words should not be
ordered aright; he will be timid in the world,
lest he should be surprised into transgression;
and even in his holy deeds he will be watchful

over his heart, lest he should mock his Lord.
This feeling of fear lest we should "slip with
our feet," is a precious feature of true spiritual
life. It is much to be regretted that it is so
lightly prized by many, in comparison with the
more martial virtues; for, despite its apparent
insignificance, it is one of the choicest fruits of
the Spirit, and its absence is one of the most deplorable evidences of spiritual decay. A heedless
spirit is a curse to the soul; a rash, presumptuous
conversation will eat as doth a canker. "Too-
bold" was never Too-wise nor Too-loving. Careful walking is one of the best securities of safe
and happy standing. It is solemn cause for
doubting when we are indifferent in our behaviour to our best Friend. When the new
creature is active, it will be indignant at the
very name of sin; it will condemn it as the
murderer of the Redeemer, and wage as fierce a
war against it as the Lord did with Amalek.
Christ's foes are our foes when we are Christ's
friends. Love of Christ and love of sin are
elements too hostile to reign in the same heart.
We shall hate iniquity simply because Jesus
hates it. A good divine * writes:—"If any
pretend unto an assurance of forgiveness through

* John Bring.

the merits of Jesus, without any experience of shame, sorrow, and hatred of sin, on account of its vile nature, I dare boldly pronounce such a pretension to be no other than a vain presumption, that is likely to be followed by an eternal loss of their immortal souls."

He that is not afraid of sinning has good need to be afraid of damning. Truth hates error, holiness abhoreth guilt, and grace cannot but detest sin. If we do not desire to be cautious to avoid offending our Lord, we may rest confident that we have no part in him, for true love to Christ will rather die than wound him. Hence love to Christ is "the best antidote to idolatry;"* for it prevents any object from occupying the rightful throne of the Saviour. The believer dares not admit a rival into his heart, knowing that this would grievously offend the King. The simplest way of preventing an excessive love of the creature is to set all our affection upon the Creator. Give thy whole heart to thy Lord, and thou canst not idolize the things of earth, for thou wilt have nothing left wherewith to worship them.

3. *If we love the Lord Jesus we shall be obedient to his commands.*—False, vain, and boast-

* James Hamilton.

ing pretenders to friendship with Christ think
it enough to talk fluently of him; but humble,
sincere, and faithful lovers of the Lord are not
content with words—they must be doing the
will of their Master. As the affectionate wife
obeys because she loves her husband, so does
the redeemed soul delight in keeping the commands of Jesus, although compelled by no force
but that of love. This divine principle will
render every duty pleasant; yea, when the
labour is in itself irksome, this heavenly grace
will quicken us in its performance by reminding
us that it is honourable to suffer for our Lord.
It will induce an universal obedience to all
known commands, and overcome that captious
spirit of rebellion which takes exception to
many precepts, and obeys only as far as it
chooses to do so. It infuses not the mere act,
but the very spirit of obedience, inclining the
inmost heart to feel that its new-born nature
cannot but obey. True, old corruption is still
there; but this does but prove the hearty wil-
lingness of the soul to be faithful to the laws of
its King, seeing that it is the cause of a perpetual and violent contest—the flesh lusting
against the spirit, and the spirit striving against
the flesh. We are *willing* to serve God when

we love his Son: there may be obstacles, but
no unwillingness. We would be holy even as
God is holy, and perfect even as our Father
which is in heaven is perfect. And to proceed
yet further, love not only removes all unwillingness, but inspires the soul with a delight in
the service of God, by making the lowest act
of service to appear honourable. A heathen *
once exclaimed, *Deo servire est regnare*—" to
serve God is to reign:" so does the renewed
heart joyfully acknowledge the high honour
which it receives by obedience to its Lord. He
counts it not only his *reasonable*, but his *delightful* service, to be a humble and submissive
disciple of his gracious Friend. He would be
unhappy if he had no opportunity of obedience—
his love requires channels for its fulness : he
would pray for work if there were none, for he
includes his duties among his privileges. In
the young dawn of true religion this is very
observable—would that it were equally so ever
after! Oh! how jealous we were lest one
divine ordinance should be neglected, or one
rule violated. Nothing pained us more than our
own too frequent wanderings, and nothing gratified us more than to be allowed to hew wood

* Seneca.

or draw water at his bidding. Why is it not so now with us all? Why are those wings, once outstretched for speedy flight, now folded in sloth? Is our Redeemer less deserving? or is it not that we are less loving? Let us seek by greater meditation upon the work and love of our Saviour, by the help of the Holy Spirit, to renew our love to him: otherwise our lamentation will soon be—"How is the much fine gold become dim! How has the glory departed!"

4. *Love to Christ will impel us to defend him against his foes.*—

"If any touch my friend, or his good name,
  It is my honour and my love to free his blasted fame
  From the least spot or thought of blame."*

Good men are more tender over the reputation of Christ than over their own good name; for they are willing to lose the world's favourable opinion rather than that Christ should be dishonoured. This is no more than Jesus has a right to expect. Would not he be a sorry brother who should hear me insulted and slandered, and yet be dumb? Would not he be destitute of affection who would allow the cha-

* Herbert.

T

racter of his nearest relative to be trampled in the dust, without a struggle on his behalf? And is not he a poor style of Christian who would calmly submit to hear his Lord abused? We could bear to be trampled in the very mire that He might be exalted; but to see our glorious Head dishonoured, is a sight we cannot tamely behold. We would not, like Peter, smite *his* enemies with the sword of man; but we would use the sword of the Spirit as well as we are enabled. Oh! how has our blood boiled when the name of Jesus has been the theme of scornful jest! how have we been ready to invoke the fire of Elias upon the guilty blasphemers! or when our more carnal heat has subsided, how have we wept, even to the sobbing of a child, at the reproach cast upon his most hallowed name! Many a time we have been ready to burst with anguish when we have been speechless before the scoffer, because the Lord had shut us up, that we could not come forth; but at other seasons, with courage more than we had considered to be within the range of our capability, we have boldly reproved the wicked, and sent them back abashed.

It is a lovely spectacle to behold the timid and feeble defending the citadel of truth: not with hard blows of logic, or sounding cannonade of rhetoric—but with that tearful earnestness, and implicit confidence, against which the attacks of revilers are utterly powerless. Overthrown in argument, they overcome by faith; covered with contempt, they think it all joy if they may but avert a solitary stain from the escutcheon of their Lord. "Call me what thou wilt," says the believer, "but speak not ill of my Beloved. Here, plough these shoulders with your lashes, but spare yourselves the sin of cursing him! Ay, let me die: I am all too happy to be slain, if my Lord's most glorious cause shall live!"

Ask every regenerate child of God whether he does not count it his privilege to maintain the honour of his Master's name; and though his answer may be worded with holy caution, you will not fail to discover in it enough of that determined resolution which, by the blessing of the Holy Spirit, will enable him to stand fast in the evil day. He may be *careful* to reply to such a question, lest he should be presumptuous; but should he stand like the three holy children before an enraged tyrant, in the very mouth of a burning fiery furnace, his answer, like theirs, would be, "We are *not careful* to answer thee in this matter. If it be so, our God whom we serve is able to deliver us out of the burning fiery furnace, and he will deliver us out of thy hand, O king! But if not, be it known unto thee, O king, that we will not serve thy gods, nor worship the golden image which thou hast set up."

In some circles it is believed that in the event of another reign of persecution, there are very few in our churches who would endure the fiery trial: nothing, we think, is more unfounded. It is our firm opinion that the feeblest saint in our midst would receive grace for the struggle, and come off more than a conqueror. God's children are the same now as ever. Real piety will as well endure the fire in one century as another. There is the same love to impel the martyrdom, the same grace to sustain the sufferer, the same promises to cheer his heart, and the same crown to adorn his head. We believe that those followers of Jesus who may perhaps one day be called to the stake, will die as readily as any who have gone before. Love is still as strong as death, and grace is still made perfect in weakness.

> Sweet is the cross, above all sweets,
> To souls enamoured with His smiles;
> The keenest woe life ever meets,
> Love strips of all its terrors, and beguiles."*

This is as true to-day, as it was a thousand years ago. *We* may be weak in grace, but *grace* is not weak: it is still omnipotent, and able to endure the trying day.

There is one form of this jealousy for the honour of the cross, which will ever distinguish the devout Christian :—he will tremble lest he himself, by word or deed, by omission of duty or commission of sin, should dishonour the holy religion which he has professed. He will hold perpetual controversy with "sinful self" on this account, and will loathe himself when he has inadvertently given occasion to the enemy to blaspheme. The King's favourite will be sad if, by mistake or carelessness, he has been the abettor of traitors : he desires to be beyond reproach, that his Monarch may suffer no disgrace from his courtier. Nothing has injured the cause of Christ more than the inconsistencies of his avowed friends. Jealousy for the honour of Christ is an admirable mark of grace.

* Madame Guion.

5. *A firm attachment to the person of Christ will create a constant anxiety to promote his cause.*—With some it has produced that burning zeal which enabled them to endure banishment, to brave dangers, and to forsake comforts, in order to evangelise an ungrateful people, among whom they were not unwilling to suffer persecution, or even death, so that they might but enlarge the borders of Immanuel's land. This has inspired the laborious evangelist with inexhaustible strength to proclaim the word of his Lord from place to place, amidst the slander of foes and the coldness of friends; this has moved the generous heart to devise liberal things, that the cause might not flag for lack of temporal supplies; and this, in a thousand ways, has stirred up the host of God, with various weapons and in divers fields, to fight the battles of their Lord. There is little or no love to Jesus in that man who is indifferent concerning the progress of the truth. The man whose soul is saturated with grateful affection to his crucified Lord will weep when the enemy seems to get an advantage; he will water his couch with tears when he sees a declining church; he will lift up his voice like a trumpet to arouse the slumbering, and with his own hand will labour

day and night to build up the breaches of Zion;
and should his efforts be successful, with what
joyous gratitude will he lift up his heart unto
the King of Israel, extolling him as much—yea,
more—for mercies given to the Church than for
bounties conferred upon himself. How diligently and indefatigably will he labour for his
Lord, humbly conceiving that he cannot do too
much, or even enough, for one who gave his
heart's blood as the price of our peace.

We lament that too many among us are like
Issachar, who was described as "a strong ass
crouching down between two burdens,"—too lazy
to perform the works of piety so imperatively
demanded at our hands: but the reason of this
sad condition is not that fervent love is unable
to produce activity, but that such are deplorably
destitute of that intense affection which grace
begets in the soul.

Love to Christ smoothes the path of duty,
and wings the feet to travel it: it is the bow
which impels the arrow of obedience; it is the
mainspring moving the wheels of duty; it is
the strong arm tugging the oar of diligence.
Love is the marrow of the bones of fidelity,
the blood in the veins of piety, the sinew of
spiritual strength—yea, the life of sincere devo-

tion. He that hath love can no more be motionless than the aspen in the gale, the sere leaf in the hurricane, or the spray in the tempest. As well may hearts cease to beat, as love to labour. Love is instinct with activity, it cannot be idle; it is full of energy, it cannot content itself with littles: it is the well-spring of heroism, and great deeds are the gushings of its fountain; it is a giant—it heapeth mountains upon mountains, and thinks the pile but little; it is a mighty mystery, for it changes bitter into sweet; it calls death life, and life death, and it makes pain less painful than enjoyment. Love has a clear eye, but it can see only one thing—it is blind to every interest but that of its Lord; it seeth things in the light of his glory, and weigheth actions in the scales of his honour; it counts royalty but drudgery if it cannot reign for Christ, but it delights in servitude as much as in honour, if it can thereby advance the Master's kingdom; its end sweetens all its means; its object lightens its toil, and removes its weariness. Love, with refreshing influence, girds up the loins of the pilgrim, so that he forgets fatigue; it casts a shadow for the wayfaring man, so that he feels not the burning heat; and it puts the bottle to the lip of thirst.

Have not we found it so? And, under the influence of love, are we not prepared by the Spirit's sacred aid to do or suffer all that thought can suggest, as being likely to promote his honour?

He who desires not the good of the kingdom is no friend to the king; so he who forgets the interests of Zion can scarce be a favourite with her Prince. We wish prosperity in estate and household to all those in whom we delight; and if we take pleasure in Jesus, we shall pray for the peace of Jerusalem, and labour for her increase.

May "the Father of lights" give unto his Church more love to her Head, then will she be zealous, valiant, and persevering, and then shall her Lord be glorified.

6. *It is a notable fact that fervent love to Jesus will enable us to endure anything he is pleased to lay upon us.*—Love is the mother of resignation: we gladly receive buffeting and blows from Jesus when our heart is fully occupied with his love. Even as a dearly-cherished friend does but delight us when he uses freedoms with us, or when he takes much liberty in our house—so Jesus, when we love him heartily, will never offend us by aught that he may do.

Should he take our gold, we think his hand to
be a noble coffer for our wealth ; should he
remove our joys, we reckon it a greater bliss to
lose than gain, when his will runs in such a
channel.   Ay, should he smite us very sorely,
we shall turn to his hand and kiss the rod.   To
believe that Christ has done it, is to extract the
sting of an affliction.   We remember to have
heard a preacher at a funeral most beautifully
setting forth this truth in parable.   He spoke
thus :—"A certain nobleman had a spacious
garden, which he left to the care of a faithful
servant, whose delight it was to train the
creepers along the trellis, to water the seeds in
the time of drought, to support the stalks of the
tender plants, and to do every work which
could render the garden a Paradise of flowers.
One morning he rose with joy, expecting to
tend his beloved flowers, and hoping to find his
favourites increased in beauty.   To his surprise,
he found one of his choicest beauties rent from
its stem, and, looking around him, he missed
from every bed the pride of his garden, the
most precious of his blooming flowers.   Full
of grief and anger, he hurried to his fellow-
servants, and demanded who had thus robbed
him of his treasures.   They had not done it

and he did not charge them with it; but he found no solace for his grief till one of them remarked:—'My lord was walking in the garden this morning, and I saw him pluck the flowers and carry them away.' Then truly he found he had no cause for his trouble. He felt it was well that his master had been pleased to take his own, and he went away, smiling at his loss, because his lord had taken them. So," said the preacher, turning to the mourners, "you have lost one whom you regarded with much tender affection. The bonds of endearment have not availed for her retention upon earth. I know your wounded feelings when, instead of the lovely form which was the embodiment of all that is excellent and amiable, you behold nothing but ashes and corruption. But remember, my beloved, THE LORD hath done it; HE hath removed the tender mother, the affectionate wife, the inestimable friend. I say again, remember your own Lord has done it; therefore do not murmur, or yield yourselves to an excess of grief." There was much force as well as beauty in the simple allegory: it were well if all the Lord's family had grace to practise its heavenly lesson, in all times of bereavement and affliction.

Our favourite master of quaint conceits* has singularly said in his poem entitled "Unkindness"—

'My friend may spit upon my curious floor."

True, most true, our Beloved may do as he pleases in our house, even should he break its ornaments and stain its glories.   Come in, thou heavenly guest, even though each footstep on our floor should crush a thousand of our earthly joys.   Thou art thyself more than sufficient re-compence for all that thou canst take away. Come in, thou brother of our souls, even though thy rod come with thee.   We would rather have thee, and trials with thee, than lament thine absence even though surrounded with all the wealth the universe can bestow.

The Lord's prisoner in the dungeon of Aberdeen thus penned his belief in the love of his "sweet Lord Jesus," and his acquiescence in his Master's will:—"Oh, what owe I to the file, to the hammer, to the furnace, of my Lord Jesus ! who hath now let me see how good the wheat of Christ is, which goeth through his mill, to be made bread for his own table.   Grace tried is better than grace, and more than grace—it is

* Herbert.

glory in its infancy. When Christ blesses his own crosses with a tongue, they breathe out Christ's love, wisdom, kindness, and care of us. Why should I start at the plough of my Lord, that maketh deep furrows upon my soul? I know that He is no idle husbandman; He purposeth a crop. Oh, that this white, withered lea-ground were made fertile to bear a crop for him, by whom it is so painfully dressed, and that this fallow-ground were broken up! Why was I (a fool!) grieved that He put his garland and his rose upon my head—the glory and honour of his faithful witnesses? I desire now to make no more pleas with Christ. Verily, He hath not put me to a loss by what I suffered; he oweth me nothing; for in my bonds how sweet and comfortable have the thoughts of Him been to me, wherein I find a sufficient recompence of reward!"

7. To avoid tiring the reader with a longer list of "the precious fruits put forth by the Sun" of love, we will sum up all in the last remark—that the gracious soul will labour after *an entire annihilation of selfishness, and a complete absorption into Christ of its aims, joys, desires, and hopes.* The highest conceivable state of spirituality is produced by a concentra-

tion of all the powers and passions of the soul
upon the person of Christ. We have asked a
great thing when we have begged to be wholly
surrendered to be crucified. It is the highest
stage of manhood to have no wish, no thought,
no desire, but Christ—to feel that to die were
bliss, if it were for Christ—that to live in
penury, and woe, and scorn, and contempt, and
misery, were sweet for Christ—to feel that it
matters nothing what becomes of one's self, so
that our Master is but exalted—to feel that
though like a sear leaf, we are blown in the
blast, we are quite careless whither we are
going, so long as we feel that the Master's hand
is guiding us according to his will; or, rather,
to feel that though like the diamond, we must be
exercised with sharp tools, yet we care not how
sharply we may be cut, so that we may be made
fit brilliants to adorn *his* crown. If any of us
have attained to this sweet feeling of self-annihilation, we shall look up to Christ as if He
were the sun, and we shall say within ourselves,
" O Lord, I see thy beams; I feel myself to be
—not a beam from thee—but darkness, swallowed up in thy light. The most I ask is, that
thou wouldst live in me,—that the life I live
in the flesh may not be my life, but thy life in

me; that I may say with emphasis, as Paul did, "For me to live is Christ."

A man who has attained this high position has indeed "entered into rest." To him the praise or the censure of men is alike contemptible, for he has learned to look upon the one as unworthy of his pursuit, and the other as beneath his regard. He is no longer vulnerable, since he has in himself no separate sensitiveness, but has united his whole being with the cause and person of the Redeemer. As long as there is a particle of selfishness remaining in us, it will mar our sweet enjoyment of Christ; and until we get a complete riddance of it, our joy will never be unmixed with grief. We must dig at the roots of our selfishness to find the worm which eats our happiness. The soul of the believer will always pant for this serene condition of passive surrender, and will not content itself until it has thoroughly plunged itself into the sea of divine love. Its normal condition is that of complete dedication, and it esteems every deviation from such a state as a plague-mark and a breaking forth of disease. Here, in the lowest valley of self-renunciation, the believer walks upon a very pinnacle of exaltation; bowing himself, he knows that he is rising immeasurably high when he is sinking into nothing, and, falling flat upon his face, he feels that he is thus mounting to the highest elevation of mental grandeur.

It is the ambition of most men to absorb others into their own life, that they may shine the more brightly by the stolen rays of other lights; but it is the Christian's highest aspiration to be absorbed into another, and lose himself in the glories of his sovereign and Saviour. Proud men hope that the names of others shall but be remembered as single words in their own long titles of honour; but loving children of God long for nothing more than to see their own names used as letters in the bright records of the doings of the Wonderful, the Councillor.

Heaven is a state of entire acquiescence in the will of God, and perfect sympathy with his purposes; it is, therefore, easy to discern that the desires we have just been describing are true earnests of the inheritance, and sure signs of preparation for it.

And now, how is it with the reader? Is he a lover of Jesus in verity and truth? or does he confess that these signs are not seen in him? If he be indeed without love to Jesus, he has good need to humble himself and turn unto the

Lord, for his soul is in as evil a condition as it can be this side hell; and, alas! will soon be, unless grace prevent, in a plight so pitiable, that eternity will scarce be long enough for its regrets.

It is more than probable that some of our readers are troubled with doubts concerning the truth of their affection for Jesus, although they are indeed his faithful friends. Permit us to address such with a word of consolation.

You have some of the marks of true piety about you,—at least, you can join in some of the feelings to which we have been giving expression,—but still you fear that you are not right in heart towards Christ. What is then your reason for such a suspicion? You reply that your excess of attachment towards your friends and relatives is proof that you are not sincere, for if you loved Jesus truly, you would love him more than these. You word your complaint thus :—" I fear I love the creature more than Christ, and if so my love is hypocritical. I frequently feel more vehement and more ardent motions of my heart to my beloved relatives than I do towards heavenly objects, and I therefore believe that I am still carnal, and the love of God doth not inhabit my heart."

Far be it from us to plead the cause of sin,
or extenuate the undoubted fault which you thus
commit; but at the same time it would be even
further from our design to blot out at once the
whole of the names of the living family of God.
For if our love is to be measured by its temporary
violence, we fear there is not one among the
saints who has not at some time or other had an
excessive love to the creature, and who has not,
therefore, upon such reasoning, proved himself
to be a hypocrite.   Let it be remembered,
therefore, that the strength of affection is rather
to be measured by the hold it has upon the
heart, than by the heat it displays at casual
times and seasons.   Flavel very wisely observes,
"As rooted malice argues a stronger hatred
than a sudden though more violent passion, so
we must measure our love, not by a violent
motion of it, now and then, but by the *depth* of
the root and the *constancy* of its actings.   Because David was so passionately moved for
Absalom, Joab concludes that if he had lived,
and all the people died, it would have pleased
him well; but that was argued more like a
soldier than a logician."

If your love be constant in its abidings, faithful in its actings, and honest in its character,

you need not distrust it on account of certain
more burning heats, which temporarily and
wickedly inflame the mind. Avoid these as
sinful, but do not therefore doubt the truthfulness of your attachment to your Master. True
grace may be in the soul without being apparent, for, as Baxter truly observes, "grace is
never apparent and sensible to the soul but
while it is in action." Fire may be in the
flint, and yet be unseen except when occasion
shall bring it out. As Dr. Sibbs observes in
his *Soul's Conflict*, "There is sometimes grief
for sin in us, when we think there is none ;" so
may it be with love which may be there, but
not discoverable till some circumstance shall
lead to its discovery. The eminent Puritan
pertinently remarks :—"You may go seeking
for the hare or partridge many hours, and never
find them while they lie close and stir not ; but
when once the hare betakes himself to his legs,
and the bird to her wings, then you see them
presently. So long as a Christian hath his
graces in lively action, so long, for the most
part, he is assured of them. How can you
doubt whether you love God in the act of
loving ? Or whether you believe in the very
act of believing If, therefore, you would be

assured whether this sacred fire be kindled in your hearts, blow it up, get it into a flame, and then you will know; believe till you feel that you do believe; and love till you feel that you love." Seek to keep your graces in action by living near to the author of them. Live very near to Jesus, and think much of his love to you: thus will your love to him become more deep and fervent.

We pause here, and pray the most gracious Father of all good to accept our love, as he has already accepted us, *in the Beloved;* and we humbly crave the benign influence of his Holy Spirit, that we may be made perfect in love, and may glorify him to whom we now present ourselves as living sacrifices, holy, acceptable unto God, which is our reasonable service.

> " Jesu, thy boundless love to me
>   No thought can reach, no tongue declare;
> O knit my thankful heart to thee,
>   And reign without a rival there:
> Thine wholly, thine alone, I am;
> Be thou alone my constant flame!
>
> O grant that nothing in my soul
>   May dwell, but thy pure love alone:
> O may thy love possess me whole,
>   My joy, my treasure, and my crown;
> Strange flames far from my heart remove;
> My every act, word, thought be love!"

TO THE UNCONVERTED READER.

Again we turn to thee; and art thou still where we left thee? still without hope, still unforgiven? Surely, then, thou hast been condemning thyself while reading these signs of grace in others. Such experience is too high for thee, thou canst no more attain unto it than a stone to sensibility; but, remember, it is not too high for the Lord. He can renew thee, and make thee know the highest enjoyment of the saints. *He alone can do it*, therefore despair of thine own strength; but *He can* accomplish it, therefore hope in omnipotent grace. Thou art in a wrong state, and thou knowest it: how fearful will it be if thou shouldst remain the same until death! Yet most assuredly thou wilt unless Divine love shall change thee. See, then, how absolutely thou art in the hands of God. Labour to feel this. Seek to know the power of this dread but certain fact—that thou liest entirely at his pleasure; and there is nothing more likely to humble and subdue thee than the thoughts which it will beget within thee.

Know and tremble, hear and be afraid. Bow thyself before the Most High, and confess his justice should He destroy thee, and admire his grace which proclaims pardon to thee. Think not that the works of believers are their salvation; but seek first the root of their graces, which lies in Christ, not in themselves. This thou canst get nowhere but at the footstool of mercy from the hand of Jesus. Thou art shut up to one door of life, and that door is Christ crucified. Receive him as God's free gift and thine undeserved boon. Renounce every other refuge, and embrace the Lord Jesus as thine only hope. Venture thy soul in his hands. Sink or swim, let Him be thine only support, and he will never fail thee.

BELIEVE ON THE LORD JESUS CHRIST, AND THOU SHALT BE SAVED.

VIII.

Love's Logic.

"The upright love Thee."—Sol. Song i. 4.

THE motives of love are in a great degree the measure of its growth. The advanced believer loves his Lord for higher reasons than those which move the heart of the young convert. His affection is not more sincere or earnest, but it is, or ought to be, more steadfast and unvarying, because experience has enabled the understanding to adduce more abundant reasons for the soul's attachment. All true love to the Redeemer is acceptable to him, and is to us an infallible evidence of our safety in him. We are far from depreciating the value or suspecting the sincerity of the warm emotions of the newly enlightened, although we prefer the more intelligent and less interested attachment of the well-instructed Christian. Let none doubt the reality of their piety because they are unable to

mount to all the heights, or dive into all the
depths, of that love which passeth knowledge.
A babe's fondness of its mother is as pleasing
to her as the strong devotion of her full-grown
son.   The graces of faith, hope, and love are to
be estimated more by their honesty than by their
degree, and less by their intellectual than by
their emotional characteristics.   Yet, without
doubt, growth in grace is as much displayed in
the Christian's love as in any other fruit of the
Spirit; and it is our belief that this growth
may in some degree be traced by the motives
which cause it, just as we trace the motion of
the shower by the position of the cloud from
which it falls.   It may be profitable to dwell
upon the motives of love for a brief season,
hoping for instruction in so doing.   We do
not pretend to enter fully into the present
subject; and, indeed, our space prevents us
as much as our incapacity.   Owen's remark will
be appropriate here:—"Motives unto the love
of Christ are so great, so many, so diffused
through the whole dispensation of God in him
unto us, as that they can by no hand be fully
expressed, let it be allowed ever so much to
enlarge in the declaration of them; much less
can they be represented in this short discourse,

whereof but a very small part is allotted unto their consideration." *

In enumerating some of the stages of spiritual growth as indicated by higher standards of motive, we pray the Holy Spirit to guide our meditations, giving us profitable wisdom and gracious enlightenment. Let us commence in entire dependance upon his aid, and so proceed from step to step as he shall be pleased to guide us. We commence with the Alpha of Love, the first ripe fruit of affection.

I. LOVE OF GRATITUDE. "We love him because he first loved us." Here is the starting point of love's race. This is the rippling rill which afterwards swells into a river, the torch with which the pile of piety is kindled. The emancipated spirit loves the Saviour for the freedom which he has conferred upon it; it beholds the agony with which the priceless gift was purchased, and it adores the bleeding sufferer for the pains which he so generously endured. Jesus is regarded as our benefactor, and the boons which we receive at his hands constrain us to give him our hearts. If enabled to receive all the doctrines of the Gospel, we

* Christologia.

bless the name of our Redeemer for his free
grace manifested in our election to eternal life;
for his efficacious grace exercised in calling us
into his kingdom; for pardon and justification
through his blood and merits, and for everlasting security by virtue of union with his divine
person.   Surely here is enough to create love
of the highest order of fervency; and if the soul
should abide for ever in contemplation of these
mighty acts of grace, without entering upon the
glorious survey of the character and perfections
of Jesus, it need never be in want of reasons for
affection.   Here are coals enough to maintain
the heavenly fire, if the Holy Spirit be but
present to fan the flame.   This order of affection is capable of producing the most eminent
virtues, and stimulating the most ardent zeal.
It is enough for every practical purpose of the
heavenly life.   But nevertheless, there is a "yet
beyond."   There are other motives which are
of a higher class in themselves, although very
seldom more potent in their influence.   This,
however, is the beginning.   "I love the Lord
because he has heard my voice and my supplication."   It is his kindness toward us, rather
than the graciousness of his nature which primarily attracts us.

The deeds of the Saviour do not so much arouse our early admiration from their intrinsic greatness and graciousness, as from the fact that *we* have a share in them. This thought at first attracts all our regard, and engrosses all our meditations. Neither the person nor the offices of Christ have as yet been fully presented to the soul,—it knows him only in his gifts, and loves him only for what he has bestowed. Call this love selfish if you will, but do not condemn it. The Saviour frowned not on the woman who loved much, because much had been forgiven, nor did he despise the offering of that heart which was first moved with affection at the casting out of its seven devils. Perhaps it is from a selfish reason that the infant casts the tendrils of its heart around its mother, but who would therefore despise its fondness? Base must be the man who should wish to eradicate such a heavenly germ because of the poverty of the soil in which it grew. Our love to God may even be heightened by due and wise self-love. "There is a *sinful* self-love, when either we love that for a self which is not ourself,—when we love our flesh and fleshly interest,—or when we love ourselves inordinately, more than God, and God only for ourselves; and there is a *lawful* self-love, when we love ourselves *in the Lord and for the Lord.*"* This lawful self-love leads us to love Christ, and to desire more and more of his grace, because we feel that so we shall be the more happy in our souls, and useful in our lives. This is in some degree earthy, but in no degree sinful, or anything but holy.

It is not needful that the foundation-stones should be of polished marble, they will well enough subserve their purpose if they act as the underlying ground-work of more excellent materials. If it be a crime to be ungrateful, then thankfulness is a virtue, and its issue cannot be contemptible. Young beginners frequently doubt their piety, because they feel but little disinterested affection for the Lord Jesus; let them remember that that high and excellent gift is not one of the tender grapes, but is only to be gathered beneath the ripening skies of Christian experience. "Do you love Christ?" is the important question, and if the answer be a firm avowal of attachment to him, it is decisive as to your spiritual condition, even though the further question, "Why do you love him?" should only receive for answer, "I love him because

* Allen's *Riches of the Covenant.*

he first loved me.' Indeed, in the loftiest stage
of heavenly life, there must ever be a great and
grateful mixture of motives in our love to our
divine Master. We do not cease to love him
for his mercies when we begin to adore him for
his personal excellences; on the contrary, our
sense of the glory of the person who is our
Redeemer increases our gratitude to him for his
condescending regard of such insignificant creatures as ourselves. Thus the ripening shock of
corn can hold fellowship with the tender blade,
since both are debtors to the sunshine. Even
the saints before the throne are in no small
degree moved to rapturous love of their exalted
King, by the very motive which some have been
ready to undervalue as selfish and unspiritual.
They sing, "Thou art worthy for thou wast
slain, and *hast redeemed us* unto God by thy
blood;" and in their song who shall ever doubt
that grace, free grace, as exhibited in their own
salvation, holds the highest place.

Oh new-born soul, trembling with anxiety, if
thou hast not yet beheld the fair face of thy
beloved, if thou canst not as yet delight in the
majesty of his offices, and the wonders of his
person, let thy soul be fully alive to the richness
of his grace and the preciousness of his blood.

These thou hast in thy possession,—the pledges of thine interest in him; love him then for these, and in due time he will discover unto thee fresh wonders and glories, so that thou shalt be able to exclaim, "The half has not been told me." Let Calvary and Gethsemane endear thy Saviour to thee, though as yet thou hast not seen the brightness of Tabor, or heard the eloquence of Olivet. Take the lower room if thou canst not reach another, for *the lowest room is in the house,* and its tables shall not be naked. But study to look into thy Redeemer's heart, that thou mayst become more closely knit unto him. Remember there is a singular love in the bowels of our Lord Jesus to his people, so superlatively excellent, that nothing can compare with it. No husband, no wife, nor tender-hearted mother can compete with him in affection, for his love passeth the love of women. Nothing will contribute more to make thee see Jesus Christ as admirable and lovely than a right apprehension of his love to thee; this is the constraining, ravishing, engaging, and overwhelming consideration which will infallibly steep thee in a sea of love to him. "Although," says Durham,* "there be much in many mouths of Christ's

* Exposition of Sol. Song.

love, yet there are few that really know and
believe the love that he hath to his people.
(1 John iii. 1.) As this is the cause that so few
love him, and why so many set up other be-
loveds beside him, so the solid faith of this and
the expectation of good from him, hath a great
engaging virtue to draw sinners to him." Study
then *his* love, and so inflame thine own; for be
thou ever mindful that the love of Jesus was
costly on his part, and undeserved on thine.

Here it will be right to mention the love which
springs from a sense of *possession* of Christ.
"O Lord, *thou art my God*, early will I seek
thee," is the vow which results from a knowledge of our possessing God as our own. As
God we *ought* to love him, but as *our* God we
do love him. It is Christ as *our* Christ, his
righteousness as imputed to *us*, and his atonement as *our* ransom, which at first cause our
souls to feel the heat of love. "I cannot love
another man's Christ," saith the anxious soul,
"he must be mine, or my soul can never be
knit unto him;" but when an interest in Jesus
is perceived by the understanding, then the
heart cries out, "My Lord and my God, thou
art mine and I will be thine." It is worth
while to be a man, despite all the sorrows of

mortality, if we may have grace to talk in the
fashion of a full assured believer, when he
rejoices in the plenitude of his possessions,
and gratefully returns his love as his only possible acknowledgment. Listen to him while he
talks in the following strain : " *My* Beloved is
mine, and I am his. The grant is clear, and my
claim is firm. Who shall despoil me of it when
God hath put me in possession, and doth own
me as the lawful heritor ? *My* Lord hath himself assured me that he is mine, and hath bid
me call his Father, *my* father. I know of a
surety that the whole Trinity are *mine*. ' I
will be *thy* God' is my sweet assurance. O, my
soul, arise and take possession ; inherit thy
blessedness, and cast up thy riches ; enter into
thy rest, and tell how the Lord hath dealt bountifully with thee. I will praise thee, O *my* God;
my King, I subject my soul unto thee. O, *my*
Glory, in thee will I boast all the day ; O, *my*
Rock, on thee will I build all my confidence.
O staff of my life and strength of my heart, the
life of my joy and joy of my life, I will sit and
sing under thy shadow, yea, I will sing a song
of loves touching MY WELL-BELOVED." This
is a precious experience, happy is the man
who enjoys it. It is the marrow of life to read

our title clear; and it is so for this reason, among others, that it creates and fosters a devout ardency of affection in the soul which is the possessor of it. Let all believers seek after it.

II. Akin to the love inspired by thankfulness, but rising a step higher in gracious attainments, is LOVE CAUSED BY ADMIRATION *of the manner in which the work of the Redeemer was performed.* Having loved him for the deed of salvation, the believer surveys the labours of his Deliverer, and finds them in every part so excellent and marvellous, that he loves him with new force as he meditates upon them. HE is altogether lovely to the soul in every office which he was graciously pleased to assume. We behold him as *our King,* and when we see the power, the justice, and the grace which attend his throne, when we witness the conquest of his enemies, and remark his strong defence of his friends, we cannot but adore him, and exclaim, "All hail, we crown thee Lord of all." If his *priestly* office engages our meditation, it is precious to view him as the faithful High Priest; remembering the efficacy of his mediation, and the prevalence of his intercession: or, if

x

the mantle of the *prophet* is viewed as worn by Him upon whose brow the crown of empire and the diadem of the priesthood are both for ever placed, how becoming does it seem upon His shoulders who is wisdom's self! In his three-fold character, in which all the offices are blended but none confused—all fulfilled, but none neglected—all carried to their highest length, but none misused,—how glorious does our Redeemer appear! Sonnets will never cease for want of themes, unless it be that the penury of language should compel our wonder to abide at home, since it cannot find garments in which to clothe its thoughts. When the soul is led by the Holy Spirit to take a clear view of Jesus in his various offices, how speedily the heart is on fire with love! To see him stooping from his throne to become man, next yielding to suffering to become man's sympathising friend, and then bowing to death itself to become his Ransom, is enough to stir every passion of the soul. To discern him by faith as the propitiation for sin, sprinkling his own blood within the vail, and nailing our sins to his cross, is a sight which never fails to excite the reverent, yet rapturous admiration of the beholder. Who can behold the **triumphs** of the Prince of Peace **and** not applaud him? Who can know his illustrious merits, and not extol him?

Doubtless this love of admiration is an after-thought, and can never be the primary acting of new-born love. The sailors rescued by the heroic daring of Grace Darling would first of all admire her as their deliverer, and afterwards, when they remembered her natural weakness, her philanthropic self-denial, her compassionate tenderness, and her heroic courage, they would give her their hearts for the manner in which the deed was done and the spirit which dictated it. In fact, apart from their own safety, they could scarcely avoid paying homage to the virtue which shone so gloriously in her noble act. Never, throughout life, could they forget their personal obligation to that bravest of women; but at the same time they would de-clare, that had it not been their lot to have been rescued from the depths, they could not have refused their heart's admiration of a deed so heroic, though they themselves had not been profited by it. We, who are saved by grace, have room enough in our Redeemer's character for eternal love and wonder. His characters are so varied, and all of them so precious, that we may still gaze and adore. The Shepherd folding the

lambs in his bosom, the Breaker dashing into
pieces the opposing gates of brass, the Captain
routing all his foes, the Brother born for adversity, and a thousand other delightful pictures
of Jesus, are all calculated to stir the affections
of the thoughtful Christian. It should be our
endeavour to know more of Christ, that we may
find more reasons for loving him. A contemplation of the history, character, attributes, and
offices of Jesus will often be the readiest way
to renew our drooping love. The more clear is
our view of Christ, the more complete will be
our idea of him; and the more true our experience of him, so much the more constant
and unwavering will be our heart's hold of him.
Hence the importance of communion with him,
which is to a great extent the only means of
knowing him.

We would here caution the reader to make
an important distinction when dwelling upon
the phase of spiritual love now under consideration. Let him carefully remember that
admiration of the moral character of Jesus of
Nazareth may exist in an unregenerate heart,
and that, apart from the love of gratitude, it is
no acceptable fruit of the Spirit: so that this
(in some senses) higher stone of the building,

leans entirely upon the lower one, and without it is of no avail. Some pretend to admire the Prophet of Nazareth, but deny him to be the Son of God; others wonder at him in his divine and human natures, but cannot lay hold on him as their Redeemer; and many honour his perfect example, but despise his glorious sacrifice. Now, it is not love to a part of Christ which is the real work of the Spirit, but it is true devotion to the Christ of God in all that he is and does. Many manufacture a Christ of their own, and profess to love him; but it is not respect to our own anointed, but to the Lord's anointed, which can prove us to be God's elect. Seek then to know the Lord, that you may with your whole soul be united to him in affection. Come, now, lay aside this volume for an hour and regale yourself with a little of His company, then will you join with the devout Hawker in his oft-repeated confession: — "In following thee, thou blessed Jesus, every renewed discovery of thee is glorious, and every new attainment most excellent. In thy person, offices, character, and relations, thou art most precious to my soul. Thou art a glorious Redeemer, a glorious Head of thy Church and people; a glorious Husband, Brother, Friend,

Prophet, Priest, and King in thy Zion. And when I behold thee in all these relative excellencies, and can and do know thee, and enjoy thee, and call thee *mine* under every one of them, surely I may well take up the language of this sweet Scripture, and say, 'Thou art more glorious and excellent than all the mountains of Prey!'" *

If you are unable to obtain a view of the Man of grief and love, ask him to reveal himself by his Spirit, and when your prayer is heard your soul will speedily be ravished with delight.

> " In manifested love explain,
>   Thy wonderful design;
>   What meant the suffering Son of Man,
>   The streaming blood divine?
>
> " Come thou, and to my soul reveal
>   The heights and depths of grace;
>   The wounds which all my sorrows heal,
>   That dear disfigured face:
>
>   Before my eyes of faith confest,
>   Stand forth a slaughter'd Lamb;
>   And wrap me in thy crimson vest,
>   And tell me all thy name."

III. SYMPATHY WITH JESUS IN HIS GREAT DESIGN is a cause as well as an effect of love to Him. Sanctified men have an union of heart with Jesus, since their aims are common Both

* See his admirable *Portions.*

are seeking to honour God, to uproot sin, to save
souls, and extend the kingdom of God on earth.
Though the saints are but the private soldiers,
while Jesus is their glorious Leader, yet they are
in the same army, and hence they have the
same desire for victory. From this springs an
increase of love; for we cannot labour with and
for those whom we esteem, without feeling ourselves more and more united to them. We love
Jesus when we are advanced in the divine life,
from a participation with him in the great work
of his incarnation. We long to see our fellow-
men turned from darkness to light, and we love
Him as the Sun of righteousness, who can
alone illuminate them. We hate sin, and therefore we rejoice in Him as manifested to take
away sin. We pant for holier and happier
times, and therefore we adore Him as the coming Ruler of all lands, who will bring a millen-
nium with Him in the day of his appearing.
The more sincere our desires, and the more
earnest our efforts, to promote the glory of
God and the welfare of man, the more will our
love to Jesus increase. Idle Christians always
have lukewarm hearts, which are at once the
causes and effects of their sloth. When the
heart is fully engaged in God's great work, it

will glow with love of the Great Son, who was himself a servant in the same great cause. Does my philanthropy lead me to yearn over dying men? Is my pity excited by their miseries? Do I pray for their salvation, and labour to be the means of it? then most assuredly I shall, for this very reason, reverence and love the Friend of sinners, the Saviour of the lost. Am I so engrossed with the idea of God's majesty, that my whole being pants to manifest his glory and extol his name? Then I shall most certainly cleave unto him who glorified his Father, and in whose person all the attributes of Deity are magnified. If a sense of unity in aim be capable of binding hosts of men into one compact body, beating with one heart, and moving with the same step—then it is easy to believe that the heavenly object in which the saints and their Saviour are both united, is strong enough to form a lasting bond of love between them.

Trusting that we may be enabled in our daily conduct to prove this truth, we pass on to another part of the subject.

IV. EXPERIENCE. Experience of the love, tenderness, and faithfulness of our Lord Jesus

Christ will weld our hearts to him. The very
thought of the love of Jesus towards us is enough
to inflame our holy passions, but experience of
it heats the furnace seven times hotter. He has
been with us in our trials, cheering and consoling
us, sympathising with every groan, and regarding
every tear with affectionate compassion. Do we
not love him for this? He has befriended us in
every time of need, so bounteously supplying all
our wants out of the riches of his fulness, that
he has not suffered us to lack any good thing.
Shall we be unmindful of such unwearying care?
He has helped us in every difficulty, furnishing
us with strength equal to our day; he has levelled
the mountains before us, and filled up the valleys;
he has made rough places plain, and crooked
things straight. Do we not love him for this
also? In all our doubts he has directed us in
the path of wisdom, and led us in the way of
knowledge. He has not suffered us to wander;
he has led us by a right way through the
pathless wilderness. Shall we not praise him for
this? He has repelled our enemies, covered our
heads in the day of battle, broken the teeth of
the oppressor, and made us more than con-
querors. Can we forget such mighty grace?
When our sins have broken our peace, stained

our garments, and pierced us with many sorrows, he has restored our souls, and led us in the path of righteousness for his name's sake. Are we not constrained to call upon all that is within us to bless his holy name? He has been as good as his word; not one promise has been broken, but all have come to pass. In no single instance has he failed us; he has never been unkind, unmindful, or unwise. The harshest strokes of his providence have been as full of love as the softest embraces of his condescending fellowship. We cannot, we dare not find fault with him. He hath done all things well. There is no flaw in his behaviour, no suspicion upon his affection. His love is indeed that perfect love which casteth out fear; the review of it is sweet to contemplation; the very remembrance of it is like ointment poured forth, and the present enjoyment of it, the experience of it at the present moment, is beyond all things delightful. Whatever may be our present position, it has in it peculiarities unknown to any other state, and hence it affords special grounds of love. Are we on the mountains? we bless him that he maketh our feet like hind's feet, and maketh us to stand upon our high places. Are we in the valley? then we praise him that his rod and staff do comfort us.

Are we in sickness? we love him for his gracious visitations. If we be in health, we bless him for his merciful preservations. At home or abroad, on the land or the sea, in health or sickness, in poverty or wealth, Jesus, the never-failing friend, affords us tokens of his grace, and binds our hearts to him in the bonds of con-straining gratitude.

It must, however, be confessed that all the saints do not profit from their experience in an equal measure, and none of them so much as they might. All the experience of a Christian is not Christian experience. Much of our time is occupied with exercises as unprofitable as they are unpleasant. The progress of a traveller must not be measured by the amount of his toil, unless we can obtain a satisfactory proof that all his toil was expended in the right path; for let him journey ever so swiftly, if his path be full of wanderings, he will gain but little by his labours. When we follow on to know the Lord in his own appointed way, the promise assures us that we shall attain to knowledge; but if we run in the way of our own devising, we need not wonder if we find ourselves surrounded with darkness in-stead of light. However, the Lord, who gra-ciously overrules evil for good, has been pleased to permit it to remain as a rule in the lives of his children, that they learn by experience,—and sure we are, that were we not dull scholars, we should in the experience of a single day discover a thousand reasons for loving the Redeemer. The most barren day in all our years blossoms with remembrances of his loving-kindness, while the more memorable seasons yield a hundredfold the fruits of his goodness. Though some days may add but little to the heap, yet by little and little it increases to a mountain. Little experiences, if well husbanded, will soon make us rich in love. Though the banks of the river do shelve but gently, yet he that is up to the ankles shall find the water covering his knees, if he do but continue his wading. Blessed is the saint whose love to his Lord hath become confirmed with his years, so that his heart is fixed, and fired, and flaming. He with his grey hairs and venerable countenance commands the attention of all men when he speaks well of the Lord Jesus, whom he hath tried and proved through more than half a century of tribulation mingled with rejoicing. As a youth his love was true, but we thought it little more than a momentary flash, which would die as hastily as it was born; but now no man can doubt its sincerity, for it is a steady flame, like the burning of a well-trimmed lamp. Experience, when blessed by the Holy Spirit, is the saint's daily income, by which he getteth rich in affection; and he who hath for a long time amassed his portion of treasure may well be conceived to be more rich therein than the young beginner, who has as yet received but little. Would to God that we were all more careful to obtain and retain the precious gems which lie at our feet in our daily experience!

The experienced believer is in advance of his younger brethren if his experience has developed itself in a deeper, steadier, and more abiding love of Christ. He is to the babe in grace what the oak is to the sapling—more firmly rooted, more strong in heart, and broader in his spread; his love, too, is to the affection of the beginner what the deep-rolling river is to the sparkling rill. Especially is this the case if he has done business on great waters, and has been buried beneath the billows of affliction. He will, if he have passed through such exercises, be a mighty witness of the worthiness of his Lord,—for tribulation unfolds the delights of covenant engagements, and drives the soul to feed upon them. It cuts away every other prop, and compels the soul to test the solidity of the pillar of divine faithfulness; it throws a cloud over the face of all created good, and leads the spirit to behold the sacred beauties of the Son of man; and thus it enables the believer to know in the most certain manner the all-sufficiency of the grace of the Lord Jesus. Tried saints are constrained to love their Redeemer; not only on account of deliverance out of trouble, but also because of that sweet comfort which he affords them whilst they are enduring the cross. They have found adversity to be a wine-press, in which the juice of the grapes of Eschol could be trodden out; an olive-press, to extract the precious oil from the gracious promises. Christ is the honeycomb, but experience must suck forth the luscious drops; he is frankincense, but fiery trials must burn out the perfume; he is a box of spikenard, but the hard hand of trouble must break the box and pour forth the ointment. When this is done, when Jesus is experimentally known, he is loved in a higher manner than the newborn Christian can aspire to talk of. Aged and mellow saints have so sweet a savour of Christ in them that their conversation is like streams from Lebanon, sweetly refreshing to him who delights to hear of the glories of redeeming love. They have tried the anchor in the hour of storm, they have

tested the armour in the day of battle, they have
proved the shadow of the great rock in the
burning noontide in the weary land; therefore
do they talk of these things, and of *Him* who is
all these unto them, with an unction and a
relish which we, who have but just put on our
harness, can enjoy, although we cannot attain
unto it at present. We must dive into the same
waters if we would bring up the same pearls.
May the great Illuminator sow our path with
light, that we may increase in knowledge of the
love *of* Christ, and in earnestness of love *to*
Christ, in proportion as we draw near to the
celestial city.

We now advance to another step, which stands
in strict connection with the subject upon which
we have just meditated.

V. COMMUNION opens up another means by
which love is excited, and its nature affected.
We love him because we have seen him, and
entered into fellowship with him. However
true and faithful the tidings which another
person may bring us concerning the Saviour, we
shall never feel love towards him in all the
power of it until we have with our own eyes
beheld him, or, rather, have laid hold on him

with our own faith. Personal intercourse with
Jesus is pre-eminently a cause of love, and it so
infallibly quickens the affections that it is impossible to live in the society of Jesus without
loving him. Nearness of life towards the
Lamb will necessarily involve greatness of love
to him. As nearness to the sun increases the
temperature of the various planets, so close
communion with Jesus raises the heat of the
affections towards him.

We hope to have another opportunity of un-
folding the sweetness of communion, and therefore we will but notice one part of it—viz.,
Christ's manifestations, as being a mighty incen-
tive to affection. Our blessed Lord, at intervals
more or less frequent, is graciously pleased to
shed abroad in the soul a most enchanting and
rapturous sense of his love. He opens the ear
of the favoured saint to hear the sweet canticles
of the bridegroom's joy, and softly he singeth
his song of loves. He manifests His heart to the
heart of his chosen ones, so that they know him
to be the sweetest, firmest, and most ardent of
lovers. They feel that he loves as a head, as a
father, as a friend, as a kinsman, as a brother,
as a husband; they behold the love of all relationships united and exceeded in the love of Christ.

They are confident that he loves them more than they love themselves; yea, that he loves them above his own life. This tends to raise their souls towards him; he becomes wholly delectable unto them, and is enshrined upon the highest throne of their hearts. Possessed with a sense of the love of their dying Lord, they feel that had they a heart as wide as eternity, it could not contain more love than they desire to give him. Thus are they impelled to daring service and patient suffering for his sake. "There is a power in this love which conquers, captivates, and overpowers the man, so that he cannot but love. God's love hath a generative power; our love is brought forth by his love." * Say, poor soul, what get you in Christ whenever you go to him? Can you not say, Oh! I get more love to him than I had before; I never approached near to him but I gained a large draught and ample fill of love to God. Out of his fulness we receive grace for grace, and love for love. In a word, by faith we behold the glory of the Lord as in a glass, and are changed into the same image—and the image of God is love. No way so ready for begetting love *to* Christ as a sense of the love *of* Christ. The

* R. Erskine.

Y

one is a loadstone to attract the other. As fire
grows by the addition of fuel, so does our love to
Christ increase by renewed and enlarged discoveries of his love to us. Love is love's food.
If, as parents, we make known our love to our
children, and deal wisely with them, it is but
natural that their affections should become
more and more knit to us; so it seems but as in
the common course of things that where much
of divine love is perceived by the soul, there will
be a return of affection in some degree propor-
tionate to the measure of the manifestation.
As we pour water into a dry pump when we
desire to obtain more—so must we have the
love of Christ imparted to the heart before we
shall feel any uprisings of delight in Him.
Hence the importance of the apostolic prayer,
that we may be able to understand with all
saints what is the breadth, and length, and
depth, and height, and to know the love of
Christ, which passeth knowledge. Beloved
fellow Christian, pray for more open discoveries
of the love and loveliness of Christ, and thus shall
thy languid passions move more readily in the
paths of obedience. We have all too much cause
to mourn the poverty of our love; let us not be
slow to seek the help of the God of Israel to

enable us to profit by all the condescending manifestations with which the Lord sees fit to favour us.

VI. LOVE TO THE PERSON OF JESUS is a most delightful state of divine life. It will be observed that the Song of the Spouse, which is doubtless intended to be the expression of the highest order of love, is composed rather of descriptions of the *person* of the Bridegroom than of any relation of the deeds which he performed. The whole language of the Book of Canticles is love, but its most overflowing utterances are poured forth upon the sacred *person* of the Well-Beloved. How do the words succeed each other in marvellous and melodious succession when the Church pours forth the fulness of its heart in praises of his beauties!— "My beloved is white and ruddy, the chiefest among ten thousand. His head is as the most fine gold, his locks are bushy, and black as a raven. His eyes are as the eyes of doves by the rivers of waters, washed with milk, and fitly set. His cheeks are as a bed of spices, as sweet flowers : his lips like lilies, dropping sweet smelling myrrh. His hands are as gold rings set with the beryl : his belly is as bright ivory overlaid with sapphires. His legs are as pillars of marble, set upon sockets of fine gold: his countenance is as Lebanon, excellent as the cedars. His mouth is most sweet: yea, he is altogether lovely." * Here it is not the crown, but the *head*, which is the theme of song; not the garment, but the unrobed body; not the shoes, but the feet. The song does not celebrate his descent from the king of ages, nor his lordship over the ministers of fire, nor his perpetual priesthood, nor his unbounded sovereignty; but it finds music enough in his lips, and beauty sufficient in his eyes without the glories which his high offices and omnipotent grace have procured for him. This indeed is true love; though the wife regards her husband's gifts, and honours his rank and titles, yet she sets her affection upon his person, loves *him* better than his gifts, and esteems him for his own sake rather than for his position among men. Let us here observe, lest we should be misunderstood, that we do not for a moment intend to insinuate that in the earlier states of the sacred grace of love, there is any lack of love *to his person*. We know that the first gushing of the fount of love is to *Christ*, and at all times the soul goes out towards

* Sol. Song v. 10—16.

him; but we make a distinction which we think
will be readily perceived, between love to the
person, for the sake of benefits received and
offices performed, and love to the person *for the
person's sake.* To suppose that a believer loves
the office apart from the person is to suppose an
absurdity, but to say that he may love the person
apart from the office is but to declare a great fact.
We love *Him* at all times, but only the heavenly-
minded love him *for his own person's sake.*

What a precious subject for contemplation is
the glorious being who is called Emmanuel, God
with us, and yet "the I am," "God over all!"
The complex person of the Mediator, Jesus
Christ, is the centre of a believer's heart. He
adores him in all the attributes of his God-head,
as very God of very God—Eternal, Infinite,
Almighty, Immutable. He bows before him as
"God over all, blessed for ever," and pays him
loving homage as the everlasting Father, the
Prince of peace; and at the same time he
delights to consider him as the infant of Bethlehem, the Man of sorrows, the Son of man,
bone of our bone and flesh of our flesh, tempted
in all points like as we are, and owning kindred
with the children of men. As man yet God,
creature yet Creator, infant and Infinite, de-

spised yet exalted, scourged though Omnipotent, dying yet eternal,—our dear Redeemer must ever be the object of wondering affection. Yea, when faith is dim and the Christian is in doubt as to his possession of his Lord, he will at times be able to feel that his thoughts of his Master's person are as high as ever. "Though he slay me, I must love him. If he will not look upon me, I cannot but bless him still. He is good and glorious, even though he damn me for ever. I must speak well of him, even if he will not permit me to hope in his mercy; for he is a glorious Christ, and I will not deny it, though he should now shut up his bowels against an unworthy creature like myself." This is the sentiment of the quickened child of God, when his heart is thoroughly occupied with a full and faithful view of his Divine Lord.

O the savour of the name of Jesus, when heard by the ear which has been opened by the Spirit! O the beauty of the person of Jesus, when seen with the eye of faith by the illumination of the Holy One of Israel! As the light of the morning, when the sun ariseth, "as a morning without clouds," is our Well-Beloved unto us. The sight of the burning bush made Moses put off his shoes, but the transporting vision of Jesus makes

us put off all the world. When once He is seen
we can discern no beauties in all the creatures
in the universe. He, like the sun, hath absorbed all other glories into his own excessive
brightness. This is the pomegranate which
love feeds upon, the flagon wherewith it is
comforted. A sight of Jesus causes such
union of heart with him, such goings out of
the affections after him, and such meltings
of the spirit towards him, that its expressions
often appear to carnal men to be extravagant
and forced, when they are nothing but the free,
unstudied, and honest effusions of its love.
Hence it is that the Song of Solomon has been
so frequently assailed, and has had its right to
a place in the canon so fiercely disputed. The
same critics would deny the piety of Rutherford,
or the reverence of Herbert. They are themselves ignorant of the divine passion of love to
Jesus, and therefore the language of the enrap-
tured heart is unintelligible to them. They are
poor translators of love's celestial tongue who
think it to be at all allied with the amorous
superfluities uttered by carnal passions. Jesus
is the only one upon whom the loving believer
has fixed his eye, and in his converse with his
Lord he will often express himself in language

which is meant only for his Master's ear, and which worldlings would utterly contemn could they but listen to it. Nevertheless love, like wisdom, is "justified of her children."

Heaven itself, although it be a fertile land, flowing with milk and honey, can produce no fairer flower than the Rose of Sharon; its highest joys mount no higher than the head of Jesus; its sweetest bliss is found in his name alone. If we would know heaven, let us know Jesus; if we would be heavenly, let us love Jesus. Oh that we were perpetually in his company, that our hearts might ever be satisfied with his love! Let the young believer seek after a clear view of the person of Jesus, and then let him implore the kindling fire of the Holy Spirit to light up his whole soul with fervent affection. Love to Jesus is the basis of all true piety, and the intensity of this love will ever be the measure of our zeal for his glory. Let us love him with all our hearts, and then diligent labour and consistent conversation will be sure to follow.

VII. RELATIONSHIP TO CHRIST, when fully felt and realised, produces a peculiar warmth of affection towards Him. The Holy Spirit is pleased, at certain favoured seasons, to open up to the understanding and reveal to the affections the nearness of Jesus to the soul. At one time we are blessed with a delightful sense of *brotherhood* with Christ. "The man is thy near kinsman," sounds like news from a far country. "In ties of blood with sinners one," rings in our ears like the music of Sabbath bells. We had said, like the spouse, "O that thou wert as my brother!" and lo! the wish is gratified. He stands before us in all his condescension, and declares he is not ashamed to call us brethren. Unveiling his face, he reveals himself as the Son of man, our kinsman near allied by blood. He manifests himself to our rejoicing spirit as "the first-born among many brethren," and he reminds us that we are "joint-heirs with him," although he is "heir of all things." The fraternity of Jesus cannot fail to quicken us to the most ardent affection, and when he himself thus confesses the relationship, our soul is melted at his speech. That sweet name "brother" is like perfume to the believer, and when he lays hold upon it, it imparts its fragrance to him. We have sometimes had such a sense of satisfaction in meditation upon this heavenly doctrine, that we counted all the honours and glories of this world to be but loss compared with the excel-

lency of it.   For this one fact of brotherhood
with Christ we could have bartered crowns and
empires, and have laughed at the worldly bar-
terer as a fool, infinitely more mad than Esau
when he took a pitiful mess of pottage as the
purchase-price of a mighty birthright.   God
the Holy Ghost has made the fulness of the
doctrine of the relationship of Jesus roll into
our soul like a river, and we have been entirely
carried away in its wondrous torrent. · Our
thoughts have been entirely absorbed in the one
transcendently glorious idea of brotherhood with
Jesus, and then the emotions have arisen with
great vehemence, and we have pressed *Him* to
our bosom, have wept for joy upon his shoulder,
and have lost ourselves in adoring love of him
who thus discovered himself as bone of our bone,
and flesh of our flesh.   We feel we must love our
brother, even nature joins her voice with grace
to claim the entire heart; and verily, in seasons
of such gracious manifestations, the claim is
fully met, and the right gladly acknowledged.

Another delightful relationship of the Lord
Jesus is that of Husband, and here he is indeed
to be beloved.   Young Christians are married to
Christ, but they have not in most cases realised
the gracious privilege; but the more enlightened

believer rejoices in the remembrance of the marriage union of Christ and his spouse. To him the affection, protection, provision, honour, and intimacy involved in the divine nuptials of the blessed Jesus with his elect are well-springs of constant joy. "Thy Maker is thy Husband" is to him a choice portion of the Word, and he feasts upon it day and night, when the gracious Spirit is pleased to enable him to lay hold upon it by faith. A tranquil, confident frame will immediately result from a satisfactory persuasion of this glorious truth, and with it there will be a fervency of affection and a continued union of heart to Christ Jesus, which is hardly attainable in any other manner.

In his conjugal relation to his Church, the Lord Jesus takes great delight, and desires that we should see the glory of it. He would have us consider him in the act of betrothing and espousing his Church unto himself: "Go forth," saith he, "O ye daughters of Jerusalem, and behold King Solomon with the crown wherewith his mother crowned him in the day of his espousals, and in the day of the gladness of his heart." *

"It is the gladness of the heart of Christ, and the joy of his soul, to take poor sinners

* Sol. Song iii. 11.

into relation with himself;"* and if so, it cannot fail to be an equal source of rejoicing to those who are thus favoured. Meditate much on thy divine relationships, and thine heart shall be much warmed thereby.

VIII. A persuasion of our UNION to Jesus must also stir up the passions to a holy flame. We are, by the decree of God, made one with our Covenant Head the Lord Jesus. From before all worlds this eternal union was most firmly settled upon a substantial basis; but our personal knowledge of it is a thing of time, and is vouchsafed to us in the appointed season by God the Holy Ghost. How swiftly doth the heart pursue its Lord when it has learned its *oneness* to Him! What man will not love his own flesh? who will not love himself? Now, when the soul perceives the indissoluble union which exists between itself and the Saviour, it can no more resist the impulse of affection than a man can forbear to love his own body. It is doubtless a high attainment in the divine life to be fully possessed with a sense of vital union to Christ, and hence the love arising from it is of a peculiarly rich and vehement character. Some pastures give richness to the flesh of the cattle which feed upon them : truly, this is a fat pasture, and the affection which feedeth upon it cannot be otherwise than excellent to a superlative degree. In fine, as an abiding sense of oneness with the Lord is one of the sweetest works of the Spirit in the souls of the elect, so the love springing therefrom is of the very highest and most spiritual nature. None can surpass it; yea, it is questionable whether so high a degree of affection can be attained by any other means, however forcible and inflaming. But set it down as a rule that we ought never to halt or sit down in any attainment of nearness to Jesus until we have brought it to such a measure that no more can be enjoyed, and until we have reached the utmost possible height therein. If there be an inner chamber in which the king doth store his choicest fruits, let us enter, for he bids us make free with all in his house; and if there be a secret place where he doth show his loves, let us hasten thither and embrace Him whom our soul loveth, and there let us abide until we see him face to face in the upper skies.

But what will be the love of Heaven? Here we utterly fail in description or conception. The

best enjoyments of Christ on earth are but as
the dipping our finger in water for the cooling
of our thirst; but heaven is bathing in seas of
bliss: even so our love here is but one drop of
the same substance as the waters of the ocean,
but not comparable for magnitude or depth. Oh,
how sweet it will be to be married to the Lord
Jesus, and to enjoy for ever, and without any interruption, the heavenly delights of his society!
Surely, if a glimpse of him melteth our soul, the
full fruition of him will be enough to burn us up
with affection. It is well that we shall have
more noble frames in heaven than we have here,
otherwise we should die of love in the very land
of life. An honoured saint was once so ravished
with a revelation of his Lord's love, that feeling
his mortal frame to be unable to sustain more of
such bliss, he cried, " Hold, Lord, it is enough, it
is enough !" But there we shall be able to set
the bottomless well of love to our lips, and
drink on for ever, and yet feel no weakness.
Ah, that will be love indeed which shall over-
flow our souls for ever in our Father's house
above ! Who can tell the transports, the raptures, the amazements of delight which that
love shall beget in us ? and who can guess the
sweetness of the song, or the swiftness of the

obedience which will be the heavenly expressions
of love made perfect? No heart can conceive
the surpassing bliss which the saints shall enjoy
when the sea of their love to Christ, and the
ocean of Christ's love to them, shall meet each
other, and raise a very tempest of delight. The
distant prospect is full of joy: what must be
the fruition of it? To answer that question we
must wait all the days of our appointed time till
our change come, unless the Lord himself
should suddenly appear in the clouds to glorify
us with himself throughout eternity.

Beloved fellow-heirs of the same inheritance,
we have thus reviewed some of the causes and
phases of the Christian grace of love; let us now
ask ourselves the question, How is it with our
love? Is it hot or cold? Is it decaying or
increasing? How stands the heart, God-ward
and Christ-ward? Is it not far too slow in its
motions, too chilly in its devotion? We must
admit it is so. Let us use the various arguments of this chapter as levers for lifting our
heavy hearts to greater heights of affection, and
then let us unitedly cry—

> " Come, Holy Spirit, heavenly Dove,
>   With all thy quickening powers;
> Come, shed abroad the Saviour's love,
>   And that shall kindle ours."

It may be that the sneering critic has been offended with all this discourse concerning love, and has turned upon his heel, protesting with vehemence that he is of a philosophic spirit, and will never endure such sickly sentimentalism. To him religion is thought, not emotion. It is a cold, speculative, unfeeling divinity which he believes, and its effects upon his mind are the reverse of enthusiastic.

Reason, "heavenly Reason," is his God, and Feeling must lie dormant beneath the throne of his great deity. We beg to remind him that the religion of the cross was intended to stir the soul with deep emotion, and that where it is truly received it accomplishes its end; but that if the passions be not moved by it, there is a strong presumption that it has never been in true operation. We do not wonder that, to the man who views religion as a mere compendium of truths for the head, it is a powerless thing, for it is intended to work in another manner. Wine may serve to cheer the heart, but who would expect to feel its exhilarating influence by pouring it upon his head. The holy Gospel makes its first appeal to man's heart, and until it be heard in that secret chamber it is not heard at all. So long as mere reason is the only listener, the melody of the cross will be unheard. Charm we never so wisely, men cannot hear the music until the ears of the heart are opened. Vinet* has thus expressed himself upon this subject:—"Ah! how can reason, cold reason, comprehend such a thing as the substitution of the innocent for the guilty; as the compassion which reveals itself in severity of punishment in that shedding of blood, without which, it is said, there can be no expiation? It will not make, I dare affirm, a single step towards the knowledge of that divine mystery, until, casting away its ungrateful speculations, it yields to a stronger power the task of terminating the difficulty. That power is the heart, which fixes itself entirely on the love that shines forth in the work of redemption; cleaves without distraction to the sacrifice of the adorable victim; lets the natural impression of that unparalleled love penetrate freely, and develop itself gradually in its interior. Oh, how quickly, then, are the veils torn away, and the shadows dissipated for ever! How little difficulty does he who loves find in comprehending love!" To the heart all divine mysteries are but simplicities, and

* See his *Vital Christianity*.

z

when reason is measuring the apparently in-
accessible heights, love is already shouting on
the summit. Let the cold, calculating worshipper
of intellect reserve his sneers for himself. Experience is one of the highest of sciences, and
the emotions claim a high precedence in the
experience which is from God. That which
these boasters contemn as an old wives' story,
is not one half so contemptible as themselves—
yea, more, the pious feelings at which they jeer
are as much beyond their highest thoughts as
the sonnets of angels excel the gruntings of
swine.

It has become fashionable to allow the title
of "intellectual preachers" to a class of men,
whose passionless essays are combinations of
metaphysical quibbles and heretical doctrines;
who are shocked at the man who excites his
hearers beyond the freezing-point of insensi-
bility, and are quite elated if they hear that
their homily could only be understood by a
few. It is, however, no question whether these
men deserve their distinctive title; it may be
settled as an axiom that falsehood is no intellectual feat, and that unintelligible jargon is no
evidence of a cultured mind. There must be
in our religion a fair proportion of believing,

thinking, understanding, and discerning, but there must be also the preponderating influences of feeling, loving, delighting, and desiring. That religion is worth nothing which has no dwelling in man but his brain. To love much is to be wise; to grow in affection is to grow in knowledge, and to increase in tender attachment is to be making high proficiency in divine things.

Look to thy love, O Christian! and let the carnal revile thee never so much, do thou persevere in seeking to walk with Christ, to feel his love, and triumph in his grace.

TO THE UNCONVERTED READER.

———————

FRIEND,—This time we will not preach the terrors of the law to thee, although they are thy deserts. We wish thee well, and if threatening will not awaken thee, we will try what wooing may accomplish, and oh ! may the Holy Spirit bless the means to thy soul's salvation.

The Lord Jesus hath purchased unto himself a number beyond all human count, and we would have thee mark who and what they were by nature.

The blood-bought ones, before their regeneration, were in the gall of bitterness and in the bonds of iniquity; they were aliens from the commonwealth of Israel, and strangers from the covenants of promise; they had chosen to themselves other gods, and were joined to idols; they walked according to the course of thi world, according to the Prince of the power of he air, the spirit that now worketh in the hildren of disobedience; they were polluted in

their blood, cast out in the open field to perish;
they were despisers of God, in league with hell
and in covenant with Death; but nevertheless they were chosen, were redeemed, and
have received the glorious title of Sons and
Daughters.

Now, Friend, if free grace has done thus with
one and another, why should it not accomplish
the same for thee? Dost thou feel thy deep
necessities? Do thy bowels yearn for mercy?
Art thou made willing to be saved in God's
way? Then be of good cheer. The promise is
thine, the blood of Jesus was shed for thee, the
Holy Spirit is at work with thee, thy salvation
draweth nigh. *He that calleth upon the name
of the Lord shall be saved.* Thy cries shall yet
be heard, since they come from a broken heart
and a contrite spirit. Remember, faith in Jesus
alone can give thee peace.

But art thou still hard and stolid, still brutish
and worldly? Then, permit the writer to weep
over thee, and bring thy case before the Lord
his God. Oh that the Lord would melt thee by
the fire of his word! Oh that he would break
thee with his hammer, and humble thee at his
feet! Alas for thee, unless this be done! Oh
that omnipotent grace would snatch thee from

the ruin of the proud, and deliver thy feet from going down into the pit! Miserable man! a brother's heart longeth after thee, and fain would see thee saved. Oh, why art thou so indifferent to thyself when others can scarce refrain from tears on thy behalf! By thy mother's prayers, thy sister's tears, and thy father's anxieties, I beseech thee give a reason for thy sottish indifference to thine eternal welfare. Dost thou now come to thyself? Dost thou now exclaim, "I will arise and go unto my Father?" Oh, be assured of a welcome reception, of gladsome entertainment, and loving acceptance.

> " From the Mount of Calvary,
> Where the Saviour deigned to die,
> What melodious sounds I hear,
> Bursting on my ravished ear!—
> Love's redeeming work is done!
> COME, AND WELCOME, SINNER, COME.
>
> Now behold the festal board,
> With its richest dainties stored;
> To thy Father's bosom press'd,
> Once again a child confess'd.
> From his house no more to roam;
> COME, AND WELCOME, SINNER, COME."

IX.

Jesus in the Hour of Trouble.

"Who passing through the valley of Baca make it a well
the rain also filleth the pools."—Ps. lxxxiv. 6.

PILGRIMAGE to an appointed shrine seems to
be an essential part of most religions. The
tribes of Israel made yearly journeys to Jerusalem, that at one great altar they might sacrifice unto the Lord their God. Borrowing the
idea, probably, from the Jews, we find false
religions inculcating the same. The disciples of
Brahma are required to undertake long and
painful journeys to the temple of Juggernaut,
or to the banks of their sacred river, the Ganges.
The Mahometan has his Kebla of worship; and,
if he be thoroughly a devout follower of the false
prophet, he must, once in his life, offer his
petitions at Mecca. And who has not heard of
the palmer plodding his weary way to the Holy

Sepulchre, or of the Canterbury pilgrim going to the tomb of Thomas à Becket?

But the religion of God, the revelation of our most merciful Father, does not thus deal with man. It prescribes no earthly pilgrimage It knows nothing of local restrictions. It declares that "neither in this mountain nor yet at Jerusalem shall men worship the Father;" that "God is a spirit," everywhere present, and as a spirit "must be worshipped," not merely by outward acts, but "in spirit and in truth."

Yet "pilgrimage" is one of the leading ideas of Christianity. Every Christian is mystically a pilgrim. His rest is not here. He is not a citizen of earth. Here he has no abiding city. He journeys to a shrine unseen by mortal eye, whither his fathers have arrived. This life-journey is his one incessant occupation. He came into the world that he might march through it in haste. He is ever a pilgrim, in the fullest and truest sense.

Nothing can be more pleasing to a thoughtful Christian than marking the footsteps of the flock, and tracing the track they have left in the blood-besprinkled way. Thus the geography of Christian life becomes an interesting study.

To enter the wicket-gate, to sit in the arbour on the hill-side, to lie in the chamber of peace in the House Beautiful, to stand on the Delectable Mountains, or walk among the spice beds of the land Beulah, yields far sweeter pleasure than fairy dreams, or tales coloured by fancy, whispered by the lips of music.

There are many fair and enchanting spots in the highway of salvation—spots which angels have visited, and which the saints have sighed to behold again and again. But some other parts of the way are not so inviting; we love not to enter the Valley of the Shadow of Death, nor to approach the mountains of the leopards, nor the lions' dens, yet must all of them be passed.

It is a precious mercy that Jesus, the heavenly Friend, is willing and able to accompany us in all our journeyings, and is the consolation of our souls in periods of blackest woe. After surveying the *Valley of Baca*, noticing the *toilsome effort* of the pilgrims in digging wells therein, and remarking the *heavenly supply* with which the pools are filled, we shall consider the grace of our Lord Jesus as exhibited to his people in their sorrowful passage through this Vale of Tears.

I. The Valley of Baca. The best description given of the Valley of Baca seems to be, that it was a defile through which a portion of the tribes had to pass on their journey to the city of their solemnities. It was a place noted for its dryness, and therefore pits were digged therein for the purpose of holding rain-water for the thirsty wayfarers as they passed through it. But, probably, the Psalmist looked not so much at the place as at its name, which signifies "Valley of Sorrow, or Tears." The Septuagint translates it, "Valley of Lamentation," and the Latin Vulgate, "Vale of Tears." We may therefore read the verse thus:—"Who passing through the vale of Tears make it a well," &c. Of this valley we may observe, first, *It is much frequented*. The way to Zion lies through its glooms. Many of God's chosen ones are carried from the breast to glory, and thus escape this dreary place, but all the rest of God's children must pass through it. Frequent are their sojourning in this "house of mourning." Not once nor twice, but many a time must they tread this valley. As numerous as their days are the causes of their griefs. The molestations of disease, the disappointments of business, the losses of adversity, and the havocs of death, combining with a thousand other ills, furnish enough material for the much tribulation through which we inherit the kingdom. All men have their times of sadness, but some seem to be always in the deep waters—their lives, like Ezekiel's roll, seem written within and without with lamentations. They can just dimly recollect happier days, but those are past long ago. They have for some time been the children of grief. They seldom eat a crust unmoistened by a tear. Sorrow's wormwood is their daily salad. Perhaps some sudden calamity has snatched away the gourd which covered their head, and, Jonah-like, they think they do well to be angry even unto death. A haze, dark and heavy, hangs like a pall before their eyes, and clothes life's scenery with sadness and gloom. Some are associated with ungodly partners, by whose unkindness their days are made bitter, and their lives a burden. Various are the causes of grief. The chains of melancholy differ in their size and material. Bound in affliction and iron, art thou saying, "He hath made my chain heavy?" Oh, child of grief, remember the vale of tears is much frequented; thou art not alone in thy distress. Sorrow has a numerous family. Say not, I am *the* man that has seen affliction, for there be others in the furnace with thee. Remember, moreover, the King of kings once went through this valley, and here he obtained his name, "the Man of sorrows," for it was while passing through it he became "acquainted with grief."

But, blessed be God, all his people are not thus clad in sackcloth and filled with bitterness. Some of them can sing for joy of heart, and, like the lark, rise to heaven's gates, carolling notes of praise. Yet, be it observed, there is not one who has not had his valley of Baca. He of flashing eye and cheerful countenance was once walking in its dark and dreary paths. He who danced before the ark had cried out of the depths unto the Lord. He whom you heard in prayer, with free heart blessing his Maker, was lately in his bed-chamber, crying out with Job, "O that my grief were weighed!" and with Jeremiah, "He hath filled me with bitterness, and made me drunken with wormwood."

Oh, mourner, say not that *thou* art a target for all the arrows of the Almighty; take not to thyself the pre-eminence of woe; for thy fellows have trodden the valley too, and upon them are the scars of the thorns and briars of the dreary pathway.

Secondly, this valley is exceedingly *unpleasant* to flesh and blood. We love to ascend the mountains of myrrh and hills of frankincense, rather than to descend into this dismal region. For tribulation is not joyous, but grievous. Disguise sorrow as we may, it is sorrow still. No pilgrim ever wished to enter here for its own sake, though there have been many who have rejoiced in the midst of its darkest and most gloomy paths. Now, let us briefly consider why this valley is so unpleasant to heaven-bound travellers. It is so because we can find no rivers of water in it. Earthly joys are continually failing us; and created cisterns, one after another, are dried up. A hot, dry wind steals away every drop of comfort, and, hungry and thirsty, our soul fainteth in us. No fruit of sweetness grows here. It well answers the description of Watts :—

> " It yields us no supply,
> No cheering fruits, no wholesome trees,
>   Nor streams of living joy."

Many rich mercies are here received by pilgrims, but these are not the fruits of the place itself, but the gifts of heaven. It is, moreover, disagreeable travelling in this valley, because the way is rough and rugged. In some parts of the

Christian journey we are led into green pastures
beside the still waters; but this valley is thorny,
stony, and flinty, and every way uncomfortable.
True, there are many labourers, called promises,
ever at work breaking the stones, and helping
passengers over its more difficult places; but notwithstanding this aid, journeying through it is
very rough work for all, but especially for those
pilgrims who are weak, and ready to halt. It is
also frequently very dark. The vale of tears is
very low, and descends far beneath the ordinary
level; some parts of it, indeed, are tunnelled
through rocks of anguish. A frequent cause of its
darkness is that on either side of the valley there
are high mountains, called the mountains of sin.
These rise so high that they obscure the light
of the sun. Behind these Andes of guilt God
hides his face, and we are troubled. Then
how densely dark the pathway becomes! Indeed, this is the very worst thing that can be
mentioned of this valley: for, if it were not
so dark, pilgrims would not so much dread
passing through it.

The soul of the traveller is also often discouraged on account of the length of the way.
Through the darkness of the place it seems as
though it had no termination, for, although it is

known that the dark river of death flows across
its extremity, but, in the night season, the
celestial city on the other side cannot be seen.
This is the Egyptian darkness which may be felt,
and, like solid piles of ebony, at such times it
appears to have an adamantine hardness in it.
Besides, this valley is much haunted. Evil
spirits are very common in it. When a man is
in the valley of Baca, Satan will soon be at him
with his fiery darts, cursed insinuations, and
blasphemous suggestions. Like the bandit, he
waylays us in the roughest and darkest part of
our way. This much deepens the horror of the
place.

Thirdly, this valley *is very healthful*. In all
the King's dominions, save alone the royal
pavilion in glory, there is no spot more conducive
to the soul's health than this. The air from the
sea of affliction is extremely beneficial to invalid
Christians. Continued prosperity, like a warm
atmosphere, has a tendency to unbind the sinews
and soften the bones; but the cold winds of
trouble make us sturdy, hardy, and well braced
in every part. Unbroken success often leads to
an undervaluing of mercies and forgetfulness of
the giver; but the withdrawal of the sunshine
leads us to look for the sun.

Fourthly, it is a very *safe place*. We are not so likely to stumble in rough ways as in smooth and slippery places. Better walk on rugged rocks than on slippery ice. If we lose our roll, it is in the harbour of ease, not in the valley of Baca. Few Christians backslide while under the rod; it is usually when on the lap of plenty that believers sin.

Fifthly, it is, therefore, a *profitable place*. Stars may be seen from the bottom of a deep well when they cannot be discerned from the top of a mountain: so are many things learned in adversity which the prosperous man dreams not of. We need affliction, as the trees need winter, that we may collect sap and nourishment for future blossoms and fruit. Sorrow is as necessary for the soul as medicine is to the body:—

> " The path of sorrow, and that path alone,
>   Leads to the land where sorrow is unknown."

The benefits to be derived in the vale of tears are greater than its horrors, and far outnumber its disadvantages. There was a fiction once of a golden cup at the foot of the rainbow: it would have been no fiction had they put the treasure in the dark cloud. In this valley of Baca there are mines of gold and of all manner of precious things ; and sometimes, even in the thick darkness, one may perceive the diamonds glitter. Full many a pilgrim has here been made rich to all the intents of bliss, and here have others had their heavenly wealth most marvellously increased.

But we proceed to observe—

II. The Toilsome Effort spoken of in the words at the head of the chapter—"They make it a well," &c. When Eastern shepherds travel, if they find no water, they dig a well, and thus obtain a plentiful supply of water for themselves and for their cattle. So did Isaac, and so also did the rulers for the people in the wilderness. When we are thirsty and there is no water to be found in the pools, we must dig deep for it. Calvin translates it,—"They, travelling through the valley of weeping, will dig a well," &c. This teaches us that—

1. *Comfort may be obtained even in the deepest trouble.* We often look for it and fancy there is none. Like Hagar, the child of our hope is given up, and we lay down to die; but why should we, when there is water to be had, if we will but seek for it ? Let no man say,

My case is hopeless; let none say, I am in the valley, and can never again know joy. There is hope. There is the water of life to cheer our fainting souls. It certainly is not possible for us to be in a position where Omnipotence cannot assist us. God hath servants everywhere, and where we think he has none his word can create a multitude. There are "treasures hid in the sand,"* and the Lord's chosen shall eat thereof. When the clouds hide the mountains they are as real as in the sunshine; so the promise and the providence of God are unchanged by the obscurity of our faith, or the difficulties of our position. There is hope, and hope at hand, therefore let us be of good cheer.

2. It teaches that *comfort must be obtained by exertion*. Well-digging is hard labour: but better dig for water than die of thirst. Much of the misery Christians feel arises from in-action. Cold numbs the hand if exercise be not used. We are bound to use every scriptural means to obtain the good we need. The sanc-tuary, the meeting for prayer, the Bible, the company of the saints, private prayer and medi-tation—these revive the soul. We must dig the wells. If there be rocky granite we must bore

* Deut xxxiii. 19.

it; we must not be disturbed from perseverance by the labour of our duties, but continue to dig still: and what a mercy! if the well has ever so small a bore the water will flow.

3. It teaches us that the *comfort* obtained by one is often of use to another; just as wells opened by former travellers would suffice for the company which came after. When we read works full of consolation, like Jonathan's rod, dropping with honey, let us remember that our brother has been here before us, and digged this well. "Songs in the Night," could only have been written by that nightingale in the thorns, Susanna Harrison. Many a "Night of Weeping," "Midnight Harmonies," an "Eternal Day," "A Crook in the Lot," a "Comfort for Mourners," has been a well digged by a pilgrim for himself, but has proved just as useful to others. Specially we notice this in the Psalms, which console us, although they were mournful odes to David. Travellers have been delighted to see the footprints of man on a barren shore, and we love to see the way-marks of the pilgrimage while passing through the vale of tears. Yea, the refuse and *débris* of the receding camp often furnish food for the stragglers behind. We may notice–

III. THE HEAVENLY SUPPLY. The pilgrims dig the well, but, strange enough, it fills from the top instead of the bottom. We use the means, but the blessing does not lie in the means, but in the God of the means. We dig the well, but heaven fills it with rain. The horse is prepared against the day of battle, but salvation is of the Lord. The means are divinely connected with the end, but they do not produce the blessing. "The rain filleth the pools," so that ordinances and duties are rather reservoirs than fountains, containing comfort, but not creating it. In vain are all the ordinances without the divine blessing; as clouds without rain, and pools without water, they yield us no supplies. When heaven smiles and pours down its showers of grace, then they are precious things; but without the celestial rain we might as much expect water from the arid waste, as a real blessing in the use of them. "All my springs are in Thee," is the believer's daily confession to his Lord,—a confession which until death must ever be upon his lips.

We now turn to our legitimate subject, from which the beauty of the text has for a while allured us, and we hasten to answer the ques-

tion, How doth Jesus behave himself toward
his people in the hour of their distresses?
Does he leave them when their friends are taken
from them? Does he desert them in the hour
of their poverty? Is he ashamed of them when
sackcloth is on their loins, and ashes upon their
heads? Do the pains of sickness affright him
from the bed? Can famine and nakedness
separate his brethren from his love? Is he the
same yesterday, to-day, and for ever? Our
answer shall be one dictated by the experience
of the saints, and confirmed in the life of the
christian reader. *The Lord Jesus is no fair-
weather friend, but one who loveth at all times
—a brother born for adversity.* This he proves
to his beloved, not by mere words of promise, but
by actual deeds of affection. As our sufferings
abound, so he makes our consolations to abound.
This he does by divers choice acts of love.

1. He affords the tried saint *clearer manifestations* of himself than usual. When he
draws the curtain around the believer on the
bed of sickness, he usually withdraws the curtain wherewith he conceals himself. He approaches nearer to the soul in its tribulation,
even as the sun is said to be nearer to the
earth in the time of winter. He sheds a clear

light on his promise when he robes his providence in darkness; and if both are alike clouded, he reveals himself the more manifestly. Affliction has often proved to be a presence-chamber, in which the King of Heaven gives audience to his unworthy subjects. As Isaac met his bride in the fields at eventide, so do true souls frequently find their joy and consolation in the loneliness of solitude, and at the sunset of their earthly pleasures. He who would see the stars sparkling with tenfold lustre must dwell in the cold regions of snow; and he who would know the full beauties of Jesus, the bright and morning star, must see him amid the frosts of trouble and adversity. Affliction is often the hand of God, which he places before our face to enable us, like Moses, to see the train of his glory as he passes by. The saint has had many a pleasant view of God's loving-kindness from the top of the hills of mercy; but tribulation is very frequently the Lord's Pisgah, from which he gives them a view of the land in all its length and breadth.

Mr. Renwick, the last of the Scottish martyrs, speaking of his sufferings for conscience' sake, says: "Enemies think themselves satisfied that we are put to wander in mosses, and upon

mountains; but even amidst the storms of these
last two nights, I cannot express what sweet
times I have had, when I had no covering but
the dark curtains of night. Yea, in the silent
watch, my mind was led out to admire the deep
and inexpressible ocean of joy wherein the
whole family of heaven swim. Each *star* led
me to wonder what He must be who is the star
of Jacob, of whom all stars borrow their
shining."

This one testimony is the type of many; it
is an exhibition of the great rule of the kingdom—"When thou passest through the rivers,
I will be with thee."

Choice discoveries of the wondrous love and
grace of Jesus are most tenderly vouchsafed
unto believers in the times of grief. Then it is
that he lifts them up from his feet, where, like
Mary, it is their delight to sit, and exalts them
to the position of the favoured John, pressing
them to his breast and bidding them lean on his
bosom. Then it is that he doth fill the cup
of salvation with the old wine of the kingdom,
and puts it to the mouth of the Christian, that
he may in some measure forget the flavour of
wormwood and grating of gravel-stones which
the draught of bitterness has placed upon his

palate and between his teeth. If Christ is more excellent at one time than another it certainly is in "the cloudy and dark day." We can never so well see the true colour of Christ's love as in the night of weeping. Christ in the dungeon, Christ on the bed of sickness, Christ in poverty, is Christ indeed to a sanctified man. No vision of Christ Jesus is so truly a revelation as that which is seen in the Patmos of suffering. As in time of war the city doubles its guards, so does Jesus multiply the displays of his affection when his chosen are besieged by trials. When Habakkuk's belly trembled, and his lips quivered, and rottenness entered into his bones, when all his earthly hopes were blasted, and his comforts removed, he had such an overcoming sense of the presence of God that he exclaimed in the midst of all his sorrows, "Yet will I rejoice in the Lord, and joy in the God of my salvation." Among the family of God none are so well versed in the knowledge of Christ's love as those who have been long in the chamber of affliction. What marvellous things have these seen, and what secrets have they heard! They have kissed the lips which others have but heard at a distance; they have pressed their heads upon the breast which others have but seen with their eyes; and they have been embraced in the arms into which others have but desired to climb. Give us the Christ of affliction, for he is Christ indeed.

2. As under sanctified affliction the manifestations of Christ are more clear, so are *his visitations more frequent*. If he pay us a daily visit when we are in our high estate, he will be with us hourly when we are cast down from our high places. As the sick child hath the most of the mother's eye, so doth the afflicted believer receive the most of his Saviour's attention, for like as a mother comforteth her children, even so doth the Lord comfort his people. Pious Brooks writes, "Oh, the love tokens, the love-letters, the bracelets, the jewels that the saints are able to produce since they have been in the furnace of affliction!" Of these they had but one in a season before, but now that their troubles have driven them nearer to their Saviour, they have enough to store their cabinet. Now they can truly say, "How precious also are thy thoughts unto me, O God! how great is the sum of them!" Mercies before came so constantly that memory could not compute their number; but now they appear to come in wave after wave, without a moment's cessation.

Happy is the man who finds the furnace as hot
with love as with affliction. Let the tried
believer look for increased privileges, and his
faithful Lord will not deceive his expectations.
He who rides upon the storm when it is tossing
the ocean, will not be absent when it is beating
about his saints. "The Lord of hosts is with
us," is not the song of them that make merry
in the dance, but of those who are struggling in
battle. "David, doubtless, had worse devils
than we, for without great tribulations he could
not have had so great and glorious revelations.
David made psalms; we also will make psalms,
and sing, as well as we can, to the honour of
our Lord God, and to spite and mock the
devil."* Surely, it would be long before our
"songs of deliverance" would end, if we were
mindful of the manifold tokens for good which
our glorious Lord vouchsafes us in the hour
of sadness. How doth he waken us morning
by morning with the turtle voice of love; and
how doth he lull us to our evening repose with
notes of kind compassion! Each hour brings
favours on its wings. He is now become an
abiding companion, that while we tarry with
the stuff we share in the spoil.† Oh, sweet

* Luther, in his *Table-talk.*   † 1 Sam. xxx. 24.

trouble, which brings Jesus nearer to us! Affliction is the black chariot of Christ, in which he rideth to his children. Welcome, shades that herald or accompany our Lord!

3. *In trying times the compassion and sympathy of Jesus become more delightfully the subject of faith and experience.* He ever feels the woes of all the members of his mystical body; in all their afflictions he is afflicted, for he is touched with a feeling of our infirmities. This golden truth becomes most precious to the soul, when, in the midst of losses and crosses, by the Holy Spirit's influence, the power of it is felt in the soul. A confident belief in the fact that Jesus is not an unconcerned spectator of our tribulation, and a confident assurance that he is in the furnace with us, will furnish a downy pillow for our aching head. When the hours limp tardily along, how sweet to reflect that he has felt the weariness of time when sorrows multiplied! When the spirit is wounded by reproach and slander, how comforting to remember that he also once said, "Reproach has broken mine heart!" And, above all, how abundantly full of consolation is the thought that now, even now, he feels for us, and is a living head, sympathising in every pang of his

wounded body. The certainty that Jesus knows
and' feels all that we endure, is one of the
dainties with which afflicted souls are comforted.
More especially is this a cheering thought when
our good is evil spoken of, our motives misrepre-
sented, and our zeal condemned. Then, in
absence of all other balms, this acts as a sovereign remedy for decay of spirit. Give us Christ
with us, and we can afford to smile in the face
of our foes.

"As to appreciation and sympathy, we do
not depend for these on fellow-worms. We
can be content to be unappreciated here, so
long as Christ understands us, and has a
fellow-feeling for us. It is for him we labour.
One of his smiles outweighs all other com-
mendation. To him we look for our reward;
and oh! is it not enough that he has promised
it at his coming? It will not be long to wait.
Do our hearts crave human fellowship and
sympathy? We surely have it in our great
High Priest. Oh, how often should we faint
but for the humanity of our divine Redeemer!
He is bone of our bone, and flesh of our flesh;
yet he has an almighty arm for our deliverance
—human to feel, divine to aid; faithful over
all our failures and imperfections. What need

we more?"* We may fancy we want some other encouragement, but if we know the value of the sympathy of Christ we shall soon find it all-sufficient. We shall think Christ alone to be enough to make a list of friends. The orator spake on so long as Plato listened, thinking one wise man enough audience for him; let us labour on, and hope on, if Jesus be our only helper. Let us, in all time of our tribulation and affliction, content ourselves with one Comforter, if all others fail us. Job had three miserable comforters; better far to have one who is full of pity and able to console. And who can do this so truly as our own most loving Lord Jesus? Moreover, it is not only true that he can do it, but he actually does do it, and that in no small degree, by making apparent the motions of his own heart. He bids us see his breast, as it heaves in unison with ours, and he invites us to read his heart, to see if the same lines of suffering be not written there.

> "I feel at my heart all thy sighs and thy groans,
> For thou art most near me, my flesh and my bones;
> In all thy distresses thy Head feels the pain,
> They all are most needful, not one is in vain."

* Vide *Shady Side*, by a Pastor's Wife.

Thus doth he gently assuage the floods of our swelling grief.

4. *The Lord Jesus is graciously pleased in many cases to give his afflicted saints an unusual insight into the deep things of his word, and an unwonted relish in meditation upon them.* Our losses frequently act toward us as if they had cleared our eyes; at any rate, sickness and sorrow have often been the fingers of Jesus, with which he applied the salve of illuminating grace. Either the understanding is more than ordinarily enlarged, or else the promises are more simply opened up and explained by the Holy Spirit. Who has not observed the supernatural wisdom of the long afflicted saint? Who has not known the fact that the school of sanctified sorrow is that in which are to be found the ripest scholars?

We learn more true divinity by our trials than by our books. The great Reformer said, "Prayer is the best book in my library." He might have added affliction as the next. Sickness is the best Doctor of Divinity in all the world; and trial is the finest exposition of Scripture. This is so inestimable a mark of the love of our blessed Lord that we might almost desire trouble for the sake of it. This proves him to be wise in his hardest dealings towards us, and therefore supremely kind; for is it not kindness which puts us to a little trouble for the sake of an immense advantage, and doth, as it were, take our money out of our coffers at home that it may return again with mighty interest? Jesus is a friend indeed!

5. *If the presence of Jesus be not felt and realised, he nevertheless sustains the soul by a secret and unseen energy which he imparts to the spirit.* Jesus is not always absent when he is unseen; but, on the contrary, he is frequently near to us when we have no assurance of his presence. Many times the man who pours oil upon the flame of our comfort .to prevent the quenching of the enemy, is behind the wall, where we cannot perceive him.* The Lord hath a heart which is ever full of affection towards his elect, and when he seems to leave them he is still sustaining them. Patience under withdrawals of his sensible presence is a sure sign of his real, though secret presence, in the soul. A blind man is really nourished by the food he eats, even though he cannot see it; so, when by the blindness of our spiritual vision, we are unable to discern the Saviour, yet his

* See Parable in Bunvan's *Pilgrim's Progress.*

grace sustains our strength and keeps us alive
in famine. The intense desire after Jesus, the
struggling of the soul with doubts and fears,
and the inward panting of the whole being after
the living God, prove beyond a doubt that Jesus
is at work in the soul, though he may be concealed from the eye of faith.   How should it,
therefore, be a matter of wonder that secretly
he should be able to afford support to the sinking saint, even at seasons when his absence is
bemoaned with lamentations and tears?   " The
real gracious influences and effects of his favour
may be continued, upholding, strengthening,
and carrying on the soul still to obey and fear
God, whilst he yet conceals his favour; for
when Christ complained, *My God, my God,
why hast thou forsaken me ?* (when as great an
eclipse in regard of the light of God's countenance was upon his spirit, as was upon the earth
in regard to the sun) yet he never more obeyed
God, was never more strongly supported than
at that time, for then he was *obeying to the
death.*"*   God's favour most assuredly rests on
his children's hearts and strengthens their spirits,
when the light and comfort of it are shut out
from their perceptions. Christ puts his children

* Goodwin's *Child of Light,* &c.

upon his lap, and healeth their wounds when, by reason of their swooning condition, they feel not his hand, and see not his smile. It is said, "All is not gold that glitters;" certainly, we may alter the proverb, for it is true spiritually that all gold does not glitter; but this dimness does not affect its intrinsic worth and value.

The old theologians used to say, " Grace may be in the heart in *esse et operari,* when not in *cognosci;* it may have a being and a working there when not in thy apprehension." Let us praise our bounteous Lord for unseen favours, and let us love our Lord Jesus for his mercies imparted in silence, unobserved.

6. *After long seasons of depression Jesus becomes sweetly the consolation of Israel by removing our load in a manner at once singularly felicitous and marvellously efficacious.* It may be that the nature or design of the trial prevents us from enjoying any comfortable sense of our Lord's love during the time of its endurance; in such cases the grace of our Lord Jesus discovers itself in the hour of our escape. If we do not see our Lord in the prison, we shall meet him on the threshold in that day which shall see him break the gates of brass and cut the bars of iron in sunder. Marvellous are

his works in the day wherein he brings us out of the house of bondage. Halyburton, after escape from a cloud and desertion, thus broke silence to a friend—"Oh, what a terrible conflict had I yesterday! but now I can say 'I have fought the good fight; I have kept the faith.' Now he has filled my mouth with a new song, 'Jehovah Jireh—in the mount of the Lord.' Praise, praise is comely to the upright. Shortly I shall get a better sight of God than ever I have had, and be more meet to praise him than ever. Oh, the thoughts of an incarnate God are sweet and ravishing! And oh, how do I wonder at myself that I do not love him more—that I do not admire him more. Oh, that I could honour him! What a wonder that I enjoy such composure under all my bodily troubles! Oh, what a mercy that I have the use of my reason till I have declared his goodness to me!" Thus it seems that the sun is all the brighter for having been awhile hidden from us. And here the reader must pardon the writer if he introduces a personal narrative, which is to him a most memorable proof of the loving-kindness of the Lord. Such an opportunity of recording my Lord's goodness may never occur again to me; and therefore now, while my soul is warm with gratitude for so recent a deliverance, let me lay aside the language of an author, and speak for myself, as I should tell the story to my friends in conversation. It may be egotism to weave one's own sorrows into the warp and woof of this meditation; but if the heart prompts the act, and the motions of the Holy Spirit are not contrary thereto, I think I may venture for this once to raise an Ebenezer in public, and rehearse the praise of Jesus at the setting up thereof. Egotism is not so frightful a thing as ungrateful silence; certainly it is not more contemptible than mock humility. Right or wrong, here followeth my story.

On a night which time will never erase from my memory, large numbers of my congregation were scattered, many of them wounded and some killed, by the malicious act of wicked men. Strong amid danger, I battled the storm, nor did my spirit yield to the overwhelming pressure while my courage could reassure the wavering or confirm the bold. But when, like a whirlwind, the destruction had overpast, when the whole of its devastation was visible to my eye, who can conceive the anguish of my spirit? I refused to be comforted, tears were my meat by day, and dreams my terror by night. I felt as I had never felt before. "My thoughts were all a case of knives," cutting my heart in pieces, until a kind of stupor of grief ministered a mournful medicine to me. I could have truly said, "I am not mad, but surely I have had enough to madden me, if I should indulge in meditation on it." I sought and found a solitude which seemed congenial to me. I could tell my griefs to the flowers, and the dews could weep with me. Here my mind lay, like a wreck upon the sand, incapable of its usual motion. I was in a strange land, and a stranger in it. My Bible, once my daily food, was but a hand to lift the sluices of my woe. Prayer yielded no balm to me; in fact, my soul was like an infant's soul, and I could not rise to the dignity of supplication. "Broken in pieces all asunder," my thoughts, which had been to me like a cup of delights, were like pieces of broken glass, the piercing and cutting miseries of my pilgrimage:—

> "The tumult of my thoughts
>   Doth but enlarge my woe;
> My spirit languishes, my heart
>   Is desolate and low.
> With every morning light
>   My sorrow new begins:
> Look on my anguish and my pain,
>   And pardon all my sins."

Then came " the slander of many "—barefaced
fabrications, libellous slanders, and barbarous
accusations. These alone might have scooped
out the last drop of consolation from my cup of
happiness, but the worst had come to the worst,
and the utmost malice of the enemy could do no
more. Lower they cannot sink who are already
in the nethermost depths. Misery itself is the
guardian of the miserable. All things combined
to keep me for a season in the darkness where
neither sun nor moon appeared. I had hoped
for a gradual return to peaceful consciousness,
and patiently did I wait for the dawning light.
But it came not as I had desired, for He who
doeth for us exceeding abundantly above what we
can ask or think sent me a happier answer to
my requests. I had striven to think of the
unmeasurable love of Jehovah, as displayed in the
sacrifice of Calvary; I had endeavoured to muse
upon the glorious character of the exalted Jesus ;
but I found it impossible to collect my thoughts
in the quiver of meditation, or, indeed, to place
them anywhere but with their points in my
wounded spirit, or else at my feet, trodden down
in an almost childish thoughtlessness. On a
sudden, like a flash of lightning from the sky,
my soul returned unto me. The burning lava

of my brain cooled in an instant. The throb-bings of my brow were still; the cool wind of comfort fanned my cheek, which had been scorched in the furnace. I was free, the iron fetter was broken in pieces, my prison door was open, I leaped for joy of heart. On wings of a dove my spirit mounted to the stars,—yea, beyond them. Whither did it wing its flight? and where did it sing its song of gratitude? It was at the feet of Jesus, whose name had charmed its fears, and placed an end to its mourning. The name—the precious name of Jesus, was like Ithuriel's spear, bringing back my soul to its own right and happy state. I was a man again, and what is more, a believer. The garden in which I stood became an Eden to me, and the spot was then most solemnly con-secrated in my most grateful memory. Happy hour. Thrice blessed Lord, who thus in an instant delivered me from the rock of my despair, and slew the vulture of my grief! Before I told to others the glad news of my recovery, my heart was melodious with song, and my tongue endea-voured tardily to express the music. Then did I give to my Well-Beloved a song touching my Well-Beloved; and oh! with what rapture did my soul flash forth its praises! but all—all were

to the honour of Him, the first and the last, the
Brother born for adversity, the Deliverer of the
captive, the Breaker of my fetters, the Restorer
of my soul. Then did I cast my burden upon
the Lord; I left my ashes and did array myself
in the garments of praise, while He did anoint
me with fresh oil. I could have riven the very
firmament to get at Him, to cast myself at his
feet, and lie there bathed in the tears of joy and
love. Never since the day of my conversion had
I known so much of his infinite excellence, never
had my spirit leaped with such unutterable delight. Scorn, tumult, and woe seemed less than
nothing for his sake. I girded up my loins to
run before his chariot, and shout forth his glory,
for my soul was absorbed in the one idea of his
glorious exaltation and divine compassion.

After a declaration of the exceeding grace of
God towards me, made to my dearest kindred
and friends, I essayed again to preach. The
task which I had dreaded to perform was another means of comfort, and I can truly declare
that the words of that morning were as much
the utterance of my inner man as if I had been
standing before the bar of God. The text
selected runs thus—" Wherefore God also hath
highly exalted Him, and given him a name which

is above every name: that at the name of Jesus
every knee should bow, of things in heaven, and
things in earth, and things under the earth; and
that every tongue should confess that Jesus
Christ is Lord, to the glory of God the Father."
May I trouble the reader with some of the
utterances of the morning, for they were the
unveilings of my own experience.

When the mind is intensely set upon one
object, however much it may by divers calamities
be tossed to and fro, it invariably returns to the
place which it had chosen to be its dwelling
place. Ye have noticed it in the case of David.
When the battle had been won by his warriors,
they returned flushed with victory. David's
mind had doubtless suffered much perturbation
in the meantime; he had dreaded alike the
effects of victory and of defeat; but have you not
noticed how his thoughts in one moment returned to the darling object of his affections?
"Is the young man Absalom safe?" said he, as
if it mattered not what else had occurred, if his
beloved son were but secure! So, beloved, is
it with the Christian. In the midst of calamities, whether they be the wreck of nations,
the crash of empires, the heaving of revolutions

or the scourge of war, the great question which he asks himself, and asks of others too, is this— "Is Christ's kingdom safe?"   In his own personal afflictions his chief anxiety is—Will God be glorified, and will his honour be increased by it?   If it be so, says he, although I be but as smoking flax, yet if the sun is not dimmed I will rejoice; and though I be a bruised reed, if the pillars of the temple are unbroken, what matters it that my reed is bruised?   He finds it sufficient consolation, in the midst of all the breaking in pieces which he endures, to think that Christ's throne stands fast and firm, and that though the earth hath rocked beneath *his* feet, yet Christ standeth on a rock which never can be moved.   Some of these feelings, I think, have crossed our minds.   Amidst much tumult and divers rushing to and fro of troublous thoughts, our souls have returned to the dearest object of our desires, and we have found it no small consolation, after all, to say, "It matters not what shall become of us; God hath highly exalted *him*, and given *him* a name which is above every name; that at the name of *Jesus* every knee should bow."

Thus is the thought of the love of Jesus in his delivering grace most indelibly impressed upon my memory; and the fact that this experience is to me the most memorable crisis of my life, must be my apology for narrating it—an apology which I trust the indulgent reader will accept.

7. Although it may be thought that we have reached the legitimate boundary of our subject, we cannot refrain from adding, that *Jesus renders himself peculiarly precious by the gracious manner in which, by bestowing an amazing increase of joy, he entirely obliterates every scar which the sword of adversity may have left in our flesh.* As the joy that a man child is born into the world is said to destroy the remembrance of the previous travail of the mother, so the glorious manifestations of the Lord do wipe out all the bitter memories of the trials of the past. After the showers have fallen from the dark and lowering skies, how pleasant is the breath of nature, how delightfully the sun peers through the thick trees, transforming all the rain-drops to sparkling gems; and even so, after a shower of troubles, it is marvellous to feel the divine refreshings of the Lord of hosts right speedily transforming every tear into a jewel of delight, and satisfying the soul with balmy peace. The soul's calm is deep and profound when the tempest has fully spent itself, for the same Jesus

who in the storm said, "It is I," will comfort his people with royal dainties when the winds have been hushed to slumber. At the heels of our sorrows we find our joys. Great ebbs are succeeded by great floods, and sharp winters are followed by bright summers. This is the sweet fruit of Christ's love,—he will not have his brethren so much as remember their sorrows with regret; he so works in them and towards them that their light affliction is forgotten in happy contemplation upon his eternal weight of glory. Happy is that unhappiness which brings with it such surpassing privileges, and more than excellent the grace which makes it so. We need a poet to sing the sweet uses of adversity. An ancient writer, whose words we are about to quote, has unconsciously produced a sonnet in prose upon this subject:—

" *Stars* shine brightest in the darkest night; *torches* are better for the beating; *grapes* come not to the proof till they come to the press; *spices* smell sweetest when pounded; *young trees* root the faster for shaking; *vines* are the better for bleeding; *gold* looks the brighter for scouring; *glow-worms* glisten best in the dark; *juniper* smells sweetest in the fire; *pomander* becomes most fragrant from chafing;

the *palm-tree* proves the better for pressing *camomile* the more you tread it the more you spread it : such is the condition of all God's children, they are most triumphant when they are most tempted ; most glorious when most afflicted ; most in the favour of God when least in man's esteem. As their conflicts, so their conquests ; as their tribulations, so their triumphs. True salamanders, they live best in the furnace of persecution ; so that *heavy afflictions* are the best benefactors to *heavenly affections*. Where afflictions hang heaviest, corruptions hang loosest ; and grace that is hid in nature, as sweet water in rose leaves, is most fragrant when the fire of affliction is put under to distil it out." *

Let each reader inquire whether this is in harmony with his experience, and if it be so, let him testify to his tried brethren that he has tasted and handled of the goodness of the Lord Jesus, and has found him full of grace to help, and power to comfort. Open thy mouth as wide in praise as thou didst in prayer, and let thy gratitude be as lasting as his love.

But if the reader cannot bear witness to the faithfulness of the Lord in the day of adversity,

* Samuel Clerk, preface to *Martyrology*.

let him tremble. If his religion has forsaken
him in his distress, let him at once doubt its
character. That is not from heaven which cannot endure the fire. If the promises afford thee
no comfort in thy trials, if thy faith doth utterly
fail, and thou findest thy profession tottering
about thine ears, look well to thyself that thou
be not deceived. We dare not say that there is
no grace in the man who finds no comfort in
the Lord in the day of evil, but we do say, with
much earnestness, there is very grave cause for
suspicion. The following sentences from the
pen of William Gurnall deserve much pondering,
they will raise a vital question in the mind of
those who have never felt the sweetness of the
promises in the hour of need :—" Promises are
like the clothes we wear. If there be heat in
the body to warm them, they warm us, but if
there be none, they give none. So where there
is living faith, the promise will afford warm
comfort; but on a dead, unbelieving heart, it
lies cold and ineffectual : it has no more effect
than pouring a cordial down the throat of a
corpse. Again, the promises do not throw out
comfort as fire throws out heat; for then we
should only need to go to them in order to be
warmed : their heat is like the fire in the flint,

which must be struck out by force, and this force can only be applied by faith." *

There is another explanation of the fact that a professor in trial sometimes finds no comfort in the promises; and as it is a little more lenient, we add it here, and desire all such persons to judge for themselves. It may be that thou hast neglected communion, and therefore‧ thy troubles weigh heavily. When a bucket is let down into a deep well, and is under the water, it is easily wound up, and seems to be light, but when once it is drawn out of the water its weight becomes excessive: it is so with our sorrows—as long as we keep them submerged in God and fellowship they are light enough; but once consider them apart from the Lord, and they become a grievous and intolerable burden. Faith will have to tug in earnest to lift our adversities when we stand alone without our Lord; want of communion will rob the promises of their comfort, and load our griefs with weights of iron.

It seems, then, that thou hast one of two faults to find with thyself,—either thou art dead, and so unable to feel the heat and comfort of the Lord's presence; or else thou hast been inactive,

* *Christian Armour.*

not improving the means whereby the fellowship of the Master may be realised. Search thine heart and know the reason. "Are the consolations of God small with thee? Is there any secret thing with thee?"* Look to thyself, for it may be thy soul is in an evil plight, and if so, be sure to give good heed unto it. Go to the Lord at once, and ask a fresh supply of life and grace. Do not seek to mimic the joy of believers, but strive for the reality of it. Rely not on thine own power. Trim thy lamp with heavenly oil. If the fire of the Roman vestals were ever extinguished, they dare not light it except at the sun; be sure that thou do not kindle a flame in thy heart with strange fire. Get renewal where thou didst get conversion, but be sure to get it, and at once. May the Holy Spirit help thee.

* Job xv. 11.

TO THE UNCONVERTED READER.

Poor sinner, how great a difference is there between thee and the believer! and how apparent is this difference when in trouble! You have trials, but you have no God to flee to; your afflictions are frequently of the sharpest kind, but you have no promises to blunt their edge; you are in the furnace, but you are without that divine companion who can prevent the fire from hurting you. To the child of God adversity brings many blessings—to you it is empty-handed; to him there ariseth light in the darkness—to you there is the darkness but no arising of the light; you have all its miseries, but none of its benefits. How dreary must your heart feel when lover and friend are put far from you, when your hopes are withered, and your joys are removed! You have no Christ to cheer you; he is not the recompence of your grief; he is not Jehovah Jireh to you. You have no Almighty arms beneath you, no

Eternal God to be your refuge, no Anointed One to be your shield. You must bear your sorrows alone, or, if any attempt to help you, their strength is incompetent for the task.

Oh, wretched man! for ever enduring the thorn, but never reaching the throne; in the floods, but not washed; burning in the fire, but not refined; brayed in the mortar, but not cleansed of foolishness; suffering, but unsanctified. What misery to have no foundation in the day of the tempest, no covert from the wind, no shelter from the storm! The saint can bear a world of trouble when the strength of Israel doth brace him with omnipotence; but thou, without the support of the Most High, art crushed before the moth, and overwhelmed when evil getteth hold upon thee. Thy present trials are too heavy for thee; what wilt thou do in the swellings of Jordan? In the day when the drops shall have become a torrent, and the small rain of tribulation has given place to the waterspouts of vengeance, how wilt thou endure the unutterable wrath of the Lamb?

Lay this to thy heart, and may the Lord enable thee to cast the burden of thy sin upon the crucified Saviour; then shalt thou have boldness to cast thy griefs there also.

X.

Jesus hiding Himself.

"Thou didst hide thy face, and I was troubled."-
Ps. xxx. 7.

"Why dost thou shade thy lovely face? oh, why
Doth that eclipsing hand so long deny
The sunshine of thy soul-enlivening eye?

"Without that light, what light remains in me?
Thou art my life, my way, my light; in thee
I live, I move, and by thy beams I see.

"Thou art my life; if thou but turn away,
My life's a thousand deaths: thou art my way;
Without thee, Lord, I travel not, but stray.

"My light thou art; without thy glorious sight,
Mine eyes are darken'd with perpetual night.
My God, thou art my way, my life, my light."

QUARLES.

THE Lord Jesus will never remove his love
from any one of the objects of his choice. The
names of his redeemed are written on his hands
and graven on his side; they are designed for
eternal felicity, and to that blessed consumma-

tion his hand and his heart are unitedly resolved to bring them. The meanest lamb of the blood-bought flock shall be preserved securely by the "strength of Israel" unto the day of his appearing, and shall, through every season of tribulation and distress, continue to be beloved of the Lord. Yet this does not prevent the great Shepherd from hiding himself for a season, when his people are rebellious. Though the Redeemer's *grace* shall never be utterly removed, yet there shall be partial withdrawals of his *presence*, whereby our joys shall be dimmed, and our evidences darkened. He will sometimes say, "I will go and return unto my place, until they acknowledge their offences which they have committed against me;" and at other seasons, for a trial of their faith, he will "for a small moment" hide himself from them.

In proportion as the Master's presence is delightful, his absence is mournful. Dark is the night which is caused by the setting of such a sun. No blow of Providence can ever wound so sorely as this. A blasted crop is as nothing compared with an absent Redeemer; yea, sickness and the approach of death are preferable to the departure of Emmanuel. Skin for skin, yea, all that a man hath will he give

for his life; and more than that would the sincere disciple be prepared to surrender for a renewal of his Lord's presence. "Oh, that I were
as in months past, as in the days when God
preserved me; when his candle shined upon my
head, and when by his light I walked through
darkness!" Such will be the sorrowful complaint of the spirit when groping its way through
the darkness of desertion. "God's hiding himself, though but for trial's sake, will so trouble
a Christian that he will quickly be a burden to
himself, and fear round about, as it is said of
Pashur.* It will make him weary of the night,
and weary of the day; weary of his own house,
and weary of God's house; weary of mirth,
and account it madness; weary of riches and
honours; yea, if it continue long, it will
make him weary of life itself, and wish for
death."† The effect is always deplorable during
the time of its duration, but the cause of it is
not always the same. There are divers reasons
for apparent desertions; we will enter upon that
interesting subject in the next chapter, and
in the present meditation we shall chiefly consider the ill effects of the absence of Christ

* Jer. xx. 3.
† Lockyer on *Christ's Communion.*

We would carefully distinguish between those withdrawals which are evidences of an offence given to our Lord, and those which are designed to be trials of our faith. Our experience under different varieties of forsakings will vary, and the following remarks, although in the main applicable to all desertions, are only intended in their detail to refer to those which are brought about by our transgressions; and even then it is not to be imagined that each case will exhibit every point which we shall now observe. Here we specially refer to those hidings of God's countenance which are brought upon us as a fatherly chastisement. And we do not here dwell upon the ultimate and blessed effects of the temporary forsakings of God, but are only to be understood to refer to the ills which, during the time, beset the soul.

Holy men may be left to walk in darkness. "Sometimes Christians are guilty of acting a part which is *offensive* to their dear Saviour, and therefore he withdraws from them. Darkness spreads itself over them, thick clouds interpose between him and their souls, and they see not his smiling face. This was the case with the Church when she was inclined unto carnal ease, rather than to rise and give her Beloved entrance. He

quickened her desires after the enjoyment of his
company, by an effectual touch upon her heart;
but he withdrew, departed, and left her to bewail her folly in her sinful neglect. Upon this
her bowels were troubled: she arose and sought
him; but she found him not. It is just with
him to hide himself from us, if we are indifferent
about the enjoyments of his delightful presence,
and give us occasion to confess our ingratitude
to him, by the loss we sustain in consequence of
it. His love *in itself* passes under no vicissi-
tude; it is always the same; that is our
security; but the *manifestation* of it to our
souls, from which our peace, comfort, and joy
spring, may be interrupted through our negligence, sloth, and sin. A sense of it, when it is
so, may well break our hearts; for there is no
ingratitude in the world like it."* We would
not be understood to teach that God punishes
his people for sin in a legal sense; this would
be a slur upon his justice; for, seeing that he
has fully punished their sin in Christ, to inflict
any penalty upon them would be demanding a
double punishment for one offence, which were
unjust. Let the chastisements be understood in
a paternal sense as correctives, and the truth is

* Brine.

gained. Sin will be chastened in the elect. "You only have I known out of all the nations of the earth, therefore, I will punish you for your iniquities." If we walk contrary to him, he will walk contrary to us. The promise of communion is only appended to obedience. "He that hath my commandments, and keepeth them, he it is that loveth me: and he that loveth me shall be loved of my Father, and I will love him, and will manifest myself to him." * Now if we walk scandalously, and indulge in known sin, no wonder though the Lord withdraw himself from us. *The joy* of his salvation must not rest with his erring ones, though the salvation itself is ever theirs. Alas for us, that our corruption should so frequently mar our communion!

Many times between conversion and the rest of eternity the Christian, through sin, will have to walk through a salt land, not inhabited, and find the songs of the Canticles hushed by the wail of the Lamentations. Yet we would fain believe that there are some who have but little cause to write their history in black letters, for their life has been one continued calm communion, with only here and there a hurried

* John xiv. 21.

interruption. We are far from believing that
the despondency, coldness, and misery produced
by a loss of the visible love of Christ ought to
make up any considerable part of the biography
of a Christian. That they do so in many cases,
we readily admit, but that it *should* be so we
never can allow. Those men who glory in what
they proudly call a deep experience,—by which
they mean great wanderings from the path
which Enoch trod when he walked with God,—
are very prone to exalt the infirmities of the
Lord's people into infallible and admirable proofs
of grace. To them an absent Christ is fine stock
in trade for a sermon upon their own superlative
wisdom; and a heart which mourns abundantly,
but loves most scantily, is to them what perfection is to the Arminian. As if the weeds of
the field were precious plants because they will
grow in good soil; as if the freckles on the face
of beauty were to be imitated by all who desire
to attain to loveliness; or as if the rocks in the
sea were the very cause of its fulness. The
deepest experience in the world is that which
deals only with the Lord Jesus Christ, and is so
sick of man, and of all within him, and so confident in the Lord Jesus, that it casts the whole
weight of the sin and sinfulness of the soul

entirely upon the Redeemer, and so rejoicing in his all-sufficiency, looks above the wants and woes of its own evil and ruined nature, to the completion of the new man in Christ Jesus. That eminent preacher, the late Rowland Hill, has well said, "I do not like Christians to live always complaining; but I do not mind how much they complain if they carry their corruptions to Jesus." This is forgotten by many; but those who are careful to practise it will have many causes for gladness.

Blessed be God, the green pastures and the still waters, the shepherd's crook and pleasant company, are objects which are quite as familiar to the believer's mind as the howling wilderness and the brandished rod—

> "The men of grace have found
> Glory begun below;
> Celestial fruits on earthly ground,
> From faith and hope do grow."

Yet, to the believer's grief, seasons of absence do occur, and those, alas, too frequently. It is our business, as the Holy Spirit shall enable us, very briefly to consider the subject of *apparent desertion on account of sin*, and may He make it useful to us.

We shall now proceed to review the mischiefs

which attend upon suspended communion. The effects of the withdrawal of the face of Jesus are the outward signs shadowing forth the secret sickness of the heart, which such a condition necessarily engenders. Although it be not fatal, yet is it exceedingly hurtful to miss the company of the Lord. As plants thrive not when the light is kept from them, but become blanched and unhealthy, so souls deprived of the light of God's countenance are unable to maintain the verdure of their piety or the strength of their graces. What a loss is a lost Christ!

During this doleful season *the believer's evidences are eclipsed;* he is in grievous doubt concerning his own condition before God; his faith is become weak, his hope well-nigh buried, and his love cold and languid. The graces which, like planetary stars, once shone upon him with light and radiance, are now dark and cheerless, for the sun has departed, the source of their light is concealed in clouds. Evidences without Christ are like unlit candles, which afford no light; like fig-trees with leaves only, devoid of fruit; like purses without gold, and like barns without wheat: they have great capabilities of comfort, but without Jesus they are emptiness itself. Evidences are like conduit-pipes—they are sometimes the channels of living water, but if the supply from the fountain-head be cut off from them, their waters utterly fail. That man will die of thirst who has no better spring to look to than an empty pitcher of evidences. Ishmael would have perished in the wilderness if his only hope had been in the bottle which his mother brought out with her from the tent of Abraham; and assuredly without direct supplies from the gracious hands of the Lord Jesus, the saints would soon be in an ill plight. Unless the God of our graces be ever at the root of them, they will prove like Jonah's gourd, which withered away when he was most in need of it. In this condition we shall find ourselves, if we lose the presence of the Lord Jesus; we shall be racked with fears, and tormented with doubts, without possessing that sovereign cordial with which in better days our sorrows have been allayed. We shall find all the usual sources of our consolation dried up, and it will be in vain for us to expect a single drop from them. Ahab sent Obadiah upon an idle errand, when in the time of great drought he said, "Go into the land unto all fountains of water, and unto all brooks : peradventure we may find grass to save the horses and mules alive, that we lose not all the beasts ;" for it was the presence and prayer of Elijah which alone could procure the rain to supply their wants; and if we, when we have lost our Master's society, seek to obtain comfort in past experiences and time-worn evidences, we shall have to weep with bitter tears because of a disappointed hope. We must regain the society of Christ, if we would restore the lustre of our assurance. An absent Saviour and joyous confidence are seldom to be spoken of together.

We know, however, that some professors can maintain a confident carriage when the presence of the Lord is withholden; they are as content without him as with him, and as happy under his frown as when in the sunshine of his smile. Between the outward appearances of strong faith and strong delusion there is frequently so little difference that the presumptuous boaster is often as highly esteemed as the assured believer: nevertheless in their inner nature there is an essential distinction. Faith believes on Jesus when his comfortable promise is not vouchsafed; but it does not render the soul indifferent to the sweetness of his society.

Faith says, "I believe Him when I do not feel
his love manifest towards me, but my very persuasion of his faithfulness makes me pant for
the light of his countenance;" but vain presumption exclaims, "Away with evidences and manifestations, I am a vessel of mercy, and therefore
I am secure; why should I trouble myself about
grace or graces? I have made up my mind
that all is right, and I will not break my slum-
bers whoever may seek to alarm me." Happy
is the man whose faith can see in the thick
darkness, and whose soul can live in the year
of drought; but that man is not far from a
curse who slights the fellowship of the Lord,
and esteems his smile to be a vain thing. It
is an ill sign if any of us are in a contented
state when we are forsaken of the Lord; it is
not faith, but wicked indifference, which makes
us careless concerning communion with Him.
And yet how often have we had cause to lament
our want of concern; how frequently have we
groaned because we could not weep as we ought
for the return of our husband who had hidden
himself from us!

When enveloped in the mists of desertion,
we lose all those pleasant visions of the future
which once were the jewels in the crown of our

life. We have no climbings to the top of
Pisgah; no prospects of the better land; no
earnests of pure delight; no foretastes of the
riches of glory, and no assurance of our title to
the goodly land beyond Jordan. It is as much
as we can do to preserve ourselves from despair;
we cannot aspire to any confidence of future
glory. It is a contested point with us whether
we are not ripening for hell. We fear that we
never knew a Saviour's love, but have been all
along deceivers and deceived; the pit of hell
yawns before us, and we are in great straits to
maintain so much as a bare hope of escape
from it. We had once despised others for what
we thought to be foolish doubts, but now that
we ourselves are ready to slip with our feet, we
think far more of the lamps which we despised*
when we were at ease, and would be willing to
change places with them if we might have as
good an opinion of our own sincerity as we have
of theirs. We would give anything for half a
grain of hope, and would be well content to be
the meanest of the sheep, if we might but have
a glimpse of the Shepherd.

*The native buoyancy of spirit which distin-
guishes the heir of heaven is in a great measure*

* Job xii. 5.

removed by the departure of the Lord. The believer is spiritually a man who can float in the deepest waters, and mount above the highest billows; he is able, when in a right condition, to keep his head above all the water-floods which may invade his peace: but see his Lord depart, and he sinks in deep mire, where there is no standing—all the waves and the billows have gone over him. Troubles which were light as a feather to him, are now like mountains of lead; he is afraid of every dog that snarls at him, and trembles at every shadow. He who in his better days could cut down an acre of foemen at a stroke, is affrighted at the approach of a single adversary. He whose heart was fixed so that he was not afraid of evil tidings, is now alarmed at every report. Once he could hurl defiance to earth and hell united, and could laugh at persecution, slander, and reproach, but he is now as timid as a deer, and trembles at every phantom that threatens him. His daily cares, which once he loved to cast upon the Lord, and counted but as the small dust of the balance are now borne upon the shoulders of his own anxiety, and are a load intolerably oppressive. He was once clothed in armour of proof, and was not afraid of sword or spear; but now that he hath lost his Master's presence, such is his nakedness that every thorn pierces him, and every briar fetches blood from him; yea, his spirit is pierced through and through with anxious thoughts which once would have been his scorn. How are the mighty fallen; how are the princes taken in a net, and the nobles cast as the mire of the street! He who could do all things can now do nothing; and he who could rejoice in deep distress is now mourning in the midst of blessings. He is like a chariot without wheels or horses, a harp without strings, a river without water, and a sail without wind. No songs and music now; his harp is hanging upon the willows. It is vain to ask of him a song, for "the chief musician upon his stringed instruments" has ceased to lead the choir. Can the spouse be happy when she has grieved her bridegroom and lost his company? No; she will go weeping through every street of the city, until she can again embrace him; her joy shall cease until again she shall behold his countenance.

It is frequently an effect of divine withdrawal that *the mind becomes grovelling and earthly*. Covetousness and love of riches attain a sad preponderance. The Lord will hide himself if we love the world; and, on the other hand, his absence, which is intended for far other purposes, will sometimes, through the infirmity of our nature, increase the evil which it is intended to cure. When the Lord Jesus is present in the soul, and is beheld by it, ambition, covetousness, and worldliness flee apace; for such is his apparent glory that earthly objects fade away like the stars in noonday; but when He is gone, they will show their false glitter, as the stars, however small, will shine at midnight. Find a Christian whose soul cleaveth to the dust, and who careth for the things of this life, and you have found one who has had but little manifest fellowship with Jesus. As sure as ever we undervalue the Saviour's company, we shall set too high an estimate upon the things of this life, and then bitterness and disappointment are at the door.

At this juncture, moreover, *the great enemy of souls is peculiarly busy;* our extremity is his opportunity, and he is not backward in availing himself of it. Now that Zion's Captain has removed his royal presence, the evil one concludes that he may deal with the soul after the devices of his own malicious heart. Accordingly, with many a roar and hideous yell, he seeks to affright the saint; and if this suffices not, he lifts his arm of terror and hurls his fiery dart. As lions prowl by night, so doth he seek his prey in the darkness. The saint is now more than usually beneath his power; every wound from the envenomed dart festers and gangrenes more easily than at other times; while to the ear of the troubled one the howlings of Satan seem to be a thousand times louder than he had ever heard before. Doubts of our calling, our election, and adoption, fly into our souls like the flies into Pharaoh's palace, and all the while the grim fiend covers us with a darkness that may be felt. Had he attacked us in our hours of communion, we would soon have made him feel the metal of our swords; but our arm is palsied, and our strokes are like blows from the hand of a child, rather exciting his laughter than his fear. Oh for the days when we put to flight the armies of the aliens! would to God we could again put on strength, and by the arm of the Lord o'erthrow the hosts of hell! Like Samson we sigh for the hair in which our great strength lieth; and when the shouts of the vaunting Philistines are in our ears, we cry for the strength which once laid our enemies "heaps upon heaps" by thousands. We must again enjoy the manifest presence of the Lord, or we shall have hard work to lift up a standard against the enemy.

It is not an unusual circumstance to find *sin return upon the conscience* at this critical season.

> " Now the heart, disclos'd, betrays
> All its hid disorders;
> Enmity to God's right ways,
> Blasphemies and murders .
> Malice, envy, lust, and pride,
> Thoughts obscene and filthy
> Sores corrupt and putrified,
> No part sound or healthy.

> " All things to promote our fall,
> Show a mighty fitness;
> Satan will accuse withal,
> And the conscience witness;
> Foes within, and foes without,
> Wrath, and law, and terrors;
> Rash presumption, timid doubt,
> Coldness, deadness, errors." *

When Israel had the sea before them, and the mountains on either hand, their old masters thought it a fit time to pursue them; and now that the believer is in great straits, his former sins rise up to afflict him and cause him renewed sorrow: then, moreover, our sins become more formidable to us than they were

* Hart.

at our first repentance; when we were in Egypt
we saw not the Egyptians upon horses and
in chariots—they only appeared as our task-
masters with their whips; but now we see
them clad in armour, as mighty ones, full of
wrath, bearing the instruments of death. The
pangs of sin, when the Lord forsakes us, are
frequently as vehement as at first conversion,
and in some cases far more so; for a conviction
of having grieved a Saviour whose love we have
once known, and whose faithfulness we have
proved, will cause grief of a far more poignant
character than any other order of conviction.
Men who have been in a room full of light,
think the darkness more dense than it is considered to be by those who have long walked in
it; so pardoned men think more of the evil of
sin than those who never saw the light.

*The deserted soul has little or no liberty in
prayer:* he pursues the habit from a sense of
duty, but it yields him no delight. *In* prayer
the spirit is dull and languid, and *after* it the
soul feels no more refreshment than is afforded
to the weary by a sleep disturbed with dreams
and broken with terrors. He is unable to
enter into the spirit of worship; it is rather an
attempt at devotion than the attainment of it.

As when the bird with broken wing strives to
mount, and rises a little distance, but speedily
falls to the ground, where it painfully limps
and flaps its useless pinion—so does the believer
strive to pray, but fails to reach the height of
his desires, and sorrowfully gropes his way
with anguishing attempts to soar on high.
A pious man once said,—" Often when in
prayer I feel as if I held between my palms the
fatherly heart of God and the bloody hand of
the Lord Jesus; for I remind the one of his
divine love and inconceivable mercies, and I
grasp the other by his promise, and strive to
hold him fast and say, ' I will not let thee go
except thou bless me.' " * But when left by
the Lord such blessed nearness of access is impossible; there is no answer of peace, no token
for good, no message of love. The ladder is
there, but no angels are ascending and descending upon it; the key of prayer is in the hand,
but it turns uselessly within the lock. Prayer
without the Lord's presence is like a bow without a string, or an arrow without a head.

The Bible, too, that great granary of the finest
wheat, becomes a place of emptiness, where
hunger looks in vain for food : in reading it,

* Gen. xxxii. 26.

the distressed soul will think it to be all threatenings and no promises; he will see the terrors
written in capitals, and the consolations printed
in a type so small as to be almost illegible.
Read the Word he must, for it has become as
necessary as his food; but enjoy it he cannot,
for its savour has departed. As well might we
try to read in the dark as to get joy from Holy
Scripture unless Christ shall pour his gracious
light upon the page. As the richest field yields
no harvest without rain, so the book of revelation brings forth no comfort without the dew
of the Spirit.

Our intercourse with Christian friends, once
so enriching, is rendered profitless, or at best
its only usefulness is to reveal our poverty
by enabling us to compare our own condition
with that of other saints. We cannot minister unto their edification, nor do we feel that
their company is affording us its usual enjoyment; and it may be we turn away from them,
longing to see His face whose absence we
deplore. This barrenness overspreads all the
ordinances of the Lord's house, and renders
them all unprofitable. When Christ is with the
Christian, the means of grace are like flowers
in the sunshine, smelling fragrantly and smiling

beauteously; but without Christ they are like flowers by night, their fountains of fragrance are sealed by the darkness. The songs of the temple shall be howlings in that day, and her solemn feasts as mournful as her days of fasting. The sacred supper which, when Christ is at the table, is a feast of fat things, without Him is as an empty vine. The holy convocation without him is as the gatherings of the market, and the preaching of his Word as the shoutings of the streets. We hear, but the outward ear is the only part affected; we sing, but

> " Hosannahs languish on our tongues,
> And our devotion dies."

We even attempt to preach (if this be our calling), but we speak in heavy chains, full of grievous bondage. We pant for God's house, and then, after we have entered it, we are but the worse. We have thirsted for the well, and having reached it we find it empty.

Very probably *we shall grow censorious,* and blame the ministry and the church when the blame lies only with ourselves. We shall begin to cavil, censure, criticise, and blame. Would to God that any who are now doing so would pause and inquire the reason of their unhappy disposition. Hear the reproof administered by one of the giants of puritanic times : " You come oft-times to Wisdom's home, and though she prepare you all spiritual dainties, yet you can relish nothing but some by-things, that lie about the dish rather for ornament than for food. And would you know the reason of this? It is because Christ is not with your spirits. If Christ were with you, you would feed on every dish at Wisdom's table, on promises, yea, and on threatenings too. 'To the hungry soul every bitter thing is sweet,' saith Solomon. All that is good and wholesome goes down well where Christ is with the spirit."* Oh, for the Master's smile to impart a relish to his dainties !

Weakness is the unavoidable result of the Lord's displeasure. "The joy of the Lord is our strength," and if this be wanting we necessarily become faint. "*His presence* is life," and the removal of it shakes us to our very foundation. Duty is toilsome labour, unless Christ make it a delight. "Without me ye can do nothing," said the Redeemer; and truly we have found it so. The boldness of lion-like courage, the firmness of rooted decision, the confidence of un-flinching faith, the zeal of quenchless love, the vigour of undying devotion, the sweetness of

* Lockyer.

sanctified fellowship—all hang for support upon the one pillar of the Saviour's presence, and this removed they fail. There are many and precious clusters, but they all grow on one bough, and if that be broken they fall with it. Though we be flourishing like the green bay-tree, yet the sharpness of such a winter will leave us leafless and bare. Then "the fig-tree shall not blossom, neither shall there be fruit in the vine; the labour of the olive shall fail, and the field shall yield no meat." "Instead of sweet smell there shall be a stink; and instead of a girdle a rent; and instead of well-set hair, baldness; and instead of a stomacher a girding of sackcloth; and burning instead of beauty."* It is then that we shall cry with Saul, "I am sore distressed, for the Philistines make war against me, and God is departed from me, and answereth me no more, neither by prophets nor by dreams."† Good it is for us that He is not clean gone for ever, but will turn again lest we perish.

Not to weary ourselves upon this mournful topic, we may sum up all the manifest effects of a loss of the manifest favour of Christ in one sad catalogue—misery of spirit, faintness in

* Isa. iii. 24.　　　　† 1 Sam. xxviii. 15.

hope, coldness in worship, slackness in duty, dulness in prayer, barrenness in meditation, worldliness of mind, strife of conscience, attacks from Satan, and weakness in resisting the enemy. Such ruin doth a withdrawing of Divine presence work in man. From all grieving of thy Spirit, from all offending of the Saviour, from all withdrawing of thy visible favour, and loss of thy presence, good Lord, deliver us. And if at any time we have erred, and have lost the light of thy countenance, O Lord, help us still to believe thy grace and trust in the merits of thy Son, through whom we address thee. Amen.

TO THE UNCONVERTED READER.

—

SINNER, if the consequences of the temporary departure of God be so terrible, what must it be to be shut out from him for ever? If the passing cloud of his seeming anger scattereth such grievous rain upon the beloved sons of God, how direful will be the continual shower of God's unchanging wrath which will fall on the head of rebellious sinners for ever and ever! Ah, and we need not look so far as the future! How pitiable is your condition NOW! How great is the danger to which you are every day exposed! How can you eat or drink, or sleep or work, while the eternal God is your enemy? He whose wrath makes the devils roar in agony is not a God to be trifled with! Beware! his frown is death; 'tis more—'tis hell. If you knew the misery of the saint when his Lord deserts him but for a small moment, it would be enough to amaze you. Then what must it be to endure it throughout eternity? Sinner, thou art hasting to hell, mind what

thou art at! Do not damn thyself, there are
cheaper ways of playing fool than that. Go
and array thyself in motley, and become the
aping fool, at whom men laugh, but do not
make laughter for fiends for ever. Carry coals'
on thy head, or dash thine head against the
wall, to prove that thou art mad, but do not
"kick against the pricks;" do not commit
suicide upon thine own soul for the mere sake
of indulging thy thoughtlessness. Be wise, lest
being often reproved, having hardened thy neck,
thou shouldest be suddenly destroyed, and that
without remedy.

XI.

The Causes of Apparent Desertion.

"Show me wherefore thou contendest with me."—
JOB x. 2.

IT would be a grievous imputation upon the
much tried children of God, if we should
imagine that their greater trials are the results
of greater sin. We see some of them stretched
upon the bed of languishing year after year—
others are subject to the severest losses i
business, and a third class are weeping the oft
repeated bereavements of death. Are all these
chastisements for sin? and are we to attribute
the excess of trouble to an enlarged degree of
transgression? Many of the Lord's people are
free from the extreme bitterness of such affliction: what is the cause of the difference? Is
it always the result of sin? We reply, Certainly not. In many cases it is, but in as many
more it is not. David had a comparatively

smooth course until after his sin with Bath-sheba, and then he commenced a pilgrimage of deepest woe; but we do not think that the trials of Job were preceded by any great fall; on the contrary, Job was never more holy than just before the enemy fell upon him. Trials have other errands besides the mortification of the flesh, and other reasons beyond that of chastisement for sin.

Since the hidings of God's countenance stand among the chief of our troubles, the previous remark will apply to them. These are, without doubt, very frequently a monition from Christ of his grief at our iniquities; but, at the same time, there are so many exceptions to this rule, that it would be unsafe, as well as untrue, to consider it to be general. A portion of the Lord's family live usually in the shade; they are like those sweet flowers which bloom no-where so well as in the darkest and thickest glades of the forest. Shall we dare to charge them with guilt on this account? If we do so, their extreme sensitiveness will lead them to plead guilty;. they will be wounded to the quick, and by their very grief and ingenuous confession, they will unwittingly refute our cruel supposition. Some of these bedarkened

travellers exhibit the rarest virtues and the
most precious graces. They are, of course,
wanting in some great points ; but in others
they so much excel that we are compelled to
admire. The white and sickly lily is exceeding fair, although she has not the ruddy health
which is the glory of the rose. We desire that
these sons and daughters of mourning may come
forth to the light, and rejoice in their Lord :
but if they shall still tarry in the land of darkness, be it far from us to charge them with
greater sin because they have less joy. We remember well the lines of the poet—

" In this wild world the fondest and the best
   Are the most tried, most troubled, and distrest." *

We will now venture to suggest some of the
reasons for the Saviour's withdrawals.

1. *Divine sovereignty* is manifested in the
communion of saints with their Lord, as well as
in every other step of the journey to heaven.
He who giveth no account of his matters, out
of his own absolute will and good pleasure may
extinguish the lamps of comfort and quench the
fires of joy, and yet give to his creature no
reason for his conduct ; yea, and find no reason
in the creature, but exercise his kingly rights in

* Crabbe.

the most uncontrolled and absolute manner.
That all men may see that their best pleasures
flow from the river of God, and are only to be
found in him, and only to be obtained through
his divine grace, he is pleased at certain seasons
to dry up the springs, to close the fountain,
and suspend the flowing of the stream; so that
even the best of men languish, and all the godly
of the earth do mourn.   Lest the green fir-tree
should exalt itself by reason of its fruitfulness,
as if it did garnish itself with beauty, the God
of our salvation allows a withering and a blight
to seize upon it that it may believe the sacred
declaration, " FROM ME IS THY FRUIT FOUND."
God's own glory is sometimes his only motive
for action, and truly it is a reason so great and
good that he who mocks at it must be a stranger
to God, and cannot be truly humbled before
him.   It may be that the sole cause of our sad
condition lies in the absolute will of God; if so,
let us bend our heads in silence, and let him do
what seemeth him good.   Unhappy is our lot
when our best Beloved is absent; but he shall
do as he pleases, and we will sigh for his return;
but we will not chide him for his absence:
"What if God will use his absoluteness and
prerogative in this his dealing with his child,

and proceed therein according to no ruled case or precedent? This he may do, and who shall cry, 'What doest thou?'" *

We think, however, that this case is but of rare occurrence, and we would, under every withdrawal, exhort the believer to look for some other cause, and only resort to this explanation when he can truly say, as in God's sight, that with diligent searching he cannot discover another. Then let him remember that such trouble shall be richly recompensed even in this life, as Job's poverty was fully restored by his double wealth.

2. Without this the believer could not enter into the depths of *fellowship with Christ in his sufferings*. The very worst of the Saviour's agonies lay in his desertion by God; the cry of "My God, my God, why hast thou forsaken me?" was the gall of the bitterness of the miseries of Jesus. Now, unless we had to endure a measure of the same excruciating torment of desertion, we could not enter into communion with him to any great degree. At the very deepest our fellowship is shallow; but give us the continued and invariable light of the Lord's countenance, and we should for ever

* Goodwin.'

E E

remain little children in fellowship. Our
Master desires that we may know him in his
death, and sympathise with him in his sufferings. That eminent divine, Richard Sibbs, thus
writes: "Now all of us must sip of that cup
whereof Christ drank the dregs, having a taste
of what it is to have God to forsake us. For
the most part, those believers who live any time
(especially those of great parts) God deals thus
with; weaker Christians he is more indulgent
unto. At such a time we know the use of a
mediator, and how miserable our condition were
without such an one, both to have borne and
overcome the wrath of God for us!" * Again,
the deeply experienced Thomas Goodwin says:
"Though no creature was able to drink off
Christ's cup to the bottom, yet taste they might,
and Christ tells them they should: 'Ye shall
drink indeed of my cup, and be baptised with the
baptism that I am baptised with,' † that is, taste
of inward affliction and desertion, as well as of
outward persecution; and all to make us con-
formable to him, that we might come to know
in part what he endured for us." ‡ Sweet
departure of Jesus, which thus enables us to

---

* Sibbs's *Bowels Opened.*   † Matt. xx. 23
‡ *Child of Light walking in Darkness.*

approach the nearer to him! of all reasons for patience none can be more powerful than this.

3. Thus, in some men, the Lord works a *preparation for eminent service.* By the experience of sharp inward trouble, the Lord's mighty men are prepared for the fight. To them the heat by day and the frost by night, the shoutings of the war, the spear and the battle-axe, are little things, for they have been trained in a sterner school. They are like plants which have lived through the severities of winter, and can well defy the frosts of spring; they are like ships which have crossed the deep and have weathered the storm, and are not to be upset by every capful of wind. . To them the loss of man's applause is of small account, for they have endured the loss of Christ's smile, and have yet trusted him. To them the contumely of a world, and the rage of hell, are nothing, for they have suffered what is a thousand times worse—they have passed under the cloud of Christ's transient forsaking. They are wise, for, like Heman, they have been "afflicted and ready to die from their youth up," * and therefore, like him, they are fit to compare with Solomon in some things, and are wiser

* Ps. lxxxviii. 15.

than he in others.*   They are useful, for Paul
saith of such men, "Brethren, if a man be
overtaken in a fault, *ye which are spiritual*,
restore such an one in the spirit of meekness,
considering thyself, lest thou also be tempted."
There are no preachers in the world like those
who have passed by the way of trouble to the
gate of wisdom.   Moses prized Hobab because
he knew how to encamp in the wilderness,† and
so we value the minister who has learned as
Hobab did, by living in the desert himself.
Luther said Temptation was one of his masters
in divinity.   We will readily trust ourselves in
the hands of a physician who has been himself
sick of our disease, and has tried the remedies
which he prescribes for us ; so we confide in the
advice of the Christian who knows our trials by
having felt them.   What sweet words in season
do tried saints address to mourners ! they are
the real sons of consolation, the truly good
Samaritans.   We who have a less rugged path,
are apt to over-drive the lambs ; but these have
nourished and brought up children, and know
how to feel for the weaknesses of the little ones.
It is often remarked that after soul-sorrow our
pastors are more gifted with words in season,

* 1 Kings iv. 31.   † Num. x. 31.

and their speech is more full of savour: this is to be accounted for by the sweet influence of grief when sanctified by the Holy Spirit. Blessed Redeemer, we delight in thy love, and thy presence is the life of our joys; but if thy brief withdrawals qualify us for glorifying thee in cheering thy saints, we thank thee for standing behind the wall; and as we seek thee by night, it shall somewhat cheer us that thou art blessing us when thou takest away thy richest blessing.

By sad experience of apparent desertion we are some of us enabled to preach to sinners with greater affection and concern than we could have exhibited without it. Our bowels yearn over dying men, for we know what their miseries must be, if they die out of Christ. If our light affliction, which is but for a moment, is yet at times the cause of great heaviness, what must an eternal weight of torment be? These thoughts, begotten by our sorrow, are very useful in stirring up our hearts in preaching, for under such emotions we weep over them, we plead with them; and, as though God did beseech them by us, we pray them in Christ's stead to be reconciled to God. For a proof thereof, let the reader turn to the Address to the Unconverted appended to this chapter;

it was written by one who for many years endured the gloom of desertion. May God bless it to sinners!

4. The Lord Jesus sometimes hides himself from us, because by his foresight and prudence he is thus able *to prevent the breaking forth of evil.* Perhaps pride would rise to an alarming height if the pining sickness of desertion did not somewhat abate its violence. If some men had all their desires the earth would need enlargement, for their pride would become intolerable to their fellows; and, certainly, while corruption still remains in our hearts, continual comfort would work somewhat in the same manner even in us. Because of the haughtiness, which so easily arises in the hearts of the Lord's people if they have a little too much feasting, "the Lord in his care and goodness is fain to hold them to hard meat, and to keep them to a spare diet." * Sometimes, also, high living would bring on carelessness of walk. We should forget that we walk by faith, and not by sight, if it were not for intervals of darkness in which sense is put to its wit's ends, and only faith is of use to us. Dependence is generally the mother of humility; as long as

* Thomas Hooker.

we feel the one we shall not be quite devoid of the other; therefore our Divine Lord, according to his own wisdom, gives us a bitter lesson in both, by stopping the supplies of joy and withholding his presence. The fact is, that in our present state much that is pleasant to us is not good for us. We are not able to endure the weight of glory, for our backs are weak, and we stagger under it. It is hard to hold a full cup with a steady hand. We are like the fire on the hearth, which can be extinguished by too much sunlight, as well as by floods of water; even joy can destroy us as well as grief. The Master said to his disciples, "I have yet many things to say unto you, but ye cannot bear them now."* The incapacity of the saint may account for the comparative fewness of his delights. "As it is with a little bark, if it should have a great mainmast and broad sailcloths, then, instead of carrying it, it would be overthrown by them; therefore men proportion their mast according to their ship or bark; and if it have skilful mariners, they strike sail when they come into the shallow or narrow seas. This is the reason why the Lord so deals with us : the soul is like the ship, and the sense of

* John xvi. 12.

God's love and mercy is like the sail that carries us on in a Christian course; and if we get but little sail of mercy and favour, we go on sweetly and comfortably; but if God gives us abundance and assurance, our cursed rotten hearts would overturn, and instead of quickening us it would overthrow us; so that, though God doth it, the fault is in ourselves." *

If we have been sorely tried and severely exercised, our trials should read us a lesson upon the evil of our nature. Let us exclaim with that long afflicted saint, Mr. Rogers, " We that have tasted so much of his displeasure have cause to rejoice with trembling; every remembrance of that doleful time must be to us a new motive to obedience, and a powerful restraint of sin; he chastens us for our profit, that we might be partakers of his holiness. Oh, what an abundance of folly must there have been lodged in our hearts that God is forced to use so sharp and so severe a method to whip it out! How benumbed were we, that nothing else could awaken us! How diseased, that nothing but a potion so bitter could promote our cure! How great was our pride, that he was forced to beat it down by so violent a stroke!

* *Soul's Implantation*, by T. Hooker.

It must have been like the pride of Israel, to whom he saith, He led thee through that great and terrible wilderness, wherein were fiery serpents, and scorpions, and drought, where there was no water; that he might humble thee, and prove thee, to do thee good in thy latter end."

5. Our Lord Jesus designs also *to try our faith*. He will see whether we can trust him or no. When we see him by sensible enjoyment there is not that space for faith which his absence causes; and, moreover, to believe what we feel to be true is no hard matter, but to credit what present experience appears to contradict is a divine act which is most honourable to the grace which enables us to do it. Our faith is the centre of the target at which God doth shoot when he tries us, and if any other grace shall escape untried, certainly faith shall not. There is no way of piercing faith to its very marrow like the sticking of the arrow of desertion in it; this finds it out whether it be of the immortals or no. Strip it of its armour of conscious enjoyment, and suffer the terrors of the Lord to set themselves in array against it, and that is faith indeed which can escape unhurt from the midst of the attack. Faith must

be tried, and desertion is the furnace, heated
seven times, into which it must be thrust.
Blest is the man who can endure the ordeal.

6. A temporary withdrawal *endears Christ
to us* upon his return, and gives the soul some
idea of the infinite value of his smile. Constant enjoyment of any good thing is too much
for our corrupt natures. Israel loathed the
angel's food, and sighed for the meaner fare of
Egypt—the garlic and the onions; but if the
manna had been stayed, how eagerly would they
have clamoured for its restoration! When rain
falls in its needed season we scarcely stay to
return thanks for the boon; but if it be withheld,
how do we bless the drops and thank the God
of heaven for them. Sunlight is never more
grateful than after a long watch in the midnight
blackness; Christ's presence is never more
acceptable than after a time of weeping, on
account of his departure. It is a sad thing
that we should need to lose our mercies to
teach us to be grateful for them; let us mourn
over this crookedness of our nature; and let us
strive to express our thankfulness for mercies, so
that we may not have to lament their removal.
Let us deal courteously, tenderly, obediently, and
affectionately, with our glorious Lord, and it

may be we shall retain him as a constant guest.

7. This also *whets our appetite for heaven*, and makes us thirst for the land of bliss. The world has a fascinating power which constrains us to love it, if all be well; but by removing the light of his face, our Lord Jesus breaks the spell, and delivers us from the overweening love of the creature. Weaning is sorrowful work, but it must be done : we must be made to groan in this body that we may be made ready for the unclothing, and the "clothing upon," by which mortality shall be swallowed up of life. In heaven they see his face, and his name is in their foreheads; this incites the saint to pant for glory, that he may obtain uninterrupted fellowship with Jesus. O how sweet it must be to behold his face without the shadow of an intervening cloud; to dwell in his house, and go no more out for ever; to lean upon his bosom, and never rise from that delightful posture! In our days of song and tabret we are still conscious that there is richer music in the upper world; but in the times of fasting and sighing, how do we cry out for the living God, and pant to appear before him. "God's house is an hospital at one end, and a palace at the

other. In the hospital end are Christ's members upon earth, conflicting with various diseases, and confined to strict regimen of his appointing. What sort of a patient would he be, who would be sorry to be told that the hour is come for his dismission from the hospital, and to see the doors thrown wide open for his admission into the presence of the King." *
Happy are the spirits who have ended their fight of faith, and now live in the raptures of a sight of Him; yea, thrice happy are the lowest of those seraphs who fly at his bidding, and do for ever behold the face of our Father which is in heaven. The drought of these dry plains stirreth us to desire the river of the water of life; the barren fig-trees of this weary land urge us to pursue a speedy path to the immortal trees upon the banks of the river of God; our clouds exhort us to fly above this lower sky up where unclouded ages roll; the very thorns and briers, the dust and heat of this world's pilgrimage and strife, are powerful orators to excite our highest thoughts to the things which are unseen and eternal. Thus the bitterness of time bids us desire the sweetness of immortality, and even prepares us for it.

* Adams's *Private Thoughts.*

In times of distress, when the withdrawal of Christ is caused by any of these causes, let the saint stay himself upon his God. The light is a pleasant thing, but faith can walk without it. It is good to have the Lord's presence, but let us remember that we are not saved by *our* enjoyments of him, but by *his* efficacy for us. We are full of sin, and in our distress we feel it, but He is full of grace and truth; let us believe His all-sufficiency, and rest in it. His blood not our peace, his merit not our comfort, his perfection not our communion,—are the pillars of our salvation. We love his company, and the manifest sense of it is sweet indeed; but, if it be denied us, nevertheless "the foundation of God standeth sure." Jesus, the yea and amen, is the same yesterday, to-day, and for ever. Our soul hangs upon him in the thick darkness, and glories in him in the storm. The promise, like an anchor, holds us fast; and, though the pilot sleeps, all must be well. It is not our eye on him which is our great protection, but his eye on us; let us be assured that although we cannot see him, he can see us, and, therefore, we are safe. Whatever our frame or feeling, the heart of Jesus is full of love—love which was not caused by our good behaviour, and is not diminished by our follies—love which is as sure in the night of darkness, as in the brightness of the day of joy. Therefore are we confident and full of hope, and we can sing with our favourite poet—

> "Away, despair; my gracious Lord doth hear,
> Though winds and waves assault my keel,
> He doth preserve it; he doth steer,
> Even when the boat seems most to reel.
> Storms are the triumph of his art:
> Well may he close his eyes, but not his heart." *

We never live so well as when we live on the Lord Jesus simply as he is, and not upon our enjoyments or raptures. Faith is never more likely to increase in strength than in times which seem adverse to her. When she is lightened of trust in joys, experiences, frames, feelings, and the like, she rises the nearer heaven, like the balloon when the bags of sand are emptied. Trust in thy Redeemer's strength, thou benighted soul; exercise what faith thou hast, and by-and-bye he shall arise upon thee with healing beneath his wings.

The next and last case has been already alluded to in the previous chapter. Sin, with its hosts, closes the rear. We do not intend to do more than instance the special iniquities

* Herbert.

which more readily than any other will cause the Master to be gone.

8. *Gross and foul offences* of any kind will drive the King from the soul very speedily. Let the believer bemire himself with lust, or put forth his hand unto violence, or speak lying or lascivious words—let him give great and scandalous cause to the enemy to blaspheme,— and, as surely as he is the Lord's child, his back shall smart for it. If we lie in the bed of Jezebel, we shall not have the company of Jesus there. As soon expect to see an angel in the sty with swine, as Christ Jesus in company with the filthy. Should we be left to commit adultery like David, we shall have our bones broken as he had; if we swear like Peter, we shall have to weep as bitterly as he; and if we flee like Jonah from the service of the Lord, we may expect to go into as great depths as he did. The sun will shine on the dunghill, but Christ will not shine on the back-slider while he is indulging in his lusts. How terrible are the agonies of the mind when some surprising sin is visited upon us! In an ancient work, as rare as its own merits, we find the following :—

" For he withdraweth his face and favour

from us, kindleth his anger against us, and
counteth us as his enemies;* the horror of his
wrath is as fire sent from above into our bones,
and is as the arrows of the Almighty, the
venom whereof drinketh up our spirit.   He
setteth our iniquities before himself, and our
secret sins in the light of his countenance;† he
setteth them also in our own sight, and our
sin is before us continually;‡ with his hand
he bindeth the yoke of our transgressions, and
with them being laid upon our neck he maketh
our strength to fail;§ bitter things doth he
write against us, and maketh us to inherit the
iniquities of our youth,‖ so that there is nothing
found in our flesh because of his anger, neither
is their rest in our bones because of our sin:
our wounds stink and are corrupt;¶ our veins
are full of burning, our heart is as wax; it
melteth in the midst of our bowels;** our bones
are parched like an hearth,†† and our moisture
is turned to a summer drought, so heavy is his
hand upon us night and day.‡‡   Then cry we
out for grief of heart; we roar like bears, and

* Job xix. 11.   † Ps. xc. 8.
‡ Ps. li. 3.   § Lam. i. 14.
‖ Job. xiii. 26.   ¶ Ps. xxxviii. 3, 5, 7
** Ps. xxii. 14.   †† Ps. cii. 3.
‡‡ Ps. xxxii. 4.

mourn like doves;* looking for judgment, but there is none—for salvation, but it is far from us; because our trespasses are many, both before him and ourselves, for which his terrors do fight against us, he visiteth us every morning,† and tryeth us every moment; setteth us as a mark against him, so that we are a burden to ourselves. Also, when we cry and shout, he shutteth out our prayer,‡ and is even angry against it,§ because our iniquities have separated between us and him, and our sins have hid his face from us, that he will not hear;‖ so loathsome are our trespasses unto him, so venomous to ourselves is the biting of those fierce serpents."

Careless living, even if we fall not into open transgression, will soon build a wall between our Lord and the soul. If daily sins are unconfessed and unrepented of, they will daily accumulate until they form "mountains of division" between our adorable Friend and our own heart. A little filth acquired every day, if it be left unwashed, will make us as black as if we had been plunged in the mire; and as sin upon the conscience turns Christ's joy out of

* Isa. lix. 11, 12.   † Job vii. 18.   ‡ Lam. iii. 8.
§ Ps. lxxx. 4.   ‖ Isa. lix. 2.

the heart, it will be impossible for us to feel the delights of communion until all our everyday sins have been washed from the conscience by a fresh application of the atoning blood. Let us take heed that we offer the morning and evening lamb, constantly looking to the blood of the Great Sacrifice, and seeking a fresh discovery of its cleansing power.

Neglect of prayer is a sad grief to the Holy Spirit, and will as soon cause the Lord to withdraw as open sin. How many of us from this cause have dropped the thread of communion, and so have lost the clue to happiness. Jesus will never reveal himself in any marked manner unto us while we neglect the throne of grace. We must seclude ourselves if we would see our Beloved. It was a sweet saying of Bernard, "O saint, knowest thou not that thy husband, Christ, is bashful, and will not be familiar in company; retire thyself by meditation into thy closet, or into the fields, and there thou shalt have Christ's embraces." Rebekah went to the well, and was met by one who gave her jewels of gold, and found her a husband; let us go to the well of prayer, and we shall meet Jesus, but those who tarry at home shall lack.

Idleness in the ways of grace will also hinder

communion.   If we travel slowly, and loiter on
the road, Jesus will go on before us, and sin
will overtake us.   If we are dilatory and lazy
in the vineyard, the Master will not smile on
us when he walks through his garden.   Be
active, and expect Christ to be with thee; be
idle, and the thorns and briars will grow so
thickly, that he will be shut out of thy door.
We should never mend our pace on Heaven's
road if our comforts did not fly ahead of us, so
as to allure us to speed, by compelling us to
pursue them.

Unthankfulness will soon strip us of our joys.
It is said of the sun, that none look at him
except he be in an eclipse; and we fear we are all
too forgetful of Christ unless he veil his face :
therefore, to chasten us for our ill manners,
and incite us to a more loving carriage towards
him, he will hide himself in darkness if we
forget his goodness.

Cowardice will also rob us of the Master's
manifest presence.   The ancient saints who at
any time, in order to avoid the stake, were led
through weakness to deny their profession,
were made sorely to rue the day that they ever
did so weak a deed.   And we, if we are ashamed
of him in the time of rebuke and reproach

must not look for any love-feasts with him
Captains cannot smile on runaway soldiers, or
even on men who quake in the moment of conflict. We must be valorous if we would be
comforted ; we must show ourselves men if we
would have Christ show himself our loving
friend. When Jonah runs from Nineveh he
must not reckon upon his Lord's company, except it be to rebuke and smite him. "In our
English chronicles we read of the rare affection
of Eleanor, the wife of Edward I., who, when
the king had been wounded with a poisoned
dagger, set her mouth to the wound to suck
out the poison, venturing her own life to preserve her husband. Such is the strength of
love in a healthy Christian, that were it necessary to suck poison out of the wounds of Jesus,
he would be content to do so." And this he
will do in a spiritual sense, for if he can in no
other way remove contempt and slander from
the cause of Christ and his church, he will
rather bear it himself than allow it to fall on
his Master. But if this noble spirit shall give
place to mean self-seeking, and carnal care of
our personal interests, the Lord will forsake the
tabernacle where we dwell, and leave us to
mourn the displeasure of our slighted friend.

Harshness to the afflicted may bring us into deep waters. If the strong cattle push the weak with their horns, and thrust with the shoulder, they must have the fatness of their strength removed, and the glory of their horns cut off, that they may learn to deal gently with the tender-hearted and timid. When we hear a strong professor dealing roughly with any of the Lord's afflicted, as sure as he is an heir of heaven he will in due time have cause to eat his words. That is an unhumbled heart which can allow hard thoughts concerning the little ones; and God will put that proud spirit into the dark until it can bear the infirmities of the weak. Be gentle, ye great in Zion, lest ye offend the poor and mean of the congregation.

Pride casts a thick shadow over the path of any believer who indulges in it. Men love not the proud—their company is a torment, and their very presence an offence; how much more obnoxious must it be to the Son of God! Especially must it be exceeding hateful in those who are indebted to grace for the very breath in their nostrils, and who, in themselves, are the most detestable of creatures, but are made the sons of God through great and unmerited mercy. When we become conceited with our

choice experiences, admirable emotions, and
marvellous discoveries, and in our imaginary
greatness grow unmindful of the Giver of these
good gifts, he will soon level us with the
ground, and make us groan out of the dust. The
smoke of the incense of our pride will blind the
eyes to Christ, and hide Christ from the saint.

Idolatrous love, whatever may be the object
of it, is so abominable, that it will shut out the
light of God's countenance in a short space,
unless it be destroyed. Rivals Jesus will not
endure; and unless we give him the highest
throne he will leave us to mourn his absence.
Love not thy wealth, thy name, thy friends,
thy life, thy comfort, thy husband, thy wife, or
thy children, more than thou lovest him, or
even so much; for he will either take *them*
from thee, or else his own delightful presence,
and the loss of either would be an evil not
worth the idolatry which will surely engender
it. Set not your affection on things of earth,
lest the comfortable enjoyment of Him who is
from above should be withdrawn from thee.

Unbelief, distrust, and worldly care, will also
provoke him to return unto his place. If we
cannot trust him with ourselves, and all that we
have, he will not confide his heart with us. A

fit of worldly anxiety has many a time cut off the streams of fellowship. Fretful trouble about many things is a fearful injury to the one thing. All the saints will confess that the fair flower of fellowship will not bloom in the atmosphere of carking care. That great rebel, Infidelity, will sometimes turn the key of the gates of Mansoul against the Prince Immanuel himself, and cause him to return to the palace of his Father. It is a high affront put upon the Lord Jesus when we presume to manage our own business instead of leaving all with him. The old puritan said, "Whenever we carve for ourselves we cut our own fingers!" He might have added, "And worse still, we highly affront the Head of the feast, and cause him to withdraw from the table." Oh! for grace to leave all with Christ; it cannot be in better hands, and our own care could never produce results which could for an instant be compared with the effects of his providential consideration.

But *carnal security* is the master-sin in this point. Hence, Bunyan makes a feast in the house of that deceitful old Diabolian, Mr. Carnal-Security, the scene of the discovery of the departure of Prince Immanuel. There is in carnal security a mixture of all other kinds of sin. It is a monster composed of the deformities of all the foul sins which man can commit. It is ingratitude, pride, worldliness, sloth, inordinate affection, evil concupiscence and rebellion in one. It is like those fabled monsters which bore a resemblance to every other creature, inasmuch as the most terrible parts of every beast were in them united into one hideous monstrosity. Now whenever self-confidence grows in the heart, and destroys our implicit dependence and our unfeigned humility, it will not be long before Christ and the soul will be far apart—so far as any comfortable communion is concerned.

It only remains to add that as we are differently constituted, certain sins will have greater power over one than another, and hence one sin may drive the Saviour from one believer, and an opposite sin may grieve him in another; indeed, any one sin, if harboured against light and knowledge, is quite sufficient to cast the mind into the doleful condition of a deserted soul. Constant watchfulness is necessary in order to the preservation of communion: but of this we will say more in another place.

It will be hard work to sustain faith when

sin is arrived at such a dangerous height; but in order that the believer may be able to do so, by the divine power of the Holy Spirit, let him reflect that his present mournful condition is no sign that he is cast away—nay, let him believe it to be the very reverse. If the Lord Jesus had not looked upon him, he would never have known how evil a thing it is to lose a sense of his love. Blind men do not miss the light when it is removed by the setting of the sun; and if the afflicted soul were wholly blind, he would not lament the hiding of the Sun of righteousness. But if this is too high a comfort, let him remember that there is still a fountain opened for sin and for uncleanness; and while he sorrows for his absent Lord let him not despair, but let him still look to the cross, and hope. Let the deserted one confess his ill-deservings, but let him remember that his sin is laid upon the head of Jesus. Punishment for sin is not in any degree mixed up with the withdrawal which he is now experiencing. The believer owes nothing to punitive justice, and therefore nothing can be exacted of him. "Though the sufferings of Christ do not secure us from sufferings, they change the nature and design of our afflictions, so that, instead of their being punishments,

they are corrections, and are inflicted not by
the sword of the Judge, but by the rod of the
Father."*   Let the believer hear the voice of
comfort:—"Thou hast not a farthing of debt
to pay to God's law; there is no indictment
against thee, nor a bill for thee to answer—
Christ has paid all."† Christ's departure is not
for thy death, but to promote thy better life. He
is not gone to demand a writ against thee, he
is but absent to make thee purge out the old
leaven, that he may come and keep the feast
with thee.

Remember also that a change in the outward
dealings of the Lord Jesus is not to be looked
upon as an alteration in his love.   He has as
much affection for us when he puts us in the
prison-house of desertion as when he leads us
into the pavilion of communion.   Immutability
will not allow of the shadow of a turning; and
as immutability is stamped as much upon the
affection of Christ as upon his divinity itself,
it follows that our variable condition produces
no change in him.

> "Immutable his will;
>   Though dark may be my frame,

---

* Jay's *Christian Contemplated.*
† Colling's *Cordial for a Dying Soul.*

> His loving heart is still
>   Unchangeably the same.
> My soul through many changes goes;
> His love no variation knows."

That holy martyr, Master John Bradford, thus comforted himself and his friends in a time of gloom—" The mother sometimes beateth the child, but yet her heart melteth upon it even in the very beating; and therefore she casteth the rod into the fire, and calleth the child, giveth it an apple, and dandleth it most motherly. And to say the truth, the love of mothers to their children is but a trace to train us up to behold the love of God towards us; and therefore saith he, ' Can a mother forget the child of her womb?' as much as to say, ' No, but if she should do so, yet will I not forget thee, saith the Lord of Hosts.' Ah, comfortable saying! —I will not forget thee."

Wait awhile, and the light which is sown for the righteous shall bring forth a harvest of delights; but water the ground with the tears of thy repentance, lest the seed should long tarry under the clods. As sure as thou art a quickened soul thou wilt, in the dreary winter of thy Lord's absence, pant for renewed communion; and be thou sure to use all means to obtain this boon.   Do as thou didst when thou didst first come to Christ.   Read and practise the directions given to the seeking sinner in the third chapter,* for they are well-adapted to thine own case, and then take the advice which follows :—

1. Hunt out and slay the sin which has caused the coolness of fellowship between thee and thy Lord.

2. Most humbly confess this sin, and ask grace to avoid it in future.

3. Come again as a poor guilty sinner to the cross of Christ, and put thy trust implicitly in him who died upon it.

4. Use thy closet and thy Bible more frequently, and with more earnestness.

5. Be active in serving Christ, and patient in waiting for him, and ere long he will appear to cheer thy spirit with floods of his surpassing love.   If all these fail thee, tarry the leisure of thy Master, and thy work shall certainly be rewarded in due time.

May God the Holy Spirit, by his divine influence, bedew with grace the pages of this chapter, that they may minister grace to the afflicted reader.

* See p. 150.

TO THE UNCONVERTED READER.

SINNER, we beseech thee listen to the warnings of one* who was for a long time sad and sick on account of the hidings of his Lord's face. He was a true and eminent saint, yet mark his sorrows, and let them awaken thee to fear the wrath to come :

"Oh, sinners! I have dearly paid for all the delight I once had in sin,—for all my indifference and lukewarmness, my cold and sluggish prayers, my lost and misimproved time. Beware that you do not provoke him, for he is a jealous God; for if you do, you shall also find that those sins which you make a slight matter of, will tear you to pieces hereafter. You will find them, when your consciences are awakened, to be a heavy and intolerable burden; they will press you down to hell itself. I could not have thought that the displeasure of God had been a thing so bitter, and so very dreadful. *It is a*

* Rev. Timothy Rogers, M.A.

*fearful thing to fall into the hands of the living
God, for he is a consuming fire :* if his anger be
kindled but a little, you cannot then fix your
mind upon any pleasant objects, nor have one
easy thought ; you cannot then go about your
business, your trade, or your secular affairs, for
your souls will be so much amazed that you will
be full of horror and consternation. Those of
us who have *felt the terrors of the Lord,* do
most earnestly persuade you to forsake every
sin ; for if you indulge in and love your
iniquities, they will set you on fire round about.
Oh, that you did but know what you do when
you sin ! You are opposing that authority that
will avenge itself of all its obstinate opposers ;
you are heaping up fuel for your own destruction ; you are whetting that sword which will
enter into your bowels ; you are preparing
yourselves for bitterness and trouble ; and
though God is patient for awhile, yet he will
not always be so : the shadows of the night are
drawing on, and the doleful time will come when
all your mirth will end in tears, and all your
false confidence and your foolish hopes will
expire and give up the ghost. And which of
you will live when God shall enter into judgment with you ? What will you do ? Where

will you go for help when he who is your
Maker,—he who has weighed your actions, and
observed your wanderings, shall call you to give
an account of all these things? If our blessed
Lord, when he came near Jerusalem, lifted up
his voice and wept, saying, *Oh, that thou hadst
known, even thou in this thy day, the things that
belong unto thy peace!* what cause have we to
mourn over our fellow-creatures, whom we see
to be in danger of misery, and, alas, they know
't not! Can we see them sleeping on the very
edge of ruin, and not be greatly troubled for
them! Oh, poor sinners, you are now sleeping,
but *the judge is at the door;* you are rolling the
pleasant morsel under your tongue, but it will
be great vexation to you in the end. How can
you rest? how can you be quiet when you have
none of your sins pardoned? No comfortable
relation to God! no well-grounded hope of
heaven! How can you, with any assurance, go
about those things that concern your buying,
your selling, and the present life, when your
poor souls, that are of a thousand times more
value, are neglected all the while! We have
felt great terrors, inexpressible sorrows, from an
angry God, and we would fain persuade you not
to run upon the thick bosses of his buckler,

not to dare his justice, not to despise his
threats as once it was our folly : but we knew
not what we did. We are *come out of great
tribulation,* and a fiery furnace, and we would
fain persuade you to avoid the like danger ; let
what we have felt be a caution to you. It was
the desire of Dives, in his misery, that he might
leave it to go thence to warn his brethren lest
they came to the same place of torment; but it
could not be granted. Some of us here come
from the very gates of hell to warn you that
you may not go thither,—nay, to warn you that
you may never go so near it as we did. We
wish you so well that we would not have any of
you to feel so much sorrow and grief as we have
felt. We were once asleep, as you are; we did
not imagine that terror and desolation were so
near when they came upon us ; and now, having
been overtaken by a storm of wrath, we come
to warn you that we see the clouds gather, that
there is a sound of much rain and of great
misery, though your eyes are so fixed on things
below, that you see it not. You must speedily
arise and seek for a shelter, as you value the
salvation of your souls; you must not put off
serious thoughts for your own safety, not for
one day, not for one hour longer, lest it be too

late.   We were travelling with as little thought
of danger as some of you, and we fell among
thieves; they plundered us of our peace and
comfort, and we were even ready to die, when
that God, whose just displeasure brought us
low, was pleased to take pity on us, and to send
his Son, as the kind Samaritan, to bind up our
wounds and to cheer our hearts; and we cannot
be so uncharitable as not to tell you, when we
see you going the same way, that there are
robbers on the road, and that if you do not
either return or change your course you will
smart for your temerity as much as we have
done.   We have been saved indeed at length
from our fears, *as by fire;* but we suffered,
while they remained, very great loss.   Some,
perhaps, will be saying within themselves, '*I
shall see no evil, though I walk in the imagina-
tions of my own heart.   These things you talk
of are the mere product of a melancholy temper,
that always presages the worst,—that is always
frighting itself and others with black and formidable ideas; and seeing I am no way inclin-
able to that distemper, I need not fear any such
perplexing thoughts.*'   But know that no brisk-
ness of temper, no sanguine courageous hopes,
no jollities nor diversions, can fence you from

the wrath of God. If you go on in sin, you must feel the bitterness of it either in this or the next world ; and that may, notwithstanding all the strength of your constitution, all the pleasures of your unfearing youth, come upon a sudden. Your souls are always naked and open before God, and he can make terrible impressions of wrath there when he will, though by your cheerfulness and mirth you seem to be at the greatest distance from it."

" Ye bold, blaspheming souls,
    Whose conscience nothing scares ;
Ye carnal, cold, professing fools,
    Whose state 's as bad as theirs.

" Repent, or you're undone,
    And pray to God with speed ;
Perhaps the truth may yet be known,
    And make you free indeed.

" The hour of death draws nigh,
    'Tis time to drop the mask ;
Fall at the feet of Christ, and cry :
    He gives to all that ask."

XII.

Communion Preserved.

" But they constrained him, saying, Abide with us, for
it is toward evening, and the day is far spent."—
LUKE xxiv. 29.

THESE disciples knew not their Lord, but
they loved the unknown stranger who spake so
sweetly of him.   Blessed are the men who discourse of Jesus; they shall ever find a welcome
in the hearts and homes of the elect. His name
to our ears is ever melodious, and we love that
conversation best which is fullest of it. We
would willingly afford the chamber on the wall,
the table, the stool, and the candlestick, to all those
who will talk continually of *Him*. But, alas!
there are too many who would blush to answer our
Saviour's question, " What manner of communi-
cations are these that ye have one to another?"*
Too great a number of professors forget the
words of the prophet, " Then they that feared

* Luke xxiv. 17.

the Lord spake often one to another: and the
Lord hearkened and heard it, and a book of
remembrance was written before him for them
that feared the Lord, and that thought upon
his name. And they shall be mine, saith the
Lord of hosts, in that day when I make up my
jewels; and I will spare them as a man spareth
his own son that serveth him."* We will not
be censorious, but we believe with an old
author, that "the metal of the bell is known
by the sound of the clapper; what is in the
well will be found in the bucket; what is in
the warehouse will be shown in the shop; and
what is in the heart will be bubbling forth at
the mouth."

We often miss our Lord's company because
our conversation does not please him. When
our Beloved goes down into his garden it is to
feed there and gather lilies;† but if thorns and
nettles are the only products of the soil, he will
soon be away to the true beds of spices. When
two walk together, and are agreed in solemn
discourse concerning heavenly things, Jesus
will soon make a third. So here, on this
journey to Emmaus, the Saviour, though they
"knew him not, because their eyes were

* Mal. iii. 16, 17.   † Cant. vi. 2.

holden," did so wondrously converse with them, that their "hearts burned within them." He who would stay a man in the street would naturally call out his name; and he who would bring Jesus into his soul must frequently pronounce his charming name.

The Lord having graciously conversed with these favoured travellers, essays to leave them, and continue his journey, but they constrain him to remain, and at their earnest suit he does so. From this pleasing little incident let us glean one or two lessons.

I. *When we have the Saviour's company for a little while we shall not be content until we have more of it.* These holy men were not content to let him go, but would have him tarry with them all night. There are certain liquors which men drink that are said to increase thirst; it is most true of this rich "wine on the lees," that the more we drink of it the more we desire. Nor will the draught be forbidden us, or prove in any way injurious, for the spouse bids us "drink, yea, drink abundantly." The soul which has enjoyed communion with Jesus will never agree that it has dwelt long enough on the mount: it will far rather build a tabernacle for itself and

its master. Never is a Christian tired of his
Redeemer's society, but, like Abraham, he
cries, " My Lord, if now I have found favour
in thy sight, pass not away, I pray thee, from
thy servant." Any plea will be urged to persuade our Lord to remain. Is it evening? we
will plead that the day is far spent, and we shall
need him to cheer our midnight hours. Is it
morning? we will tell him that we fear to
begin the day without a long visit from him.
Is it noon? we will urge that the sun is hot,
and we shall faint unless he allows us to sit
beneath his shadow. We will always find some
reason for his remaining, for love's logic is
inexhaustible. If he would become our constant guest we should never weary of his company. A thousand years would seem but as
one day if all the time we might lay our head
upon his bosom; yea, eternity itself shall need
no other source of joy since this perennial
stream is ever running. When our wondering
eyes have admired the beauties of our Saviour
for millions of years we shall be quite as willing
to continue the meditation, supremely blest with
that Heaven which our eyes shall drink in from
his wounded hands and side. The marrow of
heaven is Jesus; and as we shall never be sur-

feited with bliss, so we shall never have too
much of Jesus. Fresh glories are discovered
in him every hour; his person, work, offices,
character, affection, and relationships, are each
of them clusters of stars which the eye of contemplation will view with unutterable astonishment as they are in their order revealed to the
mind. The saint who has longest tenanted the
mansions of glory will confess that the presence
of the Saviour has not ceased to be his bliss,
nor has the freshness of the pleasure been in
the least diminished. Christ is a flower, but he
fadeth not; he is a river, but he is never dry;
he is a sun, but he knoweth no eclipse; he is
all in all, but he is something more than all.
He that longs not for Christ hath not seen
him, and by just so much as a man has tasted
of the sweetness of Jesus will he be hungry and
thirsty after more of him. Men who are content
with a manifestation once in a month will soon
become so dull that once a year will suit them;
but he who has a visit from the Saviour very
frequently will be panting for fresh views of
him every day—yea, and every hour of the day.
He will never lack appetite for spiritual things
who lives much on them. The poor professor
may be content with a few of Christ's pence

now and then, but he who is rich in grace thinks so small an income beneath his station, and cannot live unless he has golden gifts from the hand of his Lord; he will covet earnestly this best of gifts, and be a very miser after the precious things of the cross. John Owen, the most sober of theologians, falls into a perfect ecstasy when touching on this subject. In expounding Cant. viii. 6, 7, he gives us the following glowing passage: "The intendment of what is so loftily set out by so many metaphors in these verses is, 'I am not able to bear the workings of my love to thee, unless I may always have society and fellowship with thee. There is no satisfying of my love without it. It is as the grave, that still says, Give! give! Death is not satisfied without its prey. If it have not *all* it hath *nothing.*' Let what will happen, if death hath not its whole desire it hath nothing at all. Nor can it be withstood in its appointed season; no ransom will be taken. So is my love; if I have thee not wholly I have nothing. Nor can all the world bribe it to a diversion; it will be no more turned aside than death in its time. Alas! I am not able to bear my jealous thoughts; I fear thou dost not love me—that thou hast forsaken me, because I know I deserve not to be beloved. These thoughts are hard as hell; they give no rest to my soul. If I find not myself on thy heart and arm, I am as one that lies down in *a bed of coals.*" The absence of the Saviour deprives the believer of more than joy or light; it seems to destroy his very life, and sap the foundations of his being. Let us seek then to hold the king in his galleries.

II. We remark in the next place, that *if we would keep the Saviour with us, we must constrain him.* Jesus will not tarry if he is not pressed to do so. Not that he is ever weary of his people, but because he would have them show their sense of his value. In the case before us, it is said, "he made as if he would go further." This he did to try their affection. "Not," says Ness, "that he had any purpose to depart from them, but to prove them how they prized him, and accounted of his company. Therefore this ought not to be misimproved to countenance any kind of sinful dissimulation. If Solomon might make as though he would do an act that in its own nature was unlawful (to slay an innocent child),*

* 1 Kings iii. 24.

sure I am our Saviour might do that which is but indifferent in itself (whether to go or stay) without being charged with the sin of dissembling. But when Christ makes to be gone, the two disciples would not let him go, but one (as it were) gets hold on one arm, and the other on the other; there they hang till they constrain him to continue with them." These were wise men, and were, therefore, loath to part with a fellow-traveller from whom they could learn so much. If we are ever privileged to receive Jesus under our roof, let us make haste to secure the door that he may not soon be gone. If he sees us careless concerning him, and cold towards him, he will soon arise and go hence. He will not intrude himself where he is not wanted; he needs no lodging, for the heaven of heavens is his perpetual palace, and there be many hearts of the contrite where he will find a hearty welcome.

When we have the honour of a visit from Prince Immanuel let everything be done to protract it. Angels' visits are few and far between: when we have the happiness of meeting therewith, let us, like Jacob, manfully grasp the angel, and detain him, at least until he leaves a blessing. Up, Christian, with a holy bravery, and lay hold on the mercy while it is within reach! The Son of Man loves those who hold him tightly. He will not resent the familiarity, but will approve of thine earnestness. Let the loving bride of the Canticles teach thee by her example, for she glories in her deed when she sings, "I found him whom my soul loveth, I held him, and I would not let him go." True, 'tis amazing grace which can allow such a liberty with the person of so exalted a being; but seeing that he invites us to lay hold on his strength, and has sanctioned the act in others, shall we, like Ahaz, when he declined to ask a sign, refuse the favour which our Lord allows? No—

> "We will maintain our hold;
> 'Tis his goodness makes us bold."

How can we then prolong our communion with the Saviour? Let us reply to the question by sundry directions, which, by the aid of the Spirit, we will labour to follow.

1. Allow no rivals to intrude. Jesus will never tarry in a divided heart. He must be all or nothing. Search then thy heart; dethrone its idols; eject all interlopers; chastise all trespassers; yea, slay the Diabolians who lurk in thy soul. If we would enjoy uninterrupted

fellowship with the Son of God, we must institute a rigid inquisition against all kinds of sin. A little evil will at times mar our peace, just as a small stone in the shoe will spoil our walking. Tender are the shoots of this vine of communion, and little foxes will do no little injury. "The Lord thy God is a jealous God," and Jesus thy husband is jealous also. Sorely did he smite Jerusalem, because she sought affinity with other gods, and chose to herself many lovers. Keep then thy house and heart open to him, and shut to all others. With sin he cannot dwell. Canst thou expect the "angel of the covenant" to dwell with the prince of darkness? Can there be concord with Christ and Belial? Awake then, and cry "Away, ye profane," my heart is the temple of Jesus, and ye must not defile its hallowed places. If they retire not, get to thyself the scourge of repentance and self-mortification, and if it be laid on lustily they will not long abide the blows.

It behoves us to remember, also, that there are other things besides sins which may become offensive to the Saviour. The nearest friend, the partner of our bosom, or the offspring of our loins, may excite the Lord's jealousy. If these become the objects of an affection which ought to be wholly his, he will be moved to anger with us. The calf was no less an idol because it was made of gold. The brazen serpent, despite its original service, must be broken when men worship it. All things are alike cause of jealousy to Jesus if they are exalted to his throne, since no creature can in the least possess anything deserving of worship. The very mention of a rival's name will suffice to drive our blessed Lord away. He will have the name of Baali taken utterly out of our mouth; and he alone must be our Ishi.

Oh! true believer, is there no strange god with thee? Make a thorough search. Bid even thy beloved Rachel rise, for the teraph is often concealed beneath the place where she sitteth. Say not in haste, I am no idolater. The approaches of this sin are insidious in the extreme, and ere thou knowest it thou art entangled in its iron net. The love of the creature has a bewitching power over men, and they seldom know the treachery of the Delilah until their locks are shorn. Oh, daughters of Zion, let King Solomon alone have your love; rehearse his name in your songs, and write his achievements on your memories; so will he dwell in the city of David and ride through your midst in his chariot paved with love for *you*: but if ye pay homage to any save himself, he will return unto his place and make your beauteous city a byword with the enemy. Have no fellowship with strangers, if ye desire manifestations of love from the adorable Jesus. "Let none be your love and choice, and the flower of your delights, but your Lord Jesus. Set not your heart upon the world, since God hath not made it your portion; for it will not fall to you to get two portions, and to rejoice twice, and to be happy twice, and to have an upper heaven and an under heaven too. Most of us have a lover and idol besides our husband, Christ; but it is our folly to divide our narrow and little love; it will not serve for two. It is best then to hold it whole and together, and to give it to Christ; for then we get double interest for our love, when we lend it to, and lay it out upon, Christ; and we are sure, besides, that the stock cannot perish."

Let us muse on the words of the writer of *The Synagogue*—

"Peace, rebel thought, dost thou not know the king,
 My God is here?
Cannot his presence, if no other thing,
 Make thee forbear?

Or were he absent, all the standers by
      Are but his spies;
And well he knows, if thou shouldst it deny,
      Thy words were lies.
If others will not, yet I must, and will,
      Myself complain.
My God, even now a base, rebellious thought
      Began to move,
And subtly twining with me would have wrought
      Me from my love:
Fain he would have me to believe that Sin
      And thou might both
Take up my heart together for your inn,
      And neither loathe
The other's company; a while sit still,
      And part again."

2. Give the Saviour a goodly entertainment, fit for so great a prince, and thus he may be persuaded to make a longer stay. His rank, his honour, and his benevolence, entitle him to the most respectful treatment. Shall the Son of God be entertained in any but the best room of the house? Shall we offer on his altar any save the fattest of the flock and the herd? Shall we spare ourselves when he is our guest? Shall gentlemen spend all their estates that they may sumptuously feast an earthly monarch? and shall we penuriously count the cost of our love to him? Beloved, we shall have but brief glimpses of Jesus if he does not perceive our souls affected by it. A slight from his friends

grieves his spirit, and he withdraws himself. We ought to count it a cheap bargain if we could give our all to win the constant indwelling of Jesus. Princes have melted pearls into the wine wherewith they entertained monarchs, let us do the same. Let us make rich offerings to Jesus; let our duties be more faithfully discharged, our labours more willingly performed, and let our zeal be more eminently fervent. If the altar cease to smoke with incense, the heart will be made empty and void by the departure of its Lord. Self-sacrifice is sweet to our Redeemer, he loves to see his dearly-purchased people confessing that they are not their own. Oh, brethren in the Gospel, *do* more if ye would receive more; give more largely and ye shall be cheered more abundantly. The self-denying missionary, the laborious pastor, the earnest evangelist, and the indefatigable church member, are generally the persons invited to the royal banquets of Jesus. He delights to honour the men who wait at his gates with diligence, and watch for his coming with vigilance. Faithful service shall never be unrewarded by the master's notice, and continuance in well-doing shall receive as its recompence a perpetuity of approbation. Hold thou the Saviour, oh believer!

by hands ready for service and happy to obey.

3. Trust the Lord much while he is with you. Keep no secrets from him. His secrets are with you; let your secrets be with him. Jesus admires confidence, and if it be not afforded him, he will say, "Farewell," until we can trust him better. So long as we put our lips to the ear of Christ, and tell him all, he will never let us be alone. When we reveal every whit, and hide nothing from him, he is pleased with us; but when we conceal our designs, our troubles, or our fears, he frowns at our want of confidence. If thou desirest Christ for a perpetual guest give him all the keys of thine heart; let not one cabinet be locked up from him; give him the range of every room, and the key of every chamber; thus you will constrain him to remain. True faith holds the feet of Jesus and prevents his departure: when he rises to continue his journey, she cries, "Not so, my Lord, hear one more word, listen to the wants of thy servant, let at least another of my griefs find a tomb in thy loving heart. Listen to me this once, for I have somewhat to say unto thee which so deeply concerns me, that if thou dost not regard me, I know not whither to resort." Thus she will

hold her confidant by one continued series of confessions. We doubt not that our loving Lord frequently hides his face from us because we rely not enough upon him. It would be the part of wisdom to transfer our cares to him who careth for us; thus should we imitate David, who urges us to "pour out our hearts before him." Make Christ manager of thine affairs, and so please him. An old writer somewhere says, "He who runs before the cloud of divine direction goeth a fool's errand:" let us then desist from self-serving, and give ourselves up like children to the loving care of a tender parent, to be led, guided, directed, and supplied by our great Covenant Head; so will he always have business to do at our house, and will make our soul his settled rest.

4. Another method of retaining the company of our Beloved, is to bring in others of his friends to sit with us. It may be if he cometh not to us alone, he will come with them, and if perchance some ill word of ours might urge him to depart, yet, for the sake of others who sit with him, he will remain. *One* of these disciples might not have constrained Christ, but the *two effected* it. Fire will not tarry in a single coal, but if many be laid together it will

be long before it is clean gone. A single tree may not afford much shelter for a traveller, but he will rest beneath the thick boughs of the grove: so will Jesus often sit longer where many of "the trees of the Lord" are planted. Go to the assemblies of the saints, if you would keep the arm of the King of saints. Those who dwell most with the daughters of Jerusalem are most likely to have a goodly share of Emmanuel's company. Cannot my reader add his own testimony to the fact that fellowship with the saints is conducive to a continuance of fellowship with Jesus?

5. Earnest prayer is the most potent means of winning continued communion. We have found it true, that the mercy-seat is the place where the Lord meets his servants. Full often our souls have risen from depths of distress to heights of delight, by the simple appeal to heaven, which we by supplication have been allowed to make. We will speak well of the exercise of prayer; we can endorse all the titles which old divines have given it, such as—the key of heaven, and of all God's cabinets, the conduit of mercy, faith flaming, Jacob's ladder, an invisible and invincible weapon, a victory over the Omnipotent, the sweet consumption of

cares, a box of ointment broken on the head of Christ, the perfume of heaven, the mount of transfiguration, the soul's messenger, and Satan's scourge: but we will add another—it is a golden chain which holds the Saviour, and secures him to his people. Christ never lingers long with dumb souls; if there be no crying out to him, he loves not silence, and he departs and betakes himself to those hearts which are full of the music of prayer. What a marvellous influence prayer has upon our fellowship with Jesus! We may always measure one by the other. Those pray most fervently and frequently who have been constant attendants on the kind Intercessor; while, on the other hand, those who wrestle the hardest in supplication will hold the angel the longest. Joshua's voice stayed the sun in the heavens for a few hours; but the voice of prayer can detain the Sun of righteousness for months and even years.

Christian Brethren, will you slight this exhortation? Shall none of these means be tried? Are you content to suffer your Saviour to depart? Are ye careless as to his company? Then you have grave cause for fear; there is something vitally wrong. Pass not by this sad admonitory symptom; search your heart, for a sad disease is there. May the great Physician heal thee.

But surely, as joint-heir with Jesus, thou hast longings after him and sighings for his presence. Then let it be thy concern to find him, and, having found him, to constrain him to abide with thee for ever.

> " Oh, that we could for ever sit
> With Mary, at the Master's feet;
> Be this our happy choice,
> Our only care, delight, and bliss,
> Our joy, our heaven on earth be this,
> To hear the Bridegroom's voice.
>
> " Oh, that we could with favour'd John,
> Recline our weary heads upon
> The dear Redeemer's breast!
> From care, and sin, and sorrow free,
> Give us, O Lord, to find in thee
> Our everlasting rest."

In a short time it will be our joy to hold further converse with each other, upon various important points of our knowledge of Christ. We trust we shall then be privileged to enter more fully into the mysteries of communion, and in the mean time we commend our humble effort to the blessing of Heaven, trusting that some beginners will here read and learn what are the elements of that wondrous experience which falls to the lot of a Christian.

TO THE UNCONVERTED READER

WHO IS UNDER CONCERN OF SOUL.

———————

FRIEND,—You are now commencing the life of grace, for thou art just awakened to know the evil of sin. You are now feeling the guilt of your life, and are lamenting the follies of your youth. You fear there is no hope of pardon, no prospect of forgiveness, and you tremble lest death should lead your guilty soul unforgiven before its Maker. Hear, then, the word of God. Thy pains for sins are God's work in thy soul. He woundeth thee that thou mayest seek him. He would not have showed thee thy sin if he did not intend to pardon. Thou art now a sinner, and Jesus came to save sinners, therefore he came to save thee; yea, he is saving thee now. These strivings of soul are the work of his mercy; there is love in every blow, and grace in every stripe. Believe, O troubled one, that he is able to save thee unto the uttermost, and thou shalt not believe in vain. Now, in the silence of thine agony, look unto him who by his stripes healeth thee. Jesus Christ has suffered the penalty of thy sins, and has endured the wrath of God on thy behalf. See yonder crucified Man on Calvary, and mark thee that those drops of blood are falling *for thee*, those nailed hands are pierced *for thee*, and that open side contains a heart full of love *to thee*.

> "None but Jesus, none but Jesus,
> Can do helpless sinners good."

It is simple reliance on him which saves. The negro said, "Massa, I fall flat on de promise;" so if you fall flat on the promise of Jesus you shall not find him fail you; he will bind up your heart, and make an end to the days of your mourning. We shall meet in heaven one day to sing hallelujah to the condescending Lord; till then may the God of all grace be our helper. Amen.